HEART
ON FIRE

Fire & Ice Series
Book 3

FAITH O'SHEA

Cover Design by Jaycee DeLorenzo at Sweet 'N Spicy Designs
Formatted by Woven Red Author Services, www.wovenRed.ca

Heart on Fire/Sue Campbell writing as Faith O'Shea-1st Edition
ISBN ebook: 978-0-9996806-4-3
ISBN print book:978-0-9996806-5-0

To my Readers

Originally, there were four stories planned for the **Fire and Ice** series. They were written to touch on some of the issues being confronted today by undocumented residents and citizens alike. I've decided to expand it by two. The founders of the firm, Arianna Woodley and Mia Fisher, have a story to tell as well, and their voices became so loud, I couldn't ignore them. They deal more with woman's right issues, but there will be lots of research done on another event that has taken over the news, the special prosecutor's investigation.

All the heroines are strong women, lawyers who have decided to make a difference, each with their own area of expertise. They are friends and comprise the support system needed to fight in the trenches. They come from different cultures, different economic backgrounds, different parentage, and each of them live with a wound that makes them human.

Heart of Fire Consumed by Fire is the story of Em and Nick, best friends who've come to see they were always meant to be more. Of course, they have to go through some angst, heal some flaws, but in the end, love conquers all and they are stronger in themselves, by being together.

Please feel free to contact me at my website www.faithoshea.com and follow me on Facebook and Twitter.

Faith

Acknowledgments

This series **Fire and Ice** has become a labor of love. It's also become a release for some of my concerns. *Heart on Fire* touches on the immigration issue and the emboldened tactics of Immigration and Customs Enforcement, better known as ICE. They are spreading fear and anxiety throughout communities vital to our economy and our soul as a nation. I'd like to thank one of my history college professors for including a block on the immigrant city of Lawrence. It sparked a fire that is still burning today.

As always, I'd like to thank my friend and reading guru, Bunny, for her patience and persistence. All my drafts are placed in her hands, and she never fails to give me sound advice and grounded encouragement.

I'd like to thank my editor, Amy from Blue Otter Editing, for her expertise. She has become a valued partner in my writing life and I don't know what I'd do without her.

Jaycee DeLorenzo form Sweet 'N Spicy Designs has done it again. I want to thank her for her great work and the amazing covers she created for all four books of the series.

I'd also like to thank Joan Frantschuk, from Woven Red, who not only formats my work for eBook and print but who has become a valued resource.

And of course, I'd like to say thanks to my family. Jeff, Kait, Juan, Justin, Kathryn, Jaiden, Jakob, Jon-Christopher, Dominic and Liam. They surround me with the kind of love necessary for creating novels that touch the heart.

And to all who read my books, I thank you for taking time out of your life, to journey with me.

CHAPTER ONE

Emilia Spencer-Ronan pushed through the double doors of the Woodley and Fisher law firm suite with a vengeance. She was pissed, and her scowl accompanied her into the reception area and down the short hall to her office. After throwing her briefcase on her desk, she picked up the phone and followed up the earlier call she'd made as she'd exited the courthouse. Having gotten nowhere with the attendant at the deportation center, she was now calling the superintendent to see what the hell had happened. Evalina Bazorga was scheduled to appear via video this morning during her court appearance. It wasn't bad enough that her clients couldn't face the judge personally, but when things like this happened, they missed their day in court completely.

Tapping her foot, then pacing, she waited on the line for the man in charge of the corrections facility to come to the phone. Instead of the head of the jail, she got his assistant.

"Ms. Ronan."

"It's Spencer-Ronan and you better be able to fix my problem or I'm taking it to the governor."

"I'm very sorry that the video equipment was malfunctioning. It doesn't happen often. From what I understand, you were able to get the judge to postpone."

"I did, but it means more time for my client in your beautiful center, and that is not acceptable."

The sarcasm was thick. They both knew the center wasn't beautiful. Better than most in the country, but a jail was a jail, no matter what you called it or how you sliced it.

"I'm aware of that, but if she had not broken the law—"

Her voice rose in direct proportion to her blood pressure.

"Broken the law? She is the victim here, sir. She was the one assaulted. She is the one with the broken arm. She was the one who was crawling out of that house to get away from the husband who was beating her."

There were witnesses to the brutality of the attack. Nick Katsaros, her best friend, was one of them. On patrol that day, he was called in by a frightened neighbor to stop the assault. He was the one who'd written the report she read over before filing a new petition to present to the court. Evalina had had no choice but to defend herself. Her life had depended on it.

Emilia had a hard time controlling her emotion.

"Are you telling me that a woman can't fight back against her abuser?"

"No, that's not what I'm telling you. But she's undocumented and now has a pending assault charge."

Undocumented residents could be summarily deported if they'd broken the law in some way. A woman was more at risk than other perpetrators.

"Against her abuser. What is it about that that you are having trouble with?"

Em caught sight of Cami standing at her door, her look suggesting she change her tactics. She knew her law partner was right. She wasn't going to get anywhere being belligerent with the person on the other end of the line. Taking a deep breath, she tried to tamp down her anger and approach from a different perspective.

"Assistant Superintendent Bayles, I know this was not done intentionally, but my client needs to get home to her children. Their father's already been transferred to the county jail. It's my job to make sure those kids don't lose both parents to this domestic abuse issue. I hope the video equipment will be fixed soon, at least in time for my next hearing."

"I can promise you that, Attorney Spencer-Ronan. We are sorry for the delay, but some things can't be helped."

"I'd suggest you get a back-up."

"I'll run it by our accounting department. Good day."

"Good-bye."

She let the receiver slip onto the cradle and plunked herself down in her chair, just as Cami came in and took one opposite her.

"What happened?"

"The damn video machine wasn't working, so Evalina wasn't able to—" she raised her hands to make quotation marks around the words—, 'attend the hearing.' I sat outside the courtroom for over an hour waiting to be called and got the message right before I went in."

Prisoners were not guaranteed a day in court. Any petition presented by their attorney was done by means of a video conference. When the video failed to function properly, their pseudo day in court was postponed. It was no way to do business.

"What judge was presiding?"

There had been only one until the governor had assigned another to help with the backlog.

"Thankfully, it was Frechette. She was as angry about it as I was. Mumbled something about wasting the court's time."

The immigration courts were on overload, and judges were forced to give a bare minimum to each case presented. That she had read the brief meant she had lost five minutes, half the time she gave for each decision.

"Evalina's the one you got a restraining order for, isn't she?"

"Yes, for the amount of good it did her. Her husband walked right through it. The kids had to watch while their father pummeled their mother before they were whisked off to family services. It didn't help that Evalina tried to stab the son of a bitch with a kitchen knife. I went to see them yesterday and they're not doing well. The family they're with is great, but the kids are emotionally traumatized. They need their mother."

It wasn't the first time she'd handled domestic abuse cases, but when there were children involved, her hackles went through the roof.

"Where'd you get the case?"

"Saban. She was the one who got the initial call about domestic violence in the home and then got the kids into family services after the attack."

That had happened almost a month ago and now there'd be another week added to the sentence.

Cami studied her before saying, "I still don't get what Saban's doing in that capacity. From some of the stories you've told me, it's not her calling."

"It's not, but I think her supervisor has noticed. She's not working with families anymore. She handed off this case before her...demotion."

Saban Katsaros had been promoted to caseworker just six months ago and with each case handled, she made more of a mess than she'd started with. That she was back in her cubicle with paper and files was an improvement in the process. Organizational duties were more her thing than dealing with people, especially children. She didn't relate well to them. Her emotional stamina was critically low, so she created problems at the initiation of each case that had to be smoothed over. Em wondered why her supervisor had been so quick to step in. Usually the powers that be let the unqualified remain, to wreak havoc on those who weren't.

She told Cami, "She's being sent to court now as a resource. She knows her stuff, just can't put into practice with real people."

"She used to call you on a lot, didn't she?"

"Only when she needed an attorney."

"Or a babysitter."

Irritation pinched Em's eyebrows together. Nick had asked her to take Teddy tomorrow night, said he and Saban needed to talk. She knew their marriage had hit a rough patch, but it had hit a lot of them over the years. When would enough, be enough? And why was she still enabling him? She was his friend, not Nanny, Incorporated.

Her frustration meter had already been on high, and the problem with the video cam ratcheted it up a notch. It was probably why she'd handled it so poorly.

Camille slid her leg over her knee in such a graceful way, Em wondered how they'd become best friends. Totally feminine, Cami could have made her feel inadequate in comparison. Saban had the same effect and didn't go out of the way to disabuse her of that fact. Maybe if she had had that kind of allure...

"At least you don't have to work with her anymore. It must have been hard."

Shaking off the feelings that came with thoughts of the social worker, Em admitted, "Not really. She deferred to me on everything. She likes it when she can depend on someone else to do the job."

"Aren't you lucky she trusted you. Not only with her cases but with her son, as well."

With a large dose of disapproval in her voice, Em said, "Teddy's my buddy. Leave him out of this."

She didn't want to get into it. After the shit show at the courthouse, she'd didn't need to have an argument she couldn't win.

"Yes, ma'am. What are you doing tonight?"

Em released a sigh of relief.

"Just hanging out. You?"

"Maks and I are going up to the Notch. My mother wants to go over some of the wedding details."

Em sat back, a smile on her face. This was something she could feel good about. Camille had fallen head over heels with the man the FBI assigned to her right before the holidays. Cami's specialty was asylum, and the Russian had been brought into the country with detailed information about the election hacking scam that was still being investigated. The FBI was seeking data. Maxim Zhernova was seeking protection. Russians like him were being killed all over the world. Somehow, he'd managed to escape detection. Now? They hoped he'd be left alone. To think it had only been several months since they met, but the attraction had been strong, a love story, destiny, if you were to believe Cami's mother. They'd gotten engaged and the May wedding they'd planned was just a week away. She was thrilled to see her best friend so happy. That it made her own hollow love life more apparent didn't take away her feeling of contentment at Cami's upcoming nuptials.

Cami leaned forward, her features animated.

"Why don't you come up tomorrow. The snow is packed, and the skiing will be great."

Em steepled her hands under her chin and hesitated. Cami would probably lecture her about her plans. Knowing she couldn't get away with turning her down without a reason, she told her about keeping Teddy and the why behind it.

Cami's vexation was evident. "He has no idea that it must kill you to do that, does he?"

Camille was one of the few who knew her feelings for Nick went way beyond friendship. It might have started that way, but a switch had turned on somewhere over the years, and she'd developed even deeper feelings. Or maybe she was fooling herself and she'd loved him from day one.

Pulling at the corner of the file that sat atop her desk, Em sat with her eyes downcast. She didn't want to see the expression on Cami's face.

"It doesn't kill me. I love having Teddy. It's a preview of upcoming attractions when I finally have kids."

Leaning forward, Cami grabbed her hand.

"You need to fall in love with someone else to find that, Em."

After looking up to meet the intensity of the stare, Em gave her what she was looking for.

"I know. I'm working on that. I went out last week with a guy I met at Rissa's."

"And?"

"No chemistry on either side. But can't I get an A for effort?"

"I'll give you the A, but you can't quit now."

"I won't. If the opportunity presents itself, I'll take it."

She'd dated off and on over the years, but hadn't found anyone that made her heart sing. With Nick there was a forty-fucking-piece symphony.

Cami rose from her seat, seemingly satisfied that she'd made the promise.

"We're taking off a little early, so I probably won't see you until Monday."

"Have a good weekend. Say hi to Maks for me."

"I will."

Cami disappeared into the office right next door, and Em heard the rustling of papers as she collected her things before leaving for the day. Em sat in the silence, wishing she could find a lasting love like her friends. Six months ago, Nell was alone with her daughter, Cami was alone with her fear, Jelani was alone with a burning desire to find her one and only. She was alone because she loved someone who wasn't available. She didn't know how to break the spell he'd cast the day they met. But she was sick of being in a one-sided relationship, especially now, seeing Nell and Cami with men they loved, soul mates if she had to label it, just like her parents.

It was way past time to put it behind her and seriously think about opening another door.

When her cell rang, she checked caller ID and let out a staggered breath. How could she close this door if he kept pushing it open?

"Hi, Nick."

"Hey, I've got a favor to ask."

Of course, he did. It was happening more and more often, and she didn't know what she was going to do about it. She couldn't seem to say no. There had to be a dozen books on Amazon that would give instructions. Maybe it was high time to buy one.

"What is it?"

"Alec got a call about a canceled ice time, asking if we wanted it, and I was wondering…could you pick Teddy up at the rink and keep him tonight?"

It meant she'd be keeping Teddy for the weekend so Nick could play and take Saban out. Talk about having your cake and eating it, too. She was the one left cleaning up the crumbs. The fact that she loved the kid made it hard to turn him down.

She could resent this but decided that being with Teddy might chase away the blues.

"I guess. What time?"

"We need to be at the rink by eight. I'll feed him before hand, and if you want to stick around to watch for a while, he'd be up for it."

Would she? She'd attended quite a few scrimmage games in college and after, and although she didn't want to, she still enjoyed watching him play. He could have gone into the draft the year he graduated but didn't think he had the talents to make it for the long haul.

"That's prime time. Usually the big guys don't play until after ten."

"Don't know how he managed it, but I'll take it. I took on an extra shift tomorrow. This way I'll at least get some sleep."

"I'll have to go home and change, but I'll get there as close to eight as I can."

"Thanks, Em. You're a lifesaver."

She swiped to end the call, thinking he had it wrong. She was a one-pound whirly-swirl sucker.

CHAPTER TWO

Nicholas Katsaros was tying up his skates, pulling the laces tight just as he'd been taught when he was a kid. There was more aggression in his movements than usual. He was still steaming after the text from Saban. She'd had to get one more dig in before she left for wherever she was going tonight.

Playing in the over-thirty-league was his one guilty pleasure. It was his way of letting off steam, of hanging with his buds. He didn't move like he had when he was a teenager or when he was a starting center for his college team, but his love for the sport was as strong as ever. He'd been recruited for the intramural team by a friend, Alec Cleland, and over the last couple of years, they'd gotten tight. The Enforcers had a newbie who'd just joined in the last couple of months. Maxim Zhernova was a Russian transplant who just so happened to be engaged to Em's best friend. The couple was in the middle of wedding plans and they were going up north to tie up some last-minute details, so the team's new center would be away for the weekend.

When the call had come from Alec about the ice time, he was relieved that they'd be playing earlier than their usual ten o'clock time slot. It meant he'd be home earlier than usual, but it also meant Saban would have to feed Teddy and put him to bed. When he'd told her, she'd come at him with a vengeance, pissed by the last-minute change of plans. She warned him she wasn't in the mood to deal with Teddy tonight, not after the long day she had, and left it to him to find a fill-in.

He'd called Em, like he always did, pleaded his case, and trooper that she was, she'd agreed. It meant Teddy would be staying with her for another weekend. He didn't know what he'd do without her. They'd been best friends since college, and she'd stuck with him in good times and bad. The bad was coming in waves lately.

Saban was becoming an all-out witch.

Was it such a crime to want a night out with the guys? He certainly didn't complain when she called saying she was going for drinks after work. Didn't mind that she went to visit her family every single fucking weekend.

Okay, maybe he did, but he enjoyed the one-on-one time with Teddy. It was sad to say, Saban didn't. Teddy had hinted that he didn't like being alone with his mother, and he'd done his best to accommodate the little guy. He didn't think it would be a problem much longer. His marriage had imploded, and looking at it objectively, he should have seen it coming when he stopped catering to Saban's every whim. He didn't have time for it anymore or the patience. She was a grown woman, not the college girl he'd fallen in love with. Shouldn't she have matured with age? She was from a southern family, and she was the epitome of helpless female. If she'd lived a hundred years ago, smelling salts would be kept at the ready, to cure her vapors. It was her fragility that had drawn him in. Beautiful features, deep blue eyes, she'd needed him like no one else had and it'd made him want to protect her with his life. He'd been accused of having a white knight complex, but he didn't see it like that. To him it was more about taking care of her than fixing broken windmills. But lately…

"You ready?"

Alec was standing by the door of the locker room, his stick banging on the floor.

Nick looked up, letting all troubling thoughts go.

"Yeah."

He wobbled in his skates across the coated walkway until he reached the edge of the rink. Then he glided out, across the ice, feeling the freedom that comes from doing something you love. Doing his crossover, he followed the oval around, one glove under his arm as he snapped his helmet in place. Once the glove was back on, he put his stick down and played with a puck, keeping it perfectly balanced, in a to-and-fro motion. The air was cold, his breath coming out in wisps of steam, but he'd soon be overdressed from the amount of energy he'd be expending.

While gliding around the curve, he looked up into the stands and smiled. Teddy was sitting beside Em, waving at him. He flashed them both a smile. He didn't know what he'd do without her. He certainly wouldn't be here.

The expression on her face told him she was enjoying it as much as Teddy. She'd been part of his audience since college, attending almost all his games for the first two years, and she loved the sport. Things had changed when he started dating Saban. It wasn't that Em stopped coming to root the team on. She'd been going out with one of his teammates and was still a part of the group that gathered at a local watering hole after the games. Saban had stopped going after her first game, thought the players were rough around the edges, *uncouth* was the term she used, and her disdain was obvious. Her idea of a good time wasn't sitting in a cold rink, watching a bunch of guys chase a black puck around while people screamed in the stands. Soon after, Em had broken up with Jim and she was back as his number one fan. She got so caught up in the action her voice could be heard above the chaos on the ice, especially when he scored a crucial goal. She'd be hooting and screaming, making him feel like a winner. She still made him feel that way.

He was staring up at her, and she stared back as if in challenge. There was a spark that skittered in his gut. What the hell…

He was knocked off balance when Alec came up beside him and poked him with his stick. He almost tripped over his skate, still looking up, a sudden intense need pounding in his blood.

Snapping his attention away from her, he fumbled with the puck before finding his stride. He skirted around another player, zoomed down the ice, and swept the disk into the empty net.

Alec was patting him on the back. "How the hell we got your talent is beyond me. You're the league's Achilles' heel. There aren't many old-timers who could have played this for a living."

"Who are you calling old?"

"If the skate fits…"

The game was about to start, and he was standing at the face-off position, squaring off against his friend, but took a second to glance up to see Em on the edge of the bench. Then his focus was back on the puck just as it dropped. The scrimmage was under way. Hip checking Alec against the boards, he retained control of the stuttering puck as he swung around a defenseman. Alec, trying to keep up, shouted at him, "I can't believe you didn't think you were fast enough."

"I knew my limitations, never even tried for a shot in the majors."

"Went out for the marines instead."

"That was a team I knew I could make."

"Why do we has-been marines always end up in law enforcement?"

"Don't know. Are there stats?"

"You, me, Lance, Tim, Lou. Five out of fifteen. That's…a high percentage."

"Can't do the math? It's a third."

"I can do the math. Just testing you."

Alec poked his stick and stole the puck, Nick chasing after him. The play was heating up.

As always, he got lost in the zone, blocking out everything but the ice, the puck, his opponents, and the net. When there was a break in the action, the guys taking a much-needed breather, he scanned the stands. He shook his head. They were empty. He hadn't even noticed Em and Teddy leaving, hadn't said good-bye, hadn't asked Em to meet him for a drink next week, whatever night she was free. He wanted to talk to her, let her know what was going on. It was no longer his gut telling him it was over. The signs were posted all over the place.

"Hey, Nick, you still playing?"

Alec skated around with the puck waiting for him to get in position.

"Yeah, sorry."

With his mind back on the game, he scored a goal within seconds and looked back up into the stands. He wished Em was here to see it. It was pretty.

⌒

Two hours later, sweat glistening on his face, Nick stripped off his hockey gear and packed it away. He didn't really want to go home. Teddy wouldn't be there, so all he'd have to welcome him were Saban's recriminations, and he'd have to hear the litany of sins he'd committed against her this week. She'd bled him dry of all emotion. When he pushed back, her demands became more obsessive, and when he'd finally blown, she'd shown him the door. Of their bedroom. Said if he couldn't give her what she needed, she'd find someone who could. He told her to go ahead and try.

They'd reached a stalemate that was in its sixth month.

According to Saban, all it would take to go back was his undying devotion. The choice was his. He didn't like being given an ultimatum even if the terms were equitable. They weren't. She wanted to be on a pedestal and his number one priority. He thought it was way past time for her to come down from it and he was sick of all the drama. The last thing he wanted to do was relive it tonight.

His car seemed to agree. It had a mind of its own and he found himself in front of Em's, which was only a few miles away from his house. There was a light on in the family room, which meant she was still awake. He shut off his headlights and thought about going in, grabbing a beer, telling her about the game, but there was a new energy flowing through him that made him hesitate. If he didn't know any better, he'd say he was seeing her in a brand-new light.

Or was it? New?

He'd felt it the first time he met her, and thought he'd died and gone to heaven. Round face, cropped hair that was the color of brown sugar, the most beautiful hazel eyes, a great body, and an attitude that matched his. Cocky. Her athletic body was toned. She was muscular but in a feminine way, with a competitive streak that rivaled his own. Her nose was straight when he'd met her but had been broken at least once that he knew of. He'd been in the stands during college when a softball was hit straight at her, bounced off her face. It was no surprise to anyone that she stayed in the game. She'd had a shiner for a couple of weeks and he'd overheard whispers suggesting someone had hit her. The stitching on the ball left their mark over her eye, proved her story, not that it mattered. No one would dare strike her. Not because of their friendship, but because *she'd* deck anyone who tried.

When had he stopped noticing? Or rather, why had he started again?

He couldn't do this, not now. Not until he unburdened himself from the woman he'd married.

After starting the car again, he went home. When he got there, the dark suggested he'd be left alone.

Saban was either out or asleep. Not that it made a difference which. He'd have peace and that's all that counted. Not bothering to go up to the main floor of the split-level house, he went down to the basement, flicked on the TV in what was now his bedroom, surfing until he came to some hockey scores. He couldn't watch for long. He'd offered to cover for one of his cop buddies, wanting the extra money the shift would bring in. Tomorrow night, he was taking Saban out so they could discuss the end of the marriage, decide how to split things up, figure out who'd get the house, and what to do about visitation. If he was honest, he was hoping she'd agree to move out. He wanted Teddy to have the stability of the same routine, the same bedroom, playroom, school. But if she knew that, chances were, she'd fight for it tooth and nail. He didn't want to keep up the sham of a marriage. He didn't want to live in the same house, he wanted a legal separation. After stripping down to his skivvies, he crawled under the blanket, his arm under his head. Half listening to the rundown of hockey scores across the league, he wished he had rung Em's doorbell. Her mood was always infectious, and he always left her feeling good about the world. She was his happy place and he needed a dose of that right now.

He might need a dose of something else, if he was to believe his body, but he had to be careful. Em had never given him any indication that she felt that way about him. And there was no way he'd jeopardize what they had. He'd cut his dick off before damaging the most important relationship of his life.

By the next afternoon, Nick was exhausted from working six days straight. As he pulled into the garage, he was wishing he hadn't taken the extra shift. He'd banged heads with a gang member, had to chase down a purse snatcher, and had to face off with an immigrant enforcer who was trying to get him to arrest an un-documented resident. There was an unwritten law that said the local police didn't have to co-operate and he kept it as well as the written ones. Sanctuary city had to mean something for the residents to trust the community patrols.

As he made his way up the stairs into the main part of the house, he heard Teddy playing down the hall. It surprised him. Em was supposed to keep him again to-night. Wandering down to the room, he said, "Hey, bud. Whatcha doing?"

Teddy jumped up from his train set and raced over, jumping in his arms.

"I'm so glad you're home."

"Where's your mother?"

"In her room. She said she has a headache and can't deal with me right now."

Nick's heart ached at the tone. It was filled with shame.

"She said I was making too much noise playing with my train. She didn't like me going *whoo-whoo* so loud."

What the hell was Saban's problem now? It was Saturday, so she couldn't use the excuse she'd had a rough day. "When's Em coming back to pick you up?"

Teddy's head dipped in disappointment.

"She's not. Mom called her to cancel. She said she changed her mind and to bring me back right away. We were going to the movies this afternoon and now we can't."

When Teddy looked up at him, there was a well of sadness in his eyes.

Had Saban decided not to go out tonight? He'd made sure he got off duty in time to get home to change. He'd made reservations at a restaurant that he thought she'd like. They really couldn't afford to waste that kind of money, but she'd told him he'd better pick swank if he wanted her to agree.

When he'd walked by the kitchen on the way to Teddy's room, it was dark. It told him that they wouldn't be eating in. Did she want to take Teddy out with them? That was out of the question. They'd planned on talking about things that Teddy didn't need to know about. Why had she told Em they wouldn't need her tonight? He'd have to get something for Teddy to eat before too long. It was after six o'clock and the kid should be ravenous about now.

He undid his collar, began to unbutton his shirt as he walked to the room next door to Teddy's. After rapping at the door, he heard an exhale of breath and "What now, Teddy?"

"It's me."

There was a long pause before he heard, "Come in."

Saban was sitting at her vanity table putting the finishing touches on her make-up. She didn't even glance up at him. He stared at her for a minute, her movements finally registering.

"I'm confused. Are we going out or not, and if we are, why did Teddy come back?"

Putting down the mascara rod, she turned and looked at him, her eyes high-lighted by shadow and liner.

"Rachelle and I made reservations at a spa. You had your hockey last night. Now it's my turn. This week was a monster."

He could feel the animosity emanating in waves.

"We had plans. I came home early. Now you're just going to up and leave?"

She huffed as if he had no right to be upset.

"I thought it would be nice to spend the weekend being pampered. I asked her to call. They had openings and we took them."

"You didn't think it important to check in, see if I'd mind?"

"Like you did yesterday?"

"I called, Saban, and we didn't have plans. We did for tonight, so what you're doing is blowing me off."

She stared at him in her mirror, a spark of temper evident in her eyes. "We can do it next weekend. It's not like anything is going to change, is it?"

"Not in the way you mean, no."

"Then I'm going to the spa instead. You should be pleased. A massage will do wonders for my mood."

His anger began to build, and he narrowed cold, flinty eyes at her.

"How long are we going to put off the inevitable?"

She cut him a sharp look. "I don't know what you're talking about."

She was still playing her cards close to her chest. He wished she'd just get it over with and leave. She couldn't possibly believe that he would. Could she? Was that what she had in mind? She'd freeze him out until he cried uncle and moved out? She shouldn't hold her breath on that one. He'd be the one keeping Teddy and he wanted the house. He'd buy her out if he had to, if he could afford it.

As she sat fluffing her hair, she gave him a steely-eyed stare in the mirror.

"Oh, and Nick, you're not going to dump Teddy on me every time you want to go out with your friends."

"Dump him on you? He's your son. Or have you forgotten that?"

She swirled around, her eyes casting daggers.

"How could I possibly forget when you keep shoving it in my face? You want me to act like a mother, well, I do. Mine. This is how I was raised. I had nannies. We can't afford them. I do the best I can."

The best she could? That was laughable. She did minimum work where Teddy was involved. Being up on the pedestal made it hard to deal with those below. When he met her, he'd thought she was a sensitive soul, who was overwhelmed by life but what he'd come to find out was that she was only using her vast set of manipulation skills to get what she wanted. At the time, it was him.

"If this is your best—"

"You've changed and you're not the man I married. You would never have talked to me like this before."

Her scowl turned petulant.

His mood swung again, disbelief turning the anger back on.

"That's not a bad thing, Saban. People are supposed to change and grow. You haven't done either. You are exactly the same as you've always been. Immature, willful, and selfish."

He'd come to realize Saban wasn't cut out for the emotional entanglements that family involved. It was all about what she could get out of a relationship, rather than the relationship itself. She was shallow and superficial, traits he'd come to detest.

She had gotten out of her seat, was looking at him imperiously.

"You're right, I haven't. I still expect certain things from the man I'm married to. His time and attention."

He could feel the vein in his neck begin to pulse. It did that a lot lately.

"You're a spoiled little princess. You want me to take on everything that you don't like and then some."

She shook her head, the blonde curls bobbing as she did so.

"I can't talk about this anymore. You're not hearing what I'm saying which just proves my point. I need something different than what we have. I'm taking the weekend for me."

He clenched his jaw to stifle the argument simmering between them, but as her words rung in his ears, he stopped trying to contain it.

"It's always about what you want, Saban, every damn time."

"I take time for me, Nick, because you stopped doing it."

She glanced over to her suitcase, packed and waiting.

He blew out a breath and threw his hands wide. "You're not going to spend any time with Teddy this weekend?"

"He'll have you and he'll survive. I won't if I have to stay here."

She walked over and picked up the carry-all.

"I've got to go. I'm picking Rachelle up and I don't want to be late. We have to be there by nine tonight or they'll cancel our reservation."

And with that she walked out of the room, never looking back, and he didn't move until he heard the garage door open and close.

She hadn't even said good-bye to Teddy.

Dropping down to the edge of the bed, he rubbed his scalp, the buzz cut beginning to grow out. Maybe he'd take Teddy for a haircut tomorrow, get one himself. Right now, he had supper to make. Or...

He glanced up to see Teddy standing in the doorway, his mouth drooping into a frown.

"Is it my fault Mom left?"

He opened his arms and his son ran into them. Enfolding him in a hug, he said, "No. You are the most loveable boy on the planet. Just ask Em."

"I'm sorry she broke your date."

"I'm not. Now I get to spend the evening with you. I have an idea. It involves pizza and a movie. Want to hear it?"

He knew exactly what the doctor would order to change the mood. With Teddy's arms wrapped tightly around his neck, he got a muffled yes.

⁓

Em was disappointed she had to give Teddy up. They'd made plans to go to the movies, and when Saban had called, telling her to bring Teddy home, she'd argued with her, asked if she could drop him off after they were done for the day. Saban had been adamant and insisted he be home when his father got back from work. It sounded as if Saban was just being Saban and there was no method to her madness. Did Saban resent her, deep down, and not want to admit it? She'd given Nick a hard time about their friendship over the years, pleaded with him not to spend so much time with her, and he'd acquiesced periodically. She could go weeks without seeing him, although they'd text and call like they always did. When Teddy had been born, it all shifted. Not wanting to deal with a squalling, colicky infant, Saban had encouraged the relationship. If that woman needed something, she'd be whoever she needed to be to get it. Why didn't Nick ever see that side of her? Instead of getting angry, he'd placate. He was different around his wife, someone she didn't recognize, and it drove her crazy. This was just another instance of Saban's whim becoming a command performance, probably a punishment of some kind, and Teddy was getting the short end of the stick. It was probably more to prove the point that Teddy was *her* son. Em didn't need it. She knew it all too well.

Facing a long night ahead of her, she went into the kitchen, knowing she should scrounge around for some food. Why hadn't she been the one to cancel, gone skiing instead? She could still drive up if she was motivated enough. She glanced up at the clock and dithered back and forth as to whether she wanted to make the long haul around dinnertime. She didn't.

The ring of her phone grabbed her attention and she swiped, sitting on the edge of her stool at the kitchen island. Maybe she'd get the real story.

"Hi."

"Back at you. Sorry about this afternoon. I was wondering if you wanted to join Teddy and me at that movie you were going to take him to?"

She was too taken aback to answer right away but gave way to a question.

"What happened to your date with Saban?"

"She made other plans."

He sounded different. Annoyed?

"What did you do?"

Somehow her thought became words and she almost winced when she heard them out loud.

"I had the audacity to play hockey last night."

She sat up in surprise. This was a first. Where was his defense of the indefensible?

"She cancelled on you?"

"Went to a spa. She needed pampering. Right... Shit, sorry." He paused, and she heard him take a deep breath. "Teddy was bummed about the movie, so I told him we could go, thought you might want to tag along."

That's what she always did. Tag along. A third wheel who didn't have a place in the family. And yet the family didn't seem to function without her. She had to stop giving in, stop wishing it could be something it wasn't. How much longer could she pretend it didn't hurt?

"I don't think so, Nick. I might drive up to the Notch. Cami asked me to go up..."

"It's too late to drive up there tonight, Em. Go tomorrow. Come with us. We'll have fun."

She was sure they would. They always did. That's what made it so insane.

Before she could decline again, Teddy was on the line.

"Em, you've got to come with me. I don't want to see it without you."

When she'd gone on-line to check out what was up in theaters, he'd picked a story about a dog who had to get out of canine prison. He'd talked about it all morning. He was more excited about going to the movies, eating popcorn, and getting the one bag of candy she allowed than the movie itself.

"You'll be with your dad, Teddy. What could be better than that?"

"Being with you."

Her heart melted, and against her better judgment, she agreed.

"Dad, she said she'd come."

Teddy must have been in the process of handing Nick back his cell, because Nick's was the next voice she heard.

"We'll swing by and pick you up. We were going to have pizza for supper. Why don't you order it and we'll eat there?"

"Fine. I'll see you soon."

When she swiped off, she castigated herself for her lack of will-power. But when it came to Teddy, she didn't have any.

⌒

The movie was just what she'd expected, trite but cute. If a dog was the main character, it appealed to her and nothing was better than seeing a dog back with his owners. That he was put in jail appealed to Teddy's sense of the absurd. His father put criminals behind bars and he kept asking questions about the chief jailer and the inmates. The variety of dogs showcased covered the spectrum, and about a mile away from her house, Teddy started asking for a puppy.

"Why can't I have one?"

"It isn't the right time for that, Teddy. They take a lot of work."

Nick was talking to him, eye to eye in the rear-view mirror. It was heart-warming to watch their interactions. Nick was a great father. She hoped she could find a man who loved kids as much as he did.

You'd have to start looking somewhere else to find one.

"But I'd take care of it."

Teddy's voice had a tinge of whine and she smiled, glad those puppy-dog eyes weren't focused on her.

"You're too little to walk it and you can't reach the cabinets yet, so how would you feed it?"

"I could take it outside to go pee. We have a fence, so he couldn't get out. And we could put the food in the cabinet where the pans are. I can reach that."

"I'm sorry, buddy, we can't get one now. Maybe in a few years when you're older."

When he turned that adorable face to her, she gulped. "Em, can you get me a dog?"

She'd do just about anything for him and wished she could oblige, but she knew better than to make a promise she couldn't keep.

"No sweetie. I'm not home enough. It wouldn't be fair."

"But I could stay with it for you."

She turned around so she could face him when she said, "I would if I could, Teddy. I grew up with a dog and I've missed coming home to one."

She hadn't lived with anyone since Cami moved out of their rental a couple of years after they joined the firm. Just hired on, wanting to save expenses, they'd leased a condo together in the heart of the city, splitting everything equally. It was smaller than a postage stamp, but it'd served their needs. Working fourteen-hour days so you could make partner meant you didn't need anything more than a bed to crawl into. Her hours were still long, but she was glad she'd splurged on her house. It just got lonely sometimes.

Nick looked over at her and asked, "What kind of dog did you have?"

She'd never told him? She couldn't quite believe it. She'd shared most everything with him. Then again, she'd buried away the grief of those nightmarish days, so how could he know she still felt the pang of loss to this day? She rarely showed anyone her vulnerable side.

"It was a goldie. A golden retriever. Her name was Lily and she slept with me and Olivia."

Teddy's voice floated to the front of the car.

"Does she miss you?"

"Teddy, she's…She got old and she hurt, so we had to take her someplace that made her pain go away. I sure miss *her*."

"Can you bring her back?"

If only. She was the sweetest dog and Em would love nothing better than to live with her again. Lily would snuggle with her, the furry head in her lap. Dogs had a way of making everything better.

"I would if I could."

Nick looked over at her, his eyebrow arched.

"Tell us about your Lily."

A warm and fuzzy feeling hugged her heart, as it always did with thoughts of the cream-colored angel.

"She was part of my aunt's family before Olivia and I were. The first night we arrived at our new home, Lily started sleeping with us. It helped having her around. She was so sweet, and she was so lovable. She let us cry as much as we wanted without making us feel bad."

"They got another one after she was...gone, didn't they?"

"Yeah, you met him. Our old Mr. Flash was a character but not the let-me-cry-in-your-coat-kind of guy. It wasn't the same."

Now her aunt and uncle had Bailey, as well. She was a trouble-making devil but they all loved her.

Nick pulled into her drive-way. She sat for a minute, the memories of Lily bringing back a longing for something, someone to love. She finally got out but didn't leave without opening the back-seat door to give Teddy a kiss good-bye. Giving her attention to the driver, she said, "Thanks. It was fun."

"I think for all the candy you let Teddy eat, you should be the one putting him to bed."

Teddy began to unbuckle his seat belt. It seemed he took it literally.

"Sorry, bud. You're stuck with me tonight. Buckle yourself back in."

The pout was almost cute.

She waved them off before entering the darkened house, which made the memories of Lily that much stronger. She missed the old girl more than ever. There's was something about a dog greeting you when you came home that made you feel you belonged to someone. Maybe she could get one, another golden, hire a walker. She'd check some websites, look around. Think long and hard to make sure she could manage it. Maybe she'd get two. Then they'd have company. It would be twice the love.

She smiled. A feeling of warmth permeated her being at the thought of wagging tails and lots of dog kisses. She silently thanked Teddy for bringing some of those faded memories into focus.

CHAPTER THREE

By Friday, Em was ready for a weekend away. Every day had been filled with one crisis after another, jam-packed with client appointments, court appearances, new client interviews, paperwork and all the details that went into it. It seemed like there were never enough hours in the day to cover all the bases, and just when she thought she had a handle on it, another case showed up in her lap. Just yesterday, she'd walked into the courtroom for a hearing, to see a woman, dressed in blue scrubs, sitting at the defense table crying quietly. After making her way over, she introduced herself and asked what was wrong. The woman, Yolanda Hernandez, told her she'd been picked up for a driving violation and sent to the detention center. A trans-gender who was being treated for AIDS, she was being denied medication. Em's sense of justice had kicked in, and although this wasn't her area of expertise, she'd taken on the case, asking the judge for a postponement so she could look at the file. The judge had granted the request and had given her fifteen minutes to file a complaint. The complaint was deemed appropriate, and an order was given to re-prescribe the medication. The file was sitting on her left. She had a lot more work to do on it before she was satisfied.

Tuesday she'd gotten a call from a young girl whose parents had been detained while she was in school. They were deported two weeks later, which wasn't unusual. In one moment, Cara's life had split apart just like Em's had over twenty years ago. Born in the States, Cara Taibbi had legal standing here, and one of her neighbors had called to get her representation. She wanted to be emancipated, wanted out of the foster system. It was going to be an uphill battle, but at fifteen, Cara might be old enough for the courts to agree, giving the neighbor who'd brought her in temporary custody. Em still couldn't believe that children, citizens were at risk of having their families ripped away from them. It's why she'd put endless hours into helping Nell craft her Supreme Court case. They wanted a foothold, something that would give the courts leeway with their life-and-death decisions. Nell had done exactly that with her win, and because of it, Cara could petition the court to "sponsor" her parents within a year, bringing them back to the States. Age was the only limiting factor. When the justice's opinion was handed down, there had been some stipulations put in place. Restricting young children from filing suit was one of them. Sixteen was the base age, but by the time this got in front of a judge, Cara would satisfy that condition. The women at the firm looked at it as a long-overdue reform, and everyone in the office was taking advantage.

Cara was her last appointment of the day, and as she sat with her and her temporary guardian, she outlined the steps they would take to get her emancipated. Getting her folks back here would take longer, but Cara eyes glistened, thrilled she might be able to live with a family that loved her in the interim. It wasn't her own, but it was the next best thing.

Em was relieved that the week was ending on a positive note. A few of the other cases she'd worked over the last couple of days hadn't turned out so well, but it didn't mean she was going to give up. She'd have to find different avenues to pursue. Children should not be left in the care of strangers if their parents were alive. Children were returned to unfit mothers, drug-addicted fathers, environments rife with domestic abuse. None of it made sense to her. Some days the system sucked. It was her job to un-suck it.

As soon as Cara left, Em attempted to clean off her desk. She lived, by nature, in organized chaos. She knew exactly where everything was, all her files organized the way she liked them, and Liz, her assistant, had gotten used to her system, if you could call it that. She'd been with her since the beginning and they'd gotten close. She'd been trying to convince Liz to go to law school. She had the temperament for it and the skill set. Liz kept telling her she didn't want the headaches or the hours.

She glanced at her phone. Should she text Nick to say good-bye? She hadn't heard from him in a couple of days and it felt weird. She should be relieved, but instead she was...concerned? That wasn't the right word. She didn't have one for it. He'd probably made up with Saban and was busy catering to her, didn't have time to connect.

Frustration spilled out in a heavy sigh.

With the folders all neatly stacked, she went to the door, looked back once to make sure she hadn't missed anything. After clicking off the light, she went out to the lobby where, Heather, their receptionist, was just getting ready to leave for the day. The office was closing at noon, with only a skeleton staff left behind. Almost everyone from the firm would be in attendance tomorrow for Cami's big day.

She was heading straight for Franconia, having packed all her things this morning so she wouldn't have to backtrack to her house. Everyone was due in for the evening events, but she was leaving early, wanting to settle in before the festivities began. Tomorrow, Cami would become Maks' wife. She was excited for them, happy her friend had overcome all her fears about commitment and allowed Maks in.

She opened the car window and let the air circulate through the car. It would be a perfect weekend for a wedding. May didn't necessarily mean warm but the forecast indicated the temps would be above normal.

Her blue tooth signaled a call and, she held her breath. Was it Nick? She'd decided she didn't really want to talk to him, now. In the last hour, she'd developed an attitude. She was going to start sorting through some options, try to come up with a way to keep Teddy in her life, without the baggage that came with it. She was worn out from the merry-go-round of now-you-see-me-now-you-don't. The number that flashed had a four-one-three area code and that could only mean one thing. She pressed her thumb on the indicator to answer the call.

"Hello."

"Good afternoon. This is Diane from Diamond Breeders. Is this Emilia Spencer-Ronan?"

Em felt a thrill rush through her. She'd called a couple of kennels this morning, researched their methods, and had zeroed in on Diamond Breeders. She'd left a message once she'd made the decision and hoped someone would get back to her.

"It is. I'm so glad you called."

"No problem. I hope this is a good time."

"It's perfect. I'm not in my office, so I won't have any distractions."

"From what I understand you are looking for two of our puppies?"

"I am. I like the idea of two so they could keep each other company while I'm at work. It might cut down on any mischief." Wanting to reassure the woman she wouldn't be leaving them alone all day, she added, "I've already contacted a dog-walking service, I have a fenced-in back-yard they can play in and I very rarely go into the office over the weekend. I had a golden growing up and was recently reminded how much I loved my Lily."

"Our dogs never leave us, do they?"

The warm fuzzies were back.

"No, they don't."

"I assume you found us on our website?"

"Yes, and I like what I read. I know you raise the puppies at home, and the dogs are good with kids."

"You have kids?"

"No, but I have my godson a lot and I know he'd help out whenever he could."

She wasn't sure whether her friendship with Nick would survive the new parameters she was about to put into place, but she hoped it didn't affect her time with Teddy. He'd love visiting and playing with the pups.

"Pretty Girl is due to have a litter any day now. We keep the puppies here for the first three months, if not longer, so we're talking mid-to-late summer at the earliest. If you're looking for something sooner, I can only accommodate your request for one. There's a runt from our most recent litter that no one wanted. It's such a shame. She's such a sweet thing."

Such a sweet thing registered. It was just what she was looking for, not that she expected to get another Lily. She was one of a kind.

"Could I claim the one that no one wanted? I could take her now and then take one from the next litter when they're ready."

"Are you sure you want to do that, sight unseen?"

"If you say she's sweet, I believe it and I don't want her thinking she can't be loved."

"Oh, she's loved. We would have kept her. I'm almost sorry you agreed to give her a home."

"Now that I made the decision, I'd love to get her here as soon as I can. When will she be ready to leave Mom?"

"We have a pick-up date scheduled for mid-month."

"That's perfect. It'll give me time to get everything in place."

"We'll need a deposit for both, the balance due when you come and get her. I'll let you know when the next litter is born so you can pick the one you want."

The breeder was located in the western part of the state, so she'd have to make a day of it. It was where she and Nick had gone to college and she loved the laid-back vibe of the place. She got out there as often as she could, visiting old friends who still lived there. She hoped that Nick would let Teddy come with her. She knew he'd love to help her with the new addition. Maybe she'd even let him name her.

"I can give you a credit card number, but you'll have to give me time to pull over."

"Why don't I give you until tomorrow at noon to get back to me with the information. I have a couple of deposits on the next litter already, but Pretty Girl's never had less than six. We breed several different dogs over the course of a year, so no one dam has more than one litter every twelve months. We like to give them recuperation time."

She liked hearing that. No puppy mill here.

"I'm so excited. I feel like my godson right before Christmas."

"How old is he?"

"Four."

"The perfect age to become attached to a dog."

"I think so, too. Thanks again, Diane, and I'll call as soon as I get to where I'm going. I'm already in love with the little runt and don't want to lose her to someone else."

She ended the call, feeling almost giddy. She was taking control of her life, had promised herself that she'd begin making different choices, let love in. It wasn't exactly what Cami wanted for her, but it was enough. At least for now. She had a feeling her life was going to get better, that something was right around the corner.

⌒

Nick was driving around in the patrol car, his shift almost over, on the look-out for anything amiss on the streets of Boston. Fridays could be a bitch, but he loved being a cop. Loved knowing he was making a difference. Being with the guys from his precinct was like being part of a large family, where everyone had your back no matter what went down. If you needed help, you had thousands of men and women you could reach out to. He'd enjoyed being part of it, the rituals, the routines, the camaraderie. Now that his personal life was changing he was going to look into a transfer, SWAT or Narcotics being his first and second choice. It was time for a new challenge and he'd never again allow someone else to call the shots for him. He'd gone along to keep the peace, but he'd landed in the same pile of shit he would have if he hadn't.

How had he gotten so side tracked? He'd always been confident in what he wanted, and taken the steps necessary to see it done. He glanced over to Juanita, who was sitting beside him. He knew he'd miss her, miss the deep conversations they'd had while on stake-out or driving aimlessly, looking for trouble. He hoped he could trust his next partner as much.

"Nick, over there."

She issued her command as she pointed to the left of the upcoming intersection.

As he got closer, he saw what she had. A man was banging someone's head against the sidewalk. After screeching to a halt, he jumped out of the car, two steps behind Juanita. She had the cuffs on the attacker before he could get his own out, the scruffy man claiming he was the one assaulted, and that this was a big misunderstanding. Nick ignored the rant. It was par for the course. With his partner in control of the situation, he busied himself with the victim. After helping him up, assessing the damage, he turned on his radio and called for a bus. The face was a bloody pulp from the concrete facial, and his suit was ripped at the elbow.

"It seems this isn't one of your better days. The ambulance should be here soon. They'll get your face into some semblance of order."

Blood was everywhere, and Nick assessed a broken nose among other things. He seated the man on one of the benches that lined the street as the sirens blared in the distance. Juanita had already packed the soon-to-be-charged criminal in the back of the cruiser and was waiting outside the car for the ambulance to show up. The sun was out, and it was warmer than average for the beginning of May and he basked in it, knowing the next hour would be all about the paperwork. Juanita had agreed with him early in their partnership that they would only cuff those who they knew were guilty. This guy was as guilty as sin and one of the regulars. They'd already arrested him several times and he wondered if the jail time would be more significant with this collar. How many times would the courts let him go before he really hurt someone?

He glanced at the man sitting beside him and made an adjustment to that thought. He'd already done that.

When the EMTs got there, he left them to their job. The guy in the suit thanked him before Nick climbed back in the cruiser and took off for the precinct.

His shift ended just as the paperwork was wrapped and the perp locked up. Juanita said, "We're going to grab a beer at O'Reilly's. Want to join us?"

He checked his watch.

"Sure, why not. I still have time before picking Teddy up at school."

"Plans for the weekend?"

"I promised I'd take him to the aquarium. We go at least a couple of times a year. He loves the penguins."

This was the first time they'd be going without Em. Teddy was bummed but he understood. Maks and Cami were getting married and Em had to be there. He'd thought about calling her before she left, but he didn't want to ruin her weekend. And he would have. He'd needed a couple of days to calm down after his argument with Saban on Wednesday about the dog. She'd overheard Teddy asking for one again and she'd gone ballistic, yelling about what a crazy idea it was and how much a fool he'd be if he gave in. She'd gotten the idea that Em was behind it and insisted that Teddy be kept away from her and her outrageous ideas. Saban never failed to turn routine into a catastrophe. Teddy had started crying, thinking he'd never see Em again. Nick had had to deal with the repercussions of that, explaining that everything would be fine soon.

And it would be. He was going to get the ball rolling, file for divorce, finally do something to stop this craziness.

He didn't mention any of that to Teddy. It wasn't time to sit him down yet, to explain things. He was afraid that Teddy would worry that it was his fault, wonder when it was going to happen.

The kid didn't need that kind of anxiety in his life. Not that Teddy didn't know *something* was going on, but he was too young to have figured it out. That Nick had been sleeping in the bedroom downstairs in the basement since the end of last year would have spoken volumes if Teddy could read that kind of language. Instead of asking questions, Teddy was sneaking into his bed in the middle of the night. He knew it wasn't an ideal situation for him or Teddy, he just didn't have the heart or the energy to bring him back up to his room at two in the morning.

He needed some advice on how to handle it, and he knew Em would help him figure it out. She'd know what Teddy needed, would know how to make the change easier but now wasn't the time to call her. He didn't want to mess up her weekend, so he was postponing it until after the wedding.

Would she be surprised? Probably not. Em had never liked the idea of him and Saban as a couple, had declined the wedding invitation and put some space between them for months after the ceremony. He'd had to cajole her back into picking up the friendship. It had solidified after Teddy was born. She'd come to love his son as much as he did, which was why he knew she'd stand by him, offer to help. He was going to be a single parent soon and he'd need a shoulder to lean on. None was as strong as hers. And she'd know all the right things to do for Teddy, help him deal with the repercussions.

He checked his phone again, hoping, on the off chance she'd called him. They very rarely went this long without hearing from each other. There were daily texts sent back and forth, check-ins, stories, complaints. More often than not, it was Teddy who wanted to talk to her. Tell her about something that had happened at school, a show he'd watched or a game he'd played. Teddy had been asking about her in hushed whispers for the last two days and he'd told him that after the weekend, he'd set up a play date. He just hoped Em would want to play.

After he walked Juanita to her car, he left her to get his own. The drive to O'Reilly's wouldn't take long. It's why it had become the watering hole for cops. It was close to the station, the beers were cheap, and the ambience was...lacking. It fit their lifestyle. They weren't looking for atmosphere, they were looking for a place to let loose after a difficult shift. He pulled around back. A couple of cars he recognized told him some of his friends were already here. He checked his phone again just as Juanita pulled in behind him. No messages. He had a reason for not reaching out. What was hers? Was he overly obsessed with the fact that she hadn't called? The why was becoming a fire in his belly.

When Juanita rapped at his window, he got out and they walked in together, the crowd already two deep. Leaning in between the men sitting at the bar, they ordered. While waiting for his beer, he glanced around. A couple of detectives from the gang squad were playing darts, several men from his squad sitting at a table in the corner, relaxing. A couple of others were playing a game of pool. Don shouted over, "You up for a game?"

After taking the on-tap brew from the bartender, Nick went over to where they were. He could watch for the few minutes it took to drink his beer.

"Not tonight. I've got to get Teddy soon. I just came in for a quick one."

Don struck the nine ball with the cue and sent it flying into the corner pocket. As he was lining up his next shot, he said, "Bring Em in again. We'd like a chance to win our money back."

Nick wiped the foam off his mouth, took another sip.

"Even if I got her to come, you still wouldn't have a shot in hell of doing that. You'd end up losing more of your hard-earned money. She hustled me the first time I met her."

Don laughed. Made his shot, getting the three ball in.

"You're an easy mark."

"Maybe."

He smiled at the memory. Em had been playing pool at a frat house the night they met. He'd watched from a distance, and after downing three beers, he'd gone over and challenged her to a game. He'd been known to win a few here and there but with her, he was a three-time loser before she let him off the hook.

"You want to grab a beer and go outside? It's getting warm in here. I'm retiring as reigning champ, so I'm good."

"You certainly are. Where'd you learn to play?"

She'd told him when they grabbed a seat on one of the boulders that decorated the front yard of the rambling house. They'd talked for hours. He'd learned that she was from Australia, not that the accent didn't give it away, about her parents' death, about her move to America to live with her aunt and uncle. There was a pool table in the basement, and she'd learned all the tricks of the trade playing with her sister and cousins. He still played her on occasion and he still lost. Even with lack of practice, she was able to clear a table with just one or two balls, as the guys here could attest.

He went back to stand at the bar, his memories hitting him harder than they usually did. Why hadn't he taken bolder steps back then? With her? He could see her laughing, a gentle laugh that rippled the air, a full-throated laugh that affected everyone around her. The image in my mind, held the kind of power over him that was muddying his thoughts. He rested his elbow against the cuff of the bar, watching the flow of people in and out, listening to the conversation. Then guilt began to eat away at him. He could have picked up Teddy early for once, instead of coming here. The kid had stayed longer and longer hours at the preschool this week because he hadn't reached out to Em for some early pick-ups.

He downed the rest of the amber liquid, threw some money on the bar, and yelled over to Juanita that he was leaving.

Teddy was happy to see him, and all he talked about on the way home was the visit to the aquarium tomorrow. Chattering away, he covered all the issues that were important to him. What were they going to have for dinner tonight? Was he going to see Em soon? What were they going to do before bedtime? Would his mother be there when they got home?

He'd wondered that himself. And if she was, what kind of mood she'd be in. Hot or cold?

Her car was gone, and the house was dark when he went through the door and up the steps of the split-level home. Flicking on a light in the kitchen, Teddy hanging on to his leg, he saw a note laying on the counter.

Went home for the weekend. Will be back late Sunday night. Don't wait up. S.

He scrunched the letter up and threw it away. At least she'd let him know. She didn't always. He had to admit he felt relief. The scrimmage tonight had been cancelled due to the wedding, so he'd planned on staying home with Teddy. Now the two of them could just hang out, do dude things, enjoy the peace. If this was what life would be like when Saban was gone, he was all for it.

Em was seated in the local pub, along with her partners, waiting for Cami and her sister, Solange, to join them. She couldn't believe the wedding was tomorrow. Cami had shared all the preparations with her, from the invitations to the cake to the food selection and she knew the day would be beautiful. The last few months had flown by.

Tonight, they were throwing the bachelorette party. The shower had been a month ago, held at Jelani's, where they celebrated just about every occasion. With the wedding set for mid-day tomorrow, the partners were geared up to celebrate one last time together as single women. Most of them were here, along with their assistants and long-standing members of their staff, scattered among several tables. Members of Cami's family sat at various tables topped with fresh flowers and the discarded pens used for their assignment. Maks' mother and aunt, the only females on Maks' invite list, were chatting with Michelle Bissonnette's side of the family, their faces glowing with pleasure. Maks was having his own party at another location, his friends wanting to make sure he had a real American send-off. She wondered what it would entail. It couldn't get too out-of-hand. There were several G-men with him. They'd be sure to keep it all legal.

Talk flowed on around her, and she listened to the voices as familiar as her own. The significance of the night wasn't lost on any of them. They had been together since the opening of Woodley and Fisher, had become fast friends, sharing the highs and lows that came with protecting the most vulnerable. The dynamics of their friendship had already changed, with Cami spending most of her free time with Maks and Nell, with Jack. Gone were the days when it was one for all and all for one, although she had to admit the men were quite willing to join their inner circle. And it wasn't just the four of them on a crusade to save the world. There were now six. Would there ever be a seven and eight?

She glanced over to Jelani. She was the one who wanted this more than any of them. Her culture demanded family, children, close-knit ties, but it had been an elusive dream for most of her life. She had to give Jelani credit for not falling into the trap of marrying for marriage's sake. Her friend was looking for a true love, more so now that Nell and Cami had found theirs, convinced that it was possible.

Being the hostess with the mostest, Jelani had brought some games with her, and having the back room to themselves, they were able to hold a traditional event. As each guest had arrived, Jelani handed out a printable with the words *My favorite memory of the bride* and instructed them all to fill it out. Later in the night, when they were finished, Cami would read them out loud and try to guess who the memory belonged to. Chloe, Nell's daughter, had insisted they play love songs to set the mood and she'd compiled a play list.

Em had to admit there were some pretty sappy tunes, but she found herself humming along to one of them that was playing softly in the background. Just as she was hit with a bout of melancholy, Cami came in, her sister and matron of honor, Solange, with her. The smile on her face was radiant. Would Em ever find that kind of happiness? The track her mind had been spinning in suggested she wouldn't. Not if she stayed stuck in love with Nick. Getting out from under that cloud was becoming a priority.

When the food arrived, Jelani began to quiz them on some of the artists singing the love songs and most had ready answers— Ray Charles, Whitney Houston, Celine Dion, Foreigner… Chloe had put together an impressive list. There was one that had hit her hard. She didn't know why Chloe had included it. It said everything that needed to be said about her relationship with Nick. Leona Lewis wasn't the only one who was bleeding love.

She was able to take her mind off the lyrics that had lingered too long in her mind when Cami began to read some of the memories, getting overly emotional, crying at some of the stories.

Her friendship, loyalty and grace were such treasured aspects of her personality, that each memory spoke to the heart of who she was. Cami guessed most of them correctly, Em's being the easiest. It was far less sentimental that the others. She didn't do goopy well. It had to do with Maks, an accusation he'd made, and the break-up that had ensued. Cami had been devastated but had fought it off by flying out of the country to save Maks' family. When Maks' asylum hearing had come up, Cami had asked her to cover it, and although Em was livid with the man, she'd done it out of friendship. It was something she could have easily turned down, hoping that he got sent back to where he'd come from. Cami had sacrificed a lot of her own financial well-being to secure his asylum protection. The judge had had no choice but to grant it, the documentation so well-crafted, but before leaving him on the court steps that day, Em had given him a piece of her mind. She was glad he'd finally come to his senses and fought to win Cami back. They were a match made in heaven.

Cami looked up at her and said, "I trusted you with his life and I will be forever grateful that you appeared with him that day."

Admitting a truth, Em said, "His life was always in your hands. I didn't do anything more than show up. I have to admit I wanted to throttle him instead."

"I know. He told me you ripped him new one."

Cami said it with the Russian accent. Everyone burst out laughing at Maks' attempt at slang.

With each memory shared, they reveled in their closeness. They knew each other's secrets, longings, and hopes. Cami hadn't finished wiping away the last tear when Arianna stood and addressed the gathering.

"I have an announcement to make."

Jelani yelled out, "We're not sharing offices. Get over it."

Arianna smiled. As one of the founding partners of the firm, she'd been threatening that for months. With the increase in client calls due to Nell's Supreme Court win and the prevailing antagonism against immigrants, the firm had to hire more lawyers to handle the influx. Jelani knew her boss had leased space on a floor beneath them, but Jelani was issuing a warning for the future.

"As you know, I took your demands to heart. I don't want to hear any complaints about you having to travel up and down all day."

Nell assured her, "You won't hear a peep out of me."

"Good to know. Your debating skills are the ones I fear the most."

Laughter bubbled up again. After Arianna cleared her throat, she raised her glass.

"I have recently moved ahead in the polls in my quest for governor. I appreciate all the work you've done on my behalf and hope you will continue to support me."

There was an audible gasp among the staff, a round of applause from the other guests.

Mia, the other founding member, who'd been running the firm single-handedly, admitted, "It was just my luck she couldn't come up with anyone else willing to face Cox. We'll be looking to hire an office manager, so I will be able to see my kids on occasion." Looking at Jelani, she smiled. "We were thinking of giving her your office, but the thought of you hiring Nell to defend your rights, had us back off."

The ripple of laughter this time was more sedate.

Arianna had been talking about this since Christmas, refusing to let Evan Cox go unopposed, had announced at the beginning of February and was running a strong campaign against her opponent.

They all knew why. Cox was her ex-husband and they'd come up with a few choice nicknames that would have offended outsiders after hearing some of her war stories. He'd left her when she'd needed him, when she'd been given news that would have crippled anyone else. Less than a year after she married him, he left. She'd quit her job at the DA's office, and along with Mia, had started Woodley and Fisher. She hadn't looked back, putting all her time and energy into running the firm. It looked like she was willing to entangle herself in his life once again, only this time she wanted to come out the winner. It sounded like she'd do anything she could to put him in his place.

Nell offered, "Chloe's been nagging me to let her volunteer, and from what I hear Keileh has been asking, as well."

"Good to know. I'll need lots of help. Getting all the signatures took longer than we'd hoped so I'm still a little behind right now. I'll be making a swing of the state beginning next week and as you know I've handed off most of my cases to the new hires. I hope you're looking in on them like you promised, making sure they're up to speed."

Heads nodded in response.

"Think Jack will endorse me, Nell?"

"I can give him your platform and twist his arm."

"I hope it won't come to that. He knows where we stand on all the issues. We can easily contrast that with my opponent's. Anyone who knows anyone, friends, spouses, significant others who'd like to work with me, I'd be more than happy to have their help. It looks like it's going to be a highly contested race."

Mia looked around the room.

"She's campaigning. And doesn't even have to for this audience."

Jelani begged, a smile on her face, "Please don't become one of those kinds of politicians."

"Is there any other kind?"

Nell spoke up in defense of her soon-to-be-husband.

"Hey, my politician is one of the good ones."

"There are exceptions to every rule."

Arianna reclaimed her seat.

Still surprised by the turn of events, Em said, "I can talk to Nick about the police association. See if he can't set up a couple of meetings."

Cami offered, "I'm sure he'll be in touch sometime this weekend. She can give him a heads-up."

Nell, used to arguing with anyone who had a brain cell, just for the sake of debate, asked, "To talk? Because he needs something? Be more specific, please."

Cami tipped her glass back and finished off her champagne.

"I bet he calls just to see what's she's doing. The man can't seem to go a day without wanting to hear her voice. If he had a brain, he'd see what was right in front of his face."

Em's mouth dropped open thinking Cami had, had one too many glasses of wine. She was one of the friends who'd tried to talk her out of the funk she'd found herself in since the day she realized she was in love with Nick. What was she implying? Before her mind stopped whirling,

Jelani spoke, showing her disdain.

"I bet he forgets that she's out of town."

Arianna piped up, "Forgets all about the wedding."

Cami's lip stuck out in a pout.

"Who could forget about that?"

"A man. Which is what he is."

Arianna's experience had led her to the conclusion that men were…clueless assholes. They could give Evan Cox the kudos for that.

Em could feel her features stiffen at the direction the conversation was taking, and Cami must have noticed. Cami knew better than most she'd been trying to distance herself from Nick. Her friend's eyes softened, instantly filled with regret, and she went on the defensive.

"He is a good man. Great father. Damn good cop."

Arianna put her two cents in, and it always bought a compliment on large, strong and sexually attractive.

"Good-looking if you like the muscular type."

Mia giggled. "His muscles do have muscles."

Jelani added, "To top it off, he's tall, dark and handsome. I'd like one of them."

Em would, too. Square face, dark hair, penetrating brown eyes, dimples when he smiled, aquiline nose, and lips she longed to taste. Then there was his body. He was built, his hour at the gym three days a week being put to good use. But she'd never dated him, even back in college when he wasn't already taken. They were buddies and that's where it ended. For him. He'd met the woman of his dreams their junior year and he'd become untouchable. He'd married Saban years later, but in the interim, she'd remained his friend. Nothing more. She wouldn't think of doing anything to jeopardize the marriage or the relationship. It didn't mean she didn't want one of her own. And if he looked like Nick, so much the better. He was a good-looking guy.

Nell covered her hand with her own.

"You'll find someone, Em. There's a man out there for all of us. Who ever thought I'd come off the market?"

The two-carat ring on her finger flashed. Jack had bestowed it on her after the immigration ban, airport debacle, and she looked as if she still didn't believe it.

Jelani gave her a smile. The sparkler was impressive.

Em started to relax, thinking they'd been side tracked, but was appalled when they began to give odds as to whether Nick would bother her and place bets on the outcome. Nell and Jelani thought he'd forget about the wedding and call to ask her for something, Cami thought he'd call because he never went twenty-four hours without checking in, Arianna thought he'd call on her to babysit, and Mia went against the odds putting money up that he'd leave her alone. Someone had to.

She balked at joining the pool, hoping they were wrong, knowing they might be right. The fact that she hadn't heard from him for several days increased the odds. Cami would be the probable winner, knowing she and Nick texted, called, or communicated in some way every day just as she did with her other friends. Lately, she was forcing herself not to connect, to consider that he wasn't the only one out there for her, opening her mind to other kinds of happily-ever-afters. She was quiet for the rest of the night, still surprised her offer had turned into something else entirely. They'd made a game out of her relationship with Nick, at her expense.

Once in bed, she lay awake, castigating herself for the restrictive limits she'd put on dating. Tonight, they felt like a straightjacket. Until she could release the past, she'd never be able to open a new door to another kind of life. She had to put the wheels in motion and keep moving toward her new goal. But when the sun rose, and she began to dress for the ceremony, her thoughts drifted again to the man who had crippled her heart.

CHAPTER FOUR

Em stood at the front of the beautifully decorated chapel, built on the property of the Mountain Man Winery for this kind of occasion, bearing witness to the marriage of her best friend. Happiness was the order of the day, as Camille promised to love, honor and cherish her Russian. Maxim Zhernova did the same, never taking his eyes off his bride. Camille was a vision, dressed in a fitted gown that was quintessentially her, a silk creation with a lace overlay, and chiffon train. She'd chosen off-the-shoulder even though May in the mountains could be cool. Maks' expression when he first saw her coming down the aisle had been heart-warming.

Theirs was a love story made in heaven. Had to be. How else could they have come together? Why else would they have agreed to marry after only knowing each other a few months?

Her love story wasn't working out quite so well. Nick still considered her his best friend, she was godmother to his son Teddy, which made her part-time babysitter, full-time fool.

She took a deep breath, and the pungent smell of gardenias brought her back to the present. Em glanced around at her partners. They stood in phalanx around the wedding couple, each dressed in their own style. Cam had told them she'd appreciate it if they all wore the same color, and they'd honored the request. It made for an interesting mix of Bohemian for Nell, form fitting for Jelani and simple for her. Never one to like frou-frou, she'd been pleased with her own A-line gown in ice blue. The color had been voted on as the most flattering to all of them. They were something like the four musketeers, fighting together for civil rights, their clientele all female, all in need of representation. Immigration had become their focal point and each one had taken up the cause with passion and determination. Nell Warren was here with her congressman. They'd gotten back together after more than a decade-long sabbatical, their daughter Chloe doing what she could to make it happen. Jelani was the other lone wolf, although she was here with a man she'd been dating for a couple of months. She was bound and determined to find a husband to start a family with, and they'd lost count of the number of guys she'd gone out with to see it done. No one fit the bill. Yet.

When Arianna announced that Camille and Maks were husband and wife, Em didn't have to force a smile. Cami deserved her happily ever after. She'd been scarred and had refused to let love in. Until Maks. This was a joyous event, and there'd be no raining on their parade.

As soon as Cami's sister Solange handed over Cami's bouquet, the bride and groom began their walk down the aisle together. Em slipped her hand into the crook of Shane Clayton's arm, before they took their place in single file behind them. Shane had become a good friend of the groom. A member of the initial FBI bodyguard rotation, he'd been one of the first that Maks had trusted with his life.

As they stepped out into the light, she breathed in the sweet smell of ripening fruit, the scent less intoxicating than the showy fragrant flowers. The winery had come to life after the last winter frost. By May, everything was in bloom, a riotous array of color and scents. There'd never been a question of where the wedding would be held. The vineyard was owned by Cami's family, and it was the perfect place for a wedding. From the first time Em had seen the rolling green acres, plump grapes hanging from the vines, she'd thought she'd have her own ceremony here. She could never picture a different face standing by her side. It was always Nick's. She had to scrub him out of the portrait if she wanted her fairy tale to come true. She glanced around, the guests now offering their congratulations, family and friends who'd driven up for the festivities. They'd soon be moving the party to the restaurant Stone Soup, fashioned after a cask, with crisscross, metal beams and muted lighting. Everything had been planned with meticulous care by the mother of the bride, who hadn't stopped beaming since she first arrived. Michelle Bissonnette had known the couple were meant to be together since meeting Maks after he'd first arrived in the States and was more than gratified to be proven right.

As they waited for the limousine that would take Cami and Maks to the reception, they stood together, as they did for every momentous celebration, the bride and groom holding hands as if they were afraid to let go.

Em's heart swelled and dipped.

Nell said what they all felt. "You look beautiful Cami. That dress is gorgeous." Nell and Jack were planning their own wedding for late in the summer. It wouldn't be as much of a show stopper as this one. With an eleven-year-old daughter in tow, they wanted low-key and intimate. It didn't mean she didn't want to look the part, and the four of them had gone on several hunting expeditions for the perfect dress. Em felt her own loss more deeply, although she tried not to let it show.

Nell added, "Today there's a glow that wasn't there the day you tried it on."

Maks leaned in to kiss her lightly on the lips and Cami's smile turned radiant. "There is always glow about her. It is one thing I love out of many."

Seated at the dais with the others, the conversation light, the spoons tinkling musically against glass with regularity, the wine flowing freely from the vineyard's special reserves, Em joined the revelry, her mood turning festive. The meal was outstanding. The waiters and waitresses, dressed in tails or simple black dresses, served course after course until it was time to cut the cake.

Before making the first slice, Maks looked at his wife. Em felt shivers along her skin, the look of love so deep in his eyes.

"Thank you to my friends. I stand here today a free man."

Shane said aloud so everyone could hear him, "No, Maks. That's not right. You just got married. You're not free anymore."

Laughter filled the hall, and only when Maks waved his hand to quiet them did they become still.

"This is joke that I appreciate. But Shane is wrong. I have never felt so free as living here, finding love, finding new home, my mother and aunt safe from the treachery we lived under. I want to thank my wife for making it all possible. I would never know true happiness if I hadn't found her."

He bent down and kissed her tenderly, the *ahs* from the women telling him he'd said it perfectly.

Everyone was shifting into party mode as the band began to play, and Em was ready to put on her dancing shoes when her phone rang. She must have forgotten to shut it off and retrieved it from her clutch, the number displayed making her stomach ache. She wondered who'd win the bet.

Swiping to connect the caller, she said, "What, Nick?"

Without even a hello, he dove right in.

"I need you to do me a favor."

Nell and Jelani had won the bet. He'd called for a favor. He'd probably forgotten about the wedding, probably wanted her to babysit, so it seemed that Arianna might be a winner, as well. Mia had made the wrong call, so at least she wasn't the only loser among them.

Anger surged through her. It was an unfamiliar feeling. It was the first time she'd had that reaction on hearing his voice.

"I'm at Cami's wedding. Or did you forget?"

"I know. That's today. I need you tomorrow. When are you getting back?"

He had forgotten she'd be away for the entire weekend. So much for him listening to her.

"Not until Monday. I'm staying with the Bissonnettes for the weekend. Remember?"

They were her second family and had invited her to stay. She was relishing the time with them. The vacation she'd scheduled with Cami had been cancelled due to the wedding, and she hadn't figured out where to go or what to do in its place. She was going to have to find another traveling companion. Hers would be otherwise occupied for the rest of her life.

"Shit. I didn't. You can't come back early?"

There was an urgency in his voice that put her mind in rearrange mode, but she shut it down immediately.

"No. I can't. What the hell is so important it can't wait?"

Jelani was giving her the evil eye, knowing full well who she was on the phone with. After turning her back so she was no longer in the cross hairs, she took a step toward the door and privacy.

"I've been called in for an extra shift tomorrow. There's been a rash of murders, and they want extra protection out on the streets for the next couple of days."

"Where's Saban?"

There was a long pause before he simply said, "She went home for the weekend."

The anger started to percolate. How many times was she going to let him take advantage of her? She straightened her spine, got the words out. "Call *her*. She *is* Teddy's mother."

"You're the only one I can count on."

She could hear popping sounds in her head as the anger turned to a boil.

"That's kind of ass-backwards, don't you think? You're supposed to be able to count on your spouse."

"Yeah, well, I can't. She doesn't want the responsibility that goes with a kid. You know all this."

"Yeah, I know. She never has. Her emotional fragility is the reason you married her, Nick. You wanted someone to take care of. You got it, now deal with it. I'm not coming back. In fact, I'm not coming to your rescue anymore, either. Find a babysitter, or a nanny."

Or a new wife.

When she swiped to end the call, her heart was beating so fast she thought it would come out of her chest. There was a momentary pang that she'd been too quick to cut him out. She took a couple of deep breaths to find some calm, and what came with it was a sense of relief. She'd done it and she couldn't regret her decision. He'd made his choice. Now he'd have to live with it. Not her problem.

Not ever again.

⟿

Nick stared at the phone. She'd turned him down flat. He scrubbed his head with his free hand, his thoughts jumbled, his mood now taciturn. What the fuck was going on? What had happened since the movie night to cause her to turn her back on him? It wasn't bad enough that he was doing a dance of anger with Saban all week, now Em seemed to be doing a dance of her own. This wasn't like her. What was he going to do without her help? He needed it more than ever.

He got up to pace his room, his hand rubbing the buzz cut, his nerves edgy.

He just had to tell her, was all. As soon as he told her what was going on, she'd get over whatever hair was up her ass. If she knew his marriage was over, she'd insist on helping with Teddy, wouldn't she?

He left his room, went up the six steps to the main floor and into the kitchen. As he unloaded the dishwasher, he wished Em already knew. He'd tried to tell her. A month after Saban had kicked him out of their bedroom. Em had given him tickets to a Bruins game for Christmas, and of course, he'd expected her to go with him. They were on their way home, the win a good one, when he'd started to tell her about the argument that led to the exile. Her sympathetic ear must have dried up, because she'd cut him off quickly, told him she really didn't want to talk about Saban or what went on in their marriage. Her good mood had shifted, and she'd become almost sullen. She hadn't said another word for the rest of the ride home, either. Not even when he tried to talk about the goal the Bruins scored in the third period.

He hadn't broached the subject again.

Why?

Thinking back, he realized there hadn't been another opportunity. Every time he was with her, Teddy was with them, so she didn't know about the escalating tension, the missed dinners, the nights out. In her current mood, would she even care Saban was leaving him? He'd give her a couple of days to cool off, call her next week when she was back. Hope that this was just a reaction to his intrusion into her life and nothing more sinister or catastrophic.

Teddy came running out of the bathroom, pulling up his pants as he did.

"Dad, is Em coming to get me?"

After putting the last glass away, Nick refilled the dishwasher with what was in the sink and closed the door.

"No, Teddy. Remember, she's at Cami's wedding? I forgot she won't be back until Monday."

He leaned against the counter, his arms crossed, still trying to process what had happened. Teddy had a simple answer to his problem.

"Just bring me there."

He looked at the bright eyes staring at him and almost laughed. It sounded like such an easy solution.

"She's kind of busy, Teddy. Besides, it's too far away."

"She can teach me how to ski again. I kinda forgot since the last time we were there."

He lifted Teddy up in his arms, looked him in the eye.

"I'll take you up there one weekend. We can stay at the lodge, see Cami's folks. We can ski together."

He felt a small hand getting ready to curl around his neck.

"Next weekend?"

There would be no more skiing until next winter, all the ski slopes about to close out the season. Teddy didn't have a well-developed sense of time, so it would be pointless to explain it.

"No, I'll need a bit more lead time. We can look at a calendar and set a date. I'll make sure I'm not on a detail."

"Okay. Who am I staying with while you work tomorrow?"

He would have called his sister, Sara, but she worked weekends at a craft store, her husband taking over the care of their three kids. He didn't think Rick would appreciate another kid added to the bunch. His mother was leaving on a business trip tomorrow, and he knew his father wouldn't be able to deal with Teddy on his own. His brother's wife had just had a baby a couple of weeks ago, and he knew with the sleepless nights they were going through it wouldn't be fair to ask Pete and Lea to take him. He was going to have to figure out something for the long-term, especially if Em was serious and wasn't willing to take Teddy as often as she had. He'd talk to Juanita. She had a high schooler on speed dial and he might be able to get her to help him hire someone. If he ended up on the SWAT team, who knew what his hours would be, and he needed to know that Teddy was well cared for.

"Looks like I'll have to turn down the extra shift. You'll be stuck with me."

"That's okay. I like being with you."

"I like being with you too, pal. Why don't you get some of your Legos out while I get supper ready?"

"What are we having?"

"I have no idea."

He rummaged around and found a jar of spaghetti sauce, some packaged, frozen meatballs, and half a box of linguine. As he put on the water to boil, dumped the meatballs in a saucepan with the sauce, he was thinking about Teddy's solution. While he was waiting for the water to boil and the meatballs to cook, he went back downstairs to straighten up his room. His clothes were scattered all over and he sorted the mess into piles, throwing one of them into the washing machine. It was one of those chores he put off until there was nothing left in his closet. Not that he had one of them anymore. He looked around the basement. It had become his personal space. He could have taken the third bedroom, but there was a TV down here and a game console. It was everything he needed, if you didn't count a wife. Maybe going up to the Notch tomorrow wasn't a bad idea. He could try to work his way into Em's good graces again. At least see what was going on with her. He was prepared for the break with Saban, but he didn't know what he'd do if Em dropped out of his life. He had to make sure it didn't happen.

⌐

The wedding didn't wind down until the early hours of the morning but Em didn't sleep in like she'd planned. There were too many emotions going through her, too many decisions facing her now that she'd decided to exorcise Nick out of her life. At least most of it. She'd need him to understand that she couldn't continue to drop what she was doing to come running to his rescue. She had to focus on her life, start dating seriously, not just accepting one here and there, assuming it wouldn't amount to anything.

Taking to the fields, the rising sun illuminating the leafy vines tethered to posts that looked like bamboo along the tree-lined roads that traversed the winery, the breeze sliding along the pathways with her, she did some soul searching. The honeyed scent of blossoming flowers mixed with the smell of newly cut grass, and she'd found a haven of delight that made the excursion through her jumbled thoughts more bearable.

Nick hadn't called again, thank goodness, but she knew it wouldn't hold. It never did. They'd gone through this often enough for her to know he'd try again. It was up to her to resist. What made it more difficult was that he didn't know the way she felt about him. He was unaware that her feelings had changed, that they'd gone from friendship and love to being in love. It was getting harder every day to keep it hidden. If she was going to go through with this, she had to tell him. The harmony between them would ultimately be disrupted, and he'd have to keep his distance. They'd end up drifting apart. Besides, it would be too humiliating for her to sustain any kind of relationship with him once he knew. He loved his wife and it still had a way of making her ache. Saban was everything he'd ever wanted in a woman, blonde and blue-eyed, curvy, dependent, almost clingy. She got the remains, as part of their friendship. And a relationship with a precocious little boy. It wasn't enough anymore. She wanted her own child. One she could be with every day, love to distraction, one who she didn't have to return to his mother at the end of the day. She might never find love again, but she could have a child. That's what was truly missing in her life. She'd have to do some research, find a reputable donor, make some calls. By the time the house was in sight, she felt more upbeat, invigorated. She was excited about the prospect of getting pregnant, although nervous that she was doing it for all the wrong reasons. She put her hand over her eyes to act as a visor. There was a green Jeep sitting in the drive-way, the license plate number one she recognized.

He wouldn't have. Would he?

CHAPTER FIVE

She knew Nick would have as soon as Teddy came barreling down the drive, throwing himself in her arms when he reached her. And she caught him in the kind of hug he expected.

Her arms supported his butt, and his legs were hanging around her middle as he explained, "Dad didn't have anyone to watch me today 'cause you were here. He couldn't do the extra shift, so I talked him into coming up, so we could ski together. I forgot how to plow in the snow like you taught me, but I can learn again, right?"

Not wanting him to see her dismay at their arrival, she swallowed the frustration. Just when she'd given herself permission to detach, here they were. What was she going to do?

Nothing, today. She would never make Teddy feel as if she didn't want him here, but she was going to have to have a sit-down with his father so they could hash this out. She had no idea what that would look like, and she wasn't looking forward to it.

Nick was standing in the doorway when she reached it, Teddy still on her hip. He looked relaxed, a broad smile on his face. He seemed happy to see her as he opened the door and let them in. That was part of her problem. They always enjoyed being together. How was she going to turn her back on that?

She stood just outside the kitchen and watched as Michelle served up mugs of coffee and hot chocolate.

Loving commotion, Michelle was in her element and she announced cheerily, "You have visitors."

"So I see."

Michelle's gaze reached into hers, and she paused in her movements. There was a question in those warm eyes, as she realized Em didn't seem as excited as she'd expected.

"I'm making breakfast for everyone so you'll have full bellies. It's the last day of skiing up here, so I'm not sure how good the trails will be, but I bet it'll be at capacity. You are going to change your mind now, aren't you?"

Em hadn't intended to ski this weekend. She'd stayed the extra day after the wedding to relax. She'd told Michelle that last night at the tail end of the evening when everyone was getting ready to leave. Most of the guests were housed in the condos owned by the winery, but she'd been given her own room at the family homestead, the one she'd use when she visited. With Cami and Maks already gone, taking an early-morning flight out for San Francisco, she'd thought she'd have the whole day to veg out, read, maybe even nap. It wasn't going to be possible now.

Nick had the audacity to say, "I hope you don't mind. Teddy was adamant about being with you today and since we didn't have any other plans, I thought, why not?"

Why not, indeed. He'd obviously decided not to ask Saban to come back. Why did it seem he had no compunction asking Em to change plans, but not his wife? Shouldn't it be the other way around?

Unable to ask him directly, she asked instead, "Did you bring your skis?"

"Of course. Teddy helped me pack everything last night before he went to bed. I reminded him it was a long drive…"

"I told him it was shorter than to the moon and back."

She closed her eyes, pressed a kiss on his cheek and put him down. "It is by a long shot."

Teddy ran off, as Solange's kids were playing outside waiting to be called in for breakfast. Em went to the sink and washed her hands, Nick following her to lean against the counter.

"She couldn't come back?"

He'd crossed his arms over his chest, the muscles making her mouth water.

"Didn't bother to ask. I knew what the answer would be."

Getting her equilibrium back took a moment, but once the inner spasm was under control, she took a deep breath and said, "I think you better start making alternate plans. I meant what I said yesterday, Nick."

"You really don't want to see Teddy anymore?"

Her head snapped up. "I never said that. I said that I can't be dropping everything in my life to help you with yours. I don't date, I don't get to go home and put my feet up after a tough day. I want a family of my own, Nick. I can't be expected to keep sharing yours."

"Why not?"

His answer proved he was as thick as she teased him he was. She was going to have to spell it out, but not here, not now.

She skittered away, but she could feel his eyes on her as she helped Michelle fix breakfast for the bunch, which included Cami's sister, Solange, brother, Steph and their families. They ate until there wasn't a scrap of bacon, toast, or eggs left on the table.

Teddy showed his manners when he said, "That was extra delicious, Mrs. Bissonnette. Thank you."

Em smiled. *Extra delicious*. Those were her words. He was repeating what she'd say to him when he helped her bake a batch of butterscotch or oatmeal cookies. She'd thank him for his help and tell him they were extra delicious because there was a hint of Teddy in them.

Michelle looked surprised by the four-year-old's praise, maybe because her grandchildren had already escaped the table without expressing their gratitude.

"It was my pleasure, Teddy." Looking over at Em, she suggested, "Why don't you get ready? I think you should leave soon if you're going to beat the crowd."

Michelle's phone shuddered across the table. After picking it up, she squealed, "Nell posted some pictures of the wedding. Come. Look."

Nick, with Teddy in his arms, Solange and Em peered over her shoulder as she enlarged the ten- plus pictures Nell had put up on Facebook. There were several photos of Maks and Cami, their first dance, cutting the cake, throwing her bouquet.

Nick's baritone voice vibrated in Em's ear when he asked, "Who caught it?"

"We made a pact, that we'd let Nell do the honors. Maks made sure Jack caught the garter. They *are* up next."

Teddy was on tiptoe straining to catch a glimpse of the wedding. "I want to see Em. Do you have a picture of her?"

Michelle flicked through until she found what Teddy was asking for. Shifting the phone down so he could see, he all but gasped. "You look so pretty."

Em laughed. He'd never seen her all dressed up like this, in a gown, make-up, her hair in curls.

"Not my usual attire, is it?"

"You're always pretty, Em, but this one 'specially."

She leaned over and kissed his cheek.

"Thanks, Teddy. I appreciate the compliment."

She'd gotten too close for comfort to Nick and almost jerked away. Turning to Michelle she asked, "Alec and Jelani posted some earlier. Did you get them?"

Michelle looked up.

"I'm not friends with Alec but I did get Jelani's. There's one of Maks and Cami that I'm copying and getting framed."

"The one when they walked into Stone Soup?"

"Yes. I've never seen her look so happy."

Leaning in so that only Em could hear her, she whispered, "Your day will come, Em. I feel it."

There was a settling of something in her heart. Michelle was a true romantic. Em could only hope that she was right. She didn't want to think she'd live the rest of her life alone, but she was going to have to consider it a distinct possibility. She stacked the plates that belonged to her small group in the dishwasher. "Let me throw on some ski clothes. I'll be right down."

Em walked up the winding staircase of the old ski-chalet-turned-charming home, went into her room, and unpacked the pair of jeans she'd ridden up in on Friday. After stripping out of her leggings and shirt, she zipped up her pants, shrugged on the oversized sweater and vest she had with her, and slid her boots over heavy socks. It was a beautiful day, but she didn't know what the temperature would be out on the mountain. There really was nothing better than spring skiing. The snow was packed, the weather bearable. At least Teddy wouldn't freeze out there. The last time they'd come up, for Cami's birthday last year, the thermometer had hovered at twenty degrees and he'd lasted just long enough to snow plow down the bunny slope a couple of times. Nick was forced to take him into the lodge and warm him up, missing out on some awesome runs. Saban had been invited but decided last minute that she didn't want to brave the cold, so it had just been the three of them. It was just the three of them again. She wouldn't have many more of these outings if she went through with her plan. She was going to enjoy it for what it was: the last-time hurrah for the friendship.

She skipped down the stairs, a reluctant smile playing at the corners of her lips.

⌒

After an hour spent with Teddy on the beginner's slope, trying to hold in the laughter as he fell time and time again, not so much at the fall but the way he reacted to it, she let Nick go out for a couple of runs on his own. He didn't get out here as often as she did, and she didn't mind entertaining Teddy while he was gone. They were sipping hot chocolate when he came back in, his cheeks a ruddy glow, his eyes expressing his pleasure. There was a mountain range in the western part of the state, where they used to ski while in college. It wasn't as much of a challenge as Cannon, but they'd gone with a group of friends and they'd never failed to enjoy it.

He dropped down in the chair waiting for him.

"Your turn."

"No, I'm good. I've been up a lot this winter. Cami, Maks and I made it up at least once a month. He's as good a skier as she is. I got left in the dust more often than not."

Another threesome with her as tag-along.

"I can't believe that. You can hold your own with anyone."

"She was on the ski team in college remember? Softball was my thing."

Teddy seemed content, his mouth covered with a layer of brown. After taking a napkin, she uncapped her water and wet a corner of it, then wiped the moustache off. As soon as she'd finished, he asked, "Am I going to get to go to some of your games this year?"

How to answer that? She couldn't bring him with her if Nick wasn't there to watch him, unwilling to leave him in the stands alone.

Nick solved her dilemma by answering for her.

"Of course we are. Her team is expected to win the play-offs, this year."

"Cool. Have you started practicing yet?"

"Had our first one last week."

Nick took a sip of her water before asking, "When's the first game?"

"End of the month. We play the White Socks."

"We'll get the date and mark it down, Teddy. Wouldn't want to miss opening day."

She stared at Nick, wondering how she'd tell him she didn't want him there. Wondering if she'd finally be able to tell him the truth. He was smiling at her, and her heart ached. Did she really want to give up his friendship? Would that make life all better? She doubted it.

Nick tousled Teddy's hair. "You did a great job out there. Next year, we'll have to get you some more practice, maybe some lessons. I'll take you to ski at someplace local where the hills aren't nearly as high."

"Then Em can teach me how to go down like you do."

"I think that will take some time, bud."

"Not if Em shows me how."

She gave them a wan smile, knowing that this time next year she'd be in a different place. At least that was her intention. If she didn't change things now, she'd be in the same rut.

They returned to the house earlier than Teddy wanted, and after a light late lunch, Nick prepared to leave.

As she walked them out to the car, Nick warned, "Don't stay too much longer. You want to get through the Notch before dark."

He wasn't the only one who believed that was important. It was something Cami used to joke about, something her grandfather used to say. She thought it might have to do with the narrow, winding roads, and the moose that wandered the area. She never took it seriously.

"I've got some work at home that I've got to go over before tomorrow. I'll probably be a half an hour behind you. You don't have to worry."

Before getting into the car, Teddy pursed his lips, ready for her kiss good-bye. She bent down and placed a light kiss there and straightened to find Nick beside her. She barely felt his lips as they brushed hers in the same way, but the sensation jolted her right out of her senses. He'd never done that before, and even as he made light of it, a heaviness settled around her heart. He'd just made another cut and she was bleeding again.

As they pulled out, she nodded and waved, Nick's last words penetrating the shock of the kiss. "Call or text when you get home."

She stared until the car was out of sight.

Her fingers went to her lips, the buzz still penetrating layers of skin and bone. Why the hell had he done that? Why couldn't he just leave her alone? She'd finally gotten the nerve to walk away and now? Now she'd be left wondering what a deeper one would feel like.

Teddy fell asleep not soon after they got on the highway south. Nick glanced back at the sleeping form, glad he'd given in and taken the two-hour drive up to be with Em. She always made Teddy feel better. There was no drama, no need to walk on eggshells. He laughed more with her than with anyone and it felt good to see his son happy.

He fingered his brow. There was still a problem. Em seemed different today. Less animated, more serious. Most of her attention had been directed at Teddy, which wasn't unusual, but he'd never felt left out before. There were moments today, when he had. There was something going on that she wasn't telling him. Did it have to do with work? Did it have to do with him?

Her straight forward approach to things was the one thing he depended on. He never had to guess about what she was thinking, feeling, was never confused about where she stood.

Until today.

Was she angry that he'd just shown up on the Bissonnettes' doorstep? If he'd been smart, he would have checked in with her before interfering with her weekend. Especially in light, of their last conversation. Had he done it again? Just assumed she'd want to spend time with him and Teddy? If given the choice, he'd rather be with her than just about anyone else. What if he'd so totally blown it? What if he wouldn't have that option anymore?

What would his life be like?

He didn't want to find out.

As he drove, the highway clear of any traffic, his mind wandered to all the things they'd done together. They'd been coupled at one of their friend's weddings, right after graduation. He was set to go into the marines, she was set to start law school. It was the last time they'd be together, their lives diverging. They fed each other cake, danced until the last song played, ended up throwing the extra confetti at each other. She had looked as beautiful that day as she had as Cami's attendant, her eyes bright, her smile warm. They'd been inseparable in college, at least for the first two years. Everyone they knew had thought they had something going, kind of like friends with benefits. They had slept together, but it'd never turned physical. There'd been overnights at a friend's place in New Hampshire, ski weekends away, with ten of them bunking in a two-bedroom lodge, sleeping on the floor, keeping warm by means of body heat, after watching a horror movie when she was too scared to sleep alone. He'd kidded her about that for months after, but she never watched one with him again. Then there were his away hockey games, when her car would follow the bus, her friends all crowded in, the team's own cheering section. Once had been in a winter snowstorm. She'd skidded out, his heart in his mouth until she got out of it. He'd kept vigil at the back window to make sure she was sticking with them. He'd been agitated that night, wishing she and her friends had stayed home, his head not in the game, worrying about her drive back. He didn't worry as much when she drove as when she was a passenger. She was one of the most natural drivers he'd met and could handle any kind of situation. Even after a couple of beers. They'd gone to frat parties together where they'd team up and trounce anyone who challenged them at whist, pool, or darts. The classes they'd had together, criminal justice, constitutional law, and English comp were always fun. They'd write notes to each other and pass them back and forth while the professor droned on. More recently, the texts, swapping jokes, stories about a perp, a client. She was a part of his history. Shit, she was part of his DNA. If she vanished from his life, it would be like losing a limb.

A thought rattled as he pulled off the highway and headed for home.

He didn't feel this way about Saban. If she left, he'd be relieved. There'd be no more gut-wrenching stand-offs, no more catering to a woman's whims, the freedom to live the life he wanted. How had they gotten here? Hadn't he loved her to distraction? Hadn't she loved him back? Where had it all gone wrong?

When he carried Teddy into the partially lit house, the silence was welcoming. Once in Teddy's bedroom, he undressed his son, got his pajamas on without the kid waking up. He fingered a lock of Teddy's hair off his face.

"Don't worry, pal. I'll figure it all out. Everything will be okay. I promise."

As soon as he got down to his space, he put the TV on, needing the background noise to play off his restless thoughts. There was one thing that kept circling his brain. He'd made a gross error in judgment in marrying Saban. If there was a next time around, he'd need to look for someone he got along with, who had similar interests, who loved his kid, who made him laugh.

Em.

His feelings for her were intensifying or maybe resurfacing after all these years.

As if she'd heard his thought, his phone pinged. He picked it up and read the two-word text.

I'm home.

With that assurance, he knew he could get to sleep.

But by the end of the week, he wasn't sleeping at all. Em wasn't responding to his texts or answering his calls, and he was living in limbo, the place between heaven and hell.

CHAPTER SIX

Em emitted a long sigh. Things were finally back to normal. Cami had come in today, although she could have taken the last day of the week as part of her honeymoon. It was a conscious decision. Maks was already back at work and she wanted to go over the cases she'd left in her partners' hands, read through the new case files that had come in while she was away. Covering them had been more time-consuming than Em had thought it would be. Cami hadn't even been gone a full week, and her clients had multiplied like bunnies on hormones. So many refugees were arriving, asking for asylum as soon as they stepped on shore, that she didn't know how Cami handled them all.

She listened to the sounds coming from the office next door. She loved hearing the familiar voice on the phone, and she could picture Cami on her feet, pacing the area around her desk while she talked to a client, her husband, her mother, discussing a case with her assistant. She'd missed the movements that echoed through the wall, missed Cami period. They were going out after work, at Cami's suggestion. Maks was playing hockey tonight and Cami had asked if she wanted to grab a drink and dinner, then go to the rink to watch the guys scrimmage. It seemed Fridays were becoming another regular routine, their Sunday night games not enough. She accepted the dinner invite, wanting to catch her friend up on her personal life: the decision to get the dogs, the final click on the lock as she shut the door on Nick, the resulting anxiety about how that would affect Teddy. She passed on the hockey. Nick would be there, and she thought it was too soon to see him. How was she going to juggle things with Teddy if she was bound and determined to push Nick away? She was going to have to ask him out for a drink, explain things, bow out of his life. She had always been honest with him and this was the first time she'd misled him. He thought she wanted her life back, which she did, but it was more than that causing the breach in their relationship.

Putting it all on the table had an upside. She wouldn't have to interface with Saban anymore. That woman knew just what buttons to push to get her seething or feeling vulnerable. It was as if Saban knew how she felt about Nick, went out of her way to make her feel like a shit heel.

The one thing she wasn't going to share with Cami was the plan for the baby. She didn't feel strong enough yet, the decision still in hypothesis form. She'd been on a merry-go-round, going around and around trying to figure out if it was too much, too soon. Two dogs and a baby in one year might be pushing it. And if she could work out a schedule to have Teddy, she could put off the pregnancy until she was sure and ready. She wasn't going to rush into anything but had made an appointment to meet with someone from the clinic the second week in June. Just to talk. Get a feel for the process. A thought flashed across her brain at warp speed. If Nick weren't married, she might have asked him to be the sperm donor. She was glad it was gone before she could sink her teeth into it.

She swiveled her chair toward the sheet of glass that gave her a great view of downtown Boston. She watched the pedestrians being pushed along by the strong May breeze, umbrella's in varying styles and colors, a patchwork cover, against the spitting rain. Buses, taxis, and cars worked their way down the crowded street, wipers snapping as if angry they had to work so hard.

It had been a busy week. When she'd arrived in the office on Monday, there were several new cases waiting, the stories no less sad than the ones she'd left behind for the weekend. ICE had raided a factory on Saturday, and a Guatemalan was arrested. It was her friend who had called to make an appointment to see her. Tadita Ang's two-year-old son, Lael, was with his babysitter when she'd been picked up and transported cross-country to a detention center in Texas. Child Services was sent to pick up Lael, and he was placed in foster care, left at the mercy of the state. His asthma was a concern and the frantic calls made to the office were exacerbating the need to get Tadita back to Boston so she could fight for her rights. Em was looking at nine or ten days before she could make that happen, close to a year for the entire process to be completed. She'd already finished that stack of paperwork and a second for a mother detained during a different raid, this time at a textile plant. One of the volunteers from SavetheImmigrants.org was helping in the aftermath. She'd called Em about an infant she was caring for. He wasn't eating, he was dehydrated, cried all night, and she was taking him to the emergency room to see if anything could be done for him. His rights were being ignored and it was this area where she tried to do the most good. She was petitioning the court for a stay on the mother's detention so she could take care of him, the boy an American citizen.

She turned back to her desk taking in the office. As she was the last one of the four partners hired, hers was the end suite, and it was less decorative than the others. Cami's had a French flair, Nell's, strong colors and comfortable furniture, Jelani had an eclectic assortment of chairs and tables that didn't really match but came together to produce a stunning affect. Hers was a collection of family heirlooms, the desk her grandfather's. She'd sanded it down and re-stained it. She still had the business cards she'd found in the top drawer, embossed with his name and address. A lawyer back in the 1950's, he was one of the first who dealt with immigration and all it entailed. The chairs had come from her grandmother's estate.

They'd been reupholstered, the material a throwback to an earlier time, the cushions refit so they were comfortable. The side table was part of her father's office space. He'd used it as storage for all his video equipment and she could still see the lenses, camcorder, extensions, lights, bulbs lined along the surface. It was dinged in more than several places, but she'd brought it lovingly back to health. She'd begged her aunt and uncle to let her ship some things back that she wanted as keepsakes and bless their hearts, they'd agreed. The other table was at home in her bedroom.

When she glanced down at her desk, her stomach clenched. She still had one more application to complete and she had to hurry. The data collected would have to be put in some semblance of order by the time she brought them to the court house by end of day. Problem was, she was going squirrely-eyed. Perla Santiago had been picked up by ICE at a mall, her seven-year-old daughter watching as she was handcuffed and arrested. Brought to children's services, and eventually placed in foster care, the little girl wasn't eating, had taken to bed and refused to go to school. Her job, as Perla's attorney, was to get the mother released from the deportation center so she could reclaim her daughter, await trial, and then somehow convince a judge to let her stay. It was getting harder to do that. She'd ragged on Jack at the wedding, telling him Congress had to get their act together and come up with a reform bill that would work for everyone. He told her as diplomatically as possible that it was out of his hands. At least this year.

Without anyone stopping him, the president was inciting racial tension and was encouraging the Immigration and Customs Enforcement Department, better known as ICE, to take advantage of its new found powers. Not that the last president had done anything to help her cause. He'd deported a record number of undocumented residents and her case load had grown in proportion. The ripple effects of removal were ripping not only families but communities apart. Everyone was on edge, the fear of family separation real. It could mean children being placed in foster care, single mothers struggling to make ends meet or having to make the Sophie's choice of deported parents: take the children with them or leave them in the country of their birth at the risk of losing custody and never seeing them again. No parent should have to make it.

Her phone rang, and she absent mindedly answered it before checking caller ID.

"Emilia Spencer-Ronan."

"Hey, Em. It's Nick."

Shit, shit, shit, shit.

She'd kept the promise and hadn't taken one call from him all week. Now it seemed she'd sabotaged herself with her reckless disregard.

"Someone here wants to talk to you."

Before she could respond, Teddy's voice came on the line. She couldn't believe Nick's nerve.

"Hi, Em. I miss you. When am I going to see you?"

She was close to tears when she explained she was busy and couldn't get away. He'd never heard that from her before, and she was sure he wouldn't understand why everything had changed. What Nick had done was a low blow, but as soon as he asked her to pick up Teddy at the ice rink tonight, she understood.

"So that's why I got the Teddy treatment. You need me. That was mean, Nick. Even for you. I told you you're going to have to deal with your babysitting problems another way. I'm not available."

She could hear him telling Teddy to go wash his hands for dinner and then he was back, his tone one of disbelief.

"What's gotten into you, Em? You've always had time for Teddy. You used to love taking him for a few hours. And he's been asking for you."

This would be her biggest challenge. She missed the little guy, hadn't gone this long without seeing him since he'd been born. She'd had him at least one night a week, sometimes several and would pick him up from preschool early a couple others. Nick would pick him up after his shift. Sometimes, they'd eat together or go out for pizza. During the summer, Nick would bring him to her softball games, where he'd cheer her on like she was in the majors. During the winter, they skied, sledded, or went to see the Bruins play. They'd made annual trips to the zoo, the aquarium, the children's museum, gone on a duck boat tour and the swan boats. In the last two weeks they'd done almost nothing. There had been that one day up at Cannon. Could she continue to shut him out? He probably didn't understand what was going on and she didn't want him to think she'd stopped loving him.

"I'll see if I can get Olivia to pick him up this weekend. Just don't say anything to him until I know for sure she has the time."

"What you're really saying is that you don't want to see me. This has nothing to do with Teddy."

"You're not as thick as the proverbial brick. I was wrong, although it did take you over a week to get the message."

"Was it the kiss? I don't know why I did that and I'm sorry. It seemed like the thing to do after you gave Teddy one."

She drew a ragged breath, the kiss coming back in all kinds of colors and textures. So light it was almost non-existent but had sent a shot of visceral pain throughout her system. He was saying it meant nothing and she felt a deep twist in her heart.

"No, it wasn't the kiss. I know there was nothing behind it."

There was a long pause, as if he was thinking. She held her breath, wanting him to say it had meant something, that there was a reason behind it. Instead, he said, "Come on, best friend, tell me what I did to piss you off?"

She tried to mask the inner turmoil, but she was getting tired of the struggle to maintain the friendship, sick of pretending that's all she felt. She shouldn't be his best friend; that should be Saban. Camille had married her best friend, and Nell was about to. Nick should have...

She wasn't getting into it. How could she explain her feelings? She couldn't, didn't want to see a look of pity on his face. Once she told him about her decision, about the baby, maybe he'd back off. He wouldn't expect her to drop what she was doing to tend to Teddy, if she was taking care of her own child. Would he? She needed to keep the distance in place.

"You didn't do anything. I just need to have my life back. I'm so busy taking care of yours that I neglect my own. You wanted me to come back from my friend's wedding to fix your problem. Who does that?"

"I know that was wrong, but Em, you've always done it before."

His tone of voice was so matter-of-fact that she could feel the slow slide of anger gaining ground.

"Well, it's not working for me anymore. You're going to have to work things out with your wife."

"She's..."

"Nick. We're done. I don't want to hear what kind of issues Saban's dealing with. I have my own. Don't call me again. Do you hear me?"

"Loud and clear, Em. Have a good life."

She'd finally struck a nerve. Had he finally heard her?

The endless sound of emptiness buzzed in her ear.

She stared down at her cell.

What had she done?

⌒

Nicholas Katsaros had the urge to fling his cell against the wall. He was frustrated beyond all limits, having been sure this would have blown over by now. Em had never turned him down like this, not in the fifteen years he'd known her. Lately? She'd become intractable. It wasn't like her. He often called her Wonder Woman. She was able to juggle work, him, Teddy, and play time which included a couple of different sports teams. She was a natural-born athlete, no matter the game and the only ones she played were on the court or on the field.

He'd thought about asking her out every once and in a while those first two years back in college, but she was fiercely self-reliant. She would never have accepted his need to nurture, and he wasn't sure she even knew how to ask for help. And there was the fact that he didn't want to ruin the friendship. Lovers were easy to come by; best friends weren't.

"Dad, am I going to school today?"

He looked over from the spot where he'd frozen after the call, his son coming out in a pair of pants and a tee shirt. Teddy had been dressing himself for a while now, but it always impressed him that the kid knew what went with what. He couldn't dress himself as well and if he didn't need to wear his police uniform every day, he'd be at a loss.

"Yeah, pal. I'm going to make you breakfast and then I'll get dressed."

"Am I going to stay with Em tonight?"

He squatted down. He wanted to be at eye level with him before breaking the bad news.

"No, Ted. She's extra busy and can't take time off. How about we do something special when I pick you up this afternoon?"

The slight frown made his heart twinge. He needed to figure out what was going on with Em so his son would be able to see one of his favorite people. Some days he thought Teddy would prefer to be with her than—"

He was pulled away from that awful thought when Ted asked, "Like what?"

"What sounds like fun?"

"Going to the park with Em."

His eyes slipped closed. It was hard being a one-parent household. At least that's the way it had always felt. Because she was a case worker for child services, everyone thought children were close to Saban's heart. They were wrong. He still didn't know why she stuck with it. Constantly complaining about the procedures, the families, the immigration courts, she wasn't exactly living her passion. That her son was the last to get her time and attention was galling, and they'd had many discussions about her lack of maternal instinct. Em had always filled that role with Teddy, loving him as if he were her own child. When they were together, her focus was on him and him alone.

Now?

He'd done something to cause her to distance herself, but he had no idea what it was. How was he going to figure it out if she refused to talk to him? He pondered that while he made Teddy some scrambled eggs and toast. His son stood beside him, and he glanced down to see the frown hadn't left his face.

"Doesn't she love me anymore?"

He pasted a fake smile on his face, moved the pan off the burner, and picked Teddy up. "Of course, she does. She even said she was going to ask Olivia to come pick you up this weekend, so you can have a play-date."

He prayed he hadn't suggested something that would end in disappointment. But if it was him Em had the problem with—

The missing smile re-appeared, and life came back into brown eyes that were an exact replica of his own. "Really?"

"That's what she said."

He silently promised he'd do whatever he could to make sure it happened.

⌒

He shouldered his way through the doors of the precinct, still pissed after his conversation with Em. As he waded through the waiting area, every chair was filled, some of the people handcuffed, some crying, others chatting amongst themselves. Members of the squad were scurrying along the hallways, the day-shift attendant sitting tall at the desk. He was welcomed with a lot of hellos and head nods but all he did was grunt back. He groaned at the multitudes crowding the space. It must have been a busy night. Boston might not be Chicago or New York but they had their fair share of arrests, murders, and mayhem. When he got to the locker room in his department, Juanita was waiting for him. They'd been together since his rookie year and she'd become a good friend. She'd heard about the ups and downs in his life with Saban, knew Em well, and even asked outright why he'd married one and not the other.

"What has your undies in a twist this morning?"

"Em's not talking to us."

"Us as in you and Teddy?"

"Yeah. She's gone all nuclear. Refuses to keep him for me tonight. Won't pick him up from school. The kid's been left in the lurch."

He had to make a second attempt to get his padlock opened. His agitation was getting the better of him and he'd screwed up the first attempt.

Juanita leaned against the wall of steel, her arms crossed over her chest.

She asked, "What are you going to do?"

He glanced up. Her tone was mocking. He took his gun out of his locker, buckled the holder to his shoulder, secured the weapon before banging the door shut and spinning the disk on the master lock.

"Not sure. What would you suggest?"

"Carve a whole new life out for yourself. You counted on her for a lot."

He knew that. Looking up at Juanita, he admitted, "She's always been my rock."

Had been. It seemed it had shattered into tiny pieces.

"You know, Nick, she doesn't really owe you anything but friendship."

Her hand was on his arm, forcing him to face her.

"Let me give it to you from the female perspective." Her voice rose, her tone caustic. "You married the other woman."

His mouth thinned in displeasure. He was beginning to think she was right. But marry Em? She was independent, emotionally intelligent, and plowed through life as if she owned the world. She certainly didn't need him as escort.

Marrying Saban had been a reflex move to satisfy his need to be needed. She was a princess who wanted to be pampered and taken care of. He'd liked that or thought he had. It had taken a couple of years, but the allure had faded. He'd outgrown the need to have a woman on a pedestal. The fights had started at her lack of participation in Teddy's life. He'd accused her of being selfish and all he'd gotten for his efforts was the silent treatment. He'd once suggested marriage counseling, hoping they could get to middle ground, but she'd denied they needed help of any kind. If he'd just pay more attention to her, things would be fine.

Juanita knew about the marital problems, had listened and given her opinion. It seemed her opinion hadn't changed and she was willing to give him a refresher course once they were alone.

"Come on, we're going to be late. We'll talk in the car."

They went down to the briefing room for roll call, took mental notes on the outstanding incidents, were told to be on the look-out for a suspect in a robbery case, and handed a picture caught on video that was grainy and unidentifiable. With no procedural changes to go over, they were released to the streets, where they'd drive around looking for trouble.

They walked side by side out to the patrol car. Juanita was driving today so he slid into the passenger seat and buckled up.

As she pulled out of the parking space and drove to the edge of the parking lot, she gave him another thing to chew on. "I would have told you to go fuck yourself after the proposal."

Maybe she had in her own way. Refused to go to the wedding, stopped talking to him for a few months. He'd never understood her detachment.

He looked up at Juanita, telling her something she should already know.

"We never dated. It's not like I chose Saban over her."

"Yeah, just hung out all the time, best friends, good buddies. Didn't you ever want to, I don't know, kiss her? Get her between the sheets?"

His eyes flashed up to meet hers again. He had kissed her. The other day. It was the first time his lips had been anywhere close to hers. And it had been…fucking nice. Soft, full, malleable.

"No. Maybe. She was my friend, I wasn't willing to cross that line." There was an edge to his voice.

"'Cause she's not blonde, blue-eyed, and stacked? Or is it that she doesn't simper?"

Juanita seemed to be on a roll this morning. He had a feeling that if asked to pick sides, she'd choose Em's.

He didn't have a thing for blondes. It just happened that that was what Saban was, after a trip to the hairdresser. It had always looked so natural he'd never thought she got it out of a bottle. A very expensive bottle. The simpering…he couldn't argue with that.

"Em wouldn't know how to simper. She's too strong…and she wouldn't pretend to be weak for anyone."

"I don't know, Nick. She seems to have a weak spot for you and Teddy. She just expresses it differently. She shows up."

Juanita had seen how the two women interacted with him and Teddy. Saban had accompanied him to some of the precinct cook-outs, departmental softball games, outings, funerals at the beginning. When she'd started opting out, Em would step in. Juanita pointed out something he already knew. Teddy always had a much better time with Em. And Juanita was right. Em did have a weak spot, or at least she had. Now? Nothing in his life was making sense anymore. His wife was leaving him, and his best friend was declining to stay in his life.

It was like he had the plague, and everyone was running for the hills.

They had only gone a couple of blocks before Juanita had put the car in gear in front of a 7-11, where she got her daily dose of caffeine.

"Want anything?"

"No. I'm good."

"Not from where I stand." She slammed the door and walked away.

Even his partner seemed adverse to him today.

He looked out the window, taking in the people waiting for the train, reading newspapers, on cells, chatting, daily life humming away.

He'd kept Em in his life because he needed her in it. She was his buddy. When they'd gotten back in touch after she finished law school and he got out of the service, they'd picked up right where they'd left off. She'd just joined the law firm, and he'd just joined the police department, but they still found time to grab a drink, play pool, hang out like old times. When Saban had moved back to the city a couple of years later, he couldn't believe his luck. He had a woman for each arm, so to speak. One friend, one lover. It was perfect.

Somewhere along the way, his perfect life had hit a snag.

CHAPTER SEVEN

Em got to the courthouse with little time to spare. She breathed a sigh of relief as she exited the filing office, grateful that she'd been able to get her head out of her ass and there hadn't been as much of a line as she'd anticipated. Fridays were always crunch time, lawyers good at juggling their time with efficiency, but she got her docket number and the hearing was set for a month from today. If she had waited until Monday, she might have added another week to her client's jail term.

People had started filtering out of one of the court-rooms, possibly because recess had been called for the day by the sitting judge. They plugged up the flow, filling the empty space that had been available to her just moments ago. Easing her way through the throng, it was easy to identify the lawyers by the briefcases they carried, the suits they wore, even though they were wrinkled by now. Their confident strides were in stark contrast to those who seemed cowed by the proceedings. The heat still purred out of the air vents, which would blow hot until the end of the month, and she couldn't wait to get back outside, away from the smell of stale heat, sweat and fear. The benches along the corridor were filled with people, those awaiting the end of a trial or waiting to bear witness. Just as she was approaching the exit, she heard a voice from behind her and swore under her breath.

"Em, wait up."

Her stomach churned. She knew that voice. What did she want now? It seemed Nick's wife went out of her way to use her as a pin cushion, and the pricks were beginning to bleed.

Without even turning around, she answered, "Don't have time." She picked up her pace and hurried toward the double door that would take her outside. The footsteps behind her picked up as well, until they were matching hers stride for stride. Then a pull of her arm so she had to stop. Facing Saban, she waited.

"What's going on with you?"

Shifting from one leg to the other, impatient to be gone and away, Em replied, "I don't know what you mean."

"You know exactly what I mean. You never turn down a date with Teddy. Or Nick, for that matter. Are you trying to punish me?"

Turn down a date with Nick? What the hell was she implying? They'd never dated. He'd never asked her. They were together all the time, but it was never physical. Not because she didn't want it but because he didn't. It hurt as much today as it had back then. When she'd bumped into Nick after law school, they'd started hanging out like they had in college. Then Saban had showed up and Nick picked up right where he'd left off. Saban had twirled him around her little finger with her sweet nothings and feminine wiles. So naïve and inexperienced, so in need of his protection, she'd won him over hands down. His Greek forebears and their macho need to be needed had nothing on him. She couldn't play those kinds of games and had no desire to learn.

"Punish you? For what?"

Saban was staring at her, a quizzical look in her eyes. Murmuring, she said, "He hasn't told you yet. Interesting."

"Told me what?"

"Nothing."

"What do you want, Saban?"

"I asked him if you were going to be keeping Teddy tonight. He said he didn't know. You hadn't gotten back to him. You always get back to him."

She glared at Saban. Why hadn't Nick told his wife that she'd outright refused to take Teddy tonight? Was Saban pretending he hadn't for her own purposes? What the hell was going on?

"Are you? I need to know."

"I hadn't planned on it. I have my own life. I think all three of you have forgotten that."

"But Nicky's always been a part of it. You're together as much as possible. Everyone knows he'd rather be with you than me."

There was the dig. It always came. She wasn't going to let it bother her. She'd soon be out of her range and things would get better. She had to believe that.

"I've got a lot on my plate, as you well know. You've called me in on a couple of your cases and I have dozens of my own. I can't find the time right now to babysit either one of them."

She pushed through the door to get away, setting a brisk pace towards the steps that would lead her to the parking lot. She had to skirt around the protesters who were out in force today, carrying signs emblazoned with the words, IMMIGRANTS ARE AMERICANS AND REFUGEES ARE WELCOME HERE. As she moved through, she came to a complete stop.

There was a popping sound coming from her left.

She took another step, but the noise was insistent now, grabbing her attention.

Was it a jackhammer? A car backfiring?

Emilia glanced over in the direction of the sporadic beat, expecting to see a work crew. Stunned into silence, she saw a panicked crowd running helter-skelter across the plaza, small groups of people trying to make it back into the safety of the building, everyone scrambling for cover where none existed. Some had already collapsed on the pavement, dropping where they stood, blood-curling screams raising the hair on her arms, wails and moans suggesting that those lying prone on the ground were hurt and in pain or—

Out of the corner of her eye, she saw a gunman, the weapon in his hands waving back and forth in jerky motions. He was dressed in jeans and a tattered jacket, his facial expression one of intense concentration, his eyes darting pinpricks of rage. The combination of blood, acrid smoke, and fear in the unseasonal humid air, was making her sick.

When her survival instincts kicked in with Saban's hysterical cries, Em ran back and grabbed the woman who'd stalled behind her, pushing her behind one of the columns that guarded the perimeter of the building they'd exited only seconds before. The column wasn't wide enough to cover both, so she tucked Saban in front, the tremors as forceful as an earthquake as she tried to shield them both from what was to come. The pitiful moaning prevented her from thinking clearly.

Panic was roiling inside as she tried to process what was going on around her.

How could they get out of this?

Alive.

She could hear the steady *rat-a-tat* of the machine gun now as clear as day. And it was coming closer. Sounds of car horns blaring, people swearing, praying, added to the chaos vibrating in her head. Panic knotted inside her, bone-chilling numbness. With shaking fingers, she managed to get her phone out of her pocket and looked at the screen.

Who did she call? Who could stop this madness?

The sights and sounds of the Boston Marathon bombings came back to her. Having been glued to her television screen for days after, she understood now what the spectators had gone through. Even those not hurt would be forever wounded by what had gone on around them. A reedy voice brought her back to the moment.

"What should we do?"

Saban was pulling on Em's suit jacket, like a little kid needing attention, her face streaked with tears, her face etched in horror.

"Shh. Just stay still."

Dialing 9-1-1, her hands shaking so badly she had trouble punching the three numbers in, Em waited for the voice at the other end of the call. When a woman's voice gave her spiel, Em rasped out, "I'm on the plaza at the JFK…"

"Yes, ma'am. Police are on their way. Try to find cover and don't run."

When the line went dead, her brain scrambled for something Nick had once told her. Hadn't he said to run if she ever caught up in sniper fire? *Run until you find cover, stay there for as long as you can, fight…until you can't anymore?* Did that mean until she was dead?

She looked around. She'd run as far as she could. She was hiding, but she wasn't well-hidden. That left fight. But she was scared, and it had all but paralyzed her.

With the glaring absence of gun shots, Em peeked out. The shooting had stopped, but the gunman looked like he was reloading. No, that wasn't right. He wouldn't need to. Had the gun jammed? Would they be saved after all? The shooting began again but had changed beats. The AK rifle had been flung down to the ground, and another agent of death had replaced it. Who was this guy? Rambo?

She pushed herself tightly against Saban, trying to think.

Saban shrieked, trembling, hyperventilating. "Call…Nick. He'll save us."

Brushing the request off like she would a fly, the ridiculousness of the statement an indication of how much the woman depended on her husband, she shushed her.

"He'd never get here in time."

Saba's voice went up a decibel.

"Do something Em."

Another scream, another hit.

Or was that her nerves screeching for safety?

Before she could react, Saban had squeezed herself out from her protected position, into the open, as if to run. "I've got to get out of here."

"No, Saban…"

And another round of shots crackled as if alive, and Saban was shoved forward and then back as bullets riddled her body. She glanced back, her mouth open, her eyes pleading. Taking a step into the fray to drag her back, Emilia felt a burning sensation in her upper shoulder but held on to the body now in her care.

Then a voice. Deep, commanding, male.

"This is the police. Put your hands up. Drop your weapon."

From her position, as she drew off her suit jacket to wrap around Saban's wounds, trying to keep her from seeing the blood and guts gurgling out, Em saw the shooter turn toward the single cop standing at the corner of the adjacent building, his gun aimed and ready.

The gunman advanced towards the man in blue, his bullets a crescendo of noise. The policeman made the command for the second time but to no avail. One pull of the trigger is all it took. With her eyes now on the shooter, she saw him fall to the ground, a small indentation in the middle of the forehead, his weapon beside him.

After a moment of silence, a new noise rendered the air as sirens from police, ambulances, and fire engines came rushing to the scene.

Trying to ignore what was all around her, she knelt beside Saban, putting her hands over her torso, applying much-needed pressure to staunch the flow of blood that seemed to be pouring out of her. Her breathing was raspy, ragged. Saban was crying, "Stop, please. Stop. It hurts."

Taking her hand, Em squeezed it.

"Hold on. It's over. Help is coming."

"No. I…I'm not going to make it. Promise…"

The cough brought up some blood that oozed out of her mouth.

Steel-blue eyes penetrated her own. With a quiver of lips, as if she was chilled to the bone, Saban rasped out, "Now you get to have him. Promise me you'll take care of Teddy and…"

"Saban, don't…"

"I know the way...you feel about him. He's...probably the only one who doesn't..."

Another cough.

"Listen. Can you hear the sirens? Hang on..."

"You'll take care of Teddy?"

"Saban, no, you'll..."

"Promise."

Rather than have her waste her energy on a promise she didn't need to ask, Em nodded. Saban continued to stare as if she needed the words.

"I promise. Always."

"Good."

That one word was her last.

CHAPTER EIGHT

Emilia sat there, mute. Her whole body shook, her insides trembling so hard her lungs weren't giving her enough air to breathe.

What had just happened? She looked around. The pavement was pooled with blood, people crawling through it, coming out from their hiding spots. Some were clutching a part of their body as if wounded. Others were running to help those lying prone on the ground, the whimpers of the critically injured sounding as if they were coming over a loud speaker. A woman was running from the scene, screaming, now that it was safe to do so. A man had crawled over to where Em was, holding his blood-soaked hand or what was left of it. His fingers had been shot off. He looked down at Saban and gave Em a look of sympathy. Her attention was drawn away as police swarmed the area, their faces grim and somber. Still holding the small hand in hers, she noticed the arrival of ambulances, the EMTs scouring the ground for survivors, for those who needed medical attention. She glanced over at the brick building where her afternoon appearance had been a normal part of her routine, a place where she would no longer feel safe. The crowd that cowered inside began inching out, closer to the bloodbath, as if they needed to see for themselves this was real. It was late afternoon, and hundreds of pedestrians were out on the streets, most heading home, some to grab something to eat before returning to work. She'd been headed back to the office, so she could pick up Cami for the drink they were planning on.

Before Saban had forced herself on her.

She looked back down at the lifeless body. Saban looked fragile, her face completely devoid of blood, chalky white, her form lying at a weird angle. She'd be mortified if she knew she was exposed like this. Beginning to reach for the hem of her skirt to pull it down, she halted her shaking fingers. There was a voice in her head telling her not to touch anything, to leave the scene as it was. Nick's voice, as he explained how a person discovering a body made the mistake of tampering with evidence. Nick.

How was she ever going to explain this to him? To Teddy?

"Ma'am, are you hurt?"

She looked around, still trying to process what had happened. The victim with the missing digits was gone, and there was a burly man beside her, fingering the spot on her shoulder that still ached. She heard his voice echo out over the distance.

"Over here, Robin."

An EMT rushed over, her medical bag slung over her shoulder. After kneeling, she felt for a pulse on Saban's prone body and shook her head before giving her partner her attention.

After assessing Emilia's shoulder, the partner said, "Bullet wound. Not sure about the damage, possible rupture of brachial plexus. Too much blood to be sure."

He was forcing the jacket off her, ripping her blouse at the point of contact. She didn't make a move to stop him, didn't utter a sound. Disorientated to the point she couldn't identify her surroundings, she let them do their job. She scanned the area, trying to focus, the chaos around her moving in slow motion. She was numb, her control hanging by a thread. When they started moving her to the stretcher, she fought them.

"Please, I can't leave her alone. Nick might already be here. You might know him. Nick Katsaros. He's a cop."

They ignored her pleas, placing her on the stretcher and restraining her with the seat-belt like apparatus. She was still yelling at them as they put her in an ambulance, the outside noise fading away to black.

She came to as they entered the brightly lit corridor of the hospital, raised her head, taking in the doctors and nurses scurrying from room to room, stretchers lined up against the wall waiting for triage. The attendants bypassed the line, taking her to a room that had been divided by a folding partition. Was she critical? Was that why she was sent to the head of the line? With a feeling of doom, she pulled out her phone and called the law firm. She wanted them to know she was still alive.

⌐

Nick heard the ping of his phone as he raced to the scene. There'd been an all-points bulletin calling every policeman on duty to the courthouse. Some madman had opened fire in the area adjacent to City Hall. The streets would be congested with cars and pedestrians, giving the shooter hundreds of targets to choose from.

Where was Saban?

She had left without telling him anything about her agenda. He had let her go without asking. They'd outgrown the need for conversation, and Teddy had needed breakfast, his backpack refilled with extra clothes, and a lunch. By default Nick had become the primary caregiver.

Where was Em? He'd hung up on her this morning. Told her to have a good life. Could he deal with it if it was the last conversation he had with her? He was imagining the worst. They probably weren't anywhere near the plaza, but he couldn't ignore the funny feeling in the pit of his stomach.

He pressed his foot down on the accelerator as he weaved in and out of the damn traffic. Parts of Congress Street had been shut down and he slowed as he came to the gate keeper, a man in blue who would keep the media and curiosity seekers away from the scene.

No need to show his badge, he was waved through, pulling up alongside the other cruisers.

He almost swung his door into the superintendent, who stood as if waiting for him.

"Nick."

He felt prickly, the tone significant somehow.

"Superintendent Taylor."

As they faced each other, Nick was instantly alert. There was bad news here somewhere and he wasn't sure he wanted to hear it.

"I'm sorry to have to inform you..."

His heart stopped completely.

"Em?"

Taylor narrowed his eyes, his brow curling over the ridge.

"No, Nick. It's Saban."

The shock caused momentary paralysis.

"Saban was here?"

"She was, Nick. She was hit and...I'm sorry to say she didn't make it."

All sound stopped. He didn't hear the officers around him collecting evidence, the taxis beeping horns on Cambridge Street, the jackhammers that had resumed their work, people yelling and screaming.

His wife was...dead? How could that be possible? They'd argued last night, like they did every night, Teddy torn between the two, gazing up at him, his eyes pleading for them to stop.

"Her body is still here, Nick. Do you want to see her?"

He could feel the muscles jumping under his skin, the guilt eating away at the edges of his consciousness. With a nod of his head, his throat choking off all sound, he followed his supervisor to the cement post where she had been taking cover.

Bending on one knee, he felt the blood soak through his pants. There was a pool of it around the body. He took her lifeless hand in his and inspected several ragged holes, two in the chest area, one in the abdomen. Even in death she looked fragile. Small and petite, she was like a porcelain doll. It was what had drawn him to her, what had gotten old over time. He'd eventually realized he didn't want to be someone's white knight, he wanted a partnership, something she didn't know how to form. She had fought him tooth and nail when he wanted more than beat work. Cried when he wanted to join the Narcotics Unit, screamed when he wanted to join the SWAT team. Afraid he'd be killed, she'd adamantly opposed anything other than what he'd been doing over the last five years. It seemed strange that she was the one who had died.

What was he going to tell Teddy?

How would their four-year-old son take the news?

He could feel bodies pressing in, glanced up to see two men waiting, one with a body bag in his hand, the other holding on to the gurney. They must have been told to wait for his arrival and now that he'd seen, identified the body, they could dispatch it to the morgue.

He stood, giving them space to do their job, every movement a surreal one.

He'd been at numerous homicides, witnessed the routine, but this time it had a numbing feel to it. This time he knew the victim.

He felt a hand on his back and turned. Juanita was standing there.

"I'm so sorry, Nick."

He nodded his thanks at the condolences, the hollow feeling becoming more pervasive.

"How many? Anyone else we know?"

There would be attorneys, judges, court staff coming in and out of this building at this time of day and odds were the victims would be associates, friends.

"Fifteen confirmed deaths. So far. Another eleven wounded from what I've heard. The EMTs are still here. One of the bailiffs, according to Judge Rollins stepped in front, took the bullets meant for him. A couple of pedestrians, a limo driver. A couple members of a jury that had just been released for the day. Two cops, a security guard who ran out when he heard the shots, the screams. There were a couple of attorneys wounded, Nick."

His head shot in Juanita's direction.

"Which ones?"

Her stare was scaring him.

"Juanita…"

"Paula Tanner, James Packett. And Emilia."

A heavy weight settled in his chest, and it was ready to crush his heart.

"Em was shot? How badly? Is she alive?"

"She's alive. She was taken to the hospital in one of the ambulances, but I don't know the extent of the injury. Witnesses say she came out from behind the stanchion to grab the woman with her, who I assume was Saban."

His wife, letting emotion rule over reason, would have wanted to run. Em would have tried to stop her.

He looked around at the carnage. Bodies were everywhere, white sheets covering the dead, blood covering the pavers, skin, bone, and tissue in clumps underfoot. EMTs were still collecting the wounded. People were huddled in groups, crying at the scene surrounding them. It was a war zone. He should know. He'd been caught in enough of them.

The superintendent came over to where they stood. He looked as stunned as Nick felt.

"It's a mess out here. It's going to be a long night. Nick, go home, be with family. You won't be of any help."

He was right. His mind was a virtual whirling dervish, rage, guilt, regret, fear all coalesced into one giant ball of tension. He could feel his muscles tighten, his hands become fists.

"Who did this?"

It was the first time he'd even thought about the shooter.

"Hector Rojas. Thirty-five. One of the social workers who survived was part of his case. She told us his wife was undocumented and was sent back to Colombia with their son. We don't know for sure but think this was payback."

Hector had gotten what he wanted, if that was what he was seeking. There were several other mothers taken from husbands, children, families. His was one of them.

His blood started roiling. If the guy weren't dead, he would have killed him. He overheard the EMTs discussing the take-down. He met the superintendent's eyes.

"Your son's the one that took him out?"

"He is."

"Thank him for me, will you?"

With a nod, the head of the department turned to talk to some of the other policemen, taking measure of the full extent of the damage done here today.

Juanita was assigned to take him back to the station so he could get his car. He had a son to tell, calls to attend to, and a funeral to plan. But first, he had a stop to make.

⌒

"Good afternoon, Woodley and Fisher. How may I direct your call?"

"Heather, it's Em. Is anyone free?"

"Thank goodness. They've been frantic. I'll put you through to Arianna."

"Thanks."

The hustle and bustle outside the curtain made the wait seem endless. She didn't want reminders of what she'd witnessed, of what she'd been a part of.

The cool, authoritative voice that came on the line, had an edge.

"Where are you? Are you all right?"

Still shaky, still nauseous, she imposed quiet on her mind.

"I'm in the hospital. I got hit, my shoulder or my back. I'm not sure. It's not life-threatening." At least she didn't think it was. She hadn't been seen yet, which meant she wasn't one of the most critical.

"Thank God. What the hell happened out there? We're still waiting for the news conference."

"One shooter. He was taken down by Zach Taylor."

"That we know. He was in court as a witness. He snuck out the back and went around the building. He was a sniper in the marines and it seems he still has the stuff."

"If he hadn't..." She couldn't think about that. The shooter had zoned in on her, Saban's loud wail giving their location away, and it was only a matter of time before he reached her. "Have you heard how many...dead?"

When she'd been wheeled to the ambulance, she'd given up her fight to stay with the body.

She'd taken a breath and looked around. It had seemed like there were dozens of bodies strewn all over the asphalt, green space, as still as...death. She was sure it was the reason she blacked out.

"Not yet."

"Saban..." The tears started to fall. Not sobs. She wasn't the hysterical type although she could easily have given into the retching her stomach was promising. "She didn't make it."

"Oh, Em. I'm so sorry."

Arianna knew about their relationship, had given counsel, had listened.

She felt the panic rise with the bile and she heard her voice hitch up.

"I can't call Nick. I can't be the one to tell him."

A steady, calm voice asked, "Do you want me to?"

No. She was his best friend. Used to be, anyway. She couldn't pass this on to someone else.

She could hope... "He might know by now." His wife would be recognized by some of his fellow officers. They'd get word to him.

"Was he on duty today?"

"Yeah."

It was why he'd needed her to pick Teddy up after school. Who was going to do it in his stead?

"Then chances are he knows by now. Camille's been frantic. I swear she's been calling your cell every five minutes."

When Camille got on the line she cut right to the chase.

"Which hospital? I'm coming."

Normally she wouldn't have needed company, would have tried to talk her out of it. Not today.

"Mass General."

When the call ended, she was relieved. She couldn't bear being alone with her thoughts. Now, everything penetrated her mind. The emergency room was still in code red, alarms blaring, beeping machines setting off a racket, voices raised as they rushed directives, people were crying, and her senses went on overload. The ambulances were still arriving, the sirens adding more chaos to the scene, and she wondered how many had been injured. She wasn't one of the worst hurt, so she knew she'd be one of the last attended. She should be grateful but...

A doctor strode in, the stethoscope hanging from around his neck, and he went right to the box of gloves, ripping them out and thrusting his hands in before coming over to probe her wound.

"If someone else needs you more than I, please..."

"You were next. Besides, all on-call staff have arrived. The worst cases have already been rushed through."

He dabbed, poked, and prodded, and she winced at every touch. When he measured her shoulder for stability and range of motion, a shooting pain traveled down her arm and she cried out. He pulled off his gloves, sat on the stool, and faced her.

"We need to run some tests, Ms. Ronan. First up will be X-rays. The shoulder is more complicated than most people realize. It's made up of nerves, muscles, cartilage, with arteries and veins running through it. You might have some nerve damage and I want to see what the severity is. You'll recover, but there might be a loss of mobility. Compared to some of the others, you can consider yourself lucky. An AR-15 can cause severe harm, as you probably already know."

She looked up at him with glazed eyes. Lucky? She didn't think so. Lucky would have been finishing the petition earlier in the day and not being anywhere near the courthouse when the man started shooting. If Saban hadn't followed her out, would she still be alive, getting ready to go home to Nick and her son? If she hadn't been in such a hurry to get away from her, would they both have gotten away without a scratch? Had Saban really asked her to take care of her husband? Teddy? And now that she'd promised she would, what would that mean for her heart?

"Do you have any questions?"

There was just one thing she wanted to know.

"How long will I have to stay here?"

She wanted home, her bed, to feel safe again. It was her sanctuary. A renovated bungalow, with a fireplaced living room, oak flooring, and three spacious bedrooms, it was close to a hundred years old. She'd purchased it right after Teddy was born, wanting to be close by in case Nick could use her help. Saban seemed to be suffering from post-partum depression right after his birth and she wasn't doing well with the newborn. Em would never have thought about buying something so homey if it hadn't been for her godson.

The doctor explained, "Expect to stay the night, at least. It might be longer depending on what we find. If the injury is minor, we'll bandage you up and get you out of here. If it's more severe, you might be facing surgery, now or at some point down the road. I don't think it's minor."

She listened, trying desperately to process what the doctor was saying, but her mind was only willing to pick out a few choice words. Surgery? Later? She wanted to get this over with, so she could put it behind her.

"Why not immediately?"

"We like to give the body a chance to recover on its own. Many do over a period of weeks or months. Those who heal without invasive techniques have better functional outcomes."

"Okay. That makes sense. If that's the case, I'd prefer to wait."

He was busy typing at the computer terminal when he asked, "Do you have someone who can take care of you for a week or so? You'll be unable to do some things by yourself and it would greatly improve your recovery process if you took it easy."

"I live alone and don't want to interfere with anyone else's life. I'll be fine. I promise I'll take it easy."

"We'll talk more about that after the X-rays, when I know what we're dealing with."

With clipped steps he ducked around the curtain, leaving her alone but for the drip of the IV and the stinging in her shoulder.

CHAPTER NINE

Em jumped when she heard the scratch of the curtain as it was yanked aside, cowering until she saw Camille coming closer, concern etched on her face. She'd been expecting her, but the sudden movement jolted her already overloaded system.

Camille was beside her in two steps, took her hand and squeezed.

"Are you all right?"

Em shook her head as tears filled her eyes.

"I'm sorry. Ridiculous question."

Feeling exposed and vulnerable in the johnny as she waited to be taken to X-ray, she let Cami hug her good arm, grateful she didn't touch her throbbing shoulder. Tears spilled down her cheeks, and her breaths were ragged and uncontrollable. She would never forget the sounds of bullets piercing skin and ricocheting off of trees and asphalt, the smell of blood and smoke, the sight of red-splatter everywhere. Or the eyes staring up at her with no life in them.

"I can't believe this happened. That I'm here. That I was shot. Why, Cami? Why does someone do this? The carnage…" The rest of the sentiment was lost in a quivering sob.

Patting her hand, Camille shook her head. "I don't know sweetie. No matter what the reason, it didn't warrant this."

"There were so many bodies, just lying there. Did you know you see can see the blood spatter when the bullets hit, that bits of bone and muscle look like phlegm being spit on the sidewalk?"

It was horrifying.

Grabbing Cami's hand, she asked, "Was anyone else from the firm there?"

"No, thank goodness. Nell was there earlier but was already back by the time it started. Gretchen was still inside. When I checked in your office and found you gone, I asked Liz where you were. She was beside herself, knowing you'd gone in to file a petition. I kept trying to reach you, kept getting voice mail. I was a wreck waiting to hear from you. We spent a frantic amount of time tracking everyone down. And then there were the calls coming in, family of the staff wanting reassurance that their loved ones were safe. Maks must have called a dozen times wanting to know if we found you."

At the mention of family, Em bolted up, wincing as she did. "I should call Olivia. Let her know I'm here."

"She called the office right after I talked to you. She couldn't get past your voice mail and was frantic. She should be here shortly."

Olivia was the only other person who would have been worried for her. She didn't have a Maks or a Jack, whose life would be forever altered if something had happened. It made her more determined than ever to change the track she'd been running on.

But what about her promise to Saban? The one she'd made as the woman lay dying? Could she stay in Nick's life, watch him fall in love again somewhere down the road, relive the hurt and pain one more time? As her anxiety continued to build at not knowing whether she could keep her word for the first time in her life, Cami asked, "How did you get caught up in this?"

"I was just coming out…wasn't paying attention to my surroundings. Saban had…"

Her eyes flashed up to Cami's as Saban's body came back into her consciousness. "Saban got shot. She…didn't survive. She was right beside me." Would she ever be able to get that picture out of her mind? The blood, the cold hand gripped in hers, the blood trickling from her mouth?

She winced in pain as a sob tore through her.

"Why her and not me, Cam? She was the one who had so much to live for."

Making eye contact, Cami issued a severe reprimand.

"Don't you dare go down that road. I know survivor's guilt will haunt you, but don't you dare say better you than her."

"What's Teddy going to do without his mother?"

"I'm not going to answer that because I don't usually speak ill of the dead. And you're coming home with me tonight. I'm not going to leave you alone."

"You've been married less than a week. I'm not having you play nurse. If I have to, I'll stay with Olivia."

Her younger sister had a loft apartment and Em wasn't sure where she'd sleep but it would be better than invading Cami's home. She'd just moved into a new house with Maks and they weren't even settled in yet.

"Olivia's place is no bigger than a shoe box. We just bought a four-bedroom house. We have plenty of room and I know Maks won't mind."

Em knew they'd sold her condo, wanting something bigger. They were ready, willing and able to fill it with children and were already working on the first.

"Let's see what the doctor says after the X-rays. The wound might be a minor inconvenience."

At least she hoped it was. She was too active in sports to be sidelined forever because of the shooter. If her shoulder was injured what would that mean to her pitching arm.? Would she still be able to maneuver the ball in the windmill type movement? She'd been perfecting the underhand fast pitch since high school and had gotten her speed up to seventy-five miles an hour. It was her contribution to her intramural team. Who would she be without it? She'd do what she had to to make sure she got her mobility back, unwilling to give up her position. It was one of the outlets she used for all the hard and heart-breaking work she did.

She looked toward the door when they heard a commotion just outside the room, the panic beginning to rise again. When Nick raced in, he was wearing an expression of pure terror.

"Em, thank God you're all right."

Tears blinded her eyes, and in a choking voice, she said, "I'm so sorry, Nick. I tried…"

He pulled the chair closer to the bed and sat in it. Took the hand that Cami had held just moments before.

"Don't. I know. One of the witnesses said you got shot when you exposed yourself trying to keep her from running."

"You were at the scene?"

"We got an emergency alert and every car on patrol was called in. I…identified the body and the superintendent sent me home."

While brushing her cheeks with her fingers, she tried to regain some control.

"What are you going to tell Teddy?"

His misery was so apparent it was like another physical pain, this time in her heart.

"That his Mom got shot by a bad man."

His voice was harsh and raw.

That she had witnessed the scene was traumatic, that the man had taken Teddy's mother away from him, heartbreaking. She shriveled at the memory. Her voice was small when she asked, "Do you know what prompted it?"

There was bitterness hiding beneath his words as he explained what he'd been told at the plaza.

The man was an immigrant. She could just imagine the spin the news would put on it. There'd be another wave of protest to get them all out. She sighed just as a nurse and orderly came in, wheeling a gurney.

"We're transporting you down now, Ms. Spencer-Ronan. Can someone take your things? You'll be admitted as soon as we're done and won't be coming back here."

Nick became more agitated. "Where are they taking you?"

"X-ray."

"Okay, that's good. No surgery?"

The nurse answered, "Not yet. We have to wait and see what kind of damage has been done."

Cami assured her, "I'll stick around until you're out and help get you settled in your room."

Panic bubbled up. "I'm not staying overnight. I don't want to be here. I want to go home."

Nick tightened his grip on her hand, his tone as commanding as ever.

"You have to do what the doctor says, Em."

She was angry. Pissed at the injury, at Saban, at the shooter and the deportation that had prompted this. She had a scapegoat and used it.

"I can do what I want, Nick. You have nothing to say about this."

He glanced up at Cami. "Can you try to talk some sense into her?"

"I've been doing that for close to a year. She's beginning to listen to reason, so there's hope."

His brow furrowed as if he didn't understand what she was talking about. His brain was like an egg, fried and sizzled.

He watched helplessly as the attendants lifted Em up and onto the gurney and wheeled her away. Never in his life did he think she could look that small. Was she hunched in because of the pain? It made him hurt to see her so ravaged by the events of the day.

Cami turned on him as soon as Em had disappeared.

"What the hell are you doing here, Nick? Don't you have a son to take care of and a wife to bury?"

Her words were like a spray of bullets, each one piercing the thin armor of sanity he clung to.

"When I heard she'd been shot, I had to see for myself she was going to survive." Saban was dead. He couldn't bear to think he'd lost Em.

"Well, you've seen. Now you can go."

He knew he should. He had to pick Teddy up, but he couldn't pull himself away. His eyes searched the room, the florescent light flickering overhead, the discarded gloves hanging off the side of the recycle bin, the blood staining the bed sheet that must have seeped from her wound, the indentation of her body on the bed that told him, yes, she was here, in pain and shot by a crazed gunman. How extensive was the injury?

He heard himself ask, "What's the diagnosis?"

"They talked about brachial something. The only language I speak is legalese. Medical jargon is like Greek to me."

She sounded impatient, as if she didn't want to take the time to answer him, but he knew it was plain old fear she was feeling. Being Greek, it all made sense to him. It would mean there could be damage to cartilage, nerves, or muscle. Em wouldn't know what to do if she couldn't play softball. She'd been playing it since he met her and before that in high school. She'd found an intramural team when she got out of law school and been their ace pitcher for years. It would spell trouble for her if the injury caused permanent damage. This would be the first time she'd been incapacitated. How was she going to deal with it?

Not well. They couldn't trust her to—

"She won't be able to stay alone. At least for a while. She'll need rest and tending."

"Got it covered. She'll stay with us. Now, why don't you leave."

He shifted his weight to one foot, his hands went to his hips, and he flashed his eyes at her.

"What the hell have I done to make you so mad at me?"

Em didn't seem to have that market cornered.

Meeting his gaze, she said without hesitation, "You've been taking advantage of her since the day I met you. Today, she almost made the ultimate sacrifice for your wife. Thinks it would have been better if she'd died and Saban had lived. God, a world without Em in it would be…"

Cami's eyes held a sheen as if the reality of what might have happened finally hit her. He would have stepped up to comfort her, but he had a feeling it wouldn't be accepted or appreciated.

"It would be empty. I know."

And cold. He didn't like standing outside her fire. He wished he knew what he could do to get her to welcome him back into the warmth. He wanted to ask but he didn't think Camille would explain it to him.

"I've got to go pick up Teddy, call Saban's parents. But I'll be back. I want to know the prognosis. I wish I could give Teddy another couple of hours before telling him he doesn't have a mother."

She looked at him then, sympathy shining in her eyes, but said nothing. Gathering up Em's purse and clothes, she made for the door.

"I'm putting these things in my car before calling Maks and letting him know what's going on. He said he'd come wait with me until she has a room."

"Does Olivia know?"

"Yes. I already spoke to her. Her aunt and uncle need to be told but we're waiting for a little more information. I hope they don't hear the news until we know what to tell them. I don't want them rushing up."

He knew Em's Aunt Kelsey and Uncle Doug had taken her and her sister, Olivia, in when their parents died in a car crash. Em had been ten, Olivia seven. They'd been put in child services until next of kin had been contacted and could arrange a flight in from America, and it was an experience she'd never forgotten. It drove her passion, compelled her to work for children who ended up in the same spot, not from death but from an imperfect immigration system. The Ronans had flown to Australia where the Spencers had lived and taken the girls back to the States to raise as their own. It's where she got the name Spencer-Ronan, combining both to signify the impact both couples had on her life. Em had to come to love her surrogate parents as her own. They were going to be heartsick to know what had happened but grateful she'd been spared. Just like he was.

"It might be good for her to be with them, so maybe you shouldn't talk them out of coming."

"I'm not making decisions for her until I know what she wants. She'd be pissed if they came up for nothing."

"She was shot, Cami. Do you know what that does to a person?"

"It makes you mistrust your surroundings, makes you feel vulnerable, and it screws up your emotions. Few know I was attacked last year. Not a gun, a knife. Same outcome. I have more of an idea than you. You're usually on the other end of the weapon."

He stared, non-plused. Em had never told him and she told him just about everything. Or so he always thought. Maybe she saw the friendship differently than he did?

"Was it when you were working with Maks?"

There were all kinds of security issues with the Russian, and he'd had a twenty-four-seven cycle of bodyguards to keep him safe before he testified before the grand jury. It would have made sense...

"No, and I'm not discussing it with you. The point I was making is I know what she's feeling. You don't."

"I was in the marines, Camille. There wasn't a day I wasn't shot at by someone, and I've survived ambushes. I know what it's like seeing death all around you. I've also known cops who were shot on the job. Talked to them. Some of them quit the force, unable to deal with the repercussions."

Camille pursed her lips in response. He was sure she'd forgotten that part of his life, if she ever knew about it at all. At the moment, the only thing he was sure of was that his life had gone completely off the rails.

A nurse came in, interrupting their dialogue.

"I'm sorry but we need the room. We need to get the hallways clear."

Camille gathered up Em's personal effects and put them in a bag provided by the staff before she walked out ahead of him. They were greeted by the chaos they'd been able to avoid up until now. Doctors in scrubs, were rushing from room to room, nurses pushing IV poles, orderlies pushing gurneys through a throng of on-lookers. Family members crying, others talking quietly amongst themselves, the press plying hospital personnel with questions.

Nick, still in his cop uniform, was accosted by a reporter. After thrusting the microphone in his face, she said, "Jennifer Roanayne, Channel Seven News. Can you give us an update on the assault?"

Pushing the offending mic away from him, he said, "You'll have to get your information from the appropriate sources. That would be the superintendent and I'm sure he'll be holding a press conference soon."

"Are you here for a personal reason or a professional one? We heard two policemen were gunned down."

There were, but it wasn't his place to talk about them.

"No comment. If you'll excuse me, I have to go."

Going over to the curved cuff of the nurses' station, Nick, asked "You're still taking in victims from the shooting?"

"Yes, sir. We pushed through the ones who needed emergency treatment now we're dealing with the aftermath. Most of them are in shock."

"How many did you take in?"

"A half-dozen in surgery now, others in X-ray or in for cat scans, a dozen more with lesser injuries."

A woman began to wail, keening, the chilling sound signaling deep grief.

He looked at the nurse with a question in his eyes.

"There was a little girl in critical condition. She must have died from her wounds. She was only four."

His eyes closed as he thought of Teddy. What would he have done if...

He couldn't wait to pick him up from school, hug him, tell him how much he loved him, and yet, he wanted to put off the inevitable for as long as he could.

Teddy was happily playing with his friends, unaware that his life had changed, and he wished he could keep it that way. What would Teddy think? How would he react? Would he understand the concept of death, or would he not understand what this meant for his future until he was older?

What would have happened if he'd lost both his mother and his Em, which was what he called her? His Em.

Blood rushed to his head. Someone had killed Teddy's mother and hurt his best friend. That could not stand. Not in his book. An undocumented man had committed this heinous act. Anger was beginning to pierce through the shock. It followed him out to the waiting room, to his car, and all the way to the preschool. He was going to make up for Teddy's loss, one way or another.

On the way to the preschool, Nick called his parents, knowing they'd be home from work by now. When his mother answered the phone, she sounded relieved. "You're alive. We just got home, put the news right on, and they mentioned there were a couple of policemen killed by this nut."

"I wasn't wounded but..."

The words lodged in his throat. He still hadn't processed it.

"But...what, Nick?"

"Saban was in the courtyard when...the shooting started. She's dead."

He heard the intake of breath as his mother grasped what had happened. Her voice was thick with emotion.

"Oh, Nick. I'm so sorry. What can we do? How can we help?"

"I'm going over to pick Teddy up at school, then I want to go back to the hospital. Em was hit, as well. I want to check in, see what the prognosis is. Can I drop him off with you for an hour or two?"

"Oh, my God. Em, too? How badly was she hurt? Is she going to be all right?"

His parents knew Em better than Saban. They'd known her longer. She'd been part of his life, an intricate part of his life. Not only had they roomed in the same dorm, but during summers and vacations they'd both worked at his father's sporting goods store. His father never failed to remind him she was the best employee he had, used to ask him if he had any other friends like her. She had a superlative sense of responsibility. Jerry Katsaros had never doubted she'd be on time for her shift and had given her opening honors. There had always been a good rapport between them and it had continued after he married Saban. It didn't surprise him when his father had picked up the extension at the mention of Em's name, the land line still their connection to the outside world. He'd probably be more upset about Em's injuries than Saban's death. He shook that thought out of his head. His father would mourn the passing of his daughter-in-law without question.

The gruff voice asked, "What happened to Em?"

Jerry didn't know yet that his daughter-in-law was dead. Nick would leave it to his mother to relay the news.

"She's in the hospital. She got hit in the shoulder, so it depends on what kind of damage was done."

His mother asked, "Were they together?"

His father sounded confused.

"Who? Were who together?"

He heard his mother shush him before she came back on the line for his answer.

"From what I heard from witnesses, Em tried to shield her, but Saban didn't want to wait around for the shooter to advance. She got hit when she darted out."

"She was running."

"Looks like it."

That was the way she lived life. She ran away from all unpleasantness, conflict, work. Which meant they'd never really had any kind of viable relationship. He'd reached the end of his rope, gotten tired of pulling it all by himself. A divorce was coming, and he'd known it was the right thing to do, but he'd never wanted her dead.

His dad, still sounding confused asked, "Saban was part of this pandemonium?"

"Yeah, look, Mom, maybe you can tell dad the rest. I just got to the school. I'll be by soon."

"Okay, son. We'll be waiting."

CHAPTER TEN

Nick swiped off and sat for a minute. He needed to collect his thoughts, put on a brave face. He had to find the words to tell Teddy what had happened and why, although he'd never understand it himself.

He got out of the car, went through the outer door and punched in the code to get inside. The assistant director came out, her face ashen. "We've been trying to get through to you and Saban. When we couldn't reach either of you...we thought the worst. We were getting ready to call Em, make sure someone was here for Teddy. I can't tell you how good it is to see you, Nick."

He felt his eyes fill with tears and he brushed them away.

"Saban's dead, Heidi. Em was hurt, too. I came as soon as I could."

Heidi's eyes widened, and then she began to cry. "I'm so sorry, Nick. I...Will Em be okay?"

They knew her as well as Saban, she'd had Teddy so often during the week over the last couple of years, would drop him off before she went to work or pick him up if he didn't have a way to get home.

"She's in the hospital. Any advice on how to tell my son?"

Heidi had gone into her office to get a tissue, handed him one as she thought about his question.

"All I can suggest is that you just tell him the basics, answer his questions as simply as possible. He won't be able to understand completely at his age, but then again, I don't understand it completely. What possessed someone to kill like that?"

"Anger, fear, mental issues, revenge. Lots of reasons but none that make sense." This was one of the instances when the president was right. An immigrant who'd gunned down dozens of innocent people did not belong here. They needed to get people like him out. And soon.

He began to walk toward Teddy's classroom, his steps slow and measured. When he got to the door, his soon had a big grin on his face, which was pressed against the window that looked out to the hall. Teddy was in his arms as soon as he opened the door, kissing him on the cheek, asking, "Are we still doing something fun this afternoon?"

"I don't know if you think this will be fun, but I'm dropping you off at Papa and Nana's. They wanted you to come over for dinner, and I'm going to go talk to Em, see about this weekend."

His eyes lit up.

"I want to come with you."

"I'm sorry, bud, but she's somewhere they don't allow children. I have to sneak in myself, but I know how important to you it is."

Hugging him closer, his little arm around his neck, he asked seriously, "Are you going to break the law?"

"I can't do that, silly. I am the law."

Teddy's hands cupped his face.

"Don't do anything that could get you in trouble. I need you too much."

Nick held him, squeezed a little too hard, and he heard Teddy grunt, then felt him kick him in an attempt to get down. He raced over to his cubby and extracted a picture, which he was waving as he came racing back. "Can you give her this, please? I drew it for her today."

He caressed the head looking up at him.

"I bet she'll love it."

"Me, too. She'll probably put it on her refrigerator with the rest of them."

He was sure Em had saved every picture Teddy had given her, from the first crayon scrawl to the most recent, a drawing of her at her volleyball game at the end of March. She was still speaking to him then and he'd brought Teddy to her semi-final game, which her team had won. With Saban gone, his son was going to need Em more than ever, and he had to find a way to get through to her.

After throwing the backpack on the back seat and buckling Teddy in, Nick got behind the wheel, started the engine and backed out of the school parking lot. He listened to the four-year-old chatter all the way to Wilmington, where his folks lived. It was the house he'd grown up in, although it wasn't filled with a lifetime of happy memories. His mother had left his father when he was a kid, left the family behind in her search of herself. It had flattened him and his siblings, although he was the one who took it the worst. His father was an unemotional man and living without their mother's warmth had been hard on all of them. His brother and sister had looked to him as the oldest to pick up the pieces. He'd done his best to provide what they needed, sacrificing his freedom to fulfill his obligations. Thankfully, his mother found what she was looking for, because she returned after a year, a good job in hand, with a new attitude, and his parents had resumed their life together but in a different way. His mother worked as an administrative assistant for a CEO who traveled around the country giving seminars and lectures. Kathy usually went with her, but every time she packed her suitcase, he held his breath, worried that she wouldn't come back. After close to twenty years, his parents were still together and solid as a rock. It seemed the constant distress was unnecessary. When his own marriage had begun to crumble, his mother's escape made more sense. He understood better what had made her leave. Instead of following her example, he'd stuck it out, more for Teddy than himself. He'd promised in good times and in bad and he'd muddle, somehow. When it'd become obvious that Saban didn't have the same kind of commitment, he'd resigned himself to his fate but was determined to keep his son with him. He'd handled the day-to-day tasks since day one, bought his clothes, made him breakfast, got him to school and picked him up after, spent his time with him. He gave all he had to his job and his son, no longer catering to Saban and it had caused the breach in the marriage, something he regretted but wasn't willing to remediate.

Now? There was no decision to make regarding Teddy or their future. It had been taken out of his hands by a madman.

When he pulled into the drive-way, his mother was standing at the door, his father right behind her. As soon as Teddy was released, he went running to get his hugs which they gave him in abundance.

Nick's footsteps were heavy as he entered the house. It was time to break the news.

⌐

When Em was wheeled to her room, she knew no more than she had when she'd first arrived. The doctor was supposed to come in after reading the results to let her know where she stood. She knew that they were busy here today and it might take longer than she wanted. She might have to resign herself to the fact that she'd be here overnight.

Her sister, Olivia, was waiting with Camille and tears filled her eyes again at the sight of her. What if Zach hadn't arrived on the scene when he had? She might never again have seen the sister she loved so much. They had clung together after their parents died, thankfully put in the same foster home as they waited for their aunt and uncle to come and get them. Living so far away from the rest of the family, they hadn't known what to expect. Her Aunt Kelsey was her mother's sister and had been listed as next of kin on all documents, but they'd never met her husband and didn't know how willing he'd be to take on someone else's kids. He'd surprised them, taking them both into his heart, supporting them, disciplining them, and encouraging their dreams. They couldn't have asked for a more loving family to fall into, and she occasionally thanked her mother for her foresight. Her parents would have been proud of who they'd become. Both Spencer-Ronan women had done well. She was a lawyer, her sister a pediatrician.

Olivia looked worse for wear as she rushed to her side as soon as she was encased in the bed.

"Oh, my God, Em, I was so scared when I heard the news. One of my nurses got a text about it, and when I talked to Cami.... it felt the same way it did when Mom and Dad died." Olivia began to cry, and a sob tore through the grief. "I don't know what I would have done if I'd lost you, too."

Her tears elicited Em's and they began in earnest. "I'm so sorry, Liv. I didn't know whether I'd come out of it alive. Nothing was stopping him, and he just kept coming closer and closer. There was nowhere to run. We were hiding, but…"

Olivia stopped her, clutching her hand.

"Thank God Zach was there."

"If he hadn't been..."

"Don't. He was, and you are alive. That's what we have to focus on."

Brushing away the stray tears that had fallen, Olivia asked, "What's going on with your shoulder? Do we know anything yet?"

Em shook her head. She didn't know a lot, only what she'd overheard in the hallways, the nurses still bustling patients around the hospital for tests, talking in whispers, not realizing they were being overheard. There were a dozen more like her, sent to various parts of the hospital. There were fourteen dead, who'd already been transported to the morgue. It was frightening how many people had succumbed to their injuries.

The smell of antiseptic was making her stomach roil, or maybe it was the lack of food. She hadn't eaten anything since last night's dinner. Couldn't even think about putting anything in her without gagging. She glanced out the window. It was dark out, so it must be late, but she'd lost all track of time here.

"How long have I been here?"

Cami looked at her watch.

"Almost four hours. They're doing well for the number of patients they got."

"Why don't you go home? There's nothing either of you can do for me here."

She didn't like feeling vulnerable, and with the two of them cosseting her, it emphasized just how defenseless she was.

Olivia's expression was one of surprise, like how dare she even suggest it.

"I'm not leaving you. At least not until I've spoken to the doctor. I need to hear for myself what he determines the best course of action. If I know you, you'll try to get out of it."

Em fumbled for the TV remote. She wanted to know what was going on, what the news was saying.

Olivia took it from her.

"I don't think that's a good idea, hon. You've seen enough, don't you think?"

"What I remember is hazy. I need to see what's real instead of what I've come to believe is real."

"It might be a lot worse than you remember."

Looking solemnly up at her baby sister, she choked out, "Not possible."

Footsteps told her that someone was approaching so she let the remote go, hoping it was the doctor. Her expression changed from hopeful to agitated when she saw Nick enter the room.

"What are you doing here, Nick? Where's Teddy? Does he know?"

He went to take a step closer, but Olivia became a guard dog, not letting him near her.

"He's at my folks' and yes, he knows. He doesn't really understand anything more than his mother is not coming home, and it's not his fault. The assistant director at the school told me to keep it simple."

He'd explained that Saban couldn't breathe or talk. Teddy admitted he was kind of happy she wouldn't be able to yell at him anymore. It had knocked the breath out of Nick.

Olivia was fingering Em's hair back, as if wanting to soothe and comfort. She had the bedside manner down, dealing with children. She was Teddy's doctor and he'd seen firsthand how good she was at her job.

He asked, "Was that the right thing?"

She looked up at him, pressed her lips together before saying, "Yes. What kind of questions did he ask?"

"How it happened."

"And you told him the truth?"

"I told him a man did it, that the police made sure he won't be able to hurt anyone else."

She seemed satisfied with that.

"He also asked where she was. That one I didn't know how to answer."

Olivia was hovering at Em's side, as if she needed to make sure she was here and alive. He knew she'd already lived through something like this, and if something had happened to Em, Olivia would have been the last Spencer standing.

"At his age, he can't conceptualize that death is permanent. He probably thinks this is temporary, reversible." She glanced up to meet his eyes. "Don't think this is a one-time discussion. He'll probably have questions as he gets older. And what you tell him is a personal choice. A lot of people talk about heaven, God bringing the soul home. I never liked that. It would have made me angry at God for taking my parents away from me. But it's what people learn in catechism."

He listened, grateful she was sharing this. He felt so inadequate to the task and explained, "I told him I wasn't sure where she was, that I'd like to think she became part of the stars. Then he could look up every night and she'd be there."

Em looked at her sister.

"That was a good answer, wasn't it?"

Olivia nodded her approval. Cami admitted, "I'm impressed." She coolly assessed him, as if seeing something she'd never seen before. "How did he take everything?"

"Better than I hoped. I explained his routine wouldn't change much, that he'd still go to school, that I'd still pick him up after." He glanced over to Em. "He asked if you were hurt, too."

There was a look of surprise on her face. "Why would he have put that together?"

"He connects you with his mother. I'm not sure he knows who is who."

He didn't know where that thought had come from, but it had come on like a freight train. He was staring into space when Em asked, "You told him I was fine, didn't you? I don't want him scared something's going to happen to me."

She pulled herself up, the wince telling him what the move had cost her.

"You didn't tell him I was here, did you? That you were coming back to see me?"

"I had to, Em. This isn't something we could keep from him. He wants to see you, wants to know that you're okay, that you're not going to disappear on him. He wanted to come with me, but I told him I'd have you call him so he could hear it for himself. He's going to need you now, Em, more than ever. If anything ever happens to me, I want you to take him."

Camille's hackles went up and the reprimand might have been a whisper, but it held the fury of a woman pissed.

"Oh, no, you don't. You are so not putting a guilt trip on her now, Nicholas Katsaros. She's been shot, needs sleep and food and healing, not anxiety about a four-year-old's peace of mind. That's your job, not hers."

Olivia shot Cami a look that said *not now* just as the doctor entered.

They all gave him their attention.

"Ms. Spencer-Ronan."

"Dr. Agarwal. What did you find?"

The doctor took a step to the bed but directed his assessment to all in attendance as soon as Em gave her permission.

"There's a nick in the clavicle and a tear in the cartilage. Several layers of epidermis have been sheared. For as painful a recovery as that will be, it isn't as bad as we initially thought. There are a few bone chips floating under the skin, but I think they will work themselves out over time. There was no extensive muscle or nerve damage. When the bullet hit the bone, instead of burrowing into the tissue and doing a merengue dance like it should have, it skimmed across your shoulder and back like a pebble across the water. You must have been in motion, moving at the exact right time and in the right direction. A change in the trajectory would have caused major fragmentation. There was a slice in several arteries but no rupture of major blood vessels. There's nothing we can do for the bone chip, and the bone itself is in stable condition. You will need a couple of weeks' rest to give the new skin time to regrow. It means not doing anything with that shoulder for two weeks. Then I'll want you to follow up with my office before resuming your normal activities." He looked up over the bifocals that sat on his nose. "You were a very lucky woman, Ms. Spencer-Ronan. I can't stress than enough."

Before anyone got too comfortable with the news, Nick said "You might want to ask her what those normal activities include, Doctor."

⌒

The doctor took the glasses off and asked, "What do you mean?"

"She's a pitcher for a women's softball team."

He returned his attention to Em, his tone brooking no argument.

"That is out, possibly for the season. What I consider normal is driving, walking, working in small doses. No heavy lifting, no carrying groceries, no fast-pitch, no hitting."

Em gave Nick a look that could have killed him on the spot, but he wasn't letting her get away with a vague promise. He knew her pain level and she'd bite the bullet to help her team. She was still glaring when the doctor asked, "Is there someone you could stay with for the two weeks of recuperation."

Olivia didn't bat an eye before stating, "She'll stay with me."

Cami suggested a different idea. "Your place is too small, Liv. She can stay with me. We have plenty of room."

"Or she can stay with Teddy and me. We have the room and I think it would reassure Teddy that you're going to be all right. I know he'll take very good care of her."

Cami and Olivia couldn't have staged the answer better as they said in stereo, "Are you out of your mind?"

CHAPTER ELEVEN

Em was listening to them argue over who should help her with her convalescence. She wanted to stay at her house. Home. That's where she could heal the best. Who did she want to stay with her?

One name, one freckled face came to mind.

Teddy.

That little boy always lightened her heart, and if he was with her, she'd be content to do nothing but read to him, play Chutes and Ladders or Candy Land, watch him play with his trucks. She had all those things tucked away in the sunroom. She loved her sister and knew she'd have a lot more freedom during the day because she'd be at work, but Olivia would still find ways to nag her to keep still, call her twenty times a day to make sure she was following the doctor's orders. And Cami would do the same, although she'd probably hibernate in the room they assigned her while Maks was there so as not to disturb the newly married couple.

There was really no question for her, but she knew she'd be opposed on every side but one.

Her voice sounded rusty when she announced her preference.

"I want to stay with Teddy."

Both Olivia's and Camille's voices joined in argument, Nick's rising above them both.

"Look, I'm taking a week's bereavement time. I have a wake and funeral to plan, a little boy who'll need my attention. I'll be home. Neither of you will be. It makes sense for Em to stay with us for at least that long."

"Not your house. Mine."

There would be no way she'd stay at his house. Too much of Saban would be there.

She glanced over to see his expression, took him in. He still had on his uniform. He hadn't even taken the time to go home and change before coming back. This was the friend she remembered. He'd be there for her if she needed... She shriveled at the thought. That's what this was. She needed him. It was that simple. Now that Saban was gone, he'd need someone to coddle, protect. She had to remember that, even as she was letting him fulfill the role. It's not what she wanted from him. She could take care of herself.

"You want to stay at your house?"

She croaked out, "Yes."

She could tell he was digesting the idea, his forehead wrinkled in thought.

"We could do that. I know Teddy thinks of it as his second home. He'll like the idea."

Teddy had a room there, for his overnight stays. There were toys, games, and a yard outside where he could run and play.

Olivia was staring at her, as if weighing her options.

"Maybe making this decision tonight isn't a great idea."

She wavered, not sure this was the right time or place for this, but given her injury, maybe they'd cut her some slack. She studied each person. Who'd give her the hardest time?

"There's a reason I have to go home."

Olivia asked, after a brief hesitation, "And that is?"

It looked as if it would be her sister who tried to talk her out of it. Taking a deep breath, she said, "I bought a puppy and I'll need to be there to take care of her."

Olivia looked even more stressed as soon as she'd told the assembled group.

"You've what? Are you out of your mind? Do you know how much work that will be? If you were healthy, maybe, even though... God, that's too much to take on, Em."

She was taken aback by the ferocity of the outburst.

Camille offered a voice of reason and asked the practical question.

"When are you supposed to be getting her?"

She bit her lip, stalling for time. "Um, Wednesday."

Olivia wore a look of panic on her face.

"This Wednesday, as in five days from now?"

"Yeah, I've already scheduled the pick-up. I don't want to lose her... I was hoping..." She looked at Nick. She didn't know how she was going to stick with her plan when he left for the funeral, but she'd save that worry for another day.

"I was thinking that...since you're not going into work this week, that...you could take me out there? Teddy could come with us."

He rubbed his scalp, as if weighing the pros and cons. Glancing up, he must have noticed Olivia's scowl, which gave him extra pause. As if stalling for time, he asked, "Where exactly is out there?"

"North Hadley."

He'd know exactly where it was. He'd had an apartment there his junior year in college.

Olivia asked, frustration thick in her voice, "You can't explain to them that you've just been shot? Ask for a postponement?"

"Why would they care? Besides, it's the perfect time. I'll be home for at least a week and can get her settled. And I'll have help with her, if Nick doesn't change his mind about staying with me."

"Two weeks, according to the doctor." Olivia had put up her fingers stressing the point. "Two weeks, Em."

Seemed Olivia wasn't going to let the reference to just a week out of work slip past.

"If it's two, she'll help me suck it up. You know I'll get antsy to get back." She glanced up at Nick. His expression was unreadable. "Well? Would you be willing?"

He studied Olivia's face. "And, if I'm not?"

She stammered, stunned that he might turn her down, but let him know this was going to happen with or without his help.

"I'll have to work on a plan B."

"You have one of those?"

They'd always had each other's back…up until she began to distance herself. She'd let him down lately, so maybe he'd feel free to deny her request for his help. She closed her eyes before looking up into his.

"I can usually count on you and my plan A working."

She held her breath, waiting to see what he said, trying not to pay attention to Olivia and Camille, both of whom seemed unwilling to go with her scheme.

"If it's what you want, I'm willing."

There was an audible sigh of relief. She gave him a look of gratitude. "Just think how excited Teddy will be." She licked her lips and looked up at her sister. "Please don't fight me on this. I know it will help with the healing. Both mine and Teddy's. Lily did it for us years ago."

The adrenaline had worn down and she was totally zapped of energy. She'd sleep the sleep of the dead tonight. She cringed at the word *dead*.

The tears were back in her eyes, the sounds in her head replicas of the gun spraying bullets. She very rarely cried and didn't like anyone seeing her like this.

Sniffing, she said, "I'm going to be fine."

She had to keep telling herself that. Otherwise she'd lose her mind. She didn't want to be here, and she didn't want to remember what she'd seen this afternoon. It was like the Wild West, but without the guns drawn on both sides. No one had had a chance, until Zach evened the odds.

Olivia pulled her ringing cell phone out of her pocket, looked at the ID and swiped, putting it on speaker so Em could hear the conversation.

"Hi, Aunt Mom. Yes, I'm with her now."

"How is she? Should we come up?"

Em shook her head vigorously, the lump in her throat too big to get words out. She didn't want anyone hovering over her and her aunt was a nurturer at heart. She wouldn't be able to help herself from fluffing pillows and serving her tea. Em wanted neither. Her eyes sought out Nick who was standing alone in the corner of the room and she sighed. She knew that's exactly what he'd do, although he knew she didn't drink tea. He'd supply something else that would suit. She'd have to warn him she needed space to work through this.

"No. She's going to have one of us with her for the next couple of weeks. If we need to hand off her care, we'll call you."

"Are you sure. I'm going to be worried sick. I'd rather do that there than here where I'm helpless to do anything at all."

"You know our Em. She'll want to work through this her own way."

Her sister knew she didn't like to talk her feelings out. She just bit the bullet and dealt.

"If you think she needs me, call. I'll be up on the first flight out."

"I promise." Em gave Olivia a small smile for taking care of this. "I'll tell her. We love you, too. Bye Aunt Mom."

Olivia stuffed the cell back in her white doctor's coat. She must have run out of the office not even bothering to take it off before coming here.

"You heard. She'll come up if you need her."

"I know."

Her aunt and uncle had moved to North Carolina a couple of years ago, her uncle offered a district manager's job with a donut company that was headquartered there. With the kids grown and out of the house, he'd accepted. The fact that the winters were warm was part of the appeal and they'd come to love their new home. Her aunt had warned them all that when the grandbabies started coming, they were moving back, and that she'd muddle through the sleet and snow, wanting to be close by. That would be happening soon. With her cousin Sharon engaged, kids wouldn't be too far behind. The term *cousin* really didn't apply. They'd been raised as siblings, Sharon two years younger than her, a year older than Olivia. Josh was the youngest at twenty-eight. They weren't only close in age, they were a tight-knit family. She hosted Thanksgiving every year, celebrated the holiday as a family with Kelsey and Doug staying for the whole weekend.

Quiet settled over the small group, Olivia flipping through her phone for messages, Cami texting someone, probably Maks, who'd left as soon as she was assigned a room. Nick continued to watch her, and she grew uneasy under his inspection. Her eyes fluttered shut blocking him out. She didn't want to fall asleep, the nightmare a shadow behind her lids, lurking to strike. Her body disagreed, demanding sleep, and she nodded off against her will.

⌐

She awoke, sweaty, thrashing, her whole body on fire, swift shafts of pain shooting up her arm.

A male voice tried to calm her, and when she finally struggled to open her eyes, she saw him.

He'd gone home to change. His BPD tee replaced the blue uniform shirt and jeans encased his legs. His face was somber, his words a whisper of "It's okay. I'm here. You're okay, Em. I won't let anything hurt you."

She studied the dark stubble on his face, the strong jaw, angular face, the muscular biceps that came from his routine of weight lifting and pull-ups. His fingers were long and tapered. They were on her face, stroking her cheek, stirring up feelings she didn't want to have.

"What are you doing here?"

"Teddy and I stayed at my folks' house tonight and I…couldn't sleep. I decided to come in and stay with you for a couple of hours. I'm glad I did."

"You shouldn't be here, Nick. Saban…just died. You should be taking care of yourself, of the arrangements."

He scrubbed his face, as if he'd been sleeping himself and needed to wake up. Or maybe he'd remembered his wife was dead. His eyes were red-rimmed when he looked back up at her.

"Her mother's flying in. She's taken over, said she wants a proper burial for her daughter. She's insisting she take her back to South Carolina to rest in the family plot."

The anger that surged through her had to be throttled down. It wouldn't serve him well if she lambasted Saban's mother, even mentally.

"That should be your decision. Why are you letting her make it?"

He hesitated before explaining, "Saban was her only daughter. If she needs her to be close by, I can't blame her. I'd want Teddy close to me if anything happened. I don't want to go down there for the funeral but…maybe…I keep telling myself she's dead and it doesn't matter where she'd buried. I still can't believe it."

"If Mrs. Williams is coming into town, maybe I should ask Olivia…"

"No. I already told Teddy that we'll be staying at your house, and he's promised to take extra good care of you."

"But if Saban's mother is here, won't she be expecting to see Teddy?"

"She's staying at a hotel. You know kids aren't on her list of favorites."

"I still don't understand why she doesn't like being with Teddy."

Em's Grandmother Shelton had been a loving presence in her life, visiting Australia when she could, and they'd grown close in the years following her parents' death. She'd stay overnight at her house, beg her to play the piano, which she'd oblige enthusiastically, her fingers flying over the keys as she played ragtime and the blues. They'd bake cookies together, Em and Olivia sneaking pieces of uncooked dough behind her back, giggling when they got caught. Her grandmother's bedroom was indelibly inked in her mind. The bureau was lined with colorful perfume and powder bottles. She'd sniff but never spray, the scents too strong for her taste, but Olivia had tried every single one, loving the way the aroma lingered on her skin. The bed was huge and accommodated all three of them, which Jean Shelton allowed. They'd cuddle through the night, the white down comforter making her feel safe and warm. Some of her clothes were tucked away in the antique bureau that sat kitty-corner, making her feel as if she would always be welcome.

Teddy wouldn't have any of that from his mother's mother.

Nick concurred.

"I don't understand it either but she doesn't like messy, loud or rambunctious. Saban once told me that her mother would take a second look when Teddy reached high school. I'm not taking him with me if the funeral is in Greenwood. I don't want him out of his routine any more than he needs to be. I may have to leave him with my folks. I should talk to Olivia. See what she thinks."

"She'll probably tell you to leave it to Teddy. He might need the closure—" Her eyes flicked up to this, "I so dislike that word, but it might help him understand she's not coming back."

"The thing is, he hasn't asked about her again. All his questions are about you. It's good in a way, I guess, but it makes me realize he didn't really have a relationship with his mother."

His face clouded with uneasiness.

"How did you feel when your parents died?"

She knew what it was like to lose a mother, how alone you felt, how abandoned. When she was brought to the States, she and Olivia were smothered with love, and it was the only way the two of them were able to heal. Teddy was years younger than she was, so she didn't know what was going on inside of him, how he'd process it all. It had taken her a long time, and even though her aunt and uncle had been wonderful, she still missed her parents. The one saving grace for Teddy was he had his father. It had to help. Nick was one of the best she'd ever seen.

"I was older, a lot older. I understood it was permanent and I was devastated. My parents were such a big part of my life. Olivia and I cried every night for months, even though my aunt and uncle welcomed us in with open arms."

"What was your mother like?"

"Loving, strict, playful. She kept my dad's books, helped him edit his stuff, took calls, and set up appointments for him. It let her be a stay-at-home mom, who helped us with our homework, put us to bed with a hug and a kiss. My Aunt Kelsey was a lot like her, so the routine stayed the same, but I missed my mother's smile. The way she'd call me My Melia Bedelia or Mellie Moo."

She laughed at the memory. "I probably would have outgrown that at some point."

She glanced over to see his total focus on her and she became serious again. "The woman I remember was my age. She was only thirty-four when she died. So young."

Her thoughts became jagged and painful.

Nick's voice had a ragged edge when he said, "Just like Saban."

Yes, she'd been too young to die.

He knew the story of her parents' deaths. She'd told him all about it the night they met, met her aunt and uncle on a visit to the house during one of their semester breaks. He'd learned the full story later in their friendship. How her parents had been returning home from a friend's wedding. A lumber truck, going too fast, had flipped over as it was passing the Nissan Pintara the Spencers' were driving. Between being rammed by the front end of the truck and the falling lumber, the car had been crushed, and they had both died instantaneously. Em had wondered out loud if her father had had too much to drink. He wasn't a drinker by nature, but she was sure he would have imbibed at the reception. Or maybe it was late, and he wasn't paying attention to the road like he should. When the police had arrived at the house, the babysitter didn't know what to do. Tania had been young herself and didn't know enough to escort her and Olivia from the room when the officer announced the deaths. When they'd become hysterical, Tania had called her own mother, and it was Mrs. Smith who'd searched the house for a name and number to call, stayed with them that night until child services could be brought in. With no family living in the vicinity, there was nowhere else for them to go. To this day, she refused to drive anything small, drove a Range Rover just to be on the safe side. It was like a tank, and nothing could crush it, or so she believed. And she fought with everything she had in her to get children out of protective services.

A sensation of tender concern washed over her.

"Teddy's going to need a lot of love."

"I know. And I'm sorry if it's selfish of me, but I think you're one of the few who can help him through this. He adores you. If you're back in his life, he'll miss Saban less."

"You know I'll do what I can, but right now that won't be very much."

"You can be his friend. That always came easy to you."

Her stomach began to ache. Disappointment rushed through her. Being a friend to the two of them took hard work. She had to resist the temptation to be more.

Taking her hand in his, he said quietly, "Why don't you try to get back to sleep? I'll stay for a while and when the doctor releases you, I'll take you home."

She couldn't argue. She'd used up the little energy she had just talking. Doing as he asked, she let her eyes slip closed, the feel of his hand around hers reassuring.

⌒

His heart stuttered. She was pale as a ghost, her lips tight in a grimace signaling pain. He'd seen her in pain before, although nothing like this. A sprained ankle, a broken finger, a dislocated shoulder, all sports injuries that were part of the game. He sat forward, caressing her hand and watched as her breathing became more regulated, telling him she'd fallen back to sleep.

The fluttering eyelids told him it wasn't a deep one.

She was lucky to be alive. He was lucky he hadn't lost her. If he was a betting man, he would have taken odds on her surviving. That's what she did. But it was going to take everything she had to find a new sense of equilibrium. After this kind of traumatic experience, life was never the same. You had to work at feeling safe, finding happiness. He'd help her, be there for her. Just like he knew she'd be there for him.

He fell back in the chair, let out a deep sigh.

Saban was gone. Even though their marriage had been over, it was still a blow. Even though they'd lost touch, were separating, the person he'd lived with, had a child with had been killed in a brutal way. He still couldn't believe it was real. Until he looked at Em. Then it became more than real. In hazy moments, he forgot who he was mourning. Lying in this bed was the woman he couldn't live without, and he was determined to devote as much time and attention to her as she needed. The realization of this hit him like a Mack truck.

When had it happened? Had it always been this way?

A wave of remorse hit him. He *had* married the wrong woman.

Had Saban always known it? Was it part of the problem between them? They'd had their share of fights about his relationship with Em from the beginning. Saban's jealousy had been a minor irritant in an otherwise sexually satisfying union. He'd continued to hang out with Em, just like he would his hockey buddies, watching the Patriots on a Sunday afternoon during football season, skiing in the Berkshires, going for drinks after one of his hockey games. Saban learned to keep busy with other things. After college, Saban had broken it off with him, moved home, but wrote him an off-handed letter here and there, while he was in the marines. When he bumped into her while she was visiting friends in Boston a few years later, they'd picked up where they left off. She'd moved back, gotten a job, and they'd gotten engaged. He thought everything was going to work out just the way he'd intended if a bit later than he'd planned. But then Em had turned down his wedding invitation, telling him thanks but no thanks to his request she be in the wedding. Saban had acted triumphant, as if she had won a hard-earned struggle. They'd learned a few weeks after the exchange of vows that Saban was pregnant, and she was none too pleased about it. She'd been nervous about the birth, about being a mother, while he'd been over the moon. The ever-widening distance between him and Em had closed, the day Saban had Teddy. With Saban overwhelmed with the newborn, even with him doing the lion's share of the work, Em had stepped in to help, and they fell back into their comfortable roles of best friends. He'd been relieved and gratified. And disappointed. Saban's concerns were well founded. She'd been ill-equipped to deal with a child. She'd found Teddy's crying irritating, his needs too many, his colic preventing the new mother from bonding with her son. He'd never anticipated her reaction and knew instinctively that Teddy would be an only child, something he regretted. Em loved every minute she spent with his son. She gave him much-needed breaks by taking Teddy for overnights, bought a house close to theirs so she'd be nearby, decorated a room for him, and plied him with every sort of toy ever made. Losing Saban was horrifying and would impact Teddy's life but losing Em would have been debilitating.

For both of them.

It was strange, in a way, that he could never separate his feelings into more or less. He loved both women, hadn't he? He just got along better with Em. She was his side kick. They thought the same way about life, had fun together, could finish each other's sentences. They both worked to make the world a safer and better place. They'd each chosen a profession that gave them purpose, and it drove their passion. Em worked to keep families together, the families that lived in the shadows, those that lived good lives and had grown roots in their communities. He knew about some of her high-profile cases, those that paid and those that didn't. She was a name to be reckoned with as far as ICE was concerned, her diligence and well-crafted arguments turning some of their arrests on their ears. And the cases she lost? He'd lend his shoulder to cry on, knowing how each child sent into foster care hurt her on a personal level.

He glowered at the thought that it was an immigrant who caused this mass destruction, part of the citizenry she worked so hard to represent. Hector had hurt the one person who would have fought for him had he just asked. Would this event change her thirst for justice? Would she continue her fight for them or would she back away from the fight? It had changed him. He wanted to wrap his hands around that immigrant's neck and squeeze the life out of him. Watch as he coughed and sputtered for breath, feel the satisfaction of snuffing out his life. It was not a familiar feeling. He had sworn to protect the lives of others, and up until 3:47 yesterday afternoon, would have gone to his grave thinking he'd keep his oath. Now? No amount of suffering would have been enough for Hector Rojas, and he was going to find a way to get vengeance against a dead man.

With those thoughts still on his mind, he leaned back in the chair, closed his eyes and let sleep claim him.

CHAPTER TWELVE

Nick was sitting in the chair by Em's bed, his eyes closed, just coming into consciousness when he heard a rap at the door. He sat up, trying to remember where he was. And it hit him.

Hospital. Em hurt. Saban dead. Teddy, a boy without a mother.

He got up, his steps heavy, and moved towards the curtain. After pushing it aside, he found two detectives he recognized from Boston Homicide, standing there. Paul Scalera and Naji Prem were here to interrogate Em. He should have known the police would show up, but never gave it a thought. They'd have to interview everyone caught up in yesterday's events. He wasn't exactly thrilled that Em would have to relive them.

As senior detective, Paul offered his condolences. "Nick, I'm sorry about your wife."

Paul would know the kind of heartbreak he should be suffering. His wife had lost her first husband to an exploding gun. Paul had lost his partner with the same bullet.

Not knowing what to say, he nodded his thanks.

After giving him a minute to get his control back, Paul added, "Zach Taylor's my partner but Naji is standing in for him. Zach had to give up his gun until we can determine that it was a righteous kill. I don't think it will take long for Internal Affairs to make the call."

Nick stuffed his hands into his pockets. He didn't know what else to do with them. He was usually on the other end of this line of conversation.

"He saved a hell of a lot of others. We all owe him a world of thanks for taking the bastard out."

"We do. I can't imagine how many more would have died without his quick work."

"Marines have a way of assessing danger and dealing with it."

"That's my experience."

"From what I hear, he's your son-in-law."

"He is. Married to my youngest daughter, Lana." Paul glanced over to the bed. "You a friend of Em?"

Nick's eyes narrowed. Paul sounded as if he was familiar enough with Em to call her by her nickname. "You know…"

"She's on Rissa's softball team. She's been over to the house several times. Great pitcher."

He nodded as the memory floated back. Rissa Caroli was the short-stop and one hell of an athlete, as well. They'd become good friends over the years.

"Yeah. She is. And yes, we're friends. I…I couldn't sleep last night so I thought I'd come here and maybe do some good. Keep her company."

A nurse squeezed past the men and moved towards the bed, where her patient was. "You'll have to give me a couple of minutes. I have to take her vitals. Then you can talk to her."

The detectives nodded and strayed outside the curtain.

As Nick twisted his neck to get the kinks out, he ambled over to where the nurse stood. Gently, the nurse woke Em from what he hoped was a decent night's sleep. He hadn't heard another peep from her since she woke in a panic and hoped he hadn't slept too soundly that he'd missed any cry for help.

Em's eyes fluttered open, and she looked around, tried to sit up but flopped back, never making it to a sitting position.

After picking up Em's wrist, the nurse checked her pulse before introducing herself.

"My name is Sandy and I'll be your attending nurse this morning. How do you feel?"

Em's eyes were closed, but her voice held a tinge of grit.

"Like a Mack truck hit me."

A small smile snuck out. She was feistier this morning, which meant she was feeling better. He watched as the nurse went through the motions of the morning ritual.

"Close. A bullet can do the same kind of damage as a truck."

A thermometer had been stuffed in Em's mouth and the blood pressure cuff was on her arm, the machine doing the pumping, as the nurse reworked the stethoscope around her neck. She took the stick out of Em's mouth and glanced down at the reading.

"No fever. Which is good. It means there's no infection. Yet. We've given you some antibiotics that will fight it off. So far it looks like they're working. I'm not going to change the bandage until the doctor examines the wound. I'll clean you up as soon as he's finished. There's a couple of detectives here and they'd like to talk to you. Are you up for it?"

Em's eyes flashed up to meet his. There was fear there and he wished he could prevent the interview from happening. But he knew Paul and Naji were just doing their job.

"They have to talk to everyone who was in the plaza, Em."

"Will you stay?"

"They couldn't move me if they tried."

The nurse straightened out the sheet and blanket, and adjusted the bed to make her more comfortable.

He waited until Sandy was done and Em gave a nod, before pushing the curtain aside. The two men came into the perimeter of the room.

Em was studying them and then he noticed some of the tension fade away. He figured it was because she knew one of the detectives. Tears filled her eyes. "Zach. Is he okay? If he hadn't gotten there when he did...I think I was the next target."

Nick knew she was right. If Saban had spotlighted their hiding place with her attempt at escape, Rojas' sights were probably on anyone else in the area.

"He's good. Upset that he didn't get out there sooner. He was subpoenaed to testify yesterday. He was mad as hell. Ironic how things turn around in the blink of an eye."

Paul shortened the distance, notebook in hand.

"I know this isn't going to be easy, Em, but we're going to have to ask you some questions about the shooting."

She reached for Nick's hand and he grasped it tightly in his own.

"I don't see why. It's not like you need to gather testimony for a trial. He's dead."

"He is but we need to write a report about what happened, and like I said, we need evidence Zach did his job according to protocol."

"He did."

"I have to agree, but as an attorney, you know evidence in this kind of thing is crucial."

Nick noticed a flicker of apprehension in her eyes.

"I might not have the best memory of the events. It was all kind of hazy. It happened so fast that it seems more a blur of motion than real."

"I understand. We ask that you just do the best you can."

She nodded her head. Nick linked her fingers in his, hoping it would ground her.

"When did you notice what was going on?"

She closed her eyes, as if picturing the events, then opened them again.

"I had just come out of the court house. I was there to file a couple of petitions and I was on my way to the parking garage. The firm has several spots at the lot in Government Center which is closer than the one in Central Plaza. I'd been talking to someone...Saban...and kind of ran ahead. My mind wasn't really on where I was. I was kind of on automatic. I'm there so often, I..."

She shook her head. "Sorry. I'm babbling, and you don't need to know what I was thinking." She took a breath and continued. "It wasn't until I was half way across the courtyard that I heard a noise. It didn't register as anything important until I heard people screaming."

He felt her grip tighten.

"The shrieks were piercing. I got the chills hearing them. People were dropping where they stood, and all I could think of was *I have to get away.* But it was all so fuzzy, and everything was moving in slow motion. I couldn't move fast enough, and I was trembling so hard I thought my legs would give out before I found us a place to hide."

"Which direction did the shooter come from?"

"If I had to make a guess, I'd say the street. He was to my left, about thrity yards away."

"What did you do when you realized what was happening?"

"I was with…Nick's wife. We had walked out together. I remember pulling her behind one of the concrete pillars, knowing it wouldn't give us a lot of protection but the plaza was wide open and there was nowhere else to hide."

She'd entered a zone. Or maybe she was still in shock. Her eyes were glassy, but she kept going.

"I had my phone out, kept looking at it, like it was going to tell me what to do. I kept asking myself who should I call? Who could help us? Saban kept begging me to call Nick but I knew he couldn't save us. I finally called 9-1-1."

Her eyes flew up to meet his. There was fear, stark and vivid, glittering there.

His hand had swallowed hers, his fingers tightening their grip when her breathing became labored.

"I began looking around, trying to find another place to run, but there was nothing. I saw a man go down, then another, then a woman. Every time a bullet hit I could feel it. I felt a jolt of electricity. I know that doesn't make any sense, but I kept checking us both for wounds. I think I scared Saban to the point she darted from behind the stanchion, trying to get away from both me and the shooter. I grabbed her arm, tried to pull her back but…"

Her glazed eyes focused on Nick.

"I'm so sorry, Nick. I should have been more in control. I was so scared, I wasn't thinking clearly."

"I know, Em. I'm sorry I wasn't there to help you."

Paul asked quietly, "Is that when you were shot?"

"I guess so. I couldn't tell which bullets were hitting me and which ones were hitting Saban. It's like I was at the center of an explosion. Blinding light, burning pain. It felt like I'd been shocked, like I'd been electrocuted. My whole body went numb but then I noticed that Saban was bleeding."

She raised her eyes to him again, as if pleading for him to believe her. "I tried to stop it. I was pressing down on her torso, trying to keep us both out of the line of fire, but she was crying that I was hurting her. I didn't know what to do. The shots were coming closer, and…I thought…then I heard Zach's voice. I looked up, saw the shooter face his direction, but he kept on firing. Zach announced he was the police and told him to drop the gun. He had to duck back behind the building, the bullets pinging off the brick. You could see the sparks as they struck it. He yelled again that he was the police, and then I saw him come out to face the shooter, saw him take aim. The shooter just dropped to the ground. Then it seemed so quiet without all the bullets flying, but people were screaming, crying. I could hear sirens, Saban's ragged breathing. I had forgotten all about her. She was so pale, and I was so angry at myself. I had stopped trying to staunch her wounds with everything going on around me. I told her to hold on, that help was coming…"

She hesitated, glanced up at him before adding, "She asked me to take care of…Teddy. I told her I would and then she… I felt her spirit leave her. Is that crazy? How could I have felt that?"

She had broken down and Nick sat beside her on the bed and carefully put his arm around her.

Paul put his spiral notepad in his breast coat pocket.

"It sounds like Zach took all the right steps. A lot of people were so caught up in events that they didn't see or hear anything but what was going on around them. There were a couple, like you, who saw him, heard everything."

"God forgive me, I just wanted it all to end. I wanted Zach to just shoot, and when he announced who he was for the second time, I was thinking, *Just take him out, Zach. For God's sake, just shoot.* It seemed like it took forever."

"Thank you. I appreciate your willingness to talk to us. If we have any more questions, we'll be in touch, but I think we have all we need."

Before he left, Paul added, "I'm sorry you got hurt, Em. Rissa said to call if you need anything. Hopes that you make a speedy recovery."

"Thanks, Paul. I'll call her when I feel up to it."

Once they had left, Em said into his shoulder, "I want to go home. I want my bed, my blanket, my pillow…"

"I know, Em. You'll be there soon enough."

The tears hadn't abated, the sobs that tore through her no less tormented. He sat, holding her, wanting to help but not knowing how. Not yet. He didn't want to see her merely survive but get back to her fully functioning self. He knew the road to recovery would be long, dark, and lonely. He promised she wouldn't walk it alone.

"As soon as the doctor gets here, checks you out, I'll take you home."

He hadn't let go of her hand, almost brought it up to his mouth to kiss it and stopped. It was such a natural impulse, but he had to force it back. She'd probably think it was part of his white knight service and she wouldn't like it. He had to control the desire to… Shit. Desire flooded through him. When he'd made the concession to himself that she was the one he should have chosen, it had come as a mental thought. This was…a more primal expression of what he was feeling, and it had come with a rush of intensity. He resisted the urge that was becoming insistent, but kept her hand enfolded in his. He couldn't break the connection he'd come to realize was his lifeline.

Em nodded into his shoulder before laying her head back down against the pillow. When she turned her face away, he was able to release some of his own anguish at hearing her story. His wife had died in her arms, extracting the promise that Em would take care of Teddy.

Had Saban cared about him after all?

⤳

Em was facing the wall, unwilling to see the pain in Nick's eyes or any disappointment. She had let him down, stopped the critical movements that might have saved his wife. Because she was scared, deathly afraid of what was happening. Her eyes felt as if they were stuffed with sand. She hadn't cried this much since she was ten and she'd been told her parents were gone. She never thought she'd experience that kind of pain twice in a lifetime. She'd been wrong. That she'd survived before gave her a modicum of confidence that she'd survive this. She hadn't been critically hurt. Her shoulder throbbed, but she was still breathing, still alive, still able to wake up to another tomorrow. Saban wasn't as lucky, and there were others… While she was in the emergency room waiting to be seen, she'd overheard some of the gruesome stories about other survivors. A man had died shielding his wife, a bailiff had taken bullets meant for a judge, a mother had been shot covering her child. The woman in the next room was keening, her four-year-old daughter in critical condition, a bullet lodged in her tiny head. Was Em one of the lucky ones? She wasn't so sure. Some would have long-lasting physical injuries, some life-long psychological ones. The headlines would cover the story for a few days, but when they faded, would the survivors be forgotten? Who would help the them deal with the mental anguish of what they'd seen and heard?

She heard his voice, whisper-soft, close to her ear.

"You couldn't have done anything to save her, Em. I saw the body. Those bullets would have ricocheted the distance of a couple of football fields. She couldn't have survived those wounds. Don't do this to yourself."

She heaved a sigh. It stuttered out. Every bone and muscle screamed with tension. His words soothed but didn't allay her own despondency.

"I keep asking myself, what more could I have done? I don't have an answer. The noises were maddening, the bullet spray didn't stop, and I got lost in it."

"I know what that's like. I'd give anything to change what happened, but we can't. All we can do now is be grateful we're alive."

"I want to go home, Nick. Being here is a constant reminder."

"I'll take you home as soon as the doctor says it's okay. Not a minute before."

She looked down, the johnny one of her indignities.

"I need clothes to wear. They cut apart the blouse I had on yesterday…" She'd heard the slit, felt the silk fall away, hadn't cared that she was exposed, hadn't cared about anything. The sound of gunshots had stopped but she could still hear them clearly, trapped inside her mind. They'd combined with the static and squawk coming over the responders' radio and her own pounding heartbeat. Cold to the point of numb, she closed her eyes while they EMTs worked on her. Only when they'd placed her on the stretcher, put a blanket over her did she feel some warmth seep back in. As she was rushed to the hospital, she'd blacked out, her mind unable to grasp the bits and pieces of the ordeal, the pain, the despair, the fear.

From far away, a voice penetrated her re-emerging agitation.

"Olivia said she's bringing them in this morning when she comes in for rounds. She picked them up last night before she went home."

She nodded, too dazed to speak.

Her eyes slid closed, as she fought off the effects of the pain. When she opened them again, she asked, "You still willing to nurse me back to health?"

"I am…and so is Teddy. He can't wait to see you. He's given me a list of all the ways he's going to entertain you. I hope you survive it."

She began to trace an invisible pattern on the sheet.

"I've been thinking that maybe Teddy could stay with me when you go to South Carolina."

He hesitated, measuring his response.

"I think it's too soon for you to take on a four-year-old. You do remember what Teddy is like?"

She spoke with a quiet but determined tone.

"I won't be able to pick him up, but I can still…"

He rose abruptly, and he loomed over her, his hands resting on the bed, on either side of her.

"Out of the question. There's breakfast, lunch, driving him to school, retrieving him afterwards. All things you can't do yet." He was still reeling from the events, still unsure what her prognosis was. In a calmer voice he said, "But I appreciate the offer."

Not one to back down in the face of a fight, she countered, "Maybe I can work in tandem with your folks. He can stay with me at night, and they can get him back and forth to school."

He moved closer, his breath tickling her face when he said, his voice low, "My parents might be attending the wake and funeral with me. I'm not sure what I'm going to do, maybe ask my sister. You won't be up for all that he needs."

His nearness was undoing all her self-control. She didn't want to be here, hurt, she didn't want to depend on him to take care of her, didn't want to be this close. And yet she would have given anything for him to sweep her into his arms and hold her.

"I don't know. It was just a thought. They're not cutting off my arm. I'm not going to be an invalid."

"You kinda will, at least for a couple of weeks, Em."

She went to cross her arms in protest, but when she felt the hot-sheet of pain, she gave it up. Maybe he was right. Maybe she had to give into the directive that she had to stay immobile. It didn't mean she had to like it. When she swiped at the phone that was on the tray suspended over the bed, Nick came over to help her. He gave her an I-told-you-so look, reminding her how limited her movement would be for the next couple of weeks.

After turning her phone on for her, he searched the history. "There's dozens of missed calls and texts."

"Anything important?"

"There's a dozen calls from Cami. From the time stamps, she was trying to get in touch with you during the assault. There's one from Nell, Liz, Jelani, Arianna, Mia and a bunch of names I don't know. Are you looking for one in particular?"

"From my Aunt Mom?"

She'd come up with that name for her aunt one night she and Olivia were under the covers, talking late into the night after the adoption proceedings. Olivia had asked if she'd mind if she started calling Kelsey, Mom. They'd been with her for years by then. Not wanting to give her the title reserved for their biological mother, the one she still missed with all her heart, she'd come up with Aunt Mom and it stuck. Olivia slipped up sometimes and skipped the Aunt. Em knew Kelsey deserved the title and didn't take offense. She thought even Ruby would have agreed with that.

"No. The last one is from Camille."

"What does it say?"

He pulled it up and held the cell so she could read it.

Maks is making a couple of one-pot dinners for you. Let me know if you're released today and I'll bring them over.

"See, meals won't be a problem. That man can cook. Can you text her back and tell her yes, please, and thank you?"

He moved the phone away from her and got ready to do her bidding.

"I can cook, too, you know."

She almost laughed in his face. He looked insulted and it was not a look he wore well.

"It's the kind of thing that friends do for each other when there's a crisis."

When her grandmother had died, neighbors and friends dropped off all kinds of eatables for the grieving family. When planning a funeral, cooking became secondary. If there was food in the refrigerator or on the counter, you nibbled. Would there be people knocking on Nick's door? What would they do or think if he wasn't there to answer? When would he be leaving for the funeral? She felt a momentary panic at the thought of being alone at the house. Not because she didn't feel safe. She had a state-of-the-art security system, thanks to Nick but because she wasn't sure where her wayward thoughts would lead without any distractions. If Teddy didn't stay with her she'd have to find someone else to do the honors.

"Has Mrs. Williams made any plans, yet? Does she have a date in mind?"

"They have to do an autopsy and the ME's office is working overtime to get the bodies released, but it will still be a few days before she can transport it. I'd estimate it will take a week or a bit longer for everything to be in place."

"Let's see where I am in a week then before we make any decisions regarding Teddy."

"I'm not going to argue with you now. I'll let the doctor do that. And I'm sure I can count on Cami and Olivia to keep you in check."

Olivia pushed the curtain aside and asked, "What are you still doing here and what can you count on me to do?"

"She's talking crazy. Wants to take care of Teddy when I go south for the funeral."

Olivia stopped short.

"Saban's not being buried here?"

Em noticed the look of surprise on her sister's face, as if she was going to suggest he fight to keep Saban local.

"Her mother says she belongs at home."

"I thought that was here."

"She never saw it that way."

Olivia was still looking at Nick. Em wondered what she was thinking, but when she turned to address her, she knew her sister had let it go.

"Nick's right, Em. You're... We're going to have our hands full with a puppy. It's too soon for you to take over the care of a four-year-old."

Olivia would be the one to stay with her, if need be, when Nick went down south for the funeral.

Not wanting to get into an argument about something that was still a week away, she asked, "Do you have my clothes?"

"Yeah. I brought you some leggings and one of my oversized shirts. You can't wear tees or anything you have to pull over your head. At least not for a while."

"I'll take whatever you have. It's got to be better than this."

"I saw the doctor out in the hallway when I came in. You're up next, so I'll just wait around to see what he says."

She was glad Olivia had stayed. The doctor had already gone over her wound and the remedies they'd use for the healing, but today he went into a description of what kind of destruction the kinetic energy of a high velocity weapon could cause. He warned her that even though the shoulder was unaffected by the injury, there had been blood loss, several layers of epidermis had been shredded, and there was inflammation, so she needed to take it easy. Her body had been through a major trauma. With Olivia's assurance that she'd see to the patient, the doctor agreed to let her go home. He wrote out several prescriptions, one to fight infection, a sleeping pill in case her nightmares ramped up, and pain killers, but she didn't like taking them. Couldn't take them. They did a major number on her stomach and they ended up in the toilet after a bout of vomiting. She'd stick with her over-the-counter muscle relaxants. They seemed to work on everything. She wasn't going to need reminding to take it easy. She'd thought her shoulder would be so much better this morning, but she'd underestimated the impact a bullet could make. Even with minimal impairment, she was part of the walking wounded.

Once she was freshly bandaged and Nick had been given instructions on how to redress her wound, she changed into her street clothes. With doctor's orders to keep her arm in the sling and her promise to make an appointment to see him in two weeks, she was released. Bundled up in Nick's Jeep, the one she'd insisted he buy as a precaution against out-of-control lumber trucks, she leaned back, still fighting the achiness that pulsed in her arm.

CHAPTER THIRTEEN

Nick had just pulled onto Route 2 when he said, "I gave my mother the key to your house. I hope that was okay? She was going to pick up some food and bring Teddy and his things over. I texted her while the doctor was changing the dressing. She might be there before us."

She didn't have the energy to lift her head. All she could do was mutter, "Yeah, that was fine."

Glancing over, she asked, "How did Mrs. Williams take it?"

"What?"

"The fact that you're staying with me."

"She knows we're friends."

"She probably also knows I have other friends and a sister who would have stayed. She didn't give you grief about it?"

He wasn't going to get into the truth of the situation. Not now. Not until she was ready to hear it.

"Why would she? It wasn't like we were going to pal around while she was here. Saban's brother came up last night to stay with her. They'll be fine without me."

"Still haven't gotten over the fact that you refused to move to South Carolina?"

"They're actually blaming me. Said if she was living down south, nothing like this would have happened."

"Short-term memories, I take it."

Mass shootings were taking place everywhere and there wasn't one city or town that was immune to it.

"Tunnel vision."

"I can't thank you enough for being willing to do this. I would have gone stir-crazy at Olivia's."

She didn't tell him that Olivia had offered to stay at her house with her. She'd even looked a little hurt that she'd chosen Nick over her, but Nick was going to be around for the next week as part of his bereavement leave, whereas Olivia had full days of tending to children. Liv couldn't really afford to take time off, her daily schedule much more difficult to rearrange than she implied. She would know. Hers was going to take some creative planning to get her caseload covered while she was out. Cami had promised to bring some work over so she could at least prep and complete paperwork while she was convalescing. She still had use of her right hand, which would allow her to jot down notes, but she wouldn't be able to complete any e-files. She'd have to leave that to her associates. She'd talked to Liz, who was willing to come to the house for a few hours each day and help her with the client load. Mentally ticking off her upcoming court appearances, she'd have to depend on Nell, Jelani, and Cami to read over the files and go before the judge with her clients. The thought of releasing them to someone else bothered her, even though she knew they'd have the A team as back-up.

"Olivia seemed upset that you chose me to stay over her. Can you tell me what's going on? I feel as if I've been pushed outside the circle."

Coming close to death must have made her more willing to spill out part of the truth, a very small portion.

"I guess I complained a little about Saban's lack of participation. Everyone began to think I should back off and let you guys deal with your issues, especially when it interfered with my life."

"Like when I called you at the wedding?"

"Exactly. They'd taken bets on whether you would or not."

"You're kidding. Am I that predictable?"

She gave him a wan smile and nodded.

"Who won?"

"Three of them. Two thought you'd forget I was there and another was convinced you'd call for me to babysit."

"I didn't forget about the wedding…" He looked over at her sheepishly. "But I did forget you were staying another night. No wonder they're pissed at me. I'm sorry, Em. I…" When he glanced over at her, his brow was furrowed. "That shouldn't be an issue anymore."

She noticed his eyes begin to glisten.

"Nick, maybe this isn't a good idea. You've got a lot on your mind. You've got some grieving to do. Taking care of me shouldn't be another burden you have to shoulder."

"You've never been a burden. And Teddy needs you. I might be out of it from time to time, but between the two of us, we should be able to help him deal with this. He'll have your heart and my hands."

The thought of Teddy, sent shafts of fractured light through her. He was such a happy boy most of the time, and his smile could make her day. She wanted to help him. She just hoped she knew how.

⌒

Teddy was standing just inside the door when they arrived, his hands over his face, as if he was afraid of what she'd look like. Nick was deferential as he helped her up the stairs to the front door, making sure she was steady. After she made it over the threshold, Teddy raced over and hugged her legs. He was close to tears, as if seeing her alive was too much for his young mind to process. He squeezed so tightly she couldn't move. She hugged him against her with her free hand before he finally let her go.

"I'm so glad you're okay. Dad wouldn't let me come to the hospital and I couldn't wait to see you. I'm so glad you're letting us stay." He took her hand and led her into the living room, where the couch was set up for convalescence. A pillow was leaning against the arm. Her favorite throw was bunched and waiting. He lifted the fleece blanket and insisted, "You need to rest, so sit down and let me cover you."

She did, as instructed, and he tucked her in. Sitting on the floor beside her, he took her hand in his.

"I was so scared. I thought you were going to die. That's going away forever."

"Me leave you? Please. Never going to happen."

"Do you hurt? What does a bullet feel like?"

She scooted her body away from the back of the couch. The pressure was causing some pain. Licking her lips, trying to hide that fact from him, she admitted, "It hurts a little. When the bullet hit, it kind of burned."

He stared deep into her eyes, his seriousness causing her to tremble.

"I'm not going to see my Mom ever again."

Her heart did a flip, then dropped to her toes.

"I know, sweetie. I'm sorry about that."

He sat up on his haunches, rested his elbows on the edge of the couch.

"It's okay. She didn't really want to be around me, anyway."

She reached out with her good arm and fingered his hair.

"Oh, Teddy, that's not true. She loved—"

He burrowed his head in her side, his small arm wrapped around her waist.

"If you had died, I would have cried a lot."

Her eyes flashed up to Nick's, a look of total shock on his face.

⤙

Nick was flabbergasted. Teddy did understand the significance of death. At least, at some level. Had Saban made his son feel so unloved he couldn't cry for her? There had been questions but no tears. When Nick had told him about Em, he'd gotten scared, panicked that he'd never see her again. He'd begged to talk to her, clung to him until he agreed to place the call. It had gone to voice mail which had made Teddy even more anxious. He'd promised he'd get her to call as soon as he got to the hospital, which he'd done. His mother had told him, it had calmed Teddy down, but he'd been restless for most of the night, slept fitfully. The only way they could get him to bed was to give him a picture of Em and Nick. It was from their college days, when Em had come by during the holidays. It was still clutched in Teddy's hand when he'd gone downstairs for breakfast.

It shouldn't have come as such a shock that Em was the one Teddy would miss. There was evidence of that even before the shooting. Teddy never seemed to mind his mother's weekend getaways, never asked about when she was coming home. He'd just accepted them as a fact of life. But when Em had refused to see him, he'd been truly upset. It had always been this way. Em was a bigger part of his son's life than his own mother. Was that his fault or Saban's? Maybe he shouldn't have come to depend on Em for so many things. Maybe he'd enabled Saban to escape. But when she'd left, all tension left with her, so he'd almost looked forward to the absences. It was nice taking care of a child rather than a woman who behaved like a child, nice knowing he could depend on another adult to share his load.

As he watched his son cuddle, his head still in Em's lap, he remembered a scene when Teddy was just a couple of months old. His crying had reached the peak of ridiculous, and Saban had screamed at him to get the baby out of earshot. He'd put him in his car seat and driven to Em's. It was the middle of the night, but she'd gotten up, taken the swaddled bundle, and pressed him close. She'd walked Teddy around for what seemed like hours, rocked him until he eventually fell asleep. Seeing her with him then had touched something deep inside of him. The emotion was rushing back, and he was swept away by it.

He'd been sharing his life with Em. Sharing all the little details that, strung together, made a relationship. Juanita had told him as much. The only thing he should have expected from her was friendship, but he'd come to expect a whole lot more. He'd expected her to mother his child, because his wife was unable to.

When he glanced down to see Teddy still clinging to Em, he was tormented by the fact that he had taken her for granted, hadn't even realized until this tragedy, who his heart belonged to.

His mother's voice penetrated his fuzzy brain. Consumed by his thoughts, he'd forgotten she'd brought Teddy over and was still here. She must have cooked a pot of chicken soup, the aroma beginning to seep into his consciousness.

Kathy had gone over to embrace Em, taking her face between her hands and kissing her cheek, careful to leave her shoulder alone.

"I'm so glad you're okay. Jerry sends his love and says if there's anything you need, you know his number."

Em smiled up at her. "Thanks, Kathy. You give him mine as well. I'm hoping he can drop by and play some cribbage with me. I'm sure to go stir-crazy. I think I can do it one-handed."

"I will, dear."

"Nick, I'm going to get going, let you guys settle in. If you need anything at all, just call."

On the way to the door, she patted his arm. "There's soup on the stove. Your father picked up some bread this morning that I brought over. I'd offer to come right over tomorrow but I'm going to Sara's. The kids made me a cake, and they have cards."

He was at a loss at what he'd missed. A cake and cards. It wasn't her birthday, that wasn't for a couple of months, and then it hit him.

"It's Mother's Day. I'm sorry, I forgot."

"Don't go there, either. That would have been the last thing on your mind today. Or yesterday."

He'd gotten Saban a scarf from Teddy. It was in a box wrapped and tied with a bow, lying on the ledge over his make-shift bed. They'd planned on making her breakfast and Teddy had been…His fingers rubbed his forehead. Teddy hadn't been all that excited about the prospect. Had asked if he was going to see Em.

Teddy jumped up and said, "I forgot, too." He pointed his index finger at Em and said, "Don't move. I'll be right back."

Nick couldn't miss the smile on her face at the directive. She looked up at him and shrugged her good shoulder. "Like I could go anywhere?"

Not a minute later, Teddy came running back down the stairs, as fast as his legs would carry him, holding a wad of paper tissue.

"We made these in school. They were to give our moms, but Dad had already bought Mom the scarf and I wanted to give you something. So here. I hope you like it."

He presented it with a flourish of his hand.

Em gingerly pulled away the scotch tape and peeled away the tissue. Inside was a small hand made of ceramic. Inside the palm was written MY HAND IS SMALL, BUT IT FITS IN YOURS JUST RIGHT.

Her heart swelled and emotion so strong all but choked her.

"Did you make this?"

"Yup. Miss Molly does pottery and used a kin to bake it."

"I think it's called a kiln."

"Yeah, that. We all did one. I got to pick the color myself. I know you like blue."

"You're right. It's my favorite. I love it, Teddy. I'll put it on my bureau and every time I look at it, I'll think of you." She made an awkward move, but she was able to get her good arm around him for a hug.

"I love you, Em. Happy Mother's Day."

"I love you, too, Teddy. More than you'll ever know."

"It's to the moon and back, right?"

She bit her lip and nodded. There were tears in her eyes, and they fell like gentle rain.

His eyes took on a concerned look. "Why are you sad?"

"I'm not sad. These are happy tears. You took away the hurt in my shoulder."

His eyes widened.

"You're all better now?"

Taking his hand in hers, knowing it did fit just right, she said softly, "No. I still have some healing to do, but you made me forget about it."

"Maybe if I read to you, you'll forget some more."

"I just might. Shall we give it a try?"

"Yeah. What book do you want?"

"You're the reader, so you get to choose."

He raced back upstairs as Kathy got her jacket out of the closet. Recently they'd experienced the typical cornucopia of weather in New England. Yesterday had been warm and humid, but today it was behaving more like March, the wind more than a breeze, slightly less than a gale. Shrugging into it, she said, "He's such a sweet boy."

Nick walked her to the door, and asked, "Mom, I... Did you hear what he said? He didn't think his mother—."

She put her arm around him and hugged him, but he lacked the will to return it.

"You couldn't help who Saban was." Looking back to where Teddy still clung to Em she said, "He had the kind of love he needed. Just not from the source you'd expect."

Nick's gaze had followed his mother's. She was right, but he'd put everything on the wrong shoulders. They might have been the ones that could carry the weight, but she wasn't his wife. How many times had he treated her like she was? How many times had she acted like one?

His mother added, "She's gone now. In a way, it's a blessing that Teddy's not feeling pain. He won't suffer with as many aftershocks."

Teddy had come charging back down the stairs with a handful of books, and was sitting with Em, their arms around each other. "He has his Em. That's who he needs right now. I'm glad you're staying here with her."

She opened the door but before leaving, said, "I'll be available if you need me, as will Sara. She wants to know the details and if you need a place to veg, you know where she lives. My boss already gave me time off, so let me know what Laretta decides. I'll make the arrangements to travel to South Carolina with you."

"You don't have to come, Mom."

"Of course, I do. She was my daughter-in-law. How would it look if me and your father didn't show up?"

She didn't say anything about wanting to be there, which told him a lot. Her attendance would be out of obligation. To him and Teddy. She'd never befriended Saban's mother, Laretta, never brought her into the family fold. Why hadn't he seen this before? When had everything gone bad? Em was right. He was obtuse, and it was beginning to annoy the hell out of him.

CHAPTER FOURTEEN

Em's head rested on the pillow as Teddy read her one of his favorite stories. He could already sight read and at four that was impressive. She'd help him with the tough words when needed but he knew this story by heart. All she had to do was listen. Nick was up in the shower, soup was on the stove, and if she closed her eyes, she could imagine that they were a family. There were plenty of times in the past she'd done the same thing. Even Cami's mother thought they were simpatico, in tune with each other's thoughts and feelings. They got along so well a lot of people took them for a married couple. None of that mattered, because they weren't, but it compounded the feelings of disappointment and regret.

Teddy had finished his story and he came close. "I'm gonna let you sleep for a while. You need your rest. I love you." He kissed her forehead and she closed her eyes. She could hear him move to the playroom and she listened as his trucks and cars came out of the toybox, his soft voice barely discernible.

She was tired. The memory of the shooting felt like a bad dream that she couldn't banish, couldn't wake up from. The screams still echoed in her head, the bullets pinging off metal and stone. Rather than let those morbid thoughts have their sway she grasped for a good memory to take their place.

Childhood, when everything seemed perfect, before an accident turned her life upside down.

Australia. The beach. Learning to surf, her father just beginning to teach her. The laughter, the love. Bruce Spencer was as untamed as Australia. A free-spirited man, he'd traveled the continent as a videographer, capturing the moods and textures of life Down Under, recording the secrets of what some people called the last frontier: the wildlife, including kangaroos and wallabies, the geological wonders of the Great Barrier Reef, the everyday sounds of breaking surf along the vast stretch of beach. He had married her mother on a brief trip to California for a surfing competition, and Ruby had hopped the plane to Sydney, leaving her family behind, and never looked back. She'd adored her husband and made her home in his. She'd never minded his absences, knowing that he was doing what he loved, knowing he'd come back to his family more invigorated and complete than before he left. When he was home, they'd travel across the county seeing all the sights, snorkeling, wind surfing, zip-lining. It was a life packed with adventure, and her love of sports had been born and bred with him as her teacher. They'd watch rugby, cricket, football or, as Americans called it, soccer, her father like an armchair coach, telling the players what they needed to do to win the game.

Em hoarded the few things of his she'd taken with her, one of which was the last video he'd made. *Australia Untamed* had just been released, and they'd watched one of the original copies together as a family the night before he died. The video had still been in the VCR, and she'd ejected it before her aunt and uncle could whisk them away from their homeland. She remembered vividly the night he'd showed it to them, how he'd entertained them with stories about the wonders of the reef, the largest in the world, described the brilliantly colored fish that lived there, and the promise he'd made, that he'd take them snorkeling there one day when they were older. She'd promised herself that one day she'd go back, do all the things they were going to do as a family. She'd been inching closer to that trip, Olivia ready to join her whenever she garnered the nerve. The thought of seeing their gravesite was unsettling. That they were together was the only upside. Ruby would not have wanted to be separated from her husband even in death. Coming to America had been traumatic, but her aunt and uncle had done everything they could to make her and her sister feel as if they belonged. They'd encouraged her love of sports, taking her to all her practices, attending all her games, encouraged both her and her sister to talk about Ruby and Bruce whenever they wanted. The couple had become parents to the two lost girls and had adopted them as their own, merging their lives legally as well as emotionally.

Her eyes flew open when she heard Teddy call out, "Daddy where are you going?" and then heard footsteps pounding into the kitchen. "Pick me up, Daddy. Hold me."

Nick came into the room, holding Teddy, whose arms were tight around his neck.

His fear of losing another parent was making itself clear.

"So much for peace and quiet but I think you were warned."

Nick was freshly showered and shaved. He had on a good pair of pants and a button-down shirt, opened at the collar. It meant he was going somewhere. Otherwise he'd be in jeans and a tee.

She tried to shift into a sitting position and was able to manage it, with only a slight shaft of pain.

"Are you going out?"

Nick came farther into the room, shifting Teddy to his other arm.

"Yeah. Laretta called, wants to meet with me. She and Bobby want to go over some arrangements they made. I'm surprised they're keeping me in the loop. I called Cami and she's coming over, bringing some of the work you asked for, although I think you should give it a couple of days before you start back in. She said she'll stay until I get back."

He didn't look pleased by the upcoming meeting, but he never had gotten along with the Williams family. They were dead set against Saban moving away from them and it looked like their fears were warranted. It was tough losing parents. She couldn't imagine what it must be like to lose a child.

"You don't have to wait around. I'm sure Teddy and I will be fine until Cami gets here."

Teddy's arms tightened around Nick's neck.

"I don't want you to go."

"I know, pal. I'm not crazy about leaving, but I have to talk to Grandma Laretta and Uncle Bobby. You'll be with Em and Cami and I know they'll take extra-good care of you. How about I promise to bring you back some ice cream?"

Teddy buried his head in Nick's chest. "Please, don't leave us."

Nick looked up at her, his eyebrows raised in question. Teddy hadn't given him a hard time about staying with his folks last night. Now? What was going on?

Em said softly, "He's had time to sleep on it. Things are less fuzzy. It's more real today than it was yesterday and I'm sure seeing me hurt isn't helping. You're all he has left."

Nick took a seat at the end of the couch where there was some empty space, Teddy tucking his legs on either side of him. She'd pulled her knees up and her chin was resting on top of them.

Tipping Teddy's chin up, he met his eyes.

"I need you to stay with Em for me. Cami will be here, but I'm counting on you to get her what she needs and to help her eat. I'll only be gone a little while and then I'll come back. I promise, Teddy, I'll come back."

"Bad men are out there."

"They are but remember I'm one of the good guys and I carry a gun."

He'd taken an oath he'd never be without one again. He'd taken his service revolver from the station and he had a second as back up. He'd be wearing one of them from now on.

"You have it with you?"

He patted the bottom of his leg.

"I do."

"What will we do if the bad men come here?"

"Do you really think that will happen?"

"They went to the court. Why wouldn't they come here?"

"The man was mad at the courts. Have you made anyone mad lately?"

Teddy shook his head vigorously.

Nick looked over at Em and asked, "Have you?"

She copied Teddy's head shake and flinched with the effort.

"And I don't think Cami has, so you should be fine."

"Can Maks come, too?"

"Why would he make you feel safer?" Em narrowed her eyes at him and said, "And don't you dare tell me it's because he's a guy."

Sheepishly, Teddy said, "Well, he is."

Nick chuckled at the look on Em's face.

"Shall I tell him to bring his hockey stick?"

Teddy's face brightened. "Yes, please."

Em looked more than insulted.

"For your information, my softball bat would do a lot more damage. And I can swing with the best of them."

Nick knew that if someone tried to harm Teddy, hurt or not, Em would go down fighting.

Teddy wasn't so sure.

"You can't right now. And Cami couldn't hurt a fly. We need someone here who can protect you if the bad man comes back."

The revelation shouldn't have come as a surprise, and his heart swelled. Teddy wasn't afraid for him, he was afraid for Em. He probably cared for her more than any of them.

Em was busy texting, having a hard time doing it with an arm in a sling.

"If you're trying to get Cami, I'm not sure you'll catch her in time. She's probably on her way by now. She was at the office when I called, picking up those files you wanted."

Without even looking up, she continued fumbling with her phone.

"I'm texting Maks. Asking him to bring Alec if he can get away. That should relax Teddy about the whole situation."

Smart woman. Teddy knew them both, from the hockey games he'd been to. They'd even hung out when they'd gone for pizza after one of them. Teddy would feel comfortable, less fretful at being alone with her.

There was a knock at the back door before Cami came right through the kitchen, stopping long enough to deposit the bags on the counter before making her way into the family room. Her phone was in hand.

"Here are the files you wanted and thank you for inviting my husband to join us. Was it you who invited Alec along?"

"Teddy's concerned that I won't have any protection without them if Nick's going out."

"What about me?"

"According to him, you couldn't hurt a fly."

"I may look like a girl, my friend, but I can pack a punch as good as anyone."

Teddy looked up and said, "Show me your muscles."

Shrugging out of her coat, wearing a white embroidered blouse that was a vision of feminine grace and beauty, she flexed her fist and pumped her arm.

"Yeah, just like I thought. You got nothing."

Nick and Em burst out laughing, leaving Cami to look insulted.

Only when Em winced and grabbed her arm did Nick become serious again.

"I guess I'd better go. I don't want to be late."

"See you later."

His impulse was to lean down and kiss Em good-bye, tell her he'd be back soon. Instead he backed out, not believing he could want to as much as he did.

CHAPTER FIFTEEN

Nick walked into the tiled lobby of the downtown Boston hotel Laretta had booked for her stay here. She'd planned on getting back home as soon as she could, but the autopsy was holding things up. Wanting him to put pressure to bear on the medical examiner's office, she wasn't pleased when he denied her request. He was supposed to meet her in the lounge and wasn't looking forward to a harangue about all things Saban. He strode in that direction only to find she hadn't arrived yet, which wasn't a surprise. Saban was late for everything. Always saying she'd be ready in no time, putting it off until the last possible minute, she'd never failed to make him wait. She was proud to claim she was a lot like her mother.

He took a seat at the brass-rail bar and ordered a beer. It was late afternoon but still far too early for Laretta's sensibilities. He wasn't joining them for dinner, not that he expected to be invited so he didn't really care what she thought. The Red Sox game was on the TV monitor, and he watched the home team put Tampa Bay down one, two, three in the top of the third inning. He could hear customers in the background, laughter, chairs being scuffed against the tiles as someone sat down, noises from behind the bar, the whir of the blender, the drain pipe of the dishwasher, a man at the end of the bar shouting down his order. He glanced up to the glass behind the bar in between sound bites so he could observe the comings and goings, get a heads- up when Laretta walked in. Then a reflection caught him off guard and he leaned closer to the oversized mirror, wanting to get a better look. Swiveling around, he watched as Saban's best friend, Rachelle, kissed Laretta's cheek. A man imitated the gesture, following it up with a hug. He was dressed in a suit, looked familiar, but Nick couldn't place where he'd seen him before. Was he with Rachelle? Did he know Laretta well enough to offer a warm embrace? Something about the interaction was troubling but he couldn't put his finger on why. His mind shifted to several different locations, trying to pull into focus where he might have met him, but nothing came. He ran out of time to process it as soon as Laretta entered the lounge and caught sight of him. Saban's brother, Bobby was right at her side. There was no smile in way of greeting from either of them. But then again, her daughter had just died. A smile would be out of place.

After sliding off the stool, he approached, went to hug her, but she side-stepped, offering him her cheek for a quick kiss.

Primly she said, "Thank you for coming. I appreciate it. I know you have far more important things to do, so I won't keep you."

"You've taken over the services and the transport. You've left me very little to do."

"I'm sure you want to get back to your friend as soon as you can."

The way she emphasized the word *friend* incited him. Was she implying he didn't care that Saban was dead? That he was involved with Em?

"She is my friend. She was Saban's as well. Stepped out into the line of fire to prevent Saban from getting hurt."

"She failed that but managed to save herself, now didn't she?"

He bridled the anger but bit out, "If Saban had stayed in place behind the barrier, she might have survived."

"Your description of the events is telling."

"I heard it from several sources. Em grabbed her and put herself in front, stepped out to pull Saban back when she tried to run. It was too late, but the attempt was made and shouldn't be undervalued. She risked her life for your daughter."

"Are you sure? From what Saban told me, you spent a lot of time with her. Maybe she wanted to have you for herself."

He almost laughed in her face. What did she think, that Em paid the man to shoot up the plaza so she could get Saban out of the way?

"I came here to discuss Saban's funeral, not some fantasy notion that I had something going with Em. I don't. I took my vows seriously and I would never have cheated on her."

Laretta blushed, badly, and he assumed she was sorry for her outburst.

"Do you want to sit down? There's a table over there we…"

Still flustered, she shook her head.

"No. I don't have the time. I should have just called and let you know but I thought it proper to meet you in person. I've talked to the ME's office personally and they've assured me I can have the body by Tuesday. A local funeral home will be supplying the casket, which we just picked out, and will transport it to South Carolina the next day. The funeral home we're dealing with in Greenwood said they'd be ready to wake her on Friday with the burial the next day at Mary Immaculate Cemetery. I've already ordered the stone, which will be done within a month."

"I just show up, is that what you're saying? No consult on anything?"

"That's correct. I know you two were having problems, Nick. Don't deny it. Saban confided in me that she'd given her notice and was moving home the minute she finished it out."

He ignored the quick twist in his gut. Saban had already given her notice? She'd never told him that, had given him only the slightest hint that her plans were in place. He felt like a first-class fool.

"When did she confide this?"

She seemed nervous, her eyes darting to Bobby as if he could save her now. She stuttered out the words, "Last month when she came home for my birthday."

"What exactly did she say?"

Bobby stepped in, giving his mother a look that would have soured milk. "Nick, I'm sorry. My mother's upset. I don't think you need to know all of this in light of what just happened."

"I'd actually like to know, Bobby. Did she already have a job? Was she going to file for divorce?" Had she picked out another sucker?

Bobby's face turned a light shade of pink. Diverting his eyes, he informed Nick, "You were supposed to be served the day she left. The papers are at her attorneys', and she'd already signed them."

He digested this, came to a very sad conclusion. That would have been just like Saban. She wouldn't have had the decency to tell him to his face. "What were her plans for Teddy?"

"She was going to get settled and then work out an arrangement for visitation."

"That would have been over my dead body."

Laretta's eyes flew up to his, her mouth pinched in displeasure.

"Watch your language. That dead body's my daughter."

"I understand now why you want to take her back with you."

It was probably Laretta's heart's desire to see Saban back in the bosom of the family and she'd probably encouraged the separation. Well, she'd gotten what she wanted. You had to be careful about what you wished for. It didn't always turn out the way you expected it to.

"Do you want to stop by the house, see if there's anything there of hers that you want?"

Unable to look him the eye, Laretta said, "She's been taking things home with her over the last couple of months. I don't think she's left anything of value behind."

Last couple of months? She'd known she was leaving him for that long? Why hadn't she just come out and told him? Why hadn't he just moved out? Because he wanted Teddy to have the familiarity of his house, his bed, his toys.

"I take it the answer is no, then."

With a flutter of fingers, she announced, "We've got to go. I'm flying out this evening. Bobby will return to accompany the body back."

With a bitter taste in his mouth, he offered, "I could do that for you. Take the same flight down as the casket and stay until the wake and burial."

"Thank you but that doesn't make sense. Keeping Teddy there for that long would be a trial."

He braced for the reaction he knew would come.

"I'm not bringing Teddy with me."

Laretta's face paled and she stuttered, "What are you talking about? He's her son. He has to be there."

Shifting his legs, he assumed the stance of a policeman at attention, his hands linked behind his back, unwilling to placate her at Teddy's expense.

"I've talked to his teacher and his doctor. They told me to leave it to him. He doesn't want to go, and I'm not going to force him."

"But—but it's expected. What will people think?"

Lowering his voice, keeping some control over his building anger, he said, "I don't give a rat's ass what people think. If the burial was being held here, I might reconsider. That it's not is your doing. You're the one taking his mother so far away. You think it's the right thing for your daughter. I have no trouble doing what's best for my son. Good-bye, Laretta. Bobby. I'll see you next week."

With that, he turned on his heel and headed out. His temper had almost gotten the better of him. He was glad he'd controlled it. There was no point arguing with the woman and he wasn't going to spend any more time thinking about it. He was going to have to get an extension of his bereavement time or talk to his supervisor about working a couple of days before taking off again. After checking his watch, the meeting not long at all, he decided to drop by the precinct and do that. Then? He didn't want to go right back to Em's. He needed time to process what he'd been told. Saban had already filled out the divorce papers. It wouldn't have surprised him if she'd already cultivated a substitute. Saban was a woman who needed to be fawned over.

⤳

Maks and Alec had arrived not long after Nick left, bearing gifts. Unaware that Kathy had made a soup for dinner, Maks had picked up some munchables so Em would be able to eat without cooking. Sandwich meat, bread, and desserts were stuffed into a brown paper bag and when Cami answered the door, he kissed her first and announced second, "I would not think to come empty-handed."

"Thanks hon. We can add sandwiches to the soup for lunch. Come on in the kitchen with me and we'll get the stuff put away."

Teddy had hidden under the dining room table as soon as the doorbell rang. Even though he liked these guys, had asked for them to come as protection, he was still somewhat shy around people he didn't know very well.

Alec leaned down, and said, "You called in the cavalry, now you're hiding from us?"

Em smiled. Alec had a way with kids and she liked the easy way he dealt with the four-year-old.

Teddy lifted his head up and said, "What's cavalry?"

"The heroes who come to save the day."

After hesitating, Teddy climbed out from under the table and ran over to where she still sat on the sofa.

"He's the cavalry, Em."

"Looks it to me."

"You'll be safe now."

"Thank you for taking such good care of me."

"You take good care of me, so it's only fair."

She kissed his head and sat back, feeling the non-effects of over-the-counter pain management. The pills weren't doing the job like she'd hoped, but she didn't want Teddy to know how much her shoulder hurt.

Maks came in, a soccer ball in his hand. "Want to play, Teddy?"

A big smile lit up his face. "Let me check with Em." He turned his attention back to her, and said earnestly, "Will you be all right if I go outside?"

"I will. Cami's here and I think she'll pick up for you."

"Okay, but if you need me, you know where I am."

"I do. Go have fun."

Cami was standing inside the perimeter of the room as he raced past her. Laughing, she came in to join Em on the other side of the couch.

"They thought you might need a break from all his smothering."

"They're such guys."

Good ones. She was glad Cami had found love. Now if she could…

Cami's voice intruded.

"How are you? And I don't mean physically. How are you mentally?"

"Still hazy. Still tremors from the impact. But…I guess considering the alternative, I'm doing okay."

The images were still stark and vivid, but she was learning to let them have their way. When she wasn't resisting them, they tended to fade.

"What are you feeling about Nick?"

She was quick to take offense.

"What do you mean?"

"Em, I know how you feel about him. He's here with you. I want to make sure you're good with that. The invitation to stay with us is still open."

Wanting to avoid the intent of the question, Em side stepped it.

"Thanks, but if you remember, I have a puppy coming soon. I have to stay here."

"You could put that off, I'm sure. Explain things…"

Reaching out with her good arm, she clasped Cami's wrist.

"No, I need her here."

Cami bit her lip but let the argument she was geared for, go.

Em fiddled with the edge of the blanket, a tumble of confused thoughts racing through her mind.

"Before Saban died, she said something…and I need to know if she was right."

Cami sat up, annoyance flittering across her face.

"What did she say?"

The tone was caustic and Em almost stopped herself from asking, but she needed to know.

"That…Nick is the only one who doesn't know how I feel…about him. Have I been that easy to read? Have I looked like a fool?"

Cami's lips thinned, her eyes narrowed, but she didn't answer. It made the ache in her stomach yawn. "Honestly, Cam."

Cami looked into her eyes. She hoped it was the truth shining in them.

"Never a fool. Easy to read? Maybe to those who know you. You don't cater to anyone. Except Nick. I probably would have known without your saying a thing but anyone else would think you were just friends. You have never flirted with him, you've never invaded his space, never made it seem that you were longing for him. Your heart might have been on fire, but you never gave that away with your words or your actions."

"Then how did she know?" She felt her composure slipping away and her voice sounded tinny to her ears.

"I don't think she did. I think she just wanted to cause trouble."

"She was dying. Those were among her last words. What was there to gain by pointing that out?"

There was a mumble under Camille's breath, a word she couldn't hear, but her imagination gave it form. Camille was thinking, she could tell in the way she smoothed down her blouse.

"She made sure you were still tied to them."

Em's fingers tensed in her lap. A feeling of overwhelming sadness swept through her.

"I'll always be tied to Teddy. Maybe I'll have to give him up if Nick remarries but it won't break the connection."

She didn't want to think about that eventuality. It's why she had to find a way to balance things. There was no way she wasn't sticking around the next time he fell in love. It would crush her.

CHAPTER SIXTEEN

Nick sat in the car outside his house. He figured with the extra time on his hands, he'd come by and pick up a few things before heading back to Em's. The yellow and brown color combination had never been his favorite, but the price had been right, and in this city, it had been a miracle they found one that was in their range. He'd wanted to live closer to their jobs, but this was an affluent town, northwest of Boston, one of Saban's requirements. That it took each of them twenty-five to thirty minutes to get there wasn't a problem for her. Knowing just the right button to push to get her way, she'd told him it was for the school system. She'd won, knowing he'd do whatever was best for Teddy.

He got out of the car, walked up the front steps, and let himself in. Standing just inside the door, the flagstone tile still in good shape but out-of-date, he hesitated. Should he go up, or down? Was that something a person should need to decide on entering a house? For him it had become more of a conscious choice. Did he want to retreat or face the storm head on? The storm would no longer be waiting, so he slowly walked up the stairs into the main part of the house.

The family room offered no warmth. The furniture had been replaced, more formal now, the white sofa necessitating a child-free zone. He'd suggested putting down hardwood floors, but she declined his offer. It would make too much of a mess. He'd helped with some of Em's home- improvement schemes, sanding and re-staining the original oak flooring, putting three-inch decorative molding around the ceiling, painting every room in more pastel colors, and bringing her bathroom up to date. She was the queen of DIY and they had fun working together, her selection of tools a home-improvement kind of man's dream. He would have thought she'd go more for the sleek and modern look, but instead she'd created a home that was not only functional but homey as well. Here, the off-white and beige, was a stark reminder that utilitarian held no warmth. There wasn't even a TV. If he wanted to watch a game, he was relegated to the basement, which, over the last several months, had become his real home. He'd purchased a sixty-five-inch television for his thirtieth birthday. By then he was aware that the marriage was not what he'd expected. It was his way of rewarding himself for hanging in there.

He stepped into the kitchen. The sink was filled with the leftover dishes from Friday morning. His coffee cup, Teddy's cereal bowl filled with water, Saban's yogurt spoon. In the dining room, the placemat he used for Teddy was still on the table, sticky from the sugar he'd tried to sneak. He hadn't had time to clean everything up before leaving for work, figuring he could do it when he got home that night, but he'd never gotten to it. Em had plenty of clothes for Teddy at her house. He'd come here before going back to the hospital, but disturbed only his room, to pick up some of his stuff. He hadn't ventured anywhere else.

He looked around with a critical eye. This house was where he'd lived for five years, but today he didn't feel like he belonged here. He felt more at home at Em's. Had he ever truly noticed before?

Melancholy accompanied him as he walked down the hallway, peeked into Teddy's playroom, his toys scattered around, his train set out, and he could almost hear Teddy singing out *whoo-whoo* as he raced it around the track. It was always too loud for Saban's sensitive ears. He shook off the memories, took a few tentative steps, stopping at the threshold of what used to be his bedroom. He was no longer welcome here. Hadn't been for a long time. How had it all gotten away from him?

He glanced at the vanity that was lined with perfumes, nail polish, hair accessories. He walked toward it, fingered the glass top, noticed the small bowl of jewelry she kept there was missing.

She'd wanted to take over the third bedroom, make it her own space, as a walk-in closet and dressing area. He'd felt Teddy needed it more than she did. That decision might have been the beginning of the end. She wasn't pleased he'd chosen Teddy's needs over hers.

He walked over to the closet, pushed her side open to find it half-empty. What was left behind were articles of winter clothing, things she wouldn't need in the temperate climate of the south. His being banished meant her subterfuge had gone undetected. Or maybe he hadn't cared enough to notice. The bathroom was the only one to suggest she was still living here. Her shaver and shaving cream were on the edge of the counter, her deodorant, hair gel, and the electric curlers standing alongside. Her brush was there, as well as her toothbrush and toothpaste. He could almost see her tending to herself before work, getting all prettied up for whomever she might have caught in her web. It wasn't him anymore.

No way could he sleep in here. It was hers. Even if she no longer lived here, he wouldn't want to use it again. The feeling was gone. Completely. He might be sorry she was dead, but he wasn't sorry she'd been planning to leave.

He was going to call a Realtor, get an idea of what he needed to do to spruce it up without killing the bank. Maybe some paint, a good cleaning. Then list it. Would it sell quickly enough so that he could move on? Where would they go? Schools would be important with Teddy heading to kindergarten soon. Where would they stay in the meantime? Maybe Em…

He was doing it again. Depending on her to extricate him from some self-induced crisis. And this was on him. He should have made other arrangements before now. He would have weathered that part of the storm already. Compounding it all now was Saban's death. They'd still been married, 'til death do them part.

How could he move on the connection with Em, with that hanging over his head? People would talk. People who didn't know, would judge. Did he care?

He went down to the basement, got out his suitcase, packed away some of his clothes, those he'd need at Em's, those he'd need to take with him to South Carolina. He'd come back for Teddy's things later. He needed to get out of here. It had become a tomb of unwanted flashbacks.

⌐

Teddy was coming through the back door, soccer over for the day. Em noticed how flushed his cheeks were from the activity when he plopped down on the floor.

"That was fun, but I'm pooped."

"How'd you do?"

"Em, they're bigger than me. I lost every time."

She looked up and smiled at Maks.

"You do know you're supposed to control your need to win when your opponent is four?"

"*Ja*, but Alec wasn't being sportsmanlike, either. I couldn't let him get me better."

She shook her head and chuckled. She understood. It took everything in her to control her competitive streak when she played with Teddy. Nick thought her patience came naturally. It didn't.

Cami yelled out from the kitchen, "Teddy, want to come and make your own sandwich?"

"Okay. Can I make Em's, too?"

"That'd be a help. I don't know what she likes. Do you?"

Em smiled as Teddy raced off to join Cami and Maks. Cami knew what she liked better than most. She had a feeling she was just trying to make Teddy feel useful.

She tried to get comfortable but nothing she did made her arm ache less. Her face must have shown her discomfort.

Alec sat down, his hands hanging between his legs. "You won't start feeling better for a while, Em. You just got shot yesterday."

Yesterday. When all hell had broken loose. Fire and brimstone. The sulfuric smell was still lodged in her nose and throat.

"I still can't believe it. It was such a normal day. How can normal turn into hell in minutes?"

"All it takes is one nut-job."

"And a plaza full of people. What are the odds of that happening? And I keep coming back to why."

The voice that echoed in the entryway told her Nick was back.

"He's an immigrant who got screwed. The only way we stop that is by kicking them all out."

He was standing in the archway, his hands in his pockets.

Em's mouth fell open. Where had that come from? He didn't really feel like that, did he?

"The reason they get screwed is that we don't have reform. Nothing is simple, and the rules are constantly changing. We don't have to kick them out, we have to find a way to help them become naturalized."

Nick put his attention on Alec, who was now an acting supervisor with ICE.

"What are you guys doing? Not enough from the looks of things."

"We're picking up more illegals than ever before."

"The good ones or the bad?"

"You can't tell the difference until something like yesterday happens. Rojas was not on our radar."

"How could he be? They all live in the shadows. You can't find someone who's hiding underground."

Em's ire was up.

"What the hell's gotten into you?"

"Yesterday's gotten into me. People were killed, my best friend shot at. I want them all gone so this doesn't happen again."

"That's right. If *they're* gone, we won't have any more mass shootings. Have your forgotten about all the white people who've shot up plazas, music venues, restaurants, churches? I guess we'll just have to get rid of the white population as well. The crazies are in plain sight, Nick. Citizens. How do we do that?"

He scrubbed his head, which he did when he didn't have an answer.

"I don't want to hear that kind of talk while you're here. I protect these people and they are some of the best out there."

Teddy had come out to see what the shouting was about. He stood there looking scared and grim. Nick must have noticed, because he tightened his lips together so he didn't say anything further.

In a fierce voice, Teddy shouted, "Don't yell at her Dad. She's all we have left."

Nick walked over, got down on his haunches and took Teddy's hand.

"I'm sorry, pal. I'm not mad at Em, I'm angry at the man who shot her."

"Who was he?"

It was Em who answered, afraid of what Nick would say.

"He lost his wife and son, Teddy, and he was upset and hurt. He should never have done what he did, but I can understand how he felt."

Nick gave her a level look that told her he disagreed.

Teddy went over and sat on the floor between the couch and the coffee table, as close to Em as he could.

"Like I lost my mom and almost lost you?"

"Yes. Just like that."

"Then I know how he feels, too."

Em squeezed her eyes closed. She loved this little boy so much it hurt. He deserved her full attention in the coming months, so she was going to have to put her feelings aside, along with her plans. She couldn't get pregnant now. She had to make sure Teddy was going to be all right before she did that. He'd feel as if she was trying to replace him. And in a way, she guessed that was the initial reason for the decision. She wanted a child of her own. She'd been given one in the moment before Saban died. Now she had to figure out how she'd manage a life of her own while taking care of the child of her heart.

CHAPTER SEVENTEEN

Maks and Cami were back the next night. She'd slept most of the day, on Nick's orders and relished the company. Maks had whipped up a great dinner from her meager inventory. She'd meant to pick up some things at the store on Saturday but…shit happened. It was just two days ago that her world quite literally had blown-up. Would Nick be willing to run her errands for the foreseeable future?

He seemed restless, as if there was something of grave import on his mind. Did it have anything to do with the meeting with Laretta and Bobby yesterday? Would she dare to ask?

He'd told them over dinner that he'd talked to his supervisor and had been given extra bereavement time. He was thinking about taking an extra week or two off, some vacation time he'd accrued, wanting to fix up the house, make sure Teddy was acclimated to a new reality. He was used to doing things with her help, but with her out of commission, he had a lot on his shoulders.

Alec, Maks and Cami left soon after supper was eaten and the kitchen cleaned, with Cami promising to drop in tomorrow. Liz was planning on spending an hour or two a day with her. She thought it was more a directive from the higher-ups, who wanted to make sure she was overtaxing herself. Liz would be helping organize but also monitoring her movements. Em would upset with them if she didn't know the why behind it.

She settled back on the couch, having taken the opportunity to get up for dinner. It felt good to be prone again although she wouldn't admit it to anyone. She finally asked what she'd been dying to since yesterday.

"How'd the meeting with Laretta go?"

Nick was on the floor with Teddy, and they were building a cherry picker out of Legos.

"I wouldn't call it a meeting. I'd call it a brief conversation about what she's planned. I don't think it took ten minutes for her to fill me in."

Teddy, who was hovering close by, asked, "Did you tell her I'm staying with Em?"

Nick glanced at her. He looked troubled and his eyes were searching hers. Did he think she'd talked to Teddy about it, without talking to him first? She knew he hadn't made the decision yet and would never have discussed it with his son without his permission He should know her well enough by now to know she wouldn't do that.

He was looking back at Teddy now.

"I told her you're not coming with me."

Teddy inched closer, as if looking for protection.

"Was she mad?"

Nick softened his voice, trying to comfort with his words.

"It doesn't matter Teddy. You'll never have to see her again. Unless you want to."

"I don't. She doesn't like me, either."

The either was another referral to his mother and a knot formed in Em's gut. Why the hell hadn't Nick seen how cowed Teddy was by Saban? She had. It was another reason she'd drop what she was doing to take him.

Em ventured down a road she knew she shouldn't. "I talked to Olivia today and asked her to stay with me this weekend while you're gone. She agreed, very reluctantly. She is not looking forward to taking care of the puppy. Maybe we can talk later about the decision you'll need to make about another little runt."

She didn't want to come out and say it in front of Teddy, but she wanted to tell him that Olivia agreed keeping Teddy with her might be good for him. The continuity couldn't hurt.

He was distracted, and she wasn't sure he'd heard her, or what she'd implied.

Suddenly, he scooped up the Lego pieces and said, "It's time for bed, buddy. Say good-night to Em."

"Dad, please. Just a little bit longer."

As he cleared up the area where they were playing, she could tell Nick was having a hard time concentrating.

"Nope. You have school tomorrow and it's been a long day."

"Do I have to go? Can't I skip, just this once?"

As soon as the plastic storage bag was zipped, he stood, pulling Teddy up along with him.

"Sorry, bud. The doctor said to keep your routine intact. That means playing with your friends and learning new things."

"But I can learn new things here. And Em's my friend."

"I know but sleep is the best medicine for her. She had a full day yesterday and it wore her out. The next couple of days are for rest. Wednesday will consist of a long drive, a lot of puppy action, and you both need to rebuild your stamina."

He was right. She'd pushed herself the day she got home from the hospital and it had sapped her energy.

Adding to Nick's logic, she said, "You can't skip school two days this week."

"Okay. I'm not gonna fight you, 'cause I don't want you to change your mind about Wednesday."

"That's my smart boy. Give Em a kiss good-night."

After the kiss and a long hug, father and son took the stairs two at a time, Nick lifting Teddy as they went, trying to make a game out of it.

She watched them go up, still thinking about Teddy's response to his grandmother and what a shame it was that Laretta was so…hell, she was a bitch. It seemed Saban had inherited the non-maternal gene from her. Teddy deserved a mother who would appreciate his awesomeness, not belittle him at every turn. If he were her son…

Em's was startled out of her musings when her phone rang. She slipped it off the table and checked to see who was calling. She'd been fielding calls all day. Everyone from the firm had called or texted to see how she was doing. The receptionist from the doctor's office had checked in asking how she felt. Some of her softball friends had reached out, Rissa spreading the word about her injury. There weren't many others who would know that she was part of the assault. Her name hadn't been released to the press yet and she doubted it would be. The headlines would be filled with the dead. Saban's would be there, had already been announced as one of the victim's, her face appearing on air in a montage of the fourteen who'd succumbed to their injuries. It had brought it all home again. She'd blanched at the image when it was flashed on screen, sorry she'd put the news on when everyone else was preoccupied with dinner. When she cried out, Nick had come running, taken the remote out of her hand, and shut it off. His expression was grim when he said, "Laretta must have given them a picture."

She was grateful Teddy hadn't seen it. She'd have to be more careful in the future.

Knowing the number by heart now, she swiped to answer.

"Ms. Spencer-Ronan, it's Diane."

"Please call me Em, Diane. Is something wrong? Won't I be able to pick the puppy up on Wednesday?"

"Nothing's wrong but I wanted to give you first refusal on one of the puppies who was slated to be sold, who's available again."

This meant Em could get two out of this litter, something good in a world of bad. Having the dogs here with her could only accelerate the healing process. She just had to work out the logistics of how to take care of them with her arm in a sling and overprotective friends smothering her with attention. And how to break it to her entourage.

"I definitely want him. And I appreciate you're giving me the opportunity to take him."

"The little runt might feel more secure with her brother with her."

"I hope you don't mind that I have another name in mind for her."

Diane laughed and apologized. "I can't get too attached, so I refuse to give them names. I'd keep every one of them if I could."

"Do you need anything else from me?"

"Payment, but that can wait until Wednesday. I'll see you then."

"We'll be there sometime late morning."

"Perfect. Good-bye, Em."

"Bye, Diane."

She scooted down, a feeling of serenity as warm as her blanket enfolding her. Now that she was alone, she took the time to enjoy the quiet. She could give in to the pain, something she'd refused to do while people were watching. And they were watching. She'd felt everyone's eyes on her, assessing how she felt, what she needed, how they could help. She was exhausted from holding it all in. She could only hope that Nick took his time. Not only so she could enjoy the solitude but also get a handle on what he'd said when he'd returned from the meeting with Laretta. His outburst had upset her. He had never been a proponent of deportation before, had listened to her discuss her cases, seemed to have felt her pain when she lost one, when children were left behind by parents forced out of the country they'd called home. She couldn't allow him to let this fester, had to convince him that this was a random act by a random assailant. It could happen to anyone, anywhere. That it had happened to her and Saban shouldn't change his opinions about the undocumented population. It certainly hadn't changed hers. If anything, it made defending their right to be here more important than ever. She thought about the shooter as a victim, not some angry man on a mission. His story wasn't rare. There were thousands of parents out there like him, torn from his children, his wife by the instability of the system in place. Usually it was the children left behind, some left to the care of grandparents or loving aunt, others held in foster care until adoptions could be put in place. For as slow as immigration cases filtered through the courts, the agency in charge of protecting children, pushed to sever parental rights quickly and permanently. Insane as it sounded, deportation was considered neglect and abandonment. If a mother or father was not on United States soil, they could no longer care for their children. She was working with another teenager who was in the custody of child services but, at sixteen, decided he could live on his own. She'd been hired to represent him in his fight to keep a line of communication open with his sister, who was several years younger. He'd been promised visitation, but it had yet to be enforced. They had a hearing before the judge next week and she wanted to be there with him. It had taken time for her to earn his trust. He was angry, at the system, at ICE, at the courts, that had broken up his family. Could she see him picking up a gun and shooting dozens of people? No, but no one really knew what went on behind the façade.

When she heard Nick's footfalls, she braced, shut her mind down, let the pain float through her, containing it so Nick wouldn't see how she was feeling.

"Mind if I have a drink? I think I need one."

"Help yourself. You know where I keep the liquor."

He disappeared into the kitchen, came out carrying a tumbler of amber liquid. He'd gone for the gold. He settled in a seat opposite her, he took a sip and gave her a wan smile.

"He was so amped up from the company I thought he'd never settle."

"I take it he did."

"Yeah. He needed a couple of stories first. He'll probably ask you about Australia tomorrow."

"Why?"

He leaned forward, his arms braced on his legs, the glass held in two hands.

"We talked about South Carolina, where it is, where I'm going. He asked where I was from, then you. He wanted to get up and see where Australia is on a map. I told him we could show him tomorrow."

"We'll have to pull it up on the computer. I don't have a map." A well of warmth opened in her heart. "I do have an old book of folk stories I can read to him. I'll have to dig it out. It was a birthday present from my father when I was about Teddy's age."

It was one of many things she'd insisted on bringing to the States with her. Her aunt and uncle had been patient and accepting, buying a small suitcase to pack everything in. They'd gone through the house, picking apart her parents' bedroom, looking for anything she or Olivia wanted to take with them. There was a draw-string bag filled with what looked like flints. She'd come to learn the true nature of the chips of stone. They were hardened pieces of ancient lava that her father had collected over the years. His interest in the aboriginal origins of the continent had driven a lot of what he'd done. Bedtime stories were history lessons on the first people to settle on the shores of the continent, and then their movement inward. During his down time, he'd taken them to see the footprints in Willandra Lakes in New South Wales, the Gwion figures in Kimberley, West Australia, and a rock shelter in Arnhem Land. It was a gallery of art from an ancient time. She'd been too young to appreciate what he'd shown them, but it was more his reaction to the majesty of his surroundings that made the memories so vivid. His forebears were part of the British invasion back in the 1800's, his five times great-grandmother one of the convicts sent from prison to build the new nation. He loved his history and passed it on to his daughters with an enthusiasm that was catching. Reading the book to Teddy would bring back a lot of memories.

When she looked up to say something about it, Nick's eyes were filled. She'd been so consumed with her own jumbled thoughts she hadn't given much notice to his. Were they the first tears he'd shed, or had he hidden his grief from everyone?

"Nick, I'm sorry…"

In one swift movement, he was kneeling beside her, his face buried in her lap and the tears turned to sobs. Her heart almost broke in two knowing how much this must be hurting him. She placed her arms around his heaving back, held him as close as she could, wanting to take this away from him, wishing she could take it on, but this was something he had to process himself. No amount of comfort was going to take away the fact his wife was gone. All she could do was hold him while he grieved, his raw and gaping wound, deeper than her own.

⁓

He could have done this only with Em. Let it go and let it out. He never had to play the strong, silent type with her. She was never so vulnerable he had to hide what he was feeling. He could share with her who he was, in good times and bad. This had to be one of the worst. His wife was dead, and although the marriage had been over, he still felt a deep jagged wound. Being at the house hadn't helped. It was a stark reminder that his life as he knew it had gone to hell. There were such conflicting emotions that he wasn't sure how to deal with it all. Hopelessness, despair, relief, freedom. The combination of grief and guilt was the strongest. The years he'd spent loving her had been misplaced. She was a woman who couldn't be loved, didn't give enough of herself to be intimately connected. He couldn't discount who she was or what she'd done, but he also couldn't seem to shake off the anguish at her death. Guilt niggled that he hadn't been there to protect them, guilt that he was here with Em, who'd survived, and that he didn't want to be anywhere else. A deep sorrow at the death and destruction one man had created. What had Saban felt in those last few moments? Had she known she was going to die? What were her last thoughts? Were they of him? Of Teddy? For her to ask Em to take care of their son, she must have sensed…

Wiping his face with his sleeve, leaving visible remnants of his grief, he asked, "What were her last words?"

"I told you. She asked that I take care of Teddy. I tried to tell her she was going to make it, but…she made me promise. When I had, she closed her eyes…and was gone."

"Was she in a lot of pain?"

"Only when I tried to staunch the bleeding. Later, when my focus was back on her, once Zach had taken the man out, she was just very quiet."

When he'd spoken to Juanita earlier, she'd said that most of the victims had multiple gunshot wounds. Their bodies would have been destroyed by the number of bullets that penetrated. It had taken the clean-up crew all day to remove the blood from the bricks of the plaza, or what they could. There were still signs of the rampage that had taken place.

"She was bleeding out. It was as if she was aestheticized. She would have felt lethargic, light-headed."

He looked up at her, studied her expression. There was pain reflected there. Was it hers or was it for him? They'd been caught up in this together. It seemed almost comforting.

"Were you there on one of her cases? Is that why she was with you?"

"No. I had just come out of the clerk's office, was walking toward the exit when she called out to me."

"What was she doing there?"

"I have no idea. If I had to make a guess, I'd say she was there for trial. The agency seems to use her more as a resource than an actual case worker these days."

This would have been a surprise if Laretta hadn't told him what was going on. Had her supervisor put her back in her old job when she gave her notice?

"Is…Was she still working with kids?"

Saban…had complained constantly about how much working with kids, took out of her. Was that for his benefit, so he didn't figure out what was going on? She'd obviously been lying to him.

Her eyebrows came together, as if she hadn't been expecting the question. Did she know something he didn't?

"You'd have to ask her boss."

"I'm asking you. You handle a lot of cases out of that agency. You must have heard something."

Fidgeting with the edge of the blanket, she stalled. He forced the issue and asked again, "Have you heard anything?"

Her eyes came up to meet his. They were filled with distress.

"Just that her strengths were protocols and agency guidelines."

Was the word going around that she was incompetent? Saban couldn't have liked that but seemed willing to put up with it to keep the secret of her upcoming departure from getting out. Did anyone know? Did Rachelle?

"How long has she been out of the field?"

"I'm not really sure. A couple of weeks, maybe."

He blew out a breath, took a sip of his drink, and sat back. If he connected the dots, it would have been around the time she'd given her notice.

"If she didn't want to talk to you about one of her cases, what did she want?"

He doubted it had anything to do with her leaving. It didn't sound as if Em knew her deep, dark secret.

"She was upset with me, asked me why I was unwilling to babysit Teddy, told me that he missed me."

He chewed on that. Had Saban been sitting in wait for Em? Or had she just bumped into her?

"Did she follow you out expecting an answer?"

"I guess. I told her I was busy, but she didn't think that was a good enough reason."

"And that's when you heard the gunfire?"

"We were about halfway to the sidewalk. I was doing my best to get away from her, so none of it registered until then."

"Why were you trying to get away from her?"

There was agitation in every facial muscle, the dart of her eyes.

"I didn't want to have to explain myself again. She wouldn't leave it be."

"Did she realize what was going on or did you have to tell her?"

"She'd figured it out before I did, became hysterical. That's when it registered. I grabbed her by the arm and ran back to hide behind one of the stanchions in front of the building."

She was biting her lip so hard he thought it might start to bleed.

"Nick, I can't answer any more of your questions. I'm tired and I want to go to sleep."

She pushed the blanket aside, tried to get her tangled legs out from under it and couldn't. Frustration was making her movements more frenzied, so he got up and helped her escape the fleece. Picking her up in his arms, he carried up to her room, laid her on the bed and kissed her forehead. Bending over her prone body, he whispered, "I'm sorry. I didn't mean to badger you. I'm just trying to understand what happened, why she was there."

He had every intention of telling Em all about the pending divorce and all that led up to it but not until she was stronger. And not until he'd found acceptance of the way Saban had handled things.

Em's eyes were searching his, as if she was apologizing for not being able to help him.

"I don't have an answer for you, Nick. Talk to her supervisor. She'd know."

He was going to. He wanted to know when she'd given her notice, what she'd told her boss about why she was leaving. He needed answers, but he wasn't going to give Em the third degree again. Sometimes it hurt more to live than to die, and he wasn't causing her any more undue pain. There was an underlying feeling moving between them. It was more than just a spark whispering in his brain, a flicker of something he'd never felt before.

After shutting her light off, he backed out of her room and made his way to the other guest room down the hall. He sat in a chair in the corner of the room, trying to put all the pieces together. Some of them were just beginning to fall into place.

CHAPTER EIGHTEEN

Em came awake suddenly. The doorbell was ringing, Teddy was talking, and although she could tell he was trying to be quiet, the volume meter on his voice didn't have a low.

Pushing the blankets off, she pulled herself away from her pillow and swung her legs over the bed. Feeling light-headed, she took a minute to settle herself. After slipping her feet into the slippers on the floor next to her, she managed to get up and inch her way down the hall and down the stairs. The sling was uncomfortable, but she knew if she took it off, it would delay her healing time. She'd have to grin and bear it.

The grin was easy. Half-way down, she saw that Olivia had already commandeered the action, barking orders at the minions who raced to do her bidding. Clearing her mind, she cited the date, the day of the week and her name. May thirteenth, Sunday, Emilia Spencer-Ronan. She was alive, and her brain was functioning.

When she reached the bottom of the stairs, Olivia stopped and gave her a head-to-toe visual examination. Then her sister stepped toward her, taking her good arm, and helped her to the couch. The blanket had been straightened. The pillows were fluffed. As she was gently released to the soft cushions, Em asked, "You're early, aren't you?"

With one hand on her forehead, the other at her wrist, Olivia said, "I wanted to check in. Make sure you weren't at the beginning stages of infection, check the wound. I brought some shirts for you to wear. All you probably have for casual are tee shirts."

"That's not all I have, Liv. And you know it."

Olivia came closer, put her hands on her lower arms, and said, "I'm still scared shitless okay. I didn't sleep a wink last night worrying... How are you mentally?"

Em had to think about that. She'd slept well for someone with her arm in a sling and a bullet wound on her shoulder. Mentally? There were still a lot of shadows clouding her mind.

"I guess as good as can be expected three days after being an unwilling participant in a shooting spree."

She watched as her sister took a seat opposite, Olivia's look of concern touching.

"I've got the names of a couple of shrinks who might be able to help you…if you need it."

Em glanced up as Nick and Teddy came out of the kitchen. Nick was carrying a bowl of warm water and a clean cloth that Olivia must have brought with her.

Teddy came running over as soon as he noticed her sitting there. As Nick handed over the gauze and tape to Olivia's outstretched hands, he explained, "Teddy's still overly anxious. I talked to Olivia and she said another day with you couldn't hurt so he's staying home today after all."

She nodded and tried to keep up with Teddy's chatter.

"Good morning. How do you feel? Do you need anything? How can I help?"

Em cupped his cheek, her thumb tracing his cheekbone. "I feel…okay. I don't need anything right now, but I have a surprise. I was just going to tell Liv what it is."

She looked over to her sister, not knowing how she was going to take the news, but she might as well get it over with.

"The breeder called me last night—"

"And you told her what happened, and she told you to put off picking up the puppy until you're healed. Right?"

There was a look of hope in Olivia's eyes.

"Not exactly. She told me that another one became available. I'll be picking up two of them. I think they'll work far better than a shrink. Don't you?"

Teddy jumped up and twirled around, clapping his hands in eager anticipation. His smile dropped at Olivia's response.

"Oh, Em. What are you thinking?"

Em gazed lovingly at the four-year-old, glad she could give him this. Maybe it would be good for both of them.

"I'm thinking two will be better than one. I'll manage with a little help from my friends."

Nick was the one who asked, "Where was I when this happened?"

"You were upstairs putting Teddy to bed. The couple who had a deposit decided they couldn't take a dog on right now. The breeder offered him to me, and I accepted."

Olivia was angry. There was frustration thick in her voice. "Without talking to anyone? Em, this is extremely selfish and totally unlike you. Do you know how much work it's going to create for the people taking care of you? You obviously don't remember how much work they are as puppies."

She felt herself flinch at the censure. Olivia was right, but she needed this. If she was being selfish, well, they'd have to deal with it. It was a first. She always put others before herself. She wasn't willing to demur this time. She spoke with quiet determination.

"I can let them out to play, sit and watch. What's the difference between sitting here and sitting out there? I would think the sun would be good for me."

Teddy began to let his enthusiasm have free rein again.

"And I'll help. I can feed them, get what Em needs. We'll be here, right, Dad?"

"I've got to go to South Carolina, Teddy. Who's going to help then?"

"I'll be staying with her while you're gone, right?"

"No, Teddy. I was going to leave you with Aunt Sara. Em still can't do a lot of things."

Teddy's face flushed, the heat from his growing anger showing in red-flamed cheeks. He stomped his foot, his hands in fists banging against his leg.

"No, I want to stay with Em. She won't need to do anything while I'm around. I'll do it all."

Olivia now gave her a look that was not cloaked in her usual bedside manner. Her attitude was more in line with how they'd been as kids.

"See what you've started?"

Em studied her sister, whose pinched lips suggested she was still angry over the decision. She'd offered to stay with her when Nick went south, included Teddy and the new puppy in the mix. Now there were two. She didn't think it would change her mind, but by the looks of things… Then she saw a slight tilt of her lips. Maybe deep down, Olivia was as excited about the additions as she was, Lily no less an angel in her memory. She could feel her own smile coming on at the thought of the silky fur and kisses that would soon be part of her life.

"This is what I want, Liv. This. Teddy and my two puppies. They will make me feel better and you know I heal quickly. Always have."

"You've never been shot before. How do we know your magical powers will work on this?"

"Because I've decided they will."

Olivia shook her head, knowing she was right. For all the injuries sustained during her athletic career, she'd never let anything keep her down for long, and this would be no exception. At least the physical injuries. The emotional and mental ones were anyone's guess, but she knew she'd be better with love surrounding her. Lily had helped her before and would probably help this time, as well.

Em flushed from excitement.

"I'm going to have to get a crate for them. Two. One for here, one for the car. I'm hoping it will fit in the back of the Discovery." She bolted upright, anxiety rushing through her, along with a shaft of pain. "Where is my car? Is it still in the parking garage? I never gave it a thought."

She glanced at Nick, thinking he might know.

"Camille and Maks went and got it. It's out back. It's a good thing the EMTs stuck your pocketbook next to you when they transported you to the hospital. The keys were in it. Now let's get back to who is going to get a crate. Did you say you?"

His face held a look of amusement and a surge of affection pulsed through her. He was her white knight if he was willing to do this for her.

"Well, I was kind of hoping that you'd go over to the pet store for me."

Teddy went up on his tiptoes, hitting him on the chest. "Can I come, please?"

Nick lifted him up by the hands and held him against his chest. "I might need your help, so probably."

Olivia gave her a look of resignation and a brief smile.

"I've got to get to the hospital for my rounds. Let me inspect your shoulder, see if you need a fresh sponge, change the gauze. We can talk about this later."

"Thanks." Turning back to Em, she said, "Why don't we go back upstairs?"

After putting his son back down on his feet, Nick suggested instead, "Why don't I take Teddy for a bagel. I can get a coffee and it'll give you some privacy, so she won't have to retrace her steps. I thought your first order was to keep her still."

Teddy placed his hands on his father's legs, sticking like glue. His expression was grim when he looked at her.

"Is there a bullet hole in your shoulder, Em?"

"I don't think there's a hole, sweetie. Just a lot of shredded skin. Right, Liv?"

Olivia glanced down at the little boy who adored her sister. She knew him, knew he was sensitive and he just wanted to know Em was all right.

"The bullet didn't really go in, Teddy. There's no hole."

Olivia was underrepresenting the injury for his benefit. And Em was grateful. There was a large open wound that resembled a donor site from a skin graft. Layers of skin were gone, and it wasn't pretty.

"Then can I see it?"

"Not today, hon. Maybe in a week or two, when it's healed a bit more."

Nick picked him up again, refusing to let his curiosity get the better of him.

"Do either of you want coffee, muffin, bagel?"

Olivia answered.

"A coffee would be great. A large black, with lots of sugar."

Em licked her lips and asked, "You're not going to Perfect Taste, are you?"

A franchise had just opened close to where they lived. Nell had introduced her to their muffins while they were working on the Supreme Court case and their muffins were…perfect.

"That's the one that just opened on Main Street, right? We can if that's what you want."

"They have a chocolate coconut that tastes just like a Mounds candy bar. I'll have one of them. And a coffee, lots of sugar, just like Liv."

Olivia looked up, the finger that was checking the temperature of the water stilling.

"That sounds good. Just like a Mounds, huh? Where is this place?"

"Downtown. There's another one in Boston, and I think Nell said there's a third in Sommerville."

"I'll have to visit more."

Nick shifted Teddy onto his back for a piggy back ride and Teddy giggled on the way out to the car, leaving Em alone with Olivia.

As soon as they left, Olivia began to un-tape the gauze that covered the wound.

"How does it look?"

"Like you've been carved up, but the edges are a healthy pink. Which is good. I keep worrying it'll get infected."

"I told you. I'm a quick healer."

"If everyone else had your confidence and powers, some of us would be out of jobs."

After pulling latex gloves out of her bag, Olivia wriggled her hands into them and began her ministrations. When Em winced at the pressure, Olivia lightened her touch. Em soon felt the sponge being applied, felt the soft gauze of the dressing, the sticky adhesive tape on her skin. When the new bandage was on and Em was lying back against the pillows, Olivia said in observation, "I'm glad to see Teddy's doing okay. I have to admit that being here with you has helped. As his doctor, I see that as a good thing. As your sister, the jury is still out."

As she packed away her instruments, she asked, "How's Nick?"

Em closed her eyes, the sight of Nick so consumed with grief upsetting.

"He broke down last night. It was so sad. I've never seen him like that before. This must be killing him."

Olivia clipped her bag closed, set it on the floor before sitting down on the edge of a seat.

"He seems, off yes, but he's managing better than I would have thought. How were things between them?"

Em was stunned by the question. She knew they hadn't been great, but how would Olivia have guessed that? Her sixth-sense antenna must be picking up signals.

"I don't know. There were some problems but there have always been problems. Maybe they'd gotten worse."

The questions last night had been unsettling. It was as if he needed to get to the bottom of something, something that didn't make sense. The day he hadn't defended her came into clearer focus. He'd been angry about her disappearances and she'd swear he didn't know that Saban had been taken off of case files. If his tears last night hadn't been so real, she'd almost think…what? That they were fighting, disassembling?

Olivia began to help her change into fresh clothes, her sister humming while she worked. She'd always done that, even as kids. She said it made the task go faster. It had a calming effect and Em let all the unruly thoughts about Nick fade into nothing.

～

All the way to the coffee shop, Teddy was talking non-stop about the puppies. Nick couldn't believe Em had gone ahead and bought them. Them. Two. Was one for her and one for Teddy? He wouldn't put it past her to do that. She seemed to know what she was doing. The way she spoke about Lily suggested she missed her, the companionship, the unconditional love that dogs offered. Having them around would bring life into her house and would probably help her move through the trauma of the shooting. She was convinced it had helped once before, and she was counting on it to work again.

"Are we taking her out to the dog place? Can we?"

"I'm not sure we have a choice. She can't get out there by herself."

"Yeah, but you want to, don't you? You won't give her a hard time about it, will you?"

"I went to school out there. It might be fun to show you around, let you see where I lived, where I went to class."

"Then Em went there, too, right?"

"She did. Your mother, as well."

"Mom went to school with the two of you?"

"She didn't come until later but yeah."

"Were they friends?"

"I wouldn't say that. They liked different things. They didn't have a lot in common."

Saban thought it important to always be a lady. Em didn't think that sounded like fun. She was all female but lacked the prim and proper that was Saban's trademark.

"What did Em like?"

"Playing softball and volleyball, X-Box, pool, swimming, whist."

"What's whist?"

"It's a card game. Em would spend time every day in the canteen playing with her friends. You almost had to pull her away to go to class."

"Did she skip a lot?"

On the occasion that Teddy didn't want to go to school, or Nick had a day off, he'd suggest Teddy skip. He knew what it meant but it certainly didn't apply to Em. Saban was more likely to skip. Headaches, menstrual cramps, nervous tension were some of the excuses she'd use to get out of class.

"No, not ever. She took her studies seriously. She was pre-law, which was hard."

"What were you? Police?"

"I majored in criminology."

"Criminals?"

"I guess you could say that. I got really good at knowing who they are and how to arrest them."

"What did Mom like?"

He glanced up to see Teddy's curious eyes searching his. Were these the kinds of questions Oliva had talked about? Teddy wanting to know more about his mother than he did? He gave him a smile, letting him know that he'd answer anything he asked about her.

"Shopping, getting pedicures, going out to dinner with her friends. She joined a sorority and did a lot of things with the other women in the group."

It was the most traditional of the sororities. They had make-up parties, shopping sprees, afternoon teas, planned events. Sports were not something that drew Saban, and she'd avoided the ice rink as often as she could. It was too cold and too dirty.

The one night she'd attended, she sat next to the penalty box and the player kept spitting on the floor. It was the last night she'd watched him play.

What was it that had drawn him? He couldn't see it now. He'd thought she needed him, but she didn't need anything except getting her way. Had they worked because he'd given in all the time? They'd never fit seamlessly into each other's worlds, and he'd stuck out like a sore thumb at her parties. He was the most comfortable in jeans and tees, and she was always trying to get him to dress her way. Those shopping sprees had included dockers and boat shoes. She'd wasted a lot of money.

"What's a so-ror-ity?"

"It's kind of a club for women."

"Em belongs to one of them."

"She does? Which one?"

"Woodley and Fisher."

He laughed. His son was right. It was certainly a club for women. They were super heroes in his mind. There would probably never be a man working at the firm, but they'd been letting males into their inner circle lately. He wanted to be one of them.

"Can Em be my new Mom?"

Nick's eyes flashed to the rearview mirror. Eyes were staring back at him, and they reflected the seriousness of his request. Cautiously, he answered, "I'm afraid it doesn't work like that."

With a furrowed brow, Teddy asked, "Why not? Can't I choose who it is?"

A momentary feeling of discomfort niggled through him.

"Not exactly."

Teddy had folded his arms across his chest, a look of displeasure on his face.

"Do *you* get to pick again?"

He pulled up alongside the curb, in front of Perfect Taste, put the car in gear, trying to think of a way to answer the question. Unfortunately, he was the one who got to pick who his new mother would be, if he ever married again. Was Teddy implying that he hadn't done a great job to this point?

What did a four-year-old know?

In truth, probably more than he did. Teddy was the one torn between loving his mother and feeling shamed by her constant criticisms. She'd never made it easy for him to express himself.

Now Em? Teddy could throw himself in her arms, knowing she'd never turn him away, would return the squeeze every single time. He could scream, yell, kick out, and she'd let him blow off the steam, ignoring the behavior, waiting patiently for him to be done with the tantrum before wrapping him in her arms so they could discuss the problem. He could whiff a ball a hundred times and she'd throw the hundred and first with composure, knowing it was the only way he'd get better.

Teddy asked, rubbing his chest, "Do you know what's here?"

He gave Teddy his full attention, wondering where this was going.

"No what?"

"My heart." Giving his father a few seconds for that to register, Teddy added, "You're in it and so is Em, Dad."

Nick's eyes slid closed, his heart all but breaking.

The picture was becoming clearer and clearer.

Teddy had already chosen Em as his mother. A long time ago, within months of his birth. Em could rock and calm him, knew what he needed before he did, gazed into his eyes, expressing her love in so many ways. She always put his comfort before her own.

Teddy had done a better job than he had.

Maybe someday... It was far too early to think along those lines. Saban wasn't even buried yet. But years from now, he hoped Teddy could say, that he'd done a better job the second time around.

CHAPTER NINETEEN

Nick and Teddy got back just in time to hand off Olivia's coffee and muffin to go.

"Sorry, there was a line. It took forever to get to the counter."

Em fumbled the bag open and sniffed.

"That's because they're such perfect muffins."

Trying to get hers out of the bag with one hand, Em looked up in frustration but Teddy was already on his way over to help. Placing a napkin underneath, he removed the paper lining and handed it back.

She took a bite and closed her eyes to savor the taste. "Mhm. I could have one of these every day." There were a variety of flavors, so she'd never get bored. "Did you get anything?"

Teddy had a mouthful and the answer was mumbled.

"I got a whoopie pie and Dad got a Boston cream."

She glanced up at Nick, who was sitting in one of the chairs on the other side of the room, his coffee balanced on his knee as he inspected the muffin in his other hand.

"Oh, I bet that's good. Does it have a cream filling? Can I have a bite?"

He laughed, and she understood why. She had a habit of eating hers and part of his every time.

"Only if I can have a taste of yours."

She looked down at hers, then back up at his.

"Let me think about it."

He finished his off in three bites. He had an evil grin on his face when he was done.

"Took too long."

"Rack off. Tomorrow, get a dozen."

He laughed, humored her.

"Who says I'm going back tomorrow?"

"I do, because these will make me feel so much better. And I know you're all about that."

He cocked his head at her. "Maybe I've changed."

"No one could change that much in a lifetime."

The banter was back between them and it felt good. Now...she stifled a yawn. She was already tired. Was it the dread from what had happened, sitting heavily on her chest? Or just the fact that her body was healing and that meant sleep?

He must have noticed her droopy eyes. "Do you want to go back upstairs?"

Teddy was watching her, his eyes intent on her answer. She had a feeling he wanted her to stay, so she said, "No, I'm good here."

And she was. She didn't want to be isolated in another part of the house. She wanted to feel life pulsing around her, and with Teddy there was life.

She held her arm as she shimmied farther under the blanket, laid her head against the pillow.

Teddy pushed the coffee table to the side and sat down on the floor next to her. He had Nick's computer on his lap, studying whatever was up on the screen.

"Are you up for talking?"

"Mmm, what did you have in mind?"

"Dad said you were born in Australia and I kinda wanted to talk to you about that. He showed me where it was..." He turned the screen so she could see what he was looking at. It was a map of the world. His finger pointed to a spot in North America and he traced a line to the continent lying all by itself in the Pacific Ocean. "That's so far away. Why were you born there, instead of here?"

"Because that's where my mummy and daddy lived."

"Why?"

"My daddy was born there. His family lived there for a very long time."

He was thinking again.

"Did you mind being so far away?"

"I didn't know anything else. I'd never been to America."

Her parents had promised her and Olivia a visit one day, but they'd never gotten around to it. As Bruce's reputation had grown, the number of projects he'd taken on had grown, as well. He'd said he'd take on the first assignment in the States that came along so they could meet Ruby's sisters. There was one scheduled for several months after his death. She'd arrived ahead of schedule.

"What's it like?"

What would he understand? The golden-brown sand and deep blue water of the beaches, so much more beautiful than anything here? An ancient civilization over forty thousand years old? People drove on the other side of the road.

"Almost the same as here. I spoke English, went to school, had friends, lived in a city."

His hand went underneath his chin as if he was thinking, a puzzled look on his face.

"How can it be the same?"

"We live life the same way, in houses with families. There are some things that are different. It's summer there when it's winter here. We never used a clothes dryer. Instead we'd hang our clothes out in the fresh air on a clothes-line. And there's no baseball. Can you imagine?"

"But there's softball, right?"

"No. I didn't play that until I moved here."

"Really? What did you do instead?"

"I played soccer, although Aussies call it football. And something called cricket. You play with bats, balls, and two wickets as goal posts."

"Sort of like baseball on a football field?"

She laughed. "I guess it does sound like that, doesn't it?"

Maybe cricket had gotten her ready for softball. The batting part anyway. Pitching she picked up all by herself.

Wistfully she added, "And my dad taught me how to surf."

She'd had her own board, was able to maneuver some of the bigger waves, her dad guiding her along the way. She hadn't touched a surf board since...

"Why didn't they come with you? Didn't they want you around?"

A sensation of tender concern took over. She knew what he was asking, but her mother had been so different.

"My mummy and dad were killed. That's why I came to live here."

"Your mummy's dead, too?"

"She is, Teddy."

"Do you miss her?"

"I do."

He looked ashamed, the way he was hiding his head when he asked, "Will I miss mine?"

She glanced up to Nick, who'd been sitting quietly listening to the back-and-forth. She didn't want to overstep her bounds here and thought he might want to field this question.

"Come here, pal."

Teddy got up and crawled into his father's lap, laid his head against his chest. She watched as Nick stroked his back, a lump in her throat.

"Whatever you feel about it is okay."

"I kind of miss *her*. I don't miss the yelling. I didn't like that. I thought I should pick sides, but I couldn't. She'd be really mad at me if I didn't pick hers."

"I know. That was partly my fault, Teddy. I shouldn't have put you in the middle like that."

As Em sat listening, strange and disquieting thoughts raced through her mind. Saban and Nick had been fighting. She knew that. About what? Often enough that Teddy felt the tension? Was Olivia right about his...feelings? She shook her head, knowing it had to be wrong. She would have known, wouldn't she? He discussed that kind of thing with her, much to her dismay.

If Teddy was this upset...

"I like it here. There's no one fighting. Can we move in?"

She gulped. Of course they couldn't. Could they?

"Sorry, pal. We can't. This is Em's house and when she's feeling better we'll go back home."

"I don't want to live there anymore, Dad."

"We can talk about moving. But it means we'll need to sell our house first and then buy another one. It will take time."

"Can you get started today?"

"There were still things I have to figure out, like where would we live. You want to stay at your school, don't you?"

Teddy nodded his head.

"That means we can't do it today. But soon. I promise."

His brows drew together in an agonized expression, his eyes searching Em's.

"There's so many things to do. I don't know where to start."

"You're not alone, Nick. I'll help as much as I can. Of course, right now I'm limited…"

"We need you, Em. More than ever."

That should have made her feel better than it did. She knew it wasn't her he needed, but someone to help him with Teddy. And she'd be there until he found—

"I'll be there for as long as you need me."

"She loves us Dad. To the moon and back."

The eyes studying him were compelling in their intensity. He'd never noticed her look at him like that before and there was something slightly alluring in the gaze.

Then it was gone, and her eyes were the same smoky green he was familiar with. But it caught him off guard, as did the fissure of something undefined that streaked through him.

The fuzzy feeling stayed with him throughout the afternoon, the normalcy of the day so out of the ordinary. He got an up-close picture of the way Teddy and Em interacted when no one was around. At least he'd never seen them like this before. Em had put on one of Teddy's favorite movies but before she hit start, he'd raced into the sunroom, where all his toys were and dragged out a pint sized, polka dot grand piano along with a stool. Positioning it on the coffee table, he waited until Em found the clip where Johnny plays Elton John's "I'm Still Standing. When she found the right spot, he began to mimic the movements, even kicking the stool aside at just the right time, singing for all he was worth. He knew all the words, and it looked like they'd played this out before, Em singing right along with him. They repeated the scene three times before he let her rewind the movie to the beginning. Em shifted so she was in a sitting position and Teddy climbed up beside her and they watched together, singing all the songs, telling him what was coming and who was doing the vocals. Reese Witherspoon was the pig? Scarlett Johansson the porcupine? He didn't know they could sing like that. He'd never watched this movie with Teddy, hadn't known he liked it so much. There were a few other ones they had at home, that they watched occasionally but they were usually busy doing other things, like building with blocks or playing with his monster trucks. He'd never asked what he did with Em, didn't think he needed to. He knew Teddy was well taken care of, so he didn't give much thought to the details.

While they were mesmerized with the movie, he was mesmerized with watching them. No wonder Teddy loved her. He was free to be himself here. Loud, soft, rambunctious, quiet, it didn't matter. Em loved every facet of who he was. What was even more endearing was she gave him all of who she was right back.

Something else he'd never given a thought to was the house. He'd been here before, to pick up or drop off, and although he'd helped her with a lot of her projects, he had never taken the time to see how it had all come together. He knew the sunroom was painted a pale yellow, he'd had a hand in it, but he'd never noticed that the late afternoon sun streaming in through the windows made it such an airy and bright place for Teddy to play.

When he made supper, a quick meal of leftover soup and sandwiches, he examined his surroundings. The kitchen was a soft blue, with dark mahogany cabinets and a marble countertop that tied them together. The curtains kind of matched the counter, gauzy material that let the sun filter in. The counters were lined with all her necessary equipment, toaster oven, a cookie jar, a bin with potatoes and onions, and dry goods like salt and pepper for easy access. A cookbook sat on a caddy, opened to a recipe for stuffed peppers. Had she already made them? Would she make them again? And the refrigerator... He knew she told him she'd put whatever Teddy made up, but he'd never examined exactly what she'd kept. It was a story-book of Teddy over the years. A picture of him at about six months old. By then he was spending an inordinate amount of time here. One at his one-year birthday, the cake in front of him, his mouth and hands covered in white icing, and there was this year's school picture. He looked so grown-up. There were drawings, him and her, a rainbow, a coffee filter tulip, and a crayon drawn masterpiece of the three of them. Had he always wished Em was his mother? That they were a family? In a way, they were. Nick had just been too blind to see it.

The face of the refrigerator also told Em's story. A square magnet pointed out that life wasn't about finding yourself but creating yourself. She'd done a damn fine job at that. There was a Clinton button, and a picture of Hillary with the caption, GIVE A WOMAN A CHANCE TO CHANGE THE WORLD. Em had cried for two days after the election, knowing what kind of harm was about to be done to the country. Then she'd powered up and become part of the resistance, attending the Women's March in Boston with the other women from the law firm. He'd been assigned police duty and was able to chat with her a bit before she made the trek across the city. There was a magnet with Einstein's image, a saying EMPTY KITCHEN, EMPTY MIND, and one that said DO ONE THING A DAY YOU'RE AFRAID TO DO. He thought that was an Eleanor Roosevelt saying but he couldn't be sure. Em had accomplished so much, was such a warrior that he felt diminished by his own inability to make the needed changes in his life that would have made him happy. He should have created a new life instead of accepting the one he had.

After dinner, they retired to the family room, and he stood at the threshold taking it in. There wasn't room for a man cave in the house, but he didn't think one was needed. The TV was a fifty-inch, mounted on a wall, and there was a comfortable couch that was long enough for him to stretch out and watch a game. A couple of chairs made for extra seating. A book was on the coffee table with a bookmark sticking out. There was clutter, but nothing out of place. It was a room where living took place, and she never discouraged Teddy from dragging his toys in so he could play in her company. Like he had tonight.

When Em had asked Teddy to start picking up, he'd became recalcitrant, said he didn't want to, that he wasn't finished playing. Nick was about to get involved, but Em had given him a look that said butt out, and he had. With a firm but soft voice, she'd told him it was time for a bath and bed. He'd balked; she'd cajoled. Getting up from the couch, she'd bent down and picked up one of his cars and begun singing the clean-up song Teddy had taught him. He'd learned it at school and they'd sing it whenever it was transition time. The kid wasn't immediately on board, but soon, he was singing along, sadly, the pout showcasing his lack of enthusiasm for the task at hand. Within no time, Em had her family room back in order.

As soon as it was, she announced, "I'm going up. I'm kind of tired."

Probably in pain from helping Teddy with the first few toys. He'd taken over from that point, picking up the song that Em had started.

"Wait. I have to check your bandage, so don't go yet." She looked pale and he was sorry he hadn't thought to do this earlier. "Sit down. I've got to get the gauze and ointment. I'll be right back."

He watched as she plopped down to wait for him. Teddy sat beside her again, holding her hand.

He gathered the materials as quickly as he could and braced himself for the sight of the wound. His stomach churned every time he saw it. Not because he was squeamish but because he didn't like knowing she'd been hurt like that. Teddy hadn't seen it yet and he wasn't sure how he was going to keep it that way.

He didn't have to worry. Em had it covered. As usual.

"Could you sit on my lap, Ted? I need something to focus on while Dad is doing this. It kind of hurts, so if you tell me a story, I'll forget to feel any pain."

He cupped her cheeks with his hands, kissed her on the lips before agreeing.

Em had loosened the robe and he gently drew the nightgown down over her arm, baring her shoulder, so he could get to the bandage. After peeling away the tape, he pulled away the patch of gauze to see the puckered flesh along a line of ripples and bulges. He wrung the cloth, and patted the area, anticipating a flinch. He didn't get one.

Teddy had straddled Em's lap, making sure he was sitting still, and he started to tell the story about the farmer in the dell. He didn't sing it, just told it in a straight forward way, the farmer taking the wife, the wife taking the child. Then he broke off and asked, "Would you take the child?"

"I don't know. Who is this child? Do I know him?"

Nick had stopped what he was doing, afraid of what Teddy was going to ask. He hoped he wasn't going to ask her to be his mother.

"Um someone like me. Would you take him?"

"Of course, I'd take him. In a heartbeat."

"Then the child could take the dog."

"He could. Have we thought of a name for the dog yet?"

Releasing a breath, Nick began the ministrations again, applying the antibacterial ointment and covering the wound with another patch of dressing. Now that he was more relaxed with the topic of conversation, he was interested in hearing what Teddy had come up with.

"Um, Doggie?"

"That would be like calling you Boy. Sometimes people name a pet because of what they look like."

"I don't know what she'll look like. Will she be gold?"

"No, she's kind of a cream color. Can you hand me my computer?"

He scooted off her lap and picked it up from the table before handing it to her.

"Scooch back up."

He did as she asked.

She moved a finger around on the pad, did a search, and pulled up a picture of some puppies.

Teddy brought his hands together, as if ready to applaud.

"I love that she looks like that. She's so cute."

Nick was leaning over the back of the couch and had to admit, they looked adorable. Teddy's excitement was catching. He couldn't wait to meet them himself.

Teddy asked, "Can we call her Marshmallow?"

Em glanced up at Nick, her face a grimace. She wasn't overly found of the name if he was reading it correctly.

"I think Lily is a good name, don't you, Teddy?"

"Like Em's other one. Do you think she'd mind?"

Nick had finished his task and was pulling the nightgown and robe back up, his fingers tingling from the touch. Getting his mind off the soft skin he'd just tended, he began a retreat, back to the kitchen. He needed to clean the bowl and throw away the soiled bandage. He paused long enough to hear what Em said.

"I don't think so. In fact, I think she'd be honored to have another dog named after her."

When she wrapped his son in a hug, he moved forward.

When Em and Teddy were both tucked away for the night, he wandered through the house, wishing he had found the kind of life that lived here. No tension, no worries, no conflict.

Someday, he promised himself, he'd find it.

CHAPTER TWENTY

Em came awake slowly, the birds chirping outside her open window, the sheers dancing out on the breeze. Feeling a little bit better today, she lay quietly and listened to the chatter going on down the hall.

"Okay, bud. Time to get dressed for school."

"No, Dad. I want to stay here. I can skip again. My teachers won't mind."

"They probably wouldn't but you'll be out again tomorrow, and I think it's important for you to be with your friends. Besides, I'm going to insist that Em sleep a lot today and there won't be much for you to do."

"Can I go with you to pick out the dog stuff?"

"I tell you what. You go to school, I'll come get you a little earlier than usual, and we'll go to the pet store together."

"You promise you won't go without me?"

"I solemnly swear."

"Does that mean yes?"

"It does. Now, your clothes are out. All you have to do is get them on. I'll go start breakfast."

"What am I having?"

"I thought I'd make you some eggs and bacon. I know they're some of Em's favorites."

Em smiled. She'd been hoping for another muffin, but she'd never turn down bacon and eggs. Adjusting her position, she pulled herself up, unsnapped the sling, got her robe on, and re-snapped it in place. She felt stronger on her feet today, less achy, although her shoulder and back still throbbed and burned. As soon as the itch began, she'd know she was on her way to full heal although that was the one thing that would drive her crazy. She'd rather have pain than itch. Especially when she couldn't satisfy it with scratching. She'd gotten poison ivy as a kid, and her father had threatened to wrap her in plaster if she didn't stop making the rash bleed by rubbing it raw. With no nails to speak of, biting them a habit that had lessened over time, she hadn't done as much damage as she could have.

Just as she made her way to the door, Teddy came running toward her, his pj's still on. "Dad said I have to go to school. I don't like leaving you, but he's my boss."

She knew that. Nick would joke about it when things got down and dirty between them and Teddy's tantrums got to melt down stage.

"He makes a good one, at least most of the time."

He took her hand and led her down the stairs, yelling out, "Dad, Em's up. Where should I put her?"

"Wherever she wants to go, Ted. We'll leave it to her."

"You heard the man. Kitchen or couch?"

"I think kitchen. I heard something about bacon and eggs. I can't let you eat them all."

They walked down the short hall to the kitchen, where coffee was brewing, and bacon was sizzling. Her stomach growled in anticipation.

Looking over his shoulder as she came into the room, he was gut punched. She looked so fragile, so unlike his warrior, and the fragility was doing a number on his manhood. He smiled to himself. She wouldn't like where his thoughts were straying.

"I'll pick up a dozen muffins later, but I want to get Teddy to school on time."

"I appreciate that. So do my taste buds."

"Is anyone coming over today?"

"Yeah, Liz, for an hour or two, maybe Cami if she can get away."

"I've got some things I have to do, errands to run, but I'll wait to do them. It shouldn't take me long to get to the day care center and back. You won't be alone for long."

"I'm sure I'll be fine."

"If I get back and you're remodeling the kitchen, I'm going to be in trouble."

"No plans for that yet. Although, I've thought about knocking that wall out. Making it a bit more open concept."

She was pointing to the wall that stood between the dining room and kitchen.

"As long as it's not today, we're good."

"I guess it can wait."

She smiled up at him and a wave of feeling shot through him. This was the Em he knew and...loved. He might as well get used to saying it. He still worried about what she'd think. How she'd react.

As soon as plates were swiped clean of yolk and grease, he put everything in the dishwasher and told Teddy to go up and get his backpack. He'd made a lunch and needed to get it inside before he forgot.

"Dad, I like it here. Can't I stay just one more day?"

"We've already talked about this. Miss Jen might read *Make Way for Ducklings* again. I know you liked it. Can you waddle over to the stairs, show Em how ducks walk?"

He watched Em force herself to keep a straight face at Teddy's pout and the way he scrunched down and waddled across the room.

"I did it the best. Miss Jen said so."

He sounded despondent, but there was also a little pride tucked inside the statement.

"I will be waiting to hear all about your day. I can't do much of anything, so you're going to have to do it all for me."

"But I can't if I'm not here."

"But if you go to school and have fun, then you can come home and share it with me. It'll give me something to look forward to."

"Okay. If you want me to."

His head was hanging down, and he was bent over like an old man, his arms hanging limply by his sides, as he disappeared down the hall, headed for the stairs.

Nick grabbed Teddy's back pack and watched as Em climbed under the blanket on the couch.

"Is there anything you need before we go?"

"No. I'm just going to close my eyes for a minute."

꙳

When she opened them again, she could hear movements in the kitchen. She was disoriented, uncomfortable.

"Nick?"

He came walking into the room, a dish towel in his hand.

"Yeah, Em."

She looked around, the quiet unsettling.

"Where's Teddy?"

"He's at school. He kissed you, good-bye, but you never stirred. It made it easier to get him out of here."

"What time is it?"

"Just after eleven."

She was momentarily speechless. She didn't take naps. There was always too much on her mind.

"I slept that long?"

"You did."

After noticing there was a glass of water on the table, she reached over and drank down a long sip. It felt good against her throat. Nick must have gotten it for her, knowing she'd need it. The medications made her thirsty, and she was drinking water down like a drunken sailor.

"What have you been doing?"

"Made some calls, made a reservation for my flight to Carolina. Talked to Cami, Olivia, and your Aunt Mom. They tried you, but I shut your phone off. It was me or nothing."

"What did they want?"

"Just to see how you were doing." He came over and sat on the coffee table. She wondered if it would support his weight. "How *are* you doing?"

"Still hurts. It throbs and it's annoying as hell. Did you ever get shot? You never talk much about your time in the marines."

"It's hard to share with civilians. They have no idea what it's like, the things we see."

"I think I've seen."

He took her hand, thumbed the palm.

"You have."

She let the touch soothe instead of scorch.

"Do the images ever go away?"

"They fade. You have to learn to get along with them. Let them exist, but not let them take front and center."

"I've been trying to do that. Nothing's okay anymore. Every time I go back to the building, I'm going to remember."

She felt like a different kind of person. Gone was the fearless woman who fought against injustice. She was struggling here in her house. What would it feel like to be out in the world again?

Nick brushed her hair off her face, his gentle touch more than she could handle right now.

"I'll go with you the first time. It won't be easy, but I know you. You'll face your demons. You always have."

She could feel the tears threatening again.

"My demons never had an assault rifle."

"Maybe not, but you'll find a way to move through it."

"Maybe I need to buy a gun. Take lessons."

"How would that help?"

"If I'm armed…"

"The policemen were armed, and they still got shot. It doesn't guarantee anything."

"So, I just leave myself open to this kind of thing?"

"You said yourself it was an isolated incident. It's not like you're in Afghanistan with snipers around every corner."

"Is that what you faced?"

"That's what we all faced. You either survived it or you didn't."

"Did you ever suffer survivor's guilt?"

He took her hands in his own.

"Are you still thinking about Saban? Cami told me that you were sorry…that she had more to live for. Can you really say that after the way Teddy reacted?"

"He lost his mother because I couldn't…function."

"You functioned fine. You were observant, gave Paul much-needed evidence that Zach did his job, you were able to get you both to safety, you tried to keep Saban from running. No one showed more courage than you did that day. You didn't think of yourself, you thought of her. She wouldn't have done as much for you."

Her eyes shot up to see his expression. He looked pensive, brooding. Was he upset that Saban hadn't fought hard enough for her life?

"She was just too frightened."

"And you weren't?"

"Sacred shitless."

Her voice was shakier than she would have liked.

His eyes turned cold. "There's a difference between being scared and doing nothing and being scared and fighting for your life."

She was baffled by his demeanor. There was anger, not the sympathy she expected.

"Are you all right?"

"I'm fine but I don't want you to bury yourself in guilt."

He shifted his weight, his grasp on her hand tightened.

"Saban was leaving me, Em. She'd given her notice a couple of weeks ago, although I just found out. That's why I asked you so many questions. She was moving back to South Carolina with no intention of taking Teddy, if I know her at all. Not that I would have let her."

Her mind reeled with confusion. What was he saying? Why hadn't she known? Why hadn't he told her?

"What?"

"I tried telling you right after Christmas that we were having problems. You shut me down. You didn't want to hear about our issues."

She remembered that conversation. They'd been driving home from a hockey game. She'd thought he wanted to dissect what was wrong with the marriage, get her take on what he could do to improve it. She wasn't willing to go there with him.

"That was months ago."

She was appalled. He'd been a friend in need, and for her own selfish purposes, she had denied him a shoulder to lean on.

"Yeah, I know. I've been living downstairs since."

Her whole body stiffened in shock.

"You haven't…"

"It's been over a year since we had any kind of relationship. If she had left sooner, she'd be alive, living the good life in South Carolina."

Utter astonishment caused a quick intake of breath.

"What was she waiting for?"

She was probably enjoying her role as puppeteer, trying to keep him on his toes.

"I have no idea, but it makes me feel like a chump. I should have taken steps to change my situation, but I kept hoping, for Teddy's sake…"

He looked up, tears shimmering. "I was a fool to think staying was the best thing to do. Teddy would have been fine, more than fine from what I've been seeing over the last couple of days. You're more a mother to him than Saban ever was."

Her senses were spinning, her heartbeat accelerating. What was he telling her?

"But you loved her…"

He ran an agitated hand over his head.

"I'm not sure what I felt anymore. What we had doesn't fit the definition of love." He dipped his head, as if he couldn't face her. "My wife might be dead, but my marriage died long before she did. I don't know what the hell I'm feeling, Em." He looked up and into her eyes. "God forgive me, but relief is a big part of it."

Her head was swirling. How could this be? She'd thought he was head-over-heels in love with his wife and it had been a nightmare. A well of buried longing rose up and almost strangled her.

"Nick, it's okay. It's…"

He gave her a sharp look, his forehead creased in confusion.

"It's not like I wanted this. I'm relieved that there's no decision to make anymore, not that she didn't make it. I would have felt the same if she'd left. I didn't know that until—Why did I hang on so long? I wouldn't be dealing with this kind of conflict inside of me. Sorrow, grief, guilt fighting with other things I'm not proud of."

"Is that why you asked for my help so much lately?"

She'd abandoned him in his hour of need. She wished she could go back, get a re-do. She never would have left him stranded if she'd known.

"Saban was taking more and more time away, and Teddy…Teddy kept asking for you."

"I wish I had known. I would…"

"No. The other thing I've begun to see clearly is that I put too much on you, expected things from you that I shouldn't have. You deserved a life of your own and I'm sorry if I prevented you from finding it."

That's what she'd wanted. A life of her own. A child she could call hers. What she hadn't wanted to admit? She'd be tied to Nick forever, no matter the circumstances. If Saban had gone through with her plans, he would have been free. That she left them for too late meant he had to deal with the aftermath. He'd need time to sift through all he was feeling but maybe…someday…he would see…

Stop. This is foolish. He doesn't love you. Not that way. Pick another topic.

"What are you going to do, now?"

"I'm changing jobs. I don't know where I'll go but I think it's time to move on. I'm selling the house. Teddy isn't the only one who doesn't want to live there anymore. I'll need to find someone to watch Teddy on a regular basis. I can't be expecting you to take him around my schedule. He'll still want to see you, so I may ask you to pick him up from time to time, but that's for him. He wouldn't know what hit him if you disappeared from his life. Beyond that…" He studied her for a minute, as if he had something else to say. She hung onto the moment, almost breathless until he said, "I'll just have to take it day by day."

Another hurt, another scar. Now that he was unencumbered with a wife and marriage, he was distancing himself. He wasn't making more room in his life for her but less. She closed her eyes, reassured herself that she could still move forward. She had put plans in place… When she opened them, his gaze clung to hers.

"Everything's happened so fast. I know my life was going to shit in a handbasket, but now the current is flowing too fast for me to navigate."

She touched his face, her fingertips feeling the sandpaper texture of his day-old stubble.

There was a hitch in his breathing that caught her off guard and a jolt of sexual energy that rocked her to the core. Desire clawed at her but he jerked away.

Her fingers were left hanging in the air and she was quick to let them fall to her lap. An inner scream told her she shouldn't have done that.

"I'm sorry. That was uncalled for."

"Em, I... I—There's nothing to be sorry for. All you did was touch my face."

But with that one touch, he'd gotten rock hard. The feel of her fingers, the softness of the caress had sent a shaft of burning white light through his body. He could not move on this now. It was Em. He had to take it slow, work things out, get to the other side of the mayhem going on inside. What if she didn't want what he was willing to offer? What would that do to their friendship? He couldn't lose that now. He couldn't live in a future without her in it. Didn't want to. He needed her in a way he'd never needed anyone else. Why were these feelings surfacing now?

Damn you Saban. If you'd just left me like you planned, I'd be able to move forward without this feeling of guilt. No, you had to die instead. Now?

He rubbed his temples. What the hell was he thinking? What the hell was he feeling?

Too many things. All for the woman sitting on the couch, who was looking more than guilty, as if she'd done something unforgiveable. These thoughts had been infiltrating his mind since the shooting. No, before. He was only now coming to fully understand what she meant to him.

He'd never had these kinds of thoughts about her. Had he?

Maybe when they first started to get to know each other, he'd thought it might be nice to tumble into bed with her. But he'd known he'd end up tied down, something he wasn't ready for. He'd decided to keep the relationship in place rather than put it at risk. After? When they'd started hanging out again, once he was back from the middle east, he could have moved on it then. Why had Saban coming back prevented it from happening? What kind of spell had she had over him that made him turn away from the woman who... always made him feel good? Being with Em was better than being with anyone. He laughed more, played better, lived more fully. Was this what love felt like? What this what it was supposed to be? No conflict, no tension, no eggshells?

He couldn't help staring at her, studying her. When had her neck gotten so long and her skin so creamy? When had her eyes ever looked at him like this? A crackle of energy still pulsed between them and he had to get away from what it was making him feel. All it would take was to lean in to take it to another level. He wanted to feel her lips beneath his. Wanting to taste what they felt like had become an obsession burning in his blood. But she was hurt and vulnerable and it wasn't the right time to engage in any extra-curricular activities.

His could feel the crease in his forehead as he thought back to other times when...

The doorbell rang, and he jumped up, needing to get away from Em before he did something he'd regret.

Liz was standing on the other side of it, a briefcase slung over her shoulder.

"Hi. Is she up?"

"She is. She said you'd be stopping by."

"Do you think she's ready for this? I brought some case files, but I don't want to overtax her."

"You know her almost as well as I do. What do you think?"

"I think she'll go crazy if she doesn't have something to occupy her time."

"My thinking exactly."

He let her enter and followed her into the family room, where Em was sitting on the couch, just as he'd left her.

She smiled up at her assistant. "Hey, you."

"I'm here to catch you up on some things. Are you up for it?"

"Yes. I am."

Nick went to grab his coat. "I've got an errand to run and I might as well pick up Teddy early if Liz will be here with you. We'll stop at the pet store on the way home."

"No problem."

He made a hasty escape, calling Juanita as he headed for his car and she agreed to meet him for lunch.

As soon as he pulled out of the drive-way, the blue tooth signaled an incoming call from the Medical Examiner's office. Why were they calling him? Hadn't Laretta left her contact information with them?

"Hello."

"Nicholas Katsaros."

"Speaking."

"We wanted to let you know you can pick up Saban's personal effects whenever you want. They'll be in the office."

"You haven't already given them to her mother?"

"No. You're listed as next of kin. Do you want us to call her instead?"

"No. I'm on my way to pick up my son at school. I'll swing by there first and get them. Thanks for the call."

"We'll also need a signature giving us permission to release the body to the funeral home. Just go to the front desk. Everything will be there."

"Thanks."

Ending the call, he added one more thing to do before returning to Em's house. His curiosity was ripe, and this would satisfy it. He wanted to check Saban's phone for contacts, see what she'd been up to.

⌒

Juanita had suggested they meet up at the small luncheonette they frequented. The food was okay, the service was nothing to write home about, but there was a quick turnover and they were back out on patrol before anyone missed them. Not that they were ever out of reach. His radio was always turned on and there were many a day that they'd order, get a call, and leave still hungry, with less money in their pockets than they'd gone in with. He was gratified that Juanita seemed to be having a slow day. After pushing through the glass door, the bell overhead sending a signal that someone entered, he scanned the small area that was stuffed with eight tables, all taken. Even the seats at the counter were filled with the lunch crowd. Luck seemed to be smiling down on him when a family of three was getting ready to vacate a table. Like a scavenger circling, he went right over and all but forced them out. He stepped up and slid across the bench, clearing the table of creamer pots, dirty napkins, and straw wrappers.

The waitress came over and deposited a glass of water on the table and asked, "Where's your partner?"

"On her way."

"The usual?"

"Sure, but I'll have a Coke instead of coffee."

"I'll put it right in."

"Thanks."

He looked at the other people, eating their lunch as if it were an ordinary day. Would he ever have another one of them? Everything had turned upside down. His heart was doing a number on him and he didn't know what the hell he was going to do about it. The timing sucked, and he wished he could turn back the clock. He was looking at Em differently, feeling things he'd never felt before. No, that wasn't true. He'd felt them but ignored them. The kiss the other day had been impulsive. There had been pecks on the cheek, but never one on the lips. It was the lightest thing. She probably didn't even know it was a kiss. But he knew and it's all he thought about since. It was before the assault, before he knew about the divorce, the plans Saban had made. What the fuck was wrong with him? What was he going to do?"

When he heard the jingle above the door, he looked up to see Juanita, hat in hand making her way over to him.

She slid in opposite him, put her hat next to her and rested her arms on the table. "Hey, how you feeling?"

"Been better. Where's your sub?"

She nodded in the direction of the bar and stools.

"He's at the counter. He said he didn't mind."

"Miss me?"

"Of course. Who else can I boss around without caring if he likes it or not?"

She was using a lighter touch than usual, but she had to surmise there was something bothering him.

"I...I got some interesting news."

"Oh, yeah? Interesting as in good or interesting as in what the fuck?"

"I think what the fuck sums it up. Seems Saban was hiding a lot from me."

He went on to tell her what Laretta and Bobby had told him and didn't have to wait for her reaction.

Leaning in so her voice didn't travel, she said, "You've got to fucking be kidding me?"

"If only I were. Tell me why I didn't move out last year?"

When shit had begun to hit the fan, when all they'd done was fight, when she'd threatened to leave him if he didn't start paying attention.

"Because you're a moron."

"'Em jokes that I'm thick as a brick, that I don't see a lot that goes on around me."

"You see it. You just don't *think* about what goes on around you."

The waitress came over with the meal.

"You get the BLT with mayo, side of fries, and a coffee. And you, the cheese-burger, onion rings and Coke. You good?"

"With this, yeah."

With everything else in his life, not so much.

As soon as the waitress walked away, Juanita said, "I know you stayed more for Teddy than for you. Your heart was in the right place."

"If I'd have taken matters into my own hands, she'd probably be alive."

"Not your fault, Nick. And blaming yourself for it is a waste of time. I heard some interesting news recently, as well. More so now."

He'd taken a bite of the burger and waited until he swallowed before asking, "What?"

"You know Aron Tedeschi?"

"He's an assistant district attorney, right?"

Nick had testified in court during some of the trials he prosecuted. The man was a bit of a dandy, always dressed to the nines, his hair professionally coiffed, his nails manicured. He might have been picked out of a line-up as a Mafia don.

"He gave his notice. He's moving. You know where?"

He really didn't care, didn't like the guy. The up-side was he wouldn't have to see him around court anymore. The farther he moved away, the better.

"Anchorage?"

"South Carolina. I heard Aiken, South Carolina."

His eyes reached out to hers. Could it be pure coincidence that Aron was moving to within an hour of Greenwood? Nick sat up straighter. Aron was the guy with Rachelle at the hotel the day he'd met with Laretta and Bobby. He knew he'd rec-ognized him, he just didn't know from where. Seeing him outside the courtroom made it hard to place him. It certainly wouldn't have surprised him if Saban had already found his replacement. But Aron Tedeschi? He couldn't picture the guy being tolerant of kids and there was no way he'd let Teddy...

He leaned his head against the back of the bench and took a deep breath. It didn't matter anymore. Why couldn't he keep everything straight in his head?

Juanita leaned in and asked, "Do you think—"

"Yeah, I do. That guy would be just her type."

He certainly hadn't been. Why the hell had she married him? He'd never have an answer now. It was a question he should have asked, back when they started having trouble. Maybe he was just behind the eight ball and she'd reached the conclusion they weren't right for each other before he had.

Had they ever been right for each other? At the beginning maybe. They'd both wanted what the other had to give. He could take care of someone, and she could be adored. He'd outgrown the need. She hadn't. Was it Em who'd prompted that change? Teddy?

"I know you're not going to like this question. It reeks of sharing, but...do you want to talk? You have to be a mess."

"Yeah, well. I am. Pissed, guilty about being pissed. Guilty about some other things, as well."

"What? That you weren't there to save the day, Mighty Mouse?"

He pushed his plate away, the burger only half-eaten. He'd been picking at the onion rings, but they lost their appeal, too. He knew he shouldn't ask this, but he had to get another opinion and it wasn't something he could ask one of his friends. It wasn't what guys talked about.

He finally looked up and asked, "How long do you think I should wait before...wanting to be with someone?"

"Whoa. That's a question that only you can answer. Who the hell are we talking about? I haven't seen you with anyone. Are you telling me..."

"No, I haven't...screwed around. Maybe I should have. Maybe I wouldn't feel like such a...moron. I've realized...that maybe I've been in love with another woman all along."

She let out a whoosh and flopped back against the booth.

"Em."

He shouldn't be surprised she'd guessed right. Hadn't she been leading him to that since they'd partnered up?

"Seeing Teddy with her... Do you know he asked if she could be his Mom now? He pretty much told me I blew it and it was his turn to choose."

"Is this just about what you think Teddy needs? That wouldn't be fair to Em."

"No. The night of the shooting I couldn't sleep. I went to the hospital to be with her. I needed to know that she was alive, that she was going to be all right. I kept thinking that if she'd been the one to die, I would have been...leveled. It drove me crazy the week she wouldn't get back to me, refused to see me...not Teddy, me. I didn't know what I'd do without her in my life. I've survived without Saban. I'm not sure I could without Em."

"Because of the help she gives you?"

He rubbed his scalp, making raspy sounds as flesh met stubble.

"No, it's more than that. It's... Shit I don't know how to put it. I'm not good at this."

Maybe that's what it was. He didn't have to explain himself to Em. He shared things with her, but it wasn't sharing, it was talking. It was simple with her.

"You told me you didn't look at Em...like that. That needs to be part of it, Nick."

"It's crazy but since you asked about that, it's all I think about. I want to hold her."

Juanita looked ready to pounce on him, but he waved her off.

"Not to protect her. She can protect herself. She proved that. It's because I want to be that close to her. I want...everything I've had with her and more. But is it too soon? I feel like..."

"You've been separated from your wife for close to a year. It doesn't matter that you've lived in the same house. Lots of people do that, for convenience, because they can't afford to do it another way, sometimes because it's best for the kids. There's been hardly a ripple in your relationship with Em. She always had your back. What did you call her? Your rock? I don't think you have to wait long at all. And if people have a problem with it, fuck them."

"Maybe, after I get back from Greenwood, I'll...talk to her. All I keep thinking about, though, is her attempt to get me out of her life. What if I'm too late?"

"You need to find out. It might be horrible timing. She's been shot, Saban's dead, Teddy needs her. You need to make sure she understands your motives."

Her radio squawked, and she answered it.

"I've got to go." She called out to the cop at the counter, "We got a call."

She gave her attention back to Nick, took his hand.

"You made a mistake. Don't make another one."

He nodded and watched her walk out the door.

He grunted out a laugh. She'd left him with the bill. He'd consider it her fee for the counseling.

CHAPTER TWENTY-ONE

Liz had left a little while ago. She'd waited for Nick to return for as long as possible, but she had some things to take care of at the office and had to get back.

Now that Em was finally alone, she let the images of Nick do battle in her mind.

Had she read it wrong or had he felt the same electrical impulses as she had?

As soon as she'd touched his face, the tremors shot up her arm and dug deep in her belly. She'd never given herself permission to do that before and she shouldn't have today. But he'd responded. He was aroused. Was it from lack of physical intimacy? Would he have felt the same kind of feeling with anyone?

Or was there something between them after all?

If there was, the way he'd scrambled out of here as soon as Liz showed up told her he was fighting it. Or quite simply he didn't want her, not the way his body suggested.

She cringed in embarrassment. She couldn't do that, touch him like that. It wasn't going to do her any good and might even obliterate his feelings for her. They were friends. That plain and that simple. He was untouchable for all the same reasons. She didn't fulfill his fantasies, and unless she was willing to change who she was and how she approached things, she never would. She inched off the couch, needed to refill her water glass, and made her way to the kitchen. Her legs were shaky, and she couldn't determine whether it was the result of the injury or the way Nick had made her feel. Saban had been on the verge of leaving him, had filed divorce papers, was moving away. Em had thought they'd last forever. But she'd been wrong. If only that had happened, instead of what had. Neither one of them would have been hurt. Saban wouldn't have been at the court house; she wouldn't have stopped to talk to her. She would have been in her car on the way back to her office, missing the main event.

Ironic how she'd made the decision to detach from her feelings at the same moment in time that destiny stepped in. She wondered what Michelle would say to

that? Cami's mother felt strongly that hearts on fire always found a way to be together. It took two hearts for that to work. When Nick hightailed it out of here,
she knew he didn't want to want her physically. That was the problem with absti-
nence, any body would do.

She would have given anything to talk to someone about what had happened,
but she didn't want to burden anyone with this new chapter in her Nick saga. Besides, Cami was at work and handling more than usual due to her absence from the
office. Instead, she picked up one of the files Liz had left behind and began to read,
making notes in the margins as she did.

She couldn't sustain the focus.

She needed to find something to take her mind off the man who never failed to
elicit a swarm of butterflies, or was it bees? Definitely more buzz than flutter.

Getting up, adjusting the sling, she stumbled in to raid the freezer. After taking
out a pint of Ben and Jerry's Red Velvet Cake ice cream, she finagled the cover off,
grabbed a spoon, and sat at the counter. No sense wasting a bowl. She'd take it at
a slant, rather than straight up, unable to get the spoon to slice though the surface
of the frozen treat. The tub fell out of her hand and rolled across the counter. She
caught it with her good hand before it went over the edge. Determined to win this
battle, she tried again.

She scraped at it, the spoon refusing to co-operate, and instead of penetrating
the ice, skimmed across, causing her shoulder to pinch. The more she tried, the
more her arm hurt and the more frustrated she became until she found herself
sobbing at her lack of mobility.

Teddy took this moment to race in, clutching a paper in his hand, which he let
fall to the floor when he saw her.

"Dad, Dad, come quick. Em's hurt."

Pounding footsteps sounded, Nick's expression one of horror as he saw her
blubbering over the sodden mess.

With his hand on her back, he bent low to her ear, his voice ragged.

"What's the matter? Where does it hurt?"

"It doesn't," she sobbed. "It did." She looked up at him, the tears streaming
down her face. "I couldn't get the ice cream out and I wanted it."

She couldn't miss the twitch of a smile that he forced back.

"Here, let me get it for you."

He took the pint, scraped out a big teaspoon full, and offered it to her. She
opened her mouth and let him feed it to her.

There it was again. That electric spark that jumped between them.

Now the tears came in earnest and she ran from the room and up the stairs.
Dropping down on her bed, she put her head in her hand and cried her heart out.

An hour later, she went into the bathroom and washed away the remnants of
her misery, knowing she had to suck this up. Nick was going to be here for at least
another few days and she had to manage these feelings. She'd have to stay as far
away from him as the situation allowed. It was the only way she'd stay sane with
him so close and seeming so touchable.

When she opened her bedroom door, she found Teddy pacing outside of it.

"I've been so worried. Why were you crying? Dad was only trying to help."

She cupped his chin, bent down to kiss his forehead.

"I'm not used to being so helpless. That your dad had to feed me proved I am and I lost it. I didn't mean to worry you. See? I'm fine, now."

"Your eyes are red."

"They are. There's nothing I can do about that."

"Are you ready for dinner? Dad made something for us to eat. I'll feed you if you don't want Dad to do it."

She smiled down at him.

"As long as he didn't make anything frozen, I should be able to handle it myself."

She let Teddy escort her down the stairs and into the room where she'd had her melt down. The table was set, and the from the way the napkins were sitting beside the plates, she knew Teddy had helped in between his pacing. Nick was at the stove, shaking the frying pan as if he knew what he was doing. She smiled at the picture. When he turned around, his eyes bored into her and she felt a flush come on, heating her cheeks and making her blood begin to simmer. She barely made it to the chair before her knees grew so weak they'd refuse to support her. That was not a look of friendship. That was a look of something much deeper and a lot more erotic than she'd bargained for.

⌒

Nick couldn't seem to help the way his brain sizzled at her entrance. Seeing her so helpless, so unlike the woman he knew, was mind boggling. She was no longer his Wonder Woman, but more human, more touchable, and it triggered a burst of passion he'd never felt before. With anyone. Seeing her now made his senses more acute. What would she say if she knew? His heart was thudding in his chest, and there was a coiling in his gut that he'd have to ignore.

"Feeling better?"

His voice sounded hoarse to his ears and he could only hope she didn't know what he was thinking.

"Yes. I'm sorry for the…drama. I'm not used to giving in to tantrums."

He turned now and looked at her skeptically.

"Are you telling me you do get the urge every once in a while? To throw one?"

She looked put out, as if he'd discovered something new about her, which he had.

"Doesn't everybody?"

"I thought you were the exception to the rule."

She tossed her head at him, and he noticed a shadow of sadness in her eyes.

"In my line of work, it is the rule."

She'd had her fair share of disappointments, the laws being what they were. There were only so many children she could save. Being as passionate about her job as she was, it wasn't surprising she got frustrated with the lack of progress on reform. What would a different one of her tantrums look like? He had a growing desire to know. Something intense flared through him and he thought it better to change the topic.

"I made strip steak. Hope that's okay. I picked it up at the market before coming back."

Teddy chimed in, "And I mashed the potatoes. I like mashed."

"I like them, too. Especially when someone else is making them."

"And Dad said we had to have a vegetable. I picked corn."

Nick admitted, "I don't know what to do with spinach or...What's that other green stuff that's supposed to be healthy?"

Em supplied the word. "Kale?"

"Yeah. I'll have to ask Maks what he was going to do with it. I'm used to frozen but he seems to prefer fresh. You must have bought the corn. It was both frozen and something I knew what to do with."

"What you made sounds good. Thank you."

He glanced back. She was back to formality, and it was throwing him off. Why the hell had everything changed so much? Where was his Em, the one he could talk to without pause? It had to be his damn feelings. Maybe she thought he was being an asshole for coming on so soon. But it wasn't soon. It was close to fifteen years too late. But if he was reading her right by the way she looked at him, it seemed like she felt the same way. The energy pulsed between them. It wasn't just his vibe but hers as well. What if she'd always felt this way? What if she'd gotten here sooner than he had? Was that the reason she'd wanted to distance herself? She couldn't do the friendship thing anymore? She'd wanted a husband, children. But he'd kept pulling her back into his life... because he couldn't live without her. Why hadn't he seen it?

Thick. He didn't think about what was going on around him. If he had made changes months ago, things would have been settled by now.

Instead, he was preparing to go to a funeral to...what? Grieve? For a woman who'd stopped loving him, who was already hooked up with someone else. Would Aron be there? How would that all go down?

"Something smells like it's burning."

He shook himself awake and took the pan off the burner.

"Stumblebum."

"Stumblebum?"

Nick was picking out the pieces of steak that might still might be called dinner.

"Yeah, Teddy helped me come up with a new swear word."

"I'll have to remember that one. I like it. What took you so long this afternoon? Liz didn't like leaving me alone."

"Sorry, I didn't mean to take that much time, but Juanita called, and I met her at the luncheonette in the city. I should have let you know."

He wasn't going to tell her about the stop at the ME's until later. He still hadn't done a thorough search of the messages, but he'd gone through enough of them to know what Saban had been doing. Dumping him like a pail of smelly fish. He should have been enraged, hurt, confused but instead, he was numb.

He brought the plates to the stove, filled them with the fare and set them on the table.

"Are you sure you're up to eating here? You can eat on the couch."

"I don't want to eat alone. I'll manage."

He studied her complexion. It was pale. She refused the narcotics, so she wasn't out of it, but she also had to be feeling the effects of her injuries. Pain had a way of exhausting you.

"I'd say we could eat in there with you, but I don't think that would be a great idea. Teddy..."

"Teddy would be fine. But I might spill things and Mags won't be back until Friday."

He glanced up. She'd take the fall for Teddy every time. He should take lessons.

Teddy was busy mixing his corn in with his mashed potatoes, by-passing the steak all together.

"Too crunchy?"

"This is yucky, Dad. What happened? Your mind not on what you were doing?"

"As you know, Teddy, it happens from time to time."

It was something he'd said on occasion when Teddy was distracted and creating a mess.

"Yup, it does."

The meat had the texture of jerky, and after tasting a small bite, he pushed it to the side of his dish. He'd have to do better tomorrow. Em needed her strength and the only way she could get that back was by eating well. He forked some potatoes into his mouth and watched her dawdle over the meat.

"Are you sure you're up for the trip tomorrow? Teddy and I can go out and get the puppies."

The mention of the puppies animated her features. She looked like his old Em.

"And miss being the first one to hold them? I don't think so. I'll be fine."

"The doctor wouldn't be thrilled."

"I got a second opinion. Olivia is going to check in on me when we get back."

"Did she really give you the go-ahead or did you overturn her verdict?"

"She knows it won't do any good to argue with me. Besides, I think she wants to meet them, just doesn't want to seem overly excited. She loved Lily as much as I did."

She picked up a piece of meat and crunched on it like a piece of bacon. After chewing, her face giving away her distaste, she asked, "Have you made a decision about the weekend?"

"I have. I talked to your sister this afternoon on my way to pick up Teddy. If she's going to be here, doesn't mind taking you, two puppies, and a four-year-old on, who am I to turn her down?"

"Thank you. I appreciate it."

"When she explained it would be good for Teddy to keep with his routine, I couldn't say no. She's right. To pull Teddy back and forth between houses would be hard on him."

Teddy piped up, "Are you talking about me?"

"We are. You get to stay with Em while I'm gone. Thank Olivia next time you see her."

"I will. I promise I will."

He jumped off his chair and raced around the table, yelling *yippy* before stopping by Em's chair and looking her right in the eye. "I'll help. You won't have to do a thing."

CHAPTER TWENTY-TWO

The next morning the threesome got ready to travel. The crate was set up in the back of the Jeep, stuffed full, with a blanket, toys and pillows. Nick had gone a little overboard, but he'd made the mistake of taking Teddy with him and the kid kept pointing out things he thought the puppies would need. He'd purchased a fifty-pound bag of food, several bags of treats, rawhide chews, and a couple of balls that were now stored in the sunroom, along with Teddy's toys. Last night after dinner, they'd discussed where to set up the crate once it was in the house and he'd cleared the spot in the family room that Em decided on, wanting the puppies to be part of the daily activity. He was almost looking forward to this. It was something he'd never have done on his own, but he knew that Teddy would love it. When he'd changed Em's bandages this morning, he was pleased with how the wounds looked. She had an amazing immune system. Very rarely sick, she was able to cast off what took lesser mortals down. He settled her into the car and asked, "Are you comfortable?"

"Yes, thank you."

Em had been more quiet than usual since her meltdown. Absent was the usual banter between them, the jokes at each other's expense. While his heart was on fire, hers had lost all warmth.

He might have to go back to his original premise that her friendship was too important to tamper with. What he'd do with the feelings in reserve, he wasn't sure, but he knew that if she did go out and find a life of her own, it would kill him. Had she felt the same way when he'd gotten married? Was that why she'd backed away, hadn't attended the wedding? He needed to talk to her, understand her feelings before he made a total mess of an already messy situation. His thoughts were in a tangle and as he buckled Teddy in, he attempted to straighten them out. Em handed Teddy her phone so he could play a game, and then they headed west. He hadn't been out to Amherst in years. Didn't have time for it, even though one of his friends from college still lived out there. One of his old teammates had become a farmer, married a girl he'd dated in high school and they were doing quite well. Every time he talked to him, he'd promise to get out to see him. This trip would give him the opportunity, so he'd called Ben before leaving to see if he'd be around. Even though he was probably busy with the spring planting, Ben had invited him to drop by for lunch. He was looking forward to seeing him.

In between games, excited about meeting the puppies, Teddy chattered away like a magpie.

During one of Teddy's quiet times, Nick asked Em, "Have you decided on what you're going to name the other puppy?"

Her eyes were gleaming when she looked over at him, the hint of a smile on her face. She was no less excited about the prospect of meeting the puppies than Teddy.

"It's down to a couple. I think I want to see him before I attach one."

He was cruising down Route 2, which would switch to a two-lane highway once they got close to their destination. He'd taken this road so often he still knew it like the back of his hand. Em had given him the directions to the breeder's house but he wasn't going to enter it into his GPS until they hit the outskirts of the town.

"What are the choices?"

"Maybe Ripper. It means *great* in Aussie slang. My father used to use it a lot when I was a kid and…it will bring back good memories. I also like Ridley. That's the last name of the actress who plays one of the main characters in the *Star Wars* series. I can't call him Daisy, but I love the character. Rey's such a warrior."

Nick knew how much she loved that series, from the first right through to the last. She had all the DVDs and had introduced Teddy to the Death Star, Vader and Chewie. He loved them as much as she did.

Nick offered, "Why not go with Rey. It sounds like a guy's name."

Teddy shouted out, "They all start with the letter R."

Em turned to look at him. "Astute observation, young one. It seems you know your letters."

Yoda was right, the mind of a child was a marvelous thing. "Which one do you like?"

"I kinda like all of them but what if you name him Ripper, and he starts ripping things?"

"I never thought of it like that. I don't know. Maybe Ridley or Rey work better."

"What other kinds of words did your father use?"

"Let's see, if he was barbecuing chicken, he'd say, we're having chook on the barbie. When he was angry, he'd say he was as mad as a frog in a sock, or if he thought someone was lacking in brain matter, he'd say the kangaroo was loose in the paddock."

She was able to imitate the accent, as if it was on instant recall. Nick glanced over, the smile on her face reminding him of the old Em, the one he'd known when they were younger. There were no outside obligations, no one telling them what they could do or not do, and they'd lived in each other's back pocket. He'd missed her and hadn't even noticed she was gone until this minute. When had she changed? There was a disturbance in his force field when he realized it was right around the time he'd started dating Saban. She'd retreated, in increments. Had she lost her exuberance for the friendship? Had he become nothing more than an obligation?

Teddy was giggling when he asked, "Is that how you used to talk?"

The hand that was free went to her face in exclamation. "Holy dooley, I did."

"Why don't you talk like that now?"

Nick thought about how she formed some of her words, the twang behind them.

"She still has a slight accent, Teddy. You just don't realize it."

Em was clearly surprised.

"I do?"

He was amused by her reaction.

"It's not very pronounced but it didn't surprise me when you told me you were an Aussie the night we met."

Teddy tilted his head, scrunched up his face and asked, "What's an Aussie?"

Em gave Nick a scathing look as if he'd just insulted her.

"It's the shortened version of Australian. It's not Ozzie, Nick, it's Aussie."

"You can tell the difference between them? They sound, exactly, the same, to me. Here's an idea. Call him Ozzie."

She was looking at him with amused wonder and it made his heart smile.

"Maybe I will."

⌒

As soon as they got to the extension, Route 202, her stomach was churning with excitement. They weren't far now, and it would just be another twenty or thirty minutes before she met her new family. She let the term Ozzie float through her mind. It was a good name. She turned her head toward the backseat, ready to ask Teddy what he thought, but he'd fallen asleep.

Nick was smiling at her when he gestured to his son.

"That's a good thing you know. Otherwise I would have gotten *Are we there yet?* for the last twenty miles."

Her eyes twinkled. "You would have, wouldn't you? What did you plan on showing him? School?"

"I thought about it, but he wouldn't be impressed. It'd be a bunch of buildings to him. Nothing more."

They were moving slowly through the small town, over brick pavers instead of asphalt, green space all around them. She'd been offered a position at one of the local law firms when she'd graduated law school. The brother of one of her law professors had a small two-man office and had wanted her as his number two. After graduating from Suffolk Law in Boston, her sights were on a big-city firm and she'd lucked out with her hire by Arianna and Mia. They'd built the firm together, all six of them, and it had brought her friends who'd walk through fire for or with her. She'd never regretted her decision. It didn't mean she hadn't loved her time here.

"It always brings back memories when I come through."

"Do you come out a lot?"

"Once or twice a year. Usually it's to visit Chelsie or Alyssa. They both still live out here. Last fall, the dean asked me to come out and talk to the juniors about immigration law. Lecturing in the room I sat in as a student was kind of weird. I looked at all those bright, shiny faces and thought, just wait. It's not anything like they expect it to be. The law is supposed to be black and white but there's so much grey today it makes it hard knowing how to approach things."

"You seem to do okay."

"I do now but working sixty hours a week to make partner was a tough way to intern. And the learning curve? Shite, for every three wins, there was one failure."

The voice on the GPS told Nick to take a right, drive point-five miles, which he did. The announcement that they'd reached their destination knotted her stomach. She couldn't be getting cold feet now. She'd already agreed, paid for one of them, and Teddy would be devastated if she changed her mind. Nick drove down the long driveway, the old farmhouse sitting at the end with a regal bearing. After putting it into park, he got out of the car and stretched his legs. She did the same.

Nick opened the back door and began to unstrap Teddy, who woke with a start. "Are we there? Are we there?"

"We are. Let's go meet the pups."

A middle-aged woman came out to greet them, her sweater old with frayed edges but the expression on her face was welcoming.

"You must be Emilia."

She reached out a hand in hello.

"I am. These are my two friends and helpers. Nick Katsaros and his son, Teddy."

"This must be the godson you spoke about."

"In the flesh. He couldn't wait, so I brought him along."

Diane placed her arms inside the sleeves of her sweater, the May breeze shuffling through the trees.

"Follow me, and I'll get them ready."

Em walked at her side, in easy companionship.

"How can you let them go? I'm not sure I'd be able to."

"It gets harder each time, but I make sure they go to good homes. I like knowing I'm making someone's life better." There was an amused grin on her face. "We don't get too many who want two of them."

"I know it will be a lot of work, but I couldn't bear to leave one home alone."

"Which means I've made the right decision. It's why I called you first. There was a waiting list, but I bumped you to the top."

"Thank you. I appreciate it."

Diane opened the side door to the house and let Em in ahead of her. Nick and Teddy trailed behind. They were in the mudroom, but once they passed through the archway, it opened into a huge space where there were crates, water bowls, and several adult goldens wandering around. Two smaller versions came running over, jumping up, licking them.

Teddy began to giggle, which relieved her. Some children were afraid of the frantic motion. She didn't know what he was expecting and was worried their boundlessness would be overwhelming. He sat on the floor and let them crawl all over him. "Which one is Lily?"

Diane pointed her out. "She's the smaller of the two. Just the right size for you, I think."

Em squatted down, extending her good arm, and the other dog came sniffing. She petted the small animal and it turned on its back for a tummy rub. She was more than happy to oblige.

Diane was watching with interest before asking, "What happened to your arm? Did you break it?"

Teddy didn't give her a chance to downplay the injury but yipped out, "She got shot."

Nick was quick to point out, "It was during the assault at the courthouse last week. She doesn't own a gun and wouldn't know what to do with it if she did."

"Oh, my goodness. Are you sure you're ready for them? I could keep them a little longer."

Now down on her haunches, getting as close to the puppy as she could and do justice to the rub, she said, "No, but thank you for offering. My parents died when I was younger, and my Lily helped me deal with it. I know these little guys will do the same. My shoulder will be fine. It's the visuals…" She got lost for a moment, shook off the memories and added, "The doctor tells me I can resume regular activities in…less than two weeks now."

Teddy was quick to reassure the breeder, "And I'm going to help her with everything."

His Lily was on his lap, licking his face, getting stroked in return.

Glancing at Nick, Em asked, "Could you get the collars we bought and the leashes? Then we can put them in the crate. I can't wait to get these guys home."

She watched as he walked back to the Jeep to do her bidding.

"I have help for the next couple of weeks, Diane, and everyone is on board."

"If you're sure. What an awful thing. I'm so sorry."

"It was an awful thing, and the images are still pretty strong, but like I said, I'll be fine. I was lucky."

She held her breath, hoping Teddy didn't say anything about Saban but he was so engrossed with Lily, she was sure he wasn't even listening to the conversation.

When Nick came back, he helped her put the collars on and strapped on the leashes. After handing over her credit card and signing the receipt, she turned to Nick, who held two very ambitious puppies.

Em smiled and said, "I think we're good to go."

When Em reached over for Ozzie's leash, Teddy went to take the other one. When Nick refused to hand it over, he balked. "No, Dad. She's mine and I'll take her."

"She's kind of strong, Teddy and I don't want her running to the street and into trouble. How about if we both hold it."

He gave it a moment's thought before agreeing.

"Okay. I don't want her hurt and she does seem kind of wiggly."

Wrapping the leather around a couple of times, Em held on to Ozzie.

With the dogs in the crate, nestled close to each other as if they knew something was up and they were seeking security, Em was more than glad she'd gotten two. They'd have each other in the strange new environment she was taking them to. Leaning down, she whispered, "I love you both already. Everything will be fine."

Nick coaxed her back to her seat, his hand on her back, the light pressure somehow raising hers. He'd been so good to do this, and she wasn't sure how he really felt about her decision. He'd become more enthusiastic while watching Teddy play with Lily, so maybe he wouldn't mind all the work they'd entail.

She was relieved when he said, "Lily will be good for him. You were right."

"Glad you're finally seeing things clearly. I usually am."

"Yeah, well, I am thick. You've always had to explain things to me like you would to Teddy."

"I can't say you're not observant, because you're good at your job, but you do let things skate right by you sometimes."

His dark brown eyes met hers with what looked like sadness in them.

"Too many, I'm afraid. Do you mind that we're stopping at Ben's? I should have asked if you'd be up to it."

"I'm feeling pretty great right now. The shoulder is down to a minor throb, and I'm looking forward to seeing Ben and Beth."

They'd been her friends, too, for the first couple of years, then…she'd eased her way out of the tight group, finding her own.

The farm wasn't too far from the breeder's house, and within ten minutes, they pulled into the horseshoe driveway and parked in front of another old farmhouse. The paint was chipped, the wooden steps were split, but the house itself was warm and cozy. It was the kind of house where people and animals were welcome, and as the two puppies bounded in, Ben's Labrador, Sadie, was more than gracious.

Teddy went off to play outside with the other kids after lunch and they got down to some serious reminiscing.

A little over an hour later, they were back on the road, heading home.

She leaned her head back and before she knew it, Nick was gently waking her up. She came awake slowly and admitted, "I guess I was more wiped out than I thought."

"Your body is still dealing with the trauma. You now have a nap under your belt and you can sit outside for a while and watch the puppies play."

"I have to make an appointment at the vet's for the rest of their shots. Can I make it for one day that you're around? I don't know what you've decided to do. Are you going back to patrol or transferring to another department right away?"

"I'm taking another week, talking to a couple of people, seeing what I want to do. My supervisor knows what I'm planning and has given me some latitude."

Teddy had been waiting patiently but was beginning to lose it.

"Come on, Dad. Get me out of here."

"I'm coming, already."

CHAPTER TWENTY-THREE

Olivia arrived at dinnertime and ran right in to meet the new additions, not even bothering with hellos. Nick watched with amusement as the usually staid doctor got down on the floor and turned goofy. He could understand why. Dogs had that kind of effect. He'd become a dog person in a matter of hours, never realizing how they could impact a mood. Sand paper tongues had a way of taking you to a happy place, and he laughed out loud at their antics. The fact that Teddy was enthralled was a bonus.

He didn't want to leave the group assembled but he knew he should think about supper.

"Instead of cooking, why don't I run out and pick something up. I take it you're joining us, Liv?"

Without looking up, distracted by a child at play, she said, "Yes. I'm on call but I don't want to leave unless I have to."

It seemed the impact of being with the dogs was even more potent than he'd originally thought. Olivia had warmed up to him.

"What are you guys in the mood for?"

Teddy, trying to copy Em's accent, said, "Some chook on the barbie?"

It was not what you'd call spot on and Olivia's laughter bubbled up, causing Em to smile at the Aussie delivery.

"We used to have that three nights a week. Where did Teddy hear the phrase?"

Ozzie had crawled into Em's lap, with her help, and she was sitting and stroking the soft fur. It seemed he'd run out of energy for the moment and was resting. Nick wondered how long it would last. He enjoyed watching Em's contentment. It was like she was purring.

"We talked about some of Dad's sayings on the way to North Hadley."

"God, I haven't heard them in so long. It's like I've forgotten we lived there."

"You were only seven when we moved."

"I know, but there are some things I can remember distinctly, like Dad yelling *Hooroo* when he was driving away to one of his on-site projects."

"Or when he found something oddly distinct." The accent was back when Em added, "That stands out like a shag on a rock, doesn't it, you little buggers."

Nick noticed a wistful look take over the faces, as if they were back there, their father just feet away. Sadness for the loss crept over him. Em had never spoken overly much about the man, but it seemed there might have been a reason. It hurt too much.

When the doorbell rang, the dogs began scrambling toward the sound, slip-sliding across the wooden floors. He chuckled as he got up to answer it.

"Be careful, Nick. Don't let them get out."

Taking Em's warning seriously, he scooped one up just as Teddy came over to claim the other.

Maks and Cami were standing on the threshold, each holding a paper bag.

Maks lifted it by the handle and announced, "We bring food for the needy."

Cami was oohing over the squirming mass of energy and exchanged her bag for what was in Nick's possession, rubbing her face in the dog's neck.

"Hope you don't mind our barging in, but I wanted to meet them." She could hear Camille's soft laugh as she buried her neck in fur. "I might need one of these."

Em called out, "I'll give you a number to call. You can't have one of mine."

Nick and Maks disappeared into the kitchen, the steam from the take-out announcing there'd be Chinese for dinner.

Teddy stopped struggling to keep the puppy in his arms and let her down with a plop.

"Is it time to feed Lily yet? Does she eat when we do?"

"I'm going to feed them twice a day and it should be fairly consistent. I'm not usually home until six, so I wanted to wait until then. I guess it's close enough."

With Teddy's help, they got the dogs' food ready and placed it on the floor in the kitchen. Scampering paws came running and the puppies chowed down with no invitation needed.

⌒

The humans did the same as soon as the puppies were safely back in their crate.

Nick asked Maks, "How's it working for the FBI?"

"It's job. I am thinking to go to law school. I need to do undergraduate first. I've sent out application and hope for best."

Em's eyes lit up. "Maks, that's great. You'll be a natural."

"My father was attorney. I want to follow in footsteps."

Em said, "Not all of them, I hope."

His father was killed in prison after being falsely accused by the Russian government. They did what had to be done to rid the country of activists. Still were.

"Wherever they lead, Em. He was man to be proud of. I hope to be same for my children."

Cami leaned over and kissed his cheek. While they murmured love words to each other, Nick glanced over to see Em looking wistful. This was what she deserved. A man who loved her, body and soul, who she could love back the same way. Could he be that man?

It would have been so easy to love her when they were younger. He'd short-changed them both with his unwillingness to settle down, needing her as a friend more than a lover. If he'd just turned away from his adoring fans, rather than satisfy the needs of a hockey stud... He hadn't been ready for forever back then. But afterwards, when they'd bumped into each other again years later? He must have wanted a family by then, wanted to settle down. He'd proposed to Saban pretty quickly when she visited the city. Had he really thought she was the better match?

Maybe it was just the next step in their relationship. They'd been through the dating ritual, she loved his overindulgence in catering to her every whim, and he refused to marry someone who didn't need him.

His eyes were drawn to Em, who was munching on the finger food. He knew she loved her egg rolls and scallion pancakes. Cami must have, too, because there had to be three orders in front of them. She asked Maks, in between mouthfuls, "What college?"

"Suffolk. I don't want to leave city."

In between licking her fingers, she offered, "If you need a reference, let me know. It's where I went."

"Thank you. That would be appreciated. One more couldn't hurt, especially one from such an illustrious alumnus."

"I'm not sure I'm that but I know a lot of the professors there. It's a good school."

Cami wiped her sticky fingers on a napkin, as delicately as only she knew how, before asking,

"Have they called to have you guest lecture?"

"They wanted me to teach a class in their continuing ed division. I had too much on my plate and turned them down. It might have been interesting. I would have enjoyed working with young minds."

Nick looked up.

"When was this?"

"Last year. I could have been teaching Immigration Law as we speak."

Was it because of him and his constant demands on her time? Was he one thing on her plate that might have made it too heavy to take anything else on? He was sorry she hadn't mentioned it. He knew she'd make a great teacher.

"Dad, can I have some more rice?"

Teddy had been so quiet he'd almost forgotten he was sitting at the table with them.

"Sure, pal."

He scooped up a few tablespoons of the pork fried rice and put it on the plate, noticing the yawn and the droopy eyes when he did. He had a feeling the puppies weren't the only ones tired out from all the running around. He was sure Teddy would be going to bed early tonight without any complaints. Maybe it would give him a chance to talk to Em. About life, his feelings, the future.

But that wasn't to be. Olivia, Cami, and Maks stayed until Nick took Teddy up to bed. The kid had almost fallen asleep at the table and after one more push to stay up, he'd sat by the crate to say good night to Lily and Ozzie When Nick led him away, the dogs were sleeping soundly, snuggled next to each other, and Em was getting ready to go up herself. Her pallor was on the milky side.

"You've had a busy day. You must be exhausted."

"I am. Do you mind awfully if I go up, too?"

"Of course not. I'll change the bandage and tuck you in just like I do Teddy."

She hesitated, a trace of nervousness flitting across her face.

He closed his eyes and muttered a curse under his breath. Why had he said it like that? She probably didn't want him tucking her in.

She moved slowly toward the stairs, telling him, "I'll be in my room."

He followed, his arms full of Teddy. "I'll be in as soon as he's down. I don't think it's going to take long tonight."

She nodded, gave him a wan smile, and disappeared behind her door.

When he knocked ten minutes later, she told him to come in.

He opened the door a crack to see her resting on her bed, already changed into her tee and leggings, her sling flung to the side. After moving to her side, depositing all the paraphernalia on the table next to her, he quipped, "His head hadn't even touched the pillow and he was out for the count."

"He really loves them. I was afraid…their baby teeth are sharp as tacks and they bite a lot for the first few months. He didn't seem to mind at all." A crest of emotion filled her voice.

He pulled on the medical gloves he'd need to wear to tend her wound.

"You were right about them. They'll help him deal with all of this better than anything I can think of…besides you."

She scooted forward, pushed the tee she was wearing off her shoulder, giving him access to the sweet, creamy skin. He gingerly sat down behind her, using a light touch as he began to undo the tape. He used the warm cloth to bathe away the necrotic skin that was shedding around the injury site. Once that was finished, he fingered in the anti-bacterial ointment the doctor had prescribed.

After he applied the gauze, she said wistfully, "I wish I could leave it open to the air for a bit, but the tee will rub it during the night. I'll have to figure out a way now that the infection stage is almost over."

"Yes, Dr. Spencer-Ronan. When exactly did you get the degree in medicine?"

She jerked back, her good shoulder hitting him in the chest. "Don't be a cracker."

"I assume that's Aussie for…snarky? It's not exactly the nicest way to talk to someone who's helped you every step of the way."

She leaned back against him and he sucked in his breath. His mood went from amusement to turned-on in one instant.

"I appreciate it, Nick. I'm not sure I could have let anyone do as much for me. I don't like being dependent."

"I know."

She lay against him, her breathing a steady rhythm of in and out. It felt...like it should. Pure. Maybe not so innocent but a natural extension of what they felt for each other.

"When my parents died, I swore I wouldn't depend on anyone again. Liv and I lost the only two people we ever counted on and the abrupt end...nearly crushed me."

He felt a quiver move through his heart. He didn't like knowing she'd been hurt so badly as a child.

"I could tell when you and Liv were talking about your Dad. You both loved him a lot."

"He was the best. Funny, self-deprecating, smart, talented. And we never doubted that he loved us,"—she turned her head to look at him—"to the moon and back." She rested against him again. "I'm glad Mummy died with him. She wouldn't have known how to live without him."

His hand snaked around her middle and he sighed in contentment. Nothing had felt this good...in forever. She smelled like antiseptic with a whiff of coconut thrown in. His fingers itched to slide beneath her soft cotton tee, feel the silky skin beneath. Instead he pulled her closer, wanting her to know he was here with her.

That would only last a couple more days, unless she was willing to...

"I need to talk to you about some things when I get back. I can't do it until then."

He needed that behind him. Didn't think it fair to be discussing a future when his past hadn't been completely buried yet.

"Do they have to do with Teddy?"

"In a way, I guess. More me than him, though."

"I'll be here. And I promise, I'll listen."

He didn't want to release her, wanted the intimacy of the moment to last. When he heard her breathing change to soft purrs, he knew she'd fallen asleep. He stayed with her, holding her in his arms, until the sun began to come up the next morning.

She felt safe and she snuggled closer to the body behind her.

She was surprised he was still here. In the same position they were in before she fell asleep. His arms were wrapped around her waist, beneath her tee, his hand touching skin. Moving was not an option, even if she had to pee. They'd slept like this once before. With no bed left for them on a weekend away, he had brought her close, as he leaned against the wall, the floors already covered with bodies at the ski lodge. But his hand had never strayed like this. His body hadn't been nearly as solid. She'd pretended back then that they were a couple, like so many of the others scattered around them. People had thought they were doing it, and she'd often wondered why they never had. Not once had he ever given her any indication he would have liked to. It had hurt. He was known for his dating prowess back then, a first-rate hockey jock with a killer smile. She'd just accepted that he didn't find her sexually attractive. She was popular back then, on a sports team herself, got asked out a lot. She knew she had some appeal, but for some reason he found her lacking. In the end, it was probably better they never did get between the sheets. Their friendship might have been forfeited, and that would have been a tragedy. They got along too well to be adversaries.

The urge to pee became too strong to ignore, so she started easing her way off the bed just as she heard a loud shout.

"Dad, where are you?"

Teddy must have checked Nick's room to find him gone and the voice sounded panicked.

"He's in here, Teddy."

She felt Nick stir behind her, his hands going to his face and scrubbing.

"Good morning."

In a flash, she remembered about the puppies, threw off the covers and scrambled out of bed.

"I can't believe I slept through the night. I've got to get Lily and Ozzie out. They can't go more than a few hours without a pee break."

"I'll get them. I have a feeling Teddy will want to go out with us."

Now that she was on her feet, he was able to move freely. He got up and stretched. She watched the muscles flex and relax, and her mouth dried up as another part of her pooled with moisture. Forcing her eyes off the man and his body, she said, "I'll check the crate. I'm sure they peed all over it."

As he walked toward the door, he stated firmly, "I'll clean that up. You can't be crouching and moving around like that."

He laughed as he took his son by the hand. "Let's see if Teddy stays true to his word and is willing to do everything for you."

She watched him leave, his bare feet soundless on the carpet. He'd really stepped up for her. This wasn't something he'd bargained for, but he seemed to be enjoying it, which surprised her.

She listened to the sound of puppies squealing and a little boy shrieking in laughter. As she made her way down the stairs, she took in the racket. It signaled life. This was what she'd always dreamt of. It reminded her of her own family, before she lost them, with a man she loved, a child she adored, a home where she felt safe and warm. Where happiness breathed.

Could she ever find this with someone else? Did she even want to look? Maybe it was time to tell Nick how she felt. See if there was something that they could build on. Wasn't friendship the precursor to love? Didn't they already have a foundation that was solid and secure? Okay, maybe she didn't cause his heart to flutter, but maybe she could love him enough for both of them.

When she got to the bottom of the steps, the puppies came racing back in, running wild. Teddy was chasing after them, in one direction, then another. Nick was bent over the crate, taking out the blankets that had to be drenched and smelly. After crawling back out, the sodden mess in his hands, he stood and walked right to the washer that was housed next to the kitchen and dropped them in. Measuring out the liquid detergent, adding the softener, he closed the lid, pressed power, and turned to face her.

"Well, that was fun."

"Did they go when they went out?"

"They did. Are you picking up the poop or are you leaving it? The one thing I forgot to buy is poop bags."

"I have some plastic bags in one of the drawers."

"You have plastic bags? I thought you were anti-plastic."

"I am, and I recycle as much as I can. But even I need one every once in a while."

"Which drawer?"

"Third one down beside the sink."

"Come on Teddy, you'll need to learn how to do this if you're going to help while I'm gone."

"Dad, that's yucky."

"It's also part of the deal. Now come on."

"Okay. But I'm not going to like it."

"Like it's going to be my favorite morning chore?"

Teddy walked slowly towards the back door, showing his distaste for the new routine. She stifled a laugh before going to the closet to retrieve another blanket for the crate. She was glad Nick had the foresight to buy a couple. After washing the floor of the crate with disinfectant, she lined it with the soft fleece but paid for the effort with a new throb in her shoulder.

Father and son returned, looking none the worse for wear. Nick told Teddy as he began to run back to the crate, "Go wash your hands before touching anything." To Em, he said, "I threw the bag in the garbage bin. Hope that was all right."

"Better there than in here."

When he realized she'd done the residual clean-up, he turned on her.

"Why didn't you let me finish up?"

"I…I probably should have."

She was holding her arm, so he knew she'd jarred it in some way.

"Let me see your shoulder."

She offered him a view and he clucked like an old woman behind her.

"You can't do things like this yet. You've fought off infection this far. Let's not tempt fate."

"Yes, sir. But I'm not going to like it."

She was mimicking Teddy's earlier comment and he could do nothing but smile.

CHAPTER TWENTY-FOUR

In the days after picking up the puppies, there was a new routine in place. Nick was the one who got up twice during the night to let them out to pee. He'd insisted she sleep and had taken on the chore with a willingness that made her heart ache. Up for the day just after seven, he fixed Teddy's breakfast, made him lunch, and before leaving for school, made sure the dogs were secure in their crate, made the promise of a perfect muffin for breakfast.

When quiet settled, Em sat watching the puppies. They were looking at her with sad eyes, and she assumed they'd rather be running around than imprisoned. She apologized for their lack of freedom, but she couldn't take the chance of them running in two different directions.

Today marked a week since the attack. She was better than she had been, although not as well as she would have liked. She had a feeling that she'd have to take the two weeks the doctor ordered before diving back into her schedule full time. She missed the women at her firm. They'd all been calling every day, checking in, but it wasn't the same as being in the office, hearing the jokes, sharing the laughter or the tears, all depending on how an individual case went. It had been her home for a long time now. She'd created another family for herself and they were the members. She didn't know what she'd do without them. Yet, one by one, they were pairing off with someone from the outside. First, Nell, then Camille. What would she do when they were all married with children?

Last night she'd slept alone. She'd missed being wrapped in Nick's arms and the longing came rushing back with a vengeance. It had felt so right, and for a split second she'd thought about making an advance. Kissing him, moving his hand so that it was lower, wanting to feel his fingers inside of her, to quench the hunger she had for him. She wanted to make love with him, but she needed to know he wanted that, too. She didn't want it because of Teddy, or because he hadn't had relations in months. She wanted him to smile at her in that sexy way he had about him, see passion in his eyes when he looked at her, feel his body respond to hers, not in friendship but in the throes of ecstasy. Was she still hoping for something that had no way of becoming reality? If she was, she had to find out. He wanted to talk to her when he got back. She had no idea about what, he wouldn't say, but she needed to have that talk with him as well. Put it to rest or put it into action. One way or the other, she'd deal with the truth and learn to live with it. She just hoped she didn't lose him in the process.

They sidestepped each other throughout the day, as if they didn't want to get into things better left unsaid, at least for the time being, and Friday finally rolled into Saturday, bringing her closer to a resolution.

⌐

She could hear Nick's footsteps as he came down the stairs, and when she looked up, he had a suitcase in his hand, a frown creasing his forehead. He dropped the case by the door and walked over to the crate.

"Why don't we take them out before we leave."

"We?"

"Yeah, I talked to Camille while I was upstairs. She suggested I take you to the office on the way to the airport. She'll bring you back here after you both pick up Teddy at school. Maks will come to the house after he gets out of work."

She perked right up.

"I get to go to the office?"

He sat next to her, took her hand and forced a smile.

"Not to work. I don't trust you here alone. There's too much trouble you could get into on your own. Camille agreed."

She scooted off the couch and headed for the stairs. "I'll be right down. I want to change."

"You look fine just the way you are."

"But I have on jeans. I don't want to go in looking like this."

He was standing now, his hands on his hips.

"No one will see you but your friends."

"There'll be clients in the waiting room. What kind of impression will I make?"

"With your arm in the sling, I bet they can figure out you've been hurt."

"But…"

He pulled his cell out of his back pocket and scrolled for contacts.

"I can always call Cami and tell her you're pushing…"

She went rushing back to him.

"Fine. You win."

He slipped his phone back in his pocket.

"Will wonders ever cease? This is a first."

"And probably the last. Don't get comfortable with the temporary triumph."

"I know better."

"Okay. Let's get them out so we can get going."

They sat on the deck, the sun high in the sky, watching the puppies chase each other, their tails, anything that moved.

She raised her head, let the gentle breeze ruffle her hair.

"Are you picking up your folks before you head to the airport?"

He was sitting bent over, his hands hanging between his legs.

"No. My mother said they'd meet me there. I think they want to have their own car in case they decide to leave early. I don't know what I'm going to find when I get there."

She glanced over, his expression reminding her that he was going to a wake and funeral. One that would not be easy.

"Saban's mother wouldn't make it harder than it needs to be, would she?"

"It's not that. She won't be giving me a second thought. I...didn't tell you...but Saban was leaving me for someone else. That someone else will probably be there, as well."

Her jaw dropped open in surprise. "What?"

"Yeah. He was one of the assistant district attorneys, Aron Tedeschi. I'm sure you know him."

"I do. He's a piece of work."

How could Saban be willing to leave Nick for that...peacock? Although, when she thought about them together, she couldn't help thinking they made a good match. A fawn and a fawner.

But to do that to Nick?

She was pulled back into his dilemma when he asked, "So, do I stand by the casket, all dutiful, or watch as someone else does the honors? I don't know why the hell I'm even going."

"Nick, they wouldn't do that."

Not something that blatant. Laretta Williams had too much starch in her to be so dismissive of protocol.

"While I was waiting for Laretta to show up, I noticed Aron with Rachelle, and he was giving Laretta a kiss and hug good-bye. From what I heard from the ME's office, the body was being released to him and he was escorting it down. I offered but..."

The texts and messages told him all he'd needed to know. They'd been having a full-blown affair since she'd kicked him out of the bedroom, maybe even before...which meant...Aron was the one who had the right to mourn her.

He was taking in the yard and the cavorting puppies, his lips a thin line. "Juanita told me he'd transferred down to another DA's office. I don't know what he'll do now. Stay or move back."

"Hopefully, stay. I won't miss him at all."

She tugged at his shirt. Not to get his attention but to let him know she was there for him if he needed her.

"How did I get here, Em?"

You married the wrong woman.

"This isn't on you, Nick. This is on her."

"It takes two, doesn't it?"

"You've been a good husband."

"I changed the rules half-way through the game."

She didn't know how to counter that. It sounded like he had.

"Change is a given. It's how you work together through the changes that can make or break a marriage. It doesn't seem like Saban was willing to do that."

His mouth spread into a thin-lipped grimace.

"And I wasn't willing to go back to how it was. Both of us were too stubborn to work it out."

Of course he'd have wanted to work it out. He'd loved her. How would he get over the rejection, the betrayal, the death?

When the puppies came running over and raced up the steps, they took them in and crated them before leaving.

Squatting down, Em suddenly felt bereft at leaving them. The vulnerability was back, and she needed the unconditional love they offered. Her fingers felt for their snouts through an opening in the crate, their down soft and warm. "I'll be back before you even miss me."

On the way to the law firm, second thoughts were fighting for prominence. After their conversation out on the deck, she knew it was way too soon to tell Nick about her feelings. There was so much still undefined and unresolved. His emotions had to be muddled. She couldn't add to his confusion. He had to get through the upcoming wake and funeral, accept the fact that he'd never be able to work through his issues with Saban now that she was dead. He was also facing the fact that she'd chosen someone over him. What would it be like for him if he was second-chaired, if Aron was the one standing in the receiving line, replacing Nick as grieving mate? How would he handle the feelings that would evoke? He needed to sort it all out before he knew what he wanted, how to proceed.

She was glad to be out of the house. She'd brood over this all afternoon if she wasn't distracted. And she was excited she'd probably get there just in time for the afternoon break. The women always seemed to have fifteen minutes the same time every day and found themselves together with an afternoon coffee to recharge.

And that's where she found them when Nick dropped her off.

Each one of them got up and came over, hugging her in welcome.

Arianna was the first to say, "There's a strange prevailing mood when one of you isn't here."

"This from the one who just got back from a three-week campaign run. How many cities and towns did you visit?"

"It's tiring, but I have to say it's also invigorating. I think I needed a new challenge and didn't even realize it."

Nell offered, "When Jack goes out on the campaign trail next time out, I'll probably go with him, at least on a part-time basis. He thinks I'll be an asset. I think it's because I'm a woman and anyone would do."

"It does seem to be our year. We have to take advantage when we can."

Jelani amended, "Your brain is your asset, your fashion sense the trimmings."

Camille asked, breaking the mood, "So, how's Nick holding up?"

"He's been a trooper. The puppies didn't get out the first night and he had quite a mess to clean up. He did it without one word of complaint but didn't make the same mistake last night."

"I meant the trip. This can't be easy for him. Considering."

Her smile dipped. Did she share his revelations or keep them to herself? Deciding to keep it until tonight, and talk to Camille and Maks about it, she answered, simply, "It's not."

She hoped he'd be all right.

CHAPTER TWENTY-FIVE

Nick was waiting at the airport gate when his mother and father arrived, a carry-on in his father's hand. They were traveling light.

So was he. He'd been working through what he'd accept and what he wouldn't. Being required to sit among the mourners would be too much for his pride. If Aron was the one placed in the receiving line, he wouldn't stick around for the funeral. If people talked, too fucking bad. Saban had already embarked on a new life before the bullets struck. Laretta seemed to have accepted her choice and he would not be relegated to second tier.

Now it was his turn to grab hold of some happiness.

"Hello, son. How you holding up?"

"I'm doing okay, Dad. Being with Em and the puppies is helping. She's still waiting for you to come over and play cribbage with her."

"I haven't wanted to interfere in her recuperation."

"Your father's aversion is to the dogs, not the patient."

Jerry gave a weak smile.

Nick, like all kids, had wanted a dog when they were growing up, but his father hadn't and seeing it was his house, he set the rules. He was glad Teddy was getting the opportunity to bond with one. He had Em to thank for that.

The flight went without a hitch, if he didn't count the thoughts racing through his head. The closer they got to their destination, the more aggrieved he got by the whole thing. No one from the family had called him, no one had reached out even though he'd texted them which flight he was taking and the name of the hotel they'd be staying in. It had pissed him off. Royally.

When they arrived at the funeral home, he stood looking at the manicured lawns, the limousine with purple flag, the building. It was stately, as only a Southern mansion could be. There were stairs on either side, outlined in black trellis. The portico,

with four columns, looked rich in history. As he made his way up the curved archway, his parents ahead of him, he hesitated outside the door, following them in
after he'd taken a deep breath.

The entryway was carpeted in an old Persian-style rug. The antiques that lined
the walls spoke to quality and wealth. There was a sign with Saban's name on it. It
was missing the one she'd taken the day they said their vows. He wondered if Saban
herself would have pushed him this far.

His mother's exclamation told him what she thought, and her lips were rolled in
as if she didn't want to speak ill of the dead.

"We are not staying if they try to humiliate you, Nick."

"I think they already have, Kathy."

His father's voice held the anger his mother wasn't willing to share.

Soft music filtered through a sound system, and he could hear people talking in
hushed whispers along the wall just outside the viewing room.

There was a girl behind the podium, handling the sign-in book and she looked
up and smiled.

"The family has asked me to extend their gratitude to all mourners. Would you
like to sign in, please?"

"He's part of the family. No need."

His mother had already made her move into the room where the casket lay.
Large bouquets of flowers lined an alcove. Chairs were set up to the right of the
body. He scanned the row of people standing with Laretta. There was Saban's father, Robert, her brother Bobby, Bobby's wife, Stella, and Aron, who was talking
to Rachelle.

He felt a vein pulse in his forehead, the audacity of the family to cut him out
completely making his head pound. The lilies were overpowering in the humid air
and he had to force back the gag reflex. He would have chosen something a bit
subtler, but he'd had no say.

Kathy must have agreed.

"It smells like a bordello in here."

"Mom. Stop." His voice was firm and insistent.

She did but the hurumph told him she wasn't nearly finished.

There was no point for either of them to make a scene, no point for him to
pretend that he was here as Saban's husband. He'd been wiped out of her life with
an ease that amazed him.

His mother surprised him by bypassing the open casket and going right over to
Laretta. Saban's mother was busy comforting a young woman who was crying and
going on about how wonderful Saban was and what a loss this must be to her
parents.

Had she been wonderful? Had he missed something? To him she was willful,
spoiled, and pampered and it was Laretta and Bob Sr. who had enabled the selfish
behavior. He'd taken the reins from them when he married her. It had been a mistake, and when he'd changed his approach, he'd splintered his relationship with
Laretta and it had never recovered.

After waiting her turn, getting to the front of the line, Kathy Katsaros held out her hand, as if not wanting to give Laretta the chance to hug her. He shouldn't be letting his mother lead this dance, but he was interested to see what she'd say. Kathy Katsaros was not one to mince words no matter the circumstance.

"Laretta, I'm sorry for your loss. Losing a child can't be easy."

"Thank you for coming, Kathryn. I was surprised to learn that you were. You weren't close to my daughter in life. I didn't think you'd come down to mourn her death."

"For better or worse, she was my daughter-in-law and she was too young to die."

Laretta dismissed Kathryn when she reached out a hand to Nick, tears collecting in her eyes and coursing down her cheeks.

"Thank you for coming, Nick. Our girl is gone."

He cocked an eyebrow. *Thank you for coming? Our girl?* She was a girl who'd never grown up, but she certainly wasn't his anymore. The formality was almost humorous. Was it all for show?

"Laretta."

He glanced down the line to see Aron glaring at him.

"I see you've replaced me already."

"What do you mean?"

"I know about Aron. I'm surprised you dispensed with decorum. It's not like you. I would think you'd want the world to see the grieving widower."

Her tears ceased immediately, as if she could turn them on and off at will.

"Would they have seen that, Nick? I wasn't sure, so I let Saban's future husband be the one the world saw. At least he *is* grieving."

"I was planning to stay for the funeral, but seeing you have all bases covered, I might as well get back to my son."

"And your girlfriend? Don't talk to me about hypocrisy."

"She's not my... Think what you want Laretta. I'm sorry Saban's dead. I never wanted that."

"No, I don't think you did, Nick. But it's what we got."

He went down the rest of the line, spoke to Robert and Bobby, who seemed more upset by his exclusion than Laretta did.

"I didn't want this for you, Nick. It wasn't fair. I know my sister, and this was on her. I wish we could stay in touch but under the circumstances, I don't think we will. I liked you, and I'm sorry it came to this."

"Thanks, Bobby. You were the one person in the family I could talk to."

He offered his condolences to Stella and left the line, not having anything to say to Rachelle or Aron.

He stuck his arm through his mother's and father's. "We're out of here."

"Damn straight."

But before he could vacate the funeral home, Rachelle ran over, calling out, "Nick, wait up. Please."

He let his parents precede him out the door and turned to Rachelle.

"What is there to say, Rachelle?"

"I'm sorry. I tried to talk her into telling you. She was my friend but sometimes I didn't like her very much. This was one of those times. You deserved better."

"Thanks, I think. Does anyone else see the irony here? If she had just left when she wanted, she'd be alive. Why the hell did she wait so long?"

"You know Saban. She was getting her ducks in a row, making sure she had everything in place before leaving. I was convinced she thought you'd change back, give her what she was looking for. When it became apparent you weren't going to, she quit her job and cemented her relationship with Aron. He'd been asking her for months to leave you. I think she loved you, Nick."

"She had a pretty shitty way of showing it, wouldn't you say?"

All Rachelle gave him was a nod of the head. With that, he left, wiping his feet on the rug as he left, knowing he'd never be back.

⌒

Em sat on the couch, at her sister's insistence. Olivia had arrived first thing this morning, to relieve Cami and Maks. The threesome had spent a quiet night talking, watching a movie, but she felt more alone than ever. She missed Nick and wished it had all worked out another way. Now? She'd have to wait to see how the Jenga tower held. There were so many pieces, and if she moved the wrong ones, it would collapse. Just like her world.

When Ozzie tried to get up to join her, too small yet to make the jump, she picked up the squirming bundle of fur and put him on her lap. Did he already know he was hers? That Teddy had commandeered Lily, thought she was his. What would happen when he moved out, couldn't see her all the time? Another loss to contend with. Maybe she could let them stay until things were settled with their house, and they bought a new one. Where was Nick planning on going? It had been so easy for them to juggle things living so close to each other. Would his plans include her at all? So many things she wanted to talk to him about, hadn't had the courage to broach yet.

She glanced at the clock on the wall. He'd be getting ready for the wake. How would that go? She still couldn't believe that Saban had handled things the way she had. Talk about leaving one in the lurch. Would her family leave him out in the cold, as well?

Olivia came in, some Chinese leftovers warmed up on a plate. "Teddy's already eaten and wanted to go outside with Lily. I told him it was all right, but to come in when she'd done her business. I'll make sure to check on them every…ten minutes or so."

After placing the plate down, she said, "You haven't had much to eat since I got here, and you need to keep up your strength."

Ozzie was sniffing the air, looking more interested in her lunch that she was. Olivia scooped him up and petted his head.

"You are too cute. I think I might need one of these."

It was amazing how everyone who touched him wanted one. They had that effect.

"I know a great breeder."

"I might go for something smaller. We'll see. I have to figure out what I'm going to do with Scott first."

"Still on the fence about living together?"

"Yeah, and I'm losing my balance. I wonder which way I'll fall."

Scott McMillan was Olivia's boyfriend of two years. An emergency room doctor, who'd been

on duty the afternoon of the shooting. She'd seen firsthand how good he was at his job. Patient, caring, and calm in the face of crisis.

"He's talking about marriage and kids. I'm not sure I'm ready. I'm not sure I'll ever be ready."

"Is it that, or are you looking for a relationship like Mummy and Dad had? They're few and far between."

Olivia plopped down on a chair, releasing a long sigh.

"I know. I'm not sure I want one like theirs, though. Too dependent on each other for their happiness. What do you think would have happened if only one of them died?"

"The one left behind would never have been the same."

"Right. I don't want that. Mummy gave up her life, her family to be with Dad. We were too isolated in each other. It created problems for us, as well."

"Scott wouldn't expect you to do that."

"No, he wouldn't but I also wouldn't allow it. I can't even imagine what it would be like living so far away from you. To top that off, I like my life and I'm not sure sharing it would be an improvement."

Teddy came in, Lilly scampering behind him. He was performing his old man routine, his arms hanging down, his body drooped over.

"I'm pooped. Do you think Lily would mind if I go play with my toys for a while?"

"I think she'll be fine with that. Dogs are so patient, they'll wait forever for you, without a whimper."

"Good, because, I need a break."

Olivia shooed the puppies into the crate, and they cried for a minute before cuddling with each other. Teddy made sure they were fine before skipping out of the room.

Em looked longingly at him as he disappeared.

"You don't want kids?"

"I do. Someday. My biological clock is still ticking. I have time."

"I want them."

"I know. You're so good with them, with Teddy. You're a natural."

Playing with the edges of her plate, Em shared her secret.

"I...I made an appointment at a donor clinic. I'm thinking about getting pregnant."

Olivia's eyes flashed up at her.

"You can't do that, Em. Not now. Not yet."

"I'm still in the beginning stages. I...think it's time to tell Nick how I feel, but I have no idea how that's going to play out. He might still be unavailable, and I might never find another man I want to be with."

"You have to give it time. See how..."

"He's never given me any indication he loves me like that. And I can't seem to love him any other way."

"He seems to be lost right now. I can't even imagine what he's going through. Let him process things, see where he ends up."

She was sick of hoping his feelings for her would change. Not that she'd actively sought that while he was married, but now...hope was the order of the day. She couldn't live on any more of it without losing herself. She needed to move forward with the plans she'd made before things went awry.

"It's only a consultation. I haven't made any firm decisions yet. Maybe the dogs will satisfy my maternal instincts, at least for now. Then there's Teddy to consider. I don't want him to think I'm replacing him."

"He's doing well, considering. It's like he doesn't even notice she's gone."

"She didn't take up much space in his life."

"While you're his universe. Think long and hard about this, Em. It might have an adverse effect on him."

She didn't want that, but could she live her life strictly for another woman's child?

Didn't she deserve to have her own?

CHAPTER TWENTY-SIX

The sprawling airport felt like a small city, people rushing around going from here to there, queues snaking around the ropes, security forces in full view. Nick couldn't wait to get back home. Stepping around a cleaning trolley, the woman with a mop cleaning up someone's spilled drink, he moved toward the table where his parents sat, a food tray in his hands. Parceling out the sandwiches, he returned the tray to the counter before joining them. They'd been able to book a return flight, paying a premium penalty, and had a couple of hours to kill before boarding. The trip down had been a waste of his time. He'd thought about staying, going to the funeral home where there'd be a small ceremony, before going to the gravesite. A Sunday burial meant no church service, and he would have stuck out like a sore thumb, so decided against it. What good would it have done? It wouldn't have satisfied any need he had to see Saban put in the ground. He knew she was gone. Had been for months now. She'd been having an affair, riding a see-saw with Aron as well.

"You made the right decision, son. I hope you're not regretting it."

It was his father who made the statement, which surprised him. He wasn't an emotional kind of guy.

"I kinda feel sorry for Aron."

His mother paused, the roast beef sub half-way to her mouth.

"What the hell for?"

"She was playing games with both of us. I know how that felt. And I think he really loved her. He was willing to move for her, which I never was."

His mother harrumphed.

"You have a good heart. I'm still pissed. Can I ask you now, after all these years, what you saw in her?"

What had he seen?

A winning smile, her unforgettable Southern drawl, her dripping charm? Totally feminine and in need of pampering? He'd never had to second-guess what she wanted. She'd made it perfectly clear, and he'd loved catering to her at the beginning. Loved making sure she felt safe, protected, and cared for. And it had worked for a while. Only when life got more complicated had he understood how artificial it was. She'd begun to use all kinds of excuses to avoid responsibility, used his love to get what she wanted. *If you loved me, you'd take me out tonight. If you loved me, you'd let me have the third bedroom. I need more closet space, darling.*

"I wanted to take care of someone. It seems I had a half-assed backwards impression of what love was."

"Taking care of someone becomes a full-time occupation. It suffocates. Two people need to complement each other, not feed off each other."

His mother was telling him something that might have made an impact several years ago. It was coming too late to do him any good. He'd been wanting to have a conversation about his parents' marriage for decades. Maybe this was the right time to ask the right questions.

"Is that why you left? You were feeling suffocated?"

She glanced over at his father, whose expression had turned somber.

"Yes. I was someone's wife or someone's mother. I had nothing that was mine. I left because I needed to find my way back to who *I* was. I had a degree in business that I never used. Your father wouldn't hire me to work on his books or marketing, fought me about getting a job because he thought a woman's place was in the home. I didn't appreciate his sentiment. I had to leave him to prove my point. I got an apartment, found something I loved doing, then I began to travel, and I was enjoying my life again. It was challenging, and I was using my brain instead of my heart."

"Then why did you come back?"

She put the sandwich down, gave him her full attention.

"I realized there needed to be a balance. I called your dad and asked him to meet me for a drink. I always loved him, Nick. I just couldn't live the life he wanted for me. The separation was good for us."

"What you're saying is once you became independent, you felt you could be with someone without feeling hemmed in."

She nodded her head.

"I never understood that. I spent most of my life thinking you might leave again. You certainly didn't need us. I think…maybe I picked someone like Saban because if she needed me, she wouldn't desert me. Told you I had it half-assed backwards."

Her hand snaked out to grasp his wrist.

"Oh, Nick. I'm so sorry. I never… You were so young. I didn't realize…"

"I wasn't that young, Mom. I was thirteen."

She looked over to his father with love shining in her eyes. "With a little give and take, we were able to work things out, so I came home. I never intended to leave again. I had everything I wanted. You kids were always a part of that."

His father admitted, "I was wrong to keep her so tied to the house. I thought it was the man's role to take care of his family. Be the breadwinner. She was much more alive when she came back. I kicked myself in the butt for being so blind."

There was concern written on his mother's face.

"I'm sorry you were anxious about me leaving again. I wish I could go back and change it. You ended up being more scarred than I thought. Is that the reason you didn't…date Em?"

He closed his eyes, thinking that could have had something to do with it. She was too confident, too skilled at what she did. She could have left him at any time. Seemed she would have been the one to stay, independent and secure in who she was.

"How could I have gotten it all so confused? It doesn't make sense when looking back on it."

"I should have talked to you about it. I should have told you why I left and why I came back."

His dad admitted something he'd never done before.

"And I should have taken more of a hand in caring for Sara and Peter. I was lost without your mother. You picked up the slack for all of us. Too much fell on your shoulders and you were forced into being their caretaker. I'm sorry, too, Nick."

"Thanks, Dad." Although he knew it would sting, Nick added, "I think that's why I took on so much for Teddy. I wanted him to know he had someone in his corner, who loved him and would always be there."

"My mistakes made you a better father than I was, and for that I'm grateful. Someone learned from them and Teddy is the beneficiary."

Nick had to admit they had but he'd made mistakes of his own that had hurt Teddy in a similar way. He had to choose differently next time. Make sure the woman he married loved Teddy the way he deserved to be loved. Had he already found her? He thought he had.

"I've got to sort through some things, figure out the next step."

"Let Em help you."

He searched his mother's eyes, trying to read the message there. Was she suggesting what he'd already found to be true?

"I'm willing if she is. Before all of this happened, she'd been talking about finding a new life. One without me in it. I've held her back with my incessant demands on her time. I'm not sure she's going to let me back in."

"You chose a life without her in it, Nick. It had to be hard for her to sit in the back seat and watch her life go by."

"I never chose that, Mom. I've kept her in my life for a reason. She was always the one I counted on."

"You *chose* another woman, Nick. Same thing."

Juanita's voice came back to haunt him. Was that at the bottom of all of this? He'd have his answers soon. He hoped.

⟶

They landed just after ten that night. Was it too late to go back to Em's? That's where he wanted to be, so he texted her before his folks said their good-byes and left for home. They'd offered him a bed for the night. Would he have to take them up on it?

What are you doing back so early?

What do you mean? It's after ten.

You weren't due home until tomorrow night.

I wasn't welcome there. Can I come to the house?

Of course. I'll unlock the door.

See you soon.

Relieved, he kissed his parents' good-bye, and drove to the little house in Arlington that he'd come to think of as home.

She was waiting for him when he walked in and he reached her in two strides. Wrapping her in his arms, he held on for dear life.

"I'm sorry, Nick."

"For what? I'm the one who should be apologizing. I keep invading your life, keep counting on you to be there for me. I'm glad you are."

She looked up, a question in her eyes.

"I'm glad you texted. I wasn't asleep."

The dogs were yipping behind her, too young for a bark yet.

"Seems I'm not the only one who's glad you're back."

He breathed her in, coconut. It must be her shampoo, the scent so distinctly her. He didn't want to let go but the dogs might need attention.

"Should we take them out?"

"No, I did it while I was waiting for you to get here."

"I need to talk to you. I…"

She was looking at him intently and he couldn't help himself from taking her lips in his. It wasn't the kind of kiss he'd taken in the mountains, it was a full-on lip-sucking kiss that melted his brain. And she was returning it.

His hands were in her hair, the softness like silk between his fingers. Why hadn't he noticed this before? He'd pulled leaves out once, when they pile jumped after raking at her house one day, Teddy having a fit of giggles while they did. And he'd pushed it off her face while they were working out at the gym, her forehead sweaty from the workout. It had never felt like the soft rose petals it did today. And the taste of her lips was satisfying a need he didn't even know he had. Why hadn't he sampled them when they were younger? He never would have looked further. He would have had it all right here. Their breathing was labored as his tongue sought hers, and she invaded his mouth as if she'd been waiting a lifetime. He joined the assault, thrusting deeper, matching her measure for measure, wanting more, pressing for more. It was wet and wild, and he continued to kiss her with toe-curling determination.

He could feel her rapid heartbeat against his chest, heard the whimper as she opened her mouth wider to take him in. He knew she wanted this as much as he did. When she broke the kiss, her mouth was red and puffy, her eyes glazed with desire. Her breath was soft when she whispered, "Where did this come from?"

His thumbs brushed her cheekbones. His eyes searched hers. He didn't know how to answer. The magnitude of the feelings moving through him was too high, too strong to put into words. He'd never seen her as a mystery. He'd been wrong.

His loins tightened, heavy now with a desire to uncover the layers, to plunder the depths of her.

"I think it's always been there."

Her expression shifted, and his heart sputtered, thinking she was going to push him away.

"It's not because of what happened in Greenwood? It's not because you need someone to—"

"No. It only became clearer in South Carolina. Remember I told you I wanted to talk to you, but it had to wait until I got back? This is what I wanted to discuss. The way I feel about you. The way I've always felt."

She was putting up a barrier and fear was baying at it. What if she didn't reciprocate his feelings?

"I can't quite believe it. You've never given me any hint that you felt this way."

He'd been a fool, could see clearly now why he'd taken the different path.

"I...I was afraid. Afraid of losing your friendship if things didn't work out. Afraid that you were so self-sufficient you wouldn't need me. I wanted you to be my best friend for life."

She asked cautiously, "I couldn't be both?"

He scrubbed his head with his hand, pulled back before she could.

"I didn't know that's how it was supposed to work. Seeing Maks and Camille together has given me a new perspective on what it means to love someone. It doesn't have to be hard or filled with ultimatums. Loving you has always been easy. We work well as a team. I forgot that was important."

"I can't do this Nick, if you're still...dealing with what happened with Saban."

"I have to be honest. I wish it had ended in a different way. If she'd just left me when she first thought about it, it all would have been over and done with. We would have hashed things out and she would have been gone. With her death came a mixed bag of feelings that I'm still having trouble with. It doesn't have anything to do with what I feel about you."

"I can't rush this, Nick. I need to be sure this is what you want. That I'm who you want."

He pulled her closer, so she could feel his hard-on. "This doesn't tell you?"

"This tells me you're horny. It doesn't speak to what you feel for me."

"You'll have to let me show you."

His hands slid under her tee, and he moved them up slowly, skin on skin, until he captured her breasts, the feel of them setting off a thunder storm of electric current. Her moan gave him hope.

Taking her hand, he led her up the stairs to her bedroom and didn't let it go until the door was closed and they were safely shut away from the rest of the house.

Then he brought it up to his mouth and kissed her palm. "I want you, Em. Not because I'm horny, not because I need to be pumped up after getting dumped. I want you because you are the best thing that ever happened to me. You're loyal, and I can depend on you."

She was chewing on her lip, her eyes questioning.

"I sound like a puppy dog."

That's not what he meant. He'd finally realized what made their relationship so good. He could count on her, she was his partner, she completed him, but he was so mesmerized by the way her body felt he didn't take the time to explain.

Em's heart stuttered. He was still talking to her like a friend, but there was an unexpected passion that was making up for it. The kisses were hot, and his touch sent her skyrocketing somewhere in outer space. Could she be satisfied with less than what she wanted from him?

He stepped closer, his hand going behind her neck and pulling her toward him. As if wanting to savor the anticipation, he hovered with his lips a hairsbreadth away from hers, his eyes vanquishing all doubt. The tingles shot down her arms, into her torso, and exploded in the core of her. When he pulled her into him, his lips taking full possession of hers, she gave in and let him devour her. The kisses turned frenzied, their mouths letting their bodies talk for them. Until another part of their anatomy wanted a turn.

His fingers went for the buttons on her Henley tee, and he carefully pulled the hem up and over her head, being careful not to touch her injury. He seemed to be studying her as his hands molded to her curves.

She watched. It felt like she was having an out-of-body experience. Was this happening? Were those his hands caressing her? She'd wondered what it would feel like and the reality was light years away from the fantasy. It was pure ecstasy.

He bent his head. His tongue flicked at her nipple, first one then the other, his thumb taking over when he found her mouth again. And she gave in, letting herself drown in the feelings he evoked. The coil in the pit of her belly was spiraling outward, creating tiny tremors that coursed through her body.

"Em, let me love you." His voice was ragged, but there was an edge of command in his tone.

With those whispered words, she gave in, knowing she might never have another opportunity to feel this way. Years of wanting, of desire would finally find release. Her hands lay flat against his chest, and she could feel the pounding of his heart. He wanted her. On some level, anyway. Moving her hands around his neck, she pressed closer, letting him know she was willing.

He eased her back, sat her at the edge of the bed, and removed her leggings. His hands slid along her thighs, his palms calloused, the texture intoxicating. When they reached her sweet spot, he opened her up, his thumb massaging her clit, so soft and slowly that the sensations continued to build, reaching a peak she'd never climbed before. Her head fell back, the tension mounting, as the ripples of pleasure shot through her. She'd never let a man get this close, never this intimate, but with Nick, it seemed natural. He'd owned her heart, and now, it seemed he owned her body.

When he stopped, she tensed. The tension eased when he rose to remove his clothes. With each layer of clothing he took off, the wanting grew. He was magnificent. Solid muscle, the contours defined, his abdomen a perfect specimen of manhood. He lifted her up and placed her in the center of the bed before lying beside her. He continued the exploration of her body and her breath hitched as she became more enflamed, more restless to have him inside of her. Turning into him, she pulled him close, and he slid on top of her, sensing her need. The wide expanse of his chest surrounded her in a muscular vortex of feeling. His penis strained against her, as if demanding entrance. Her legs slid apart and she felt the tip of his manhood, and a rush of desire clawed at her insides. Arching up, she gave him the access he needed, and he plunged in in one wild thrust. And then he stilled.

Had he remembered who she was? Had he finally gained control over his hormones? She should have stopped him when she had the chance, not allowed herself the dream. It seemed he didn't want her after all. When she moved, he held her fast.

There was a flash of some unspoken emotion in his eyes. "What are you doing?"

There was a thread of mania in her voice when she said, "This isn't going to work."

He tightened his hold. "What do you mean? It's working fine. Too fine. I'm so close to the edge I'm going to blow before I want to. You feel…like silk, wet silk. I've never…"

Without finishing his sentence, he began to move again, his strokes sure and steady, fast, agonizingly slow. She could feel the tremors in her legs, and she tensed as his head bent to take her mouth in his.

His kisses were incendiary, and her heart was on fire. She moved against him, brushing her nipples against his chest, writhing beneath him, wanting this torture to end. He broke the contact of their mouths, pushed his hands up and underneath her, and she arched up to meet him, thrust for thrust. She felt her quivering flesh seize as the orgasm took hold. He was murmuring her name, as he convulsed, riding her until the last spasm dissipated, and then held her close, so they remained as one.

⌒

He didn't want to let her go, wanted her again, with a fervor that rocked him. In his arms lay his future but she was also his past. A past he cherished, and it was the kind of foundation he could build a brand-new life on. Teddy would have the mother he wanted and maybe they could have more children. He knew Em wanted them, and he wanted to be the one to give them to her.

When he rolled to his side, he took her with him, kept her in the hollow of his shoulder. He closed his eyes, the sensation of her flesh against him overwhelming. He breathed in her scent, the coconut now mixed with their lovemaking, her skin soft beneath his fingertips.

He kissed her brow, snuggling her closer.

"Why did it take us so long to get here?"

"I think you'd be the one to answer that."

He didn't know how, without discussing things better left unspoken. What they'd just experienced was too fragile.

"I'm thick?"

"I think it's more than that…"

He put his finger on her lips and asked the question burning in his gut.

"Where do we go from here, Em?"

He looked down to read something shimmering in her eyes. Was it fear? Indecision?

"I don't know. I think it's too soon for you to make that decision. This could be nothing more than an aftershock of what happened."

A heavy weight settled in his chest and his heart began to ache. She didn't believe this was real. Could he blame her?

"You want to take some time? Want to be sure of how I feel?"

"I have to, Nick. I can't trust this yet. There's too much still in the way."

Her words hit him like body blows. Now that he knew what he wanted, what he needed, who he was made to love, he didn't want to waste any time. But that was his problem.

"Em, I know I fucked up badly. If time is what you need, then time is what I'll give you. I know my feelings won't change. What about yours?"

She raised her eyes to him, those beautiful hazel-green eyes that he'd never really seen before.

They bedazzled him.

"I love you, Nick. Heart and soul. I'm beginning to think since college but...you never.... I keep asking myself, where is this coming from? Why now?"

Her words were like a quiver of arrows to his heart. She'd loved him that long. While he'd been agonizing over his marriage, trying to figure out the right thing to do, for him and Teddy, she'd been there, wanting more. Why had he been too blind to see it?

"When you make a colossal mistake, you begin to analyze what went wrong, what you could have done to avoid it, try to learn from it so it doesn't happen again. There were so many mis-steps along the way...but the one thing that stayed constant? You. I didn't understand what it meant, until recently."

"What you're feeling might not be enough to sustain a more in-depth relationship. There has got to be some residual baggage you haven't unpacked yet. You can't just jump into bed with me and think it's all behind us."

Was she right? He had to admit his world had been shaken upside down. Not only with the death but all that had come to light afterwards. Maybe they should take it slow, maybe...

"Can we see where this goes?"

"I'm not sure I can put my heart at risk like that. If you find this was a mistake, if you fall in love with someone else..."

He slid down, kissed her quivering lips to stop her from speaking. When she accepted his mouth on hers, he began to stroke her body again, bringing her to another release, another combustible mating. When she fell asleep, her head on his shoulder, he didn't think he'd ever felt this happy, content. He knew in his heart he'd never leave her. Now he just had to convince her of that.

CHAPTER TWENTY-SEVEN

Em slid out of bed the next morning and left the room on tiptoe. No kiss, no hug, no indication they had rocked each other's world last night. And he had rocked her world. She needed to get up before he realized where he was and who he'd loved last night. He'd told her she was in the picture when he thought about his life, and she had been, but was it front and center? Could he love her the way she loved him, or would she remain trusted friend? These were questions she needed answers to before she embarked on what could be a treacherous path. For her heart.

She was half-way down the hall when Teddy came racing out of his room.

"I thought you were up. Are we going to take Lily out?"

He slipped his hand into hers, and her heart skipped a beat. Seemed both Katsaros' males had the power to do that.

When they got the puppies out, they frolicked in the yard, their antics bringing a smile to her face. When Nick stepped out to join them, he went to put his arm around her, but she stepped away.

"Not in front of Teddy, okay?"

Teddy didn't need to know that there was a chance of them being a family. If it didn't work out, he'd be left with another loss and she knew what that would do to him. Once back inside, she acted as if nothing had happened, barely giving him a glance and showing no outward signs of affection. At least none that Olivia and Teddy would notice. Teddy was so thrilled that his dad was back, he probably wouldn't have anyway, but Olivia... She glanced over to her sister sitting in front of the kitchen window, the sun streaming in, texting. She was surprised Olivia hadn't said anything, but she knew it was coming. Nick had just taken Teddy upstairs to get dressed.

Getting up from her seat, Olivia said, "As long as Nick's here, I might as well go home. Scott texted and asked if I wanted to take a drive to the beach. It's such a beautiful day, I thought, why not."

It was a good beach day. Not for sunbathing, but for walking along the dunes, and she envied her sister the opportunity.

Olivia had come to stand beside her at the sink, her arms folded across her chest. "Do you want to talk about last night?"

Em swished the sponge around the inside of the pan a little more aggressively than she needed to.

"There's nothing to talk about."

"Are you going to be okay?"

"I'm going to be fine."

"I know you, sis. You've been in love with him for as long as you've known him…or close enough to it. Last night was probably a dream come true, but I want you to take care of your heart for me."

She jerked her head up, stunned. How did her sister know about last night? What had she given away?

"Don't look so surprised. I didn't get right to sleep last night. I know he came back earlier than expected and I heard…you…talking."

Em let the pan slide out of her hand, and it plunked into the sink. She closed her eyes, wanting to shut out what she was feeling, before casting her eyes toward her sister.

"I don't know what to do but I'm not giving my heart away until I know what he really feels, until after some of the aftershocks have worn down."

Olivia put her hand on her arm, leaned in to remind her, "Hon, he already has it. Just be careful, okay?"

Em nodded as she picked the pan back up, rinsed it, and leaned it on her coffee cup to dry.

Before she could reassure her sister she was going to be okay, Teddy came hurriedly down the stairs, the puppies scampering into the living room after him, slip-sliding on the wooden floors. She'd have to get some rubber-backed rugs to put out so they got better traction.

Nick went to the cabinet to get a glass and some water out of the dispenser. After taking a long sip, he asked, "Are you sticking around, Liv?"

"No. With you here, I can go home and relax. This is like being in a zoo, with the animals running it."

"She's going to the beach with Scott. Do you think we could take a ride, walk it? It sounds too good to pass up."

"What does your doctor think?"

Em looked at her sister.

"As usual, the woman is a healing machine. I still can't believe it even though she's been like this since we were kids. She should be fine if she sticks to walking. No surfing, no volleyball, no sprinting."

"I know that." After a pause, she said, "I think it might be time for a new surfboard."

Olivia looked up, stunned.

"Really?"

Her sister knew how intricately surfing was tied to their father, had tried to talk her into taking it up again years after they moved to America. She'd always declined to discuss it.

"I think it's time. With all the talks we've had about Dad recently, it's made me want to try it again. It will make me feel closer."

Not understanding the significance of the announcement, Teddy became animated. "Will you teach me?"

She tousled his hair.

"If your father says it's okay, sure. But I won't be able to do anything until my shoulder is fully healed."

Nick couldn't say anything more than, "Will wonders never cease. Feel the same way about softball?"

"I can't pitch yet, but soon. We have a practice Tuesday night. I'm going."

When she saw the expression on her sister's face, she reassured her, "Not to play. I'm still part of the team and want to be there. I can always be third-base coach during the first few games."

Olivia turned toward Nick.

"You go with her, make sure she's not telling me a white lie."

"I will. Teddy always enjoys watching."

"Okay. I'll be going then."

She leaned over and kissed Em on the cheek. "Stay safe."

"I plan on it."

Throughout the morning, she became pre-occupied with the time, checking her watch every ten minutes, waiting for the exact hour Saban was scheduled for burial. She also watched Nick's reaction, looking for signs of distress. She knew him well enough to know what they'd be, and he'd been transparent. As the hours ticked away, he'd grown somber, rubbed his head, gone outside on the deck while the dogs were playing and just stared out in the distance. Even Teddy couldn't distract him from his mood. The fear that she was right, that it was far too soon for him to make a new commitment, encapsulated her. After last night, she would have liked nothing better than waking up and shouting to the world what had happened between them. He was a skillful lover but there was still too much in the way for them to be together. He might want it. It might be easy, like he said. But she didn't want half measures. She wanted it all and she was sure disappointment was waiting around the bend. At least she'd soon have work to occupy her time, would be able to deal with her clients who had far bigger problems than she did.

Her injury had healed remarkably well and she'd almost convinced Olivia that she could return to work on Monday. She'd call Dr. Agarwals' office and ask if she could get in earlier to see him. Get the green light for returning to the firm. She needed something to take her mind off of Nick, off the recurring nightmare that he'd come to his senses and back away.

While fixing Teddy's lunch, his favorite, macaroni and cheese, she watched father and son out the window. Teddy was running around, the puppies chasing him. Nick didn't seem to notice.

He stayed in a zone while Teddy ate, while she cleaned up.

After the kitchen was cleaned, Em began to pack a small cooler with water and juice boxes. They didn't plan to be gone long, but she liked to be prepared for any eventuality.

Nick asked, "Should we take the puppies?"

It seemed he was finally aware of his surroundings, noticed what she was doing. She hoped he was still willing to go to the beach. She needed to feel the sand beneath her feet, smell the salty air.

"They might like that."

They'd kept one of the crates in the car for transportation purposes. Once Lily and Ozzie got bigger, were less rambunctious, she'd take it out. They both wouldn't fit in it for long.

Teddy was excited that they were including the dogs. He didn't like to be away from them for long and talked about the day that they could sleep in his room with them. She didn't have the heart to remind him that he might not be staying here. She didn't trust it for herself yet, either, so she'd shut down all Nick's attempts to hug or kiss her. It had taken a force of will.

Nick got behind the wheel of the Range Rover and asked, "Reservoir?"

It was a small area tucked in the city that had a playground and picnic area. He knew Em took Teddy there on occasion and had passes to get in.

"Doesn't open until next month. It'll have to be Revere."

⌒

Setting off in the direction of Revere Beach, figuring it would take about twenty to thirty minutes to get there depending on traffic, either way he went, he decided to take the less-traveled, Route 16. The windows were down, the air warm, and Teddy was quiet for a change.

He glanced over for the hundredth time, trying to gauge her mood. He'd been watching her all morning and she was off. He wished he could ask her what she was thinking, feeling. Olivia had made it impossible earlier, and he wouldn't be able to until later, when Teddy was otherwise occupied. It felt so right to be here with her, playing family. It had always felt right. The three of them had some good times behind them and he could only hope there'd be more of them in the future. His future. He glanced over again, wanting to tell her, wanting to be there already, needing to know this was what he thought it was. Stable, reliable, infused with the kind of passion and love he hadn't known existed.

Once they were on the beach, both holding on to a leash, Teddy finally willing to walk by their side after insisting he could hold on to Lily, he snuck her free hand into his. He didn't let her pull it away. He liked the way it fit in his, and he linked his fingers with hers, swaying his arm back and forth in contentedness.

He breathed in the air coated with brine, took in the expanse of the ocean.

"This was a good idea."

When she glanced over, he took her in, the glow from the sun surrounding her, creating an aura of bright. How could he have ignored her beauty?

"I love the beach. My father used to take us almost every day if he was around."

"What are they like…Down Under?"

"Different. White sand, sparkling blue water. The best in the world, from what experts say."

"Did it take you long to acclimate here?"

"Longer than it should have. I had a hard time letting go of home, or where I thought home was."

"Did you ever think of moving back?"

"Lots at the beginning. Then, well, this became home, and the memories would have been too invasive. There was nothing for me there anymore. The people I loved and who loved me were here."

"Maybe we could go one day. You can show me around. Give me a guided tour of the school you went to, the house you lived in."

"Maybe go the gravesite. I haven't been there since their bodies were laid in the ground." She looked out over the horizon. "My aunt picked a quiet spot under some trees, knowing how much my father loved nature." She lifted their enjoined hands and fingered a loose tendril that kept getting in her eyes. "I cried so hard and so long. I didn't want to leave them, wanted to sit under one of the trees forever. Olivia took my hand, led me away. She was the only one who could have coaxed me into my new life."

She was giving him a glimpse into the pain she'd felt as a child, something she'd never done before. Sharing this part of her life gave him an insight into her self-reliance, why she thought it important not to depend on anyone. Could she ever come to depend on him the way he wanted her to? Not as champion but as lover, friend…husband?

Teddy had gone down to the water's edge, and he watched closely, making sure he stayed away from the waves and undertow.

"Will you take Teddy to see Saban's grave?"

Without taking his eyes off his son, he answered, "If he wants to go, maybe. I don't see it, but who knows what questions he'll ask when he gets older."

On the verge of calling Teddy back, he relaxed when his son came racing toward them.

Jogging alongside, Teddy asked, "What are we going to do later?"

"I haven't though that far ahead. Why?"

"We always do something when we're together."

"We're doing something now."

"I know. I like it. Can we do it again tomorrow?"

"I'm back at work tomorrow. You're back at school."

"Who's going to stay with Em?"

"I'm feeling much better now, Teddy. I'm hoping to go back into my office for a few hours. Maybe I can pick you up before nap."

"Then I can go home with you? Play with Lily?"

He glanced down, knowing he had to set the record straight, also knowing Teddy was not going to be happy about it.

"We've got to talk about that, Ted. We're going to have to go home at some point."

Teddy stopped abruptly and gave him a penetrating look.

"No. I don't want to. I want to move in with Em. Don't you?"

Handing Lily's leash to Em, he picked Teddy up so he could explain the reasons they couldn't do that, but before he could get a word out, Em interrupted.

"You originally agreed to stay for two weeks, so if you want…"

"You're willing to keep us for another one?"

"If it works for you. I know you want to get your house on the market. Maybe you can take this week to put things in place and I can keep Teddy with me while you do."

Was she willing to let him stay with her? Or was this for Teddy?

"If you're sure you don't mind."

She looked at him then, the light burning in her eyes telling him what he wanted to know. He gulped, impatient now for what he'd find in her arms.

~

It took forever for Teddy to settle that night. The puppies were over excited after their trip to the beach, and they were whining and scrapping with each other in the crate. He didn't think he'd ever be alone with Em, but when quiet came, he sank down next to her on the couch and pulled her close.

He brushed his lips against her forehead, and asked, "Do we need to talk? You seemed kind of pre-occupied this morning. I want to know what you were feeling."

"I thought the same thing about you. Were you thinking about…the burial?"

It meant she had been. What to say? He had glanced at his watch at some point and realized it would have already taken place. Did he feel a shift in the universe? No. He still felt the calm and steady beat in his life with Em. Her distance had put him in a funk, and he spent the morning wondering if she was going to turn a future with him down.

"It hit me at one point, but she was gone from my life before this. Do I regret coming back early? Do I regret last night? The answer to both questions is no."

She cupped his face with her hands, her eyes searching his.

"Nick, you have to be feeling more than that."

He was getting exasperated. There was no underlying grief, no deep questions. Not after last night.

He blew out a breath. "Why are you making this more difficult than it is? I don't have the kind of issues with this that you think I do."

"How can you not?"

It sunk in that the line of questioning wasn't for him. It was for her. She was the one with issues and she'd pretty much explained them to him already.

"The separation happened months ago. This isn't new. Her death? Yeah, that one got me. It wouldn't be normal if it didn't. But I'm not agonizing over what she'd put in place, what she had planned, or that she was having an affair. I told you, I was feeling relief. That was tough to deal with in the face of what happened."

She was massaging her forehead and she looked flustered.

"I'd love a glass of wine. It might help."

"Em, I'm not sure…"

"I'm not on painkillers and it would do a lot to take the edge off. I had one with Liv last night. The doctor seemed okay with it."

She'd refused the narcotics, and he figured one glass couldn't hurt. After he had opened a bottle and poured two glasses, he brought them back and reclaimed his seat next to her.

"This is bothering you more than me. Tell me why."

Her voice held an edge.

"Your wife just died, you just found out she was cheating on you, had already put a new life in place, you've taken up with someone who's been nothing more than a friend for over a decade… Should I go on?"

"Is it the part where I've taken up with a friend that's causing the most trouble for you?

"Yes, it's that part. Why? I keep wanting to know why. You should be taking time to process this."

"Men don't process, Em."

"And that's why things get fucked up."

He didn't want to talk anymore. He wanted to feel her body against his. It was when he felt the most balanced, less vulnerable.

He took her glass away, placed it on the coffee table, and pulled her into his lap. His lips found hers and he kissed her with all the love he felt, hoping she'd read it right.

The next morning when he got ready for work, he still wasn't sure that she had.

CHAPTER TWENTY-EIGHT

Em pushed through the double doors at Woodley and Fisher with her good arm, feeling better already. This was where she felt the most confident, and she tried to wash away the feelings the last two nights had wrought.

She was scared. Petrified that Nick was making love to her for all the wrong reasons. He hadn't processed what had happened. He couldn't have. She was still struggling with the assault, the deaths, and the aftermath.

Heather called out, "Hey, Em. You're a week early, aren't you?"

"According to my doctor, maybe. I think it's the best medicine around. How's things?"

"Busy, as usual. Cami came in about twenty minutes ago. She took all your call slips. Jelani and Nell are both in court this morning."

"I'll check in with her, then. Thanks."

She walked around the curved wall, and when Liz, sitting at her desk in the office across from hers, saw her, she jumped up and came out to greet her.

"What…"

"I know. I'm not going to repeat. Follow me."

When she peeked in to see Cami on the phone, she took a step back, but Cami motioned her in with her free hand. After finishing up the call, she stood, scowling at her.

"I know. I'm going to say this once and then you've both got to leave it. I feel fine. I have no infection or fever." She'd skip the part about the aches and pain. They were a given but they weren't going to stop her from getting back to life. "My injury is healing well and I'm bored. I'm back. If I get tired, I'll leave."

Both knew her too well to argue.

Looking squarely at Cami, she asked, "And how long did you take after your…injury?"

Losing the attitude, Cami admitted, "Not as long as the doctor suggested."

"That's who we are. So, may I have my messages? And my files?"

Her hand was out, her stance brooking no argument.

"Fine. Here are your messages. Liz has your files. I've got some notes in the margins, questions for you. She was going to take them over to you today. Guess she'll have to change her agenda."

Turning to Liz, Em said, "With me. You can take me through the mark-ups."

The day flew by but by mid-afternoon her stamina had run down. Nell was just walking in and did a double take as she passed her office.

She put her hand up in a stop motion.

"I'm leaving, so no lectures."

"I wasn't going to lecture you. I just wanted to say hi, welcome back."

She felt her shoulders relax. Every single person that worked here had given her a hard time. Arianna and Mia the worst.

"Thank you. You're the first."

"No welcome?"

"No. You'd think they were ready to give my office away and my coming back put a dent in their plans."

Nell smiled. "They're just worried. More about the psychological ramifications than physical."

"I'm not ready to go to the court house yet. That one's going to take it out of me."

"It was kind of eerie going back. We all used the buddy system for the first few days. We'll all go with you if you want us to."

"Thanks. Nick promised he'd go as well. I'd rather have the three of you. More intimidating."

"We do walk with swagger."

Em gave her a smile tinged with exhaustion.

"How's Jack?"

"He's good. Frustrated, pissed, beside himself with what's going on and no power grip on the pulse. Seems a few of the chairs on select committees are dragging their feet. It's as if they're all complicit in some way and refuse to help the investigation along at all."

"Maybe they are."

"Twitter seems to agree."

"Maybe we'll get out of this alive."

"I sure hope so. I won't keep you. Go home, get some rest."

She went to walk on, then stopped. "Oh, how are the puppies?"

"A handful but precious. I don't regret my decision."

"I'm going to keep Chloe away from your house for a while. She's gotten into her head that we need one, too. She thinks if we get a guard dog, she can stay by herself. I haven't been able to get her to understand that's not necessarily an outcome."

Em laughed. If Nell couldn't get the point across, she doubted anyone could.

After packing up her briefcase, she hefted it up over her shoulder. Her good one, but the weight affected the other and she swore under her breath. Taking it by the handles, she walked out of the lobby and to her waiting car. She'd promised to get Teddy early, and although it wasn't before nap, it would still be before his usual pick-up time. He'd just woken up when she arrived, and rather than being sulky because she was later than he'd wanted, he was excited to be going back to her house and Lily.

⌒

When Nick got back to Em's, he found the domestic kind of picture he'd hoped for all his life. At least from the time his mother had left. Up until then, it was just like this. He thought Kathy had liked her life. Were there warning signs? Had his father seen any? If his father had lightened up, encouraged her to go to work, maybe they could have averted the whole experience. He looked for some indication that this wasn't what Em wanted: dressed in jeans and a button-down, short-sleeve shirt, cooking dinner, a little boy at the table playing with his metal cars, the puppies underfoot, a satisfied smile on her face. The aroma was inviting, the sight heartwarming, and he was prompted to drop a light kiss on Em's cheek.

"Smells good."

He was relieved that she didn't skirt away from him.

"Thanks."

The broiler was on, the chicken crackling under the coil. He looked at her and smiled.

"A poor man's chook on the barbie?"

She wiped the moisture from her brow and admitted, "A lazy one's. I didn't feel like getting the grill going."

"Did you wear yourself out today?"

"Maybe."

She gave him the truth, which surprised him.

"You could have waited for me. I would have cooked for us tonight."

"I didn't know what time you'd be back, and I was getting hungry. So was my partner in crime over there."

Not one to be ignored, Teddy piped up, "Hi, Dad. How was your day?"

He walked over to Teddy and tousled his hair.

"It went well, thanks, bud. And yours?"

"Em picked me up after nap so I had a 'ceptional one."

"That's exceptional, and I'm glad to hear it."

Turning to Em, he added, "You could have texted. I could have picked him up."

"He was on my way home. I thought he could help me with Lily and Ozzie. He ran them ragged when we got back, and I think they might be ready for the crate."

"Let me change, then I can help with whatever."

"Okay. Everything's almost done, so you get clean-up duty."

"Going with my talents, huh?"

"Why not?"

He left and climbed the stairs and went up to the bedroom he'd claimed the first night he stayed. He was hoping that he'd be sleeping in a different one tonight, but he had to take his time, not rush her. Stripping out of his uniform, he yanked on his jeans that were lying across the bed and pulled out a tee shirt from his duffel. Em had given him the shirt years ago, a Life is Good shirt with a hockey player shooting a puck. It was one of his favorites although beginning to fray around the collar.

When he got back downstairs, dinner was on the table, the dogs were resting in their home, Teddy was already eating, and there was a beer ready and waiting for him. This had to be heaven.

The next morning Nick was waiting in the patrol car while Juanita went in to grab them lunch at the luncheonette they frequented in another part of the city. Thinking. Last night hadn't gone exactly as he would have liked. It had gone from heaven back to limbo. He'd been relegated to the original bedroom assigned him, and he'd left Em at her doorway, reluctantly. Em wanted to give herself time to adjust to this new reality, still unsure that his feelings weren't some aberration that had sprung up over the past week. He didn't know what he'd do to reassure her, but it was going to take more than time.

His cell phone alerted him to an incoming call, and when he looked at the ID, he swiped immediately.

"Hey, Em. What's up?"

There was a pause before her shaky voice came over the line.

"I...need you to come get me."

He sat up, starting the engine, willing to leave without Juanita if necessary.

"Where are you?"

"I'm...I'm inside the court house. I thought I'd...be okay...but..." The sob that came next grabbed his heart and punched him in the gut.

"It's okay, Em. I'll be there as soon as I can. Stay right where you are."

He'd noticed Juanita strolling over to where he was parked, and by the time she got to the door, he was already in reverse.

She was barely in the car when he backed up and out of the space, hightailing it over to the JFK building as if there was a five-alarm fire and he was the only one equipped to put it out.

The boxes jumped off her lap, but she grabbed them before they spilled all over the floorboard.

"What the hell? Did we get a call?"

"It's Em. She's stuck, and I have to go get her."

He had her attention now.

"Stuck where?"

"She went over to the JFK before she was ready. I told her I'd go with her the first time. Why doesn't that woman ever listen?"

"She's not used to needing help. I'm surprised she called you."

"Who the hell else was she going to call?"

"One of her partners?"

His siren was going, and he whipped around cars that had done the right thing and pulled over, harassed those that hadn't. Within ten minutes he pulled up to the plaza and barely got the car in park before he was sprinting toward the front door.

Em was crouching in a corner, and when he went to help her up, her body was shaking, her lips a pink-toned blue. When he wrapped his arms around her, she sobbed against his chest.

"I'm sorry. I—"

"No need. Let's sit down."

There were a couple benches along the glass walls and he sat her down, without letting her go.

She'd been clutching her briefcase, and he heard it drop to the floor before she gripped him around his middle.

Licking her lips, she explained, "I walked across the courtyard with no problem. Thought I'd be fine. But when I was finished filing the petition, started for the door to go to the garage for my car, I panicked. I stared outside, saw the whole thing happen again, and I couldn't get my legs to move. I just wanted to hide."

As he stroked her back, he murmured, "It's perfectly normal, Em. You had a traumatic experience. If it didn't impact the way you see things, I'd be worried."

"This is where I do my business. I can't…"

"You won't. I told you that I'd come with you. Why didn't you call me?"

"I can't be pulling you off duty every time I have a panic attack. You have people to protect. I can't believe I did it this time."

"This was one of the reasons the doctor wanted you to give yourself more time to recuperate. It's not just the physical wounds, it's the psychological ones, too."

"I'm not a victim, Nick. I don't think like that."

"No, you're not. You're one of the strongest women I know."

"I don't feel strong right now."

"It's there. You came here all by yourself. A lot of others won't ever come back."

"I have no choice." Drawing in a deep breath, she stuttered, "Help me to my car please."

He was planning on dispensing with the car and getting her to where she'd feel safe.

"I'll take you home."

"No. I need to go through the paces, have to take the steps across the plaza. I can do it if you're with me. I know you won't let anything hurt me."

He picked up her briefcase as she put her hand in the crook of his arm, her weight against him, and she followed his slow steps out to the pavers, but they hadn't gone fifteen feet when she stopped.

"That was where I hid. Where…"

"I know, Em. I'm glad you had the foresight to hide."

Her head slanted as she took in the circular pillar.

"It looks so narrow. How could I have thought being behind that would protect us?"

He kissed the top of her head, a shudder at how close he came to losing her, passing through him.

"There was nowhere else for you to go."

She looked up at him, her lips trembling.

"There wasn't."

He stroked her arm with his hand, and he could feel the trembles that still had control over her body. He stood with her until she was ready, holding her close, letting her know she was safe in his arms. While moving at the same pace, matching her footsteps as she walked across the plaza, toward the parking garage, he noticed Juanita standing by the cruiser, her hands on her hips, ready and waiting if he needed her. He nodded in her direction and kept Em moving toward her goal, to the edge of the open space, down the sidewalk, and up the ramp to the garage.

"Where are you parked?"

"Second tier."

He followed her directions, and soon her car was in sight.

"Where are your keys?"

"In my pocket book. Here, let me. You'll never find them."

He did as she asked because he knew she was right. Her bag was filled with everything one might need for any emergency.

As she pulled them out, the keys shook, a natural side effect from her shaking limbs.

"Do you want me to drive?"

"No. I need to do this."

"I'm following you back. Where are you going? Home or to the office?"

"The office. I won't stay long. I just need to file the copy of the petition and make a call."

He called Juanita on his cell and he waited until she brought the patrol car to the ramp at the exit.

He waited long enough for Em to get in, turn on the engine and back out. Juanita was ready to follow as soon as he took his place in the passenger seat.

"Will she be okay?"

"If I know anything, I'd say the answer is yes. How long she takes to get there is anybody's guess."

They followed at a sedate speed and pulled up in front of the office building that housed the law firm.

"I'll wait here. You see her safely inside."

"Thanks, partner."

He went into the front entrance and waited the five minutes it took Em to park her car in the underground garage and take the elevator up.

When she saw him, she said, "You didn't have to come in. I should be fine now."

"I'm coming up with you. I want to talk to Camille."

Her eyes shot up to meet his, and he could read the war of emotions she was battling.

"No, please, you can't tell her. I don't want anyone to know. They'll worry."

He could feel a muscle of tension flick in his jaw. She could not afford to fight him on this.

"You need a buddy system if you're not willing to call me. She should know that."

She bit down hard on her lower lip, and he could tell she was fighting off her feelings of vulnerability.

"Nick. Please. I'm fine now."

He walked her over to the elevator, pushed the up button, and as soon as it opened, he let her go in alone.

She was standing in the corner, protecting herself, when she whispered, "Thank you."

The doors swished closed in his face.

As soon as they did, he pulled out his cell and called Camille. He explained what had happened, swore her to secrecy and she promised she wouldn't let Em go over to the court-house alone until she was ready to.

She thanked him for the call with more warmth than he'd heard from her in months.

On the way out to join Juanita, he made another call.

"You have time for a drink after work tonight?"

CHAPTER TWENTY-NINE

Em picked up Teddy from school again, not that she minded. After the travesty of an afternoon, she needed his smile and energy. Nick had called asking how she was and if she'd mind if he grabbed a drink with Alec after work. Said he wouldn't be long. He knew she had a practice tonight. She appreciated the courtesy, but what he did with his life, was his call. She'd planned on taking Teddy with her knowing she couldn't join the exercises. After taking the puppies out for a hard run, the afternoon sun feeling good, she changed out of her suit and threw on a pair of jeans and a tee. She was finally able to wear them again and there was nothing sweeter than being comfortable.

After fixing up a quick meal of grilled cheese sandwiches, which took longer than it should have, her arm still in the sling, she cleaned the kitchen and got ready to leave just as Nick drove in.

He was half-way out of his car when he asked, "You weren't going to wait for me? I told you I wouldn't be late."

"I didn't know what late meant."

"Do I have time to change? I don't like going in uniform."

"Sure. We'll wait."

True to his word, he was down again in minutes, looking all kinds of good.

She took a moment to appreciate him before asking, "You didn't happen to speak to Cami today, did you?"

"Why?"

"She was extremely solicitous when I got back. Made me promise I'd let her know if I was going over to the court house again."

"She's your best friend. She had to know how that would affect you."

"You didn't answer my question."

"I'm taking the fifth. Now, do you want to be late?"

"It doesn't really matter. That's why I waited for you. I can't do anything but watch. If I'd had a serious practice, you would have been left in the dust."

He relaxed. She wasn't going to go mental jacket on him and there had been a brief hint of humor in her voice. He smiled and said, "Good to know."

⌒

The next day, back in her office, Em promised herself she'd go to the court house every day. It was bad enough she couldn't use her muscles, or help her team, last night's practice particularly painful. It was hard for her to sit, watch and envy. Her team mates were glad to see her but insisted she wait until the doctor gave the go-ahead for her to resume pitching. As their ace, she didn't want to let them down and she wasn't sure she'd listen to all the well-intentioned advice. She wasn't going to allow any physical or psychological issues to prevent her from moving forward. Gathering up her courage, she slid away from the desk and pulled her purse out of the drawer.

Liz must have noticed, her office opposite hers on the other side of the short hall, and called out, "Where are you going?"

Cami must have heard the question because within seconds she was standing just outside the door.

"Yeah, where are you going?"

Figuring she might as well be truthful, she said, "Court house."

Cami gave her a stern look.

"Not alone, you aren't."

"I have to…"

"Not alone. Wait right here."

Em weighed her options. She could slip out while Cami was collecting her things or wait for her friend. She didn't like where the scales were tilting but when Cami, accompanied by Nell and Jelani converged in the hall, she gave them a warm smile. By all appearances, purses slung over their shoulders, they were going with her. This was friendship. They weren't going to let her face her demons without them. The feeling of solidarity hit her with waves of gratitude.

Nell brushed the bangs off her face and announced, "Where you lead, we follow."

Cami said softly, "At least until you're well enough to handle it yourself."

Jelani, not to be left silent, agreed. "One of us will be with you every single time."

Em could feel tears fill her eyes, and she wiped them away quickly. This was not like her. She didn't cry.

"Don't you have clients?"

Nell assured her, "Light day."

Em almost laughed through a sob. "There's no such thing."

Jelani took hold of her arm and led her out to the lobby, where there were several clients waiting to be seen. "We'll manage."

Nell opened the door, and all four of them stepped over to the elevator.

"Hani, Liz, Sikha, and Vivian will hold down the fort. If they need assistance, Arianna and Mia are here. This won't take long."

Nell drove, and she parked in the same municipal lot as Em had the day of the shooting.

As they got out of the car, Cami took a breath. "This is what got my nerves humming. Dark, underground spaces. I never understood why. I was attacked in a hotel room, by someone I knew. It never made sense, but fear has a way of screwing with your mind."

Cami hadn't mentioned the close call until months after it happened and had somehow managed to deal with it all by herself. Em had to stop being such a wimp.

Jelani glanced at Cami. "I'm not trying to diminish what you went through, Cam, but seeing the destruction around you has to be more difficult to deal with. Thinking you're going to die, and thinking you're going to die because people are dropping like flies around you...I'm not sure how I would have dealt with it. Em did well. She walked away alive."

"Only because of Zach."

"No, because you did all the right things. It's the panic you held in that's coming out, now."

They stood at the edge of the plaza, taking in the open space.

"I can still see the bodies and I'm still struggling with that. I want to hide, not deal with any of it, but I can't do that. Not to myself, not to my clients. Will I ever stop reliving it?"

The relentless sight of the carnage wasn't abating. The sounds of gunfire penetrated her mind at the oddest times.

Cami was the one who said, "I don't know, Em. The memories won't ever go away. But I hope they fade in time."

They walked the distance to the door without incident, went in, and stood at the windows, looking out. Em knew that Gretchen had been in here, safe, when the gunfire began, and she'd taken a week off to settle her nerves. Just being a witness to the scene caused a major disruption in perspective. She had survived, and she wasn't going to allow Hector to continue to scare her. Leaving would be the test. This was where she'd lost all nerve yesterday. She looked at Cami when she asked, "You ready?"

"I'm ready."

Once outside, Cami and Nell flanked her, Jelani was on the other side of Nell. Em imagined them as a phalanx of women warriors who would march together into battle, no matter the outcome. It warmed her soul.

Able to keep the hyperventilating in check, Em felt Cami's hand slide into hers and took several deep breaths and proceeded to walk the plaza, her shoulders back, her emotions under control.

When she was back in her office, her next appointment not for another half-hour, she gazed out the window, thinking.

She'd needed the three women, hadn't even known it, until they were there for her. She didn't even have to ask. This was what she'd had as a child. Love and protection. When it had been taken so drastically, she'd vowed never to depend on anyone like that again. And she hadn't.

Nick had suggested she share her feelings with them, but she'd ignored his advice. She shouldn't have. Being able to count on someone was a gift, and she'd never seen it that way until today. She was not only going to shake off her fears of death, she was determined to shake off the fear of being dependent, to fix what was broken inside. These friends hadn't allowed her to push them away. Neither had her adoptive parents. She'd never given in to trust them completely. Never sure they wouldn't be taken way as quickly and easily as her birth parents. Doug had been so patient. Unwilling to let her shut herself away in isolated grief, he'd encouraged her to participate in life. He was the one who'd enrolled her in softball when she was in middle school. Had taken her to her first practice, agreed to coach so she'd feel more secure, taught her to pitch. He'd been there, as solid as a rock. Yet she'd kept him at arm's length. Coming to love him as deeply as she could anyone, she was unable to trust him to be there forever. Had she done the same with Nick? Was that why she'd never taken any steps to expand the relationship in college or later, when he was still free? Being a best friend and having him gravitate out of her life was better than loving someone deeply and having them taken away...or leave.

But was it?

The day she realized she was in love with him had caused a heartache so deep she'd pulled away. He'd come over to her dorm room, excited about a woman he'd met at the book store, who was from the south, and he'd gone on and on about how feminine she was. They were juniors by then and had spent the last two years doing everything together. Or almost everything. The feelings evoked as he'd talked about his new love, had shaken her to her very soul. She'd never realized there'd been a deep well of love hiding in the friendship until she knew she'd lost him. There had been a couple of months after law school when she thought about making a move, but she knew she'd never be what he wanted. She wasn't a fragile flower, wouldn't let herself become one. Knowing she could never satisfy him the way he needed, she'd withdrawn. When he'd gotten back together with Saban, it hadn't been a surprise, but it had hurt as much as before. She'd refused to attend his wedding, and for as much as she'd known it hurt him, she couldn't stand and watch him pledge his heart to someone else. Their carefree way of being together had ended with the marriage, but their connection only seemed deepen after Teddy's birth. He'd needed her. She'd loved the infant and hadn't found anyone to replace him. They'd hung out, but she'd kept herself in reserve, the fight to keep her feelings in exhausting. If it hadn't been for Teddy, she would have distanced herself from the heartache years ago.

Now? Nick said he wanted what she did. But could she trust it? It could be the residual effects of what he'd been through. What if she woke up one day and he changed his mind? Another loss. That loss would be...too big.

Was she going to deny herself the chance to find out? There was nothing standing in her way anymore. Except her own insecurity.

That night, after Nick put Teddy to bed, she told him about what her friends had done. She also gave in and let him love her. If there was a sad ending, so be it. There couldn't be a happy one if she wasn't willing to risk it all.

They were lying in bed, Em sleeping peacefully beside him. She had led him into her bedroom last night and let him love her. He'd never known such pleasure. There was a true sharing of heart and soul, something he hadn't even known existed. In college it had been all about the sex. Later…it had been all about how well he could satisfy. He had, or at least believed he had, but there had been a lack of warmth, a lack of…intimacy.

Em had been rough tonight. Intense. Heat surged through him at the memory of her riding him, climaxing hard, her silky sex convulsing around his shaft. Her kiss ignited a bone-melting fire that set his blood to boiling. He'd never felt such heat. Always more concerned with the woman's orgasm than his own, he was more servile than assertive, but Em had tempted that side of himself he rarely let show. She'd been seductive, and he'd taken full advantage of her forwardness. And she'd blown him away. He'd never felt so replete. This was what love was, what passion was like.

He smoothed her hair between his fingers, more enamored of her than ever. He wanted to be in this same place with her when he was old and grey…and feeble.

He smiled when he thought about what her friends had done for her today. She wouldn't have called him again. He knew that for a fact. Seeing her so helpless yesterday had unhinged him, and she knew it. She didn't like people knowing she was vulnerable, but yesterday she was unable to mask it. If he was going to help her, it would have to be in some other way. It had prompted the call to Alec. He wanted people like Hector Rojas gone, deported, back where they belonged so they couldn't commit crimes against his loved ones ever again.

He hadn't expected the meeting with Alec to go the way it had. They'd discussed things that were disturbing, things that had surprised him, but it wasn't going to deter him. He'd been seeking an avenue for revenge, and Alec was willing to hand him the opportunity to walk it.

How would Em react when she found out? He already knew the answer to that, but it wasn't going to deter him. He was going to keep her safe from harm no matter what it took.

He pulled her closer. With her lying in his arms, the gnawing ache in his gut eased. He closed his eyes at how she felt against his flesh, all warm and soft. Why the hell hadn't they ever consummated their relationship before this? His soul mate had been right in front of him and he'd never seen it, never felt the spark…never realized how perfect her mouth was, how soft her skin was, how plush her body. The sparks from her kisses went off like skates against a sharpener, creating all kinds of shooting flares. Maybe he had seen it, felt something momentous happening the first night he'd met her. Her cheeks were pink from the cold, her eyes a sparkling spectrum of greens, browns, and blues but she was sending out a vibe, one that said, *Don't mess with me*. And he hadn't. With each successive time he'd bumped into her around campus, they'd talk more, grab lunch, walk to class until they'd fallen into a deep friendship that he refused to put at risk. If she didn't need him, she could easily walk away. He couldn't take the chance.

Now, he was willing to risk it all. She felt too right in his arms.

He wanted to make plans, secure their future. Had she told him tonight she wanted that, as well?

He couldn't read it any other way. Or maybe he just didn't want to.

CHAPTER THIRTY

Em emitted a contented sigh.

She'd lowered her inhibitions and found everything she'd ever dreamed of in Nick's arms. Every Over the last couple of days, they'd made passionate love, with no barriers between them and she'd never known sex could be so good. She now knew why Nell had rated hers with Jack an eleven. It was over the top and exquisitely satisfying.

Teddy was thriving, the puppies driving everyone to distraction but adding a special brand of love to the dynamics of the threesome, and she'd gotten over the worst part of her fears. No longer walking a tightrope, she'd found her balance. The doctor still hadn't cleared her to play softball and thought it was much too early to pitch. She'd thrown a bit during their last practice and decided the doctor might be right. The itch had started, which meant it was healing, and she was taking medication for it, but it would still be awhile before she could resume these kinds of activities. Nick hadn't been overly thrilled, and he'd watched her with a concentrated focus. He'd breathed an audible sigh of relief when she'd told him she was giving herself more time before getting out on the mound.

Today, the three of them were going to Mia's house for her husband Nate's birthday party. He'd hit the big four-oh and Mia had talked him into inviting their friends over to share it with him. Some members of the FBI would be there, along with Alec, who'd been transferred to Homeland Security as an ICE supervisor. In command of a unit she doubted she'd ever face him in court, which would have worried her. She didn't like to shred her friends but would if the situation dictated it.

"Come on, Teddy, let's get a move on."

"Okay, Dad. I'll be down in a minute. The shirt Em gave me to wear has all kinds of buttons."

"If you need help, just ask."

"I need help."

She watched as Nick took the stairs two at a time to do as asked. And smiled, her heart warmed by Nick's willingness to do anything for his son.

It was a pot luck kind of day, and she'd made some of her buffalo chicken wings which were always a hit. After packing up some carrots, celery and blue cheese dressing, she slipped two bottles of wine she'd picked up after work on Friday into the large brown bag. They knew they couldn't stay long, the puppies still needing to go out every few hours, but she was going to push it and see how well they did. She had blankets to spare if they couldn't go as long as she hoped.

While Teddy sat by the crate, saying good-bye to Lily, a slight frown on his small face, Nick whispered into her ear, "This is the first time we'll be with your friends as a couple."

She looked up from what she was doing.

"Are we a couple?"

He leaned in and kissed her cheek, her nose, her mouth.

"We are definitely a couple."

He nuzzled her neck just as Teddy came into the kitchen.

"How come you guys kiss all the time now? You never did that before."

"I got jealous. You do it all the time."

"Oh. Okay. Lily's sad we're leaving."

Em gave him a warm smile. "She'll be fine. She needs to get used to being without people around. I'll be going back to work full time soon. That's why we brought Ozzie home with her, so she'd have company."

Any sadness Teddy felt at leaving seemed to vanish as soon as he was with the other kids at Mia's house. They raced around outside, played on the swings, and Mia's older son, David seemed more than happy to entertain them. It was usually Chloe who took on that role, but she had gone to New York City with her grandmother for the weekend. Eloise had promised her a day of shopping and a night at a Broadway play. Jack had somehow gotten tickets for *Hamilton* and Chloe was more excited about that than the shopping part. They wouldn't be getting back until after the party was over.

The women were congregated in the kitchen, the men in the family room. It seemed like that's how it always worked out. She knew Nick would be fine. Alec was one of his best friends, Maks was a hockey mate, and Jack was a politician at heart. He could get along with just about everyone.

It was later, when she had gone to the bathroom, that the afternoon lost all its glow. She stayed in the shadows, not intending to snoop until she caught the drift of the conversation.

"Are you going to talk the decision over with her?"

She recognized Alec's voice and she wondered who he was speaking to, until she heard Nick's reply.

"Em won't fight me. And on the outside chance she does? It won't matter. I'm never going to let a woman dictate what I do for a living again."

Her fear blossomed into full-out panic. Had he just dumped her into a category she didn't deserve? She took a step out of the alcove so that Nick could see her. As calmly as she could, she asked, "What are you talking about?"

Alec had the good sense to slip away.

Standing his ground, something she'd rarely seen him do with her, he announced, as if proud of it, "I'm working for Homeland Security for a couple of weeks. I want to see if it's a good fit."

She felt the earth rumble under her feet.

What happened to the SWAT team? Narcotics? Why this now? Why this at all?

Her voice broke when she asked, "You're what?"

Drawing in a deep breath, he reminded her, "I've been thinking about this since Hector Rojas took out all those people. I think I mentioned it before."

Now the bottom was falling out of her stomach. And her world.

"One of whom was your wife."

His brow furrowed and he seemed to lose some of the cockiness.

"And you. You could have been killed as easily as anyone."

Her chin angled up, and she met his gaze.

"I wasn't. I knew there had to be some issues you were burying."

"I haven't buried them. I think I made how I feel very clear."

"You honestly believe that, by deporting immigrants, things will get better?"

"There'll be one less Hector Rojas to commit mass murder."

"And one more child who'll live without a parent. You'll be doing to other children exactly what Rojas did to Teddy."

She took a step away from him, as if seeing him in a new light.

"I can't fight you. I have no right to do that. But I also won't live with you while you're ripping families apart. I guess you need to decide what's more important to you."

She didn't do ultimatums, but that's exactly what she'd thrown down.

"What the hell, Em? All of a sudden, you're telling me what I can and cannot do? You've never done that before. It's more Saban's style than yours."

She jerked back as if he'd slapped her in the face.

"You can do what you damn well please, but I won't sit at a defense table representing a man or woman you've detained. I want to be with someone who's in the fight with me, not against me."

She spun away from him, but he snagged her arm.

"Em, I need to do this."

"For Saban? Because it's not for me. Still can't break the habit of protecting her, can you?"

"No, that's not it."

"I think it is. You were besotted with her and she hasn't been in the grave a week. I knew I couldn't trust this, you. I think you better make arrangements to move out."

"Unless I bend to your will."

His cockiness came back in spades and she could tell he was pissed. Tough shit.

"Un-fucking-believable. Is that what you think this is? A power play? Well, you're wrong. This has to do with me and what I want in a partner. It isn't this."

He had no fucking idea what this meant, which meant nothing had changed. He couldn't love her if he was still seeking justice for his wife's death. Flustered now by her mistake in trusting this, her mind a jumble of tangled thoughts and emotions, she said, "You can do what the fuck you want, Nick. I don't really care anymore."

But she did. Her heart was breaking but she'd never let him see that. Love was disappointing. It hurt you in places you didn't know you had, in the recesses of your mind and soul. She hadn't been what he'd wanted, not if he was still thinking of...

His voice caught. "What am I going to tell Teddy?"

Was it all about Teddy? Was this whole charade a means to an end for him? Getting Teddy well?

"That it's time to go home."

"But Lily..."

"Is my dog, just like Teddy is your child. Get him one of his own if you're so worried about him."

She took out her phone and texted Uber. She wasn't going home with him, and she couldn't celebrate in the mood she was in. She hoped her friends would understand.

"I'll have to come pick up our stuff."

"You can do that tomorrow while I'm at work."

Without a backward glance, she went to explain why she was leaving to the women still in the kitchen, and after they each ripped Nick a new one, she waited outside for the Uber driver to show up.

⌒

Nick stood there, his hands scrubbing at his buzz-cut head before wandering back into the family room, stunned into silence.

"Didn't go as planned, did it?"

Alec was the first one to approach him, the only one who knew what had happened.

"I don't get it. We never fight."

Maks came over and asked what was going on. "The women have turned nasty."

Once he explained it, Nick added, "My fault. I guess I should leave."

Nate, who'd been entertaining the men, pointed out what they all knew. "Won't improve the mood, now. I told Mia I didn't want a party. They never seem to end well."

Jack offered, "Still, if Nell gets her stiletto tongue sharpened, you'll wish you had."

Nick had lived with sharp, cutting words, and it had made life hell. Jack didn't seem to mind.

"Ever use it on you?"

"Oh, yeah. Until I smartened up."

"So, this is a woman thing?"

"Nell has a strong sense of what is right and wrong. She goes into battle with whatever weapon works. I respect her opinion regardless of how she wields it.

That made Nick pause. Em had a strong sense of that, too. Was breaking off with him the weapon she was using to make him see the light? But he'd seen it, in the remnants of her fear and the permanent scars as she walked across the plaza. This had to do with protecting others, her. Something he'd dedicated his life to.

What the hell was he going to tell Teddy? It sounded like Em had turned her back on him, as well.

"Want me to ask Cami if she'll watch Teddy tonight?"

He'd forgotten about the hockey game, but he didn't think Maks was using very good judgment if he was offering to do that. The women would be pissed at him and Cami more so than the rest.

"I'll have to skip it tonight."

His phone pinged, and he quickly scanned Em's message.

Have Cami drop Teddy off before the game. You can pick him up tomorrow.
He can stay?
I don't want him in the middle of this. We'll work something out.
Between you and me?
Visitation for Teddy.
Call me.

He was still waiting for the call when he left for hockey. Kept checking his phone as he drove to the rink. And checked again before heading to his parents' house, where he was spending the night.

Nothing.

⌒

When Em got home, she put herself on auto-pilot, took the dogs out, got them supper, let them scamper around. They were getting big enough to attempt the stairs, and she was going to have to get a gate soon. She didn't want them to have access to the whole house just yet. She went to the kitchen and poured herself a glass of wine, swirled it before taking a sip. She knew it wasn't the cure, but it couldn't hurt to try to numb her senses.

She couldn't believe Nick was thinking of joining ICE. He knew her opinion, had heard her dark jokes about no-heart-ice-men. How could he possibly think they could remain together if that was the road he was traveling? He knew most of her clients came from detainment and deportation. Would she have to cross-exam him during some of her trials? Pick him apart as she tried valiantly to keep a family together? She'd told him the truth. She had to be with someone who was fighting on the same side. Like he had been for years as a local patrolman. He'd spent his energy building trust in the communities he served. Talked at schools, gave presentations, refused to work with Homeland Security to detain or deport. He knew the value of the undocumented, tried to help shape a safe environment where they could live and breathe in peace, helped them navigate their lives within the framework of the law. Why the radical departure from who he'd been? It could only be the result of the shooting. And who had been killed.

She wandered through the house, so empty without Teddy, without Nick's presence. Her mind had become pure pandemonium. How could he do this to them?

After what he'd promised. He couldn't have meant it, not if he'd been planning on this course of action. What had the last week been about? An attempt by a man betrayed to return to the land of the living? He couldn't possibly care about her or her heart, because he'd just trampled it.

Her mood had deteriorated to the point of no return when Cami came in with Teddy a little before seven p.m. He ran over to her and gave her a hug, asking, "Why did you leave?"

He was able to lift her spirits a ripple, but she knew he'd be gone soon and she'd have lost a connection so important to her healing and well-being, but she couldn't let him see her so conflicted. He'd seen so much of that already. Kissing him on the head, she said, "I had to come home and take the puppies out. You know they can't go long without peeing."

He was looking up at her, sincerity shining in his brown eyes.

"I would have come with you."

"You were having fun and I thought it would be better for you to stay."

"Can I take Lily out for a while?"

She said, "Sure," before asking Cami, "Are you staying, leaving?"

"I'll stay. Wine?"

"Sounds good although I might need something stronger."

She poured two glasses, told Teddy to let the rug rats out, and headed out to the back deck. After they took seats at the patio table, Teddy running around the back-yard, chased by nipping teeth, Cami got right to it.

"What the hell happened?"

"I told you, he's going to be working with ICE."

"And you couldn't talk him out of it?"

"He's never going to let a woman dictate his choice of a career ever again."

She'd tried to get his voice right.

"Stupid man for saying it out loud."

She gave a rueful half laugh.

"Crazy how, as soon as we hooked up, our friendship evaporated. I thought it might make the relationship deeper, better. I was wrong. He would never have come down on me like that before. He would have listened as I gave him the salient points of his error in judgment. Instead, I get lumped in with Saban. I was so fucking pissed I couldn't see straight."

She could feel the tears in her eyes, which indicated that pissed wasn't the only feeling coursing through her. "I knew this would happen. I told him there had to be residual issues. He told me emphatically that there were none. And I'd started to believe him. Now we don't even have a friendship anymore. What am I going to do?"

"I don't know, sweetie. Give it time. Maybe he'll see the error of his ways."

"Then what? He declines the job offer and we try again? Not only will things be unresolved, but he'll think I'll use threats to get my way. I'm not trying to get him to bend to my will. It's just wrong on so many levels." She glanced up to meet Cami's eyes. "It's as if he doesn't understand my commitment to keep families together, which means he has no idea about who I am."

"He knows. Better than most. He's just got a blind spot right now."

"You're right. It's the same blind spot he's always had, and I'm done trying to work around it."

"What are you going to do about Teddy?"

"Set up visitation, if he agrees. I'll always love that little boy and I don't want him hurt by any of this."

When Cami left, she tucked Teddy into bed, got the dogs settled for the night, and took another glass of wine to bed with her. It was all she'd have for company.

She ignored the calls that came in before shutting her phone off. She had to think through what she wanted, and as soon as she arrived at the office after dropping Teddy off at day care, she texted what she thought was a sensible visitation schedule. Wednesdays she'd pick Teddy up, keep him overnight, and drop him off at school, and she'd also keep him Sunday night, so he could play hockey. Friday, he was on his own.

He sent her a three-word text in return.

Fine with me.

CHAPTER THIRTY-ONE

Nick lay in bed, another night spent in his parent's house. Why had he texted those three words instead of trying to explain, trying to get her to understand?

Fine with me.

It hadn't been fine with him. Nothing was fine anymore. He missed Em with a ferocity he didn't know how to deal with, but at least it seemed that she was going to keep her connection to Teddy. All his son wanted right now was to be with Em and Lily. He'd asked him at least a hundred times why they had to move. The tears had almost been Nick's undoing. He had a feeling that Teddy had cried with her, as well, because she amended her visitation schedule to include Fridays. But there would be no interaction with him. He couldn't drop off or pick up. The school would be the point of departure and arrival during the week, and on Saturdays, Olivia would drop Teddy at his folk's house. The divide was a concrete wall between them.

Maybe if he'd been able to tell her himself, instead of her overhearing it, it would have ended better. Maybe he could have softened the blow. Maybe he shouldn't have said what he was thinking out loud. She'd never told him what to do before, didn't have a manipulative streak in her body. She told it like it was and left it up to the recipient to rethink their perspective.

His rubbed his ribs. His whole body was a massive ache, most of it from the abuse he'd taken during the hockey game last night. When you hit hard, you got hit harder. He felt like a train had hit him going full speed. And then there was his heart. Em had done more than bruise it. Her text, so cold and civil, had almost changed his mind. Then his ego had stepped in. No way was he going to back down now. He needed to see for himself if this would work. It was an extension of what he'd been doing since joining the force, getting the bad guys off the street.

Crawling out of bed after a restless night, he got ready to start his new day, in his new capacity.

As he stood in the shower, he wondered who'd help Em now that he was out of her house. She'd been unable to shower without a plastic protective patch covering her wound, something he'd applied. He'd tended her injury, changed the gauze. The exposed skin wasn't pretty, and he knew it had to be painful. Would Olivia stop in every day to check on it?

"Do you want breakfast, Nick?"

His mother's voice carried up the stairs like it had when he was a kid. She'd gotten back from her business trip on Saturday afternoon and wouldn't be leaving again for another week and she'd agreed to let him stay until he got his house settled and on the market. He'd been avoiding her, knowing she'd want an explanation as to why he was here.

"Just coffee, Mom."

"Are you sure? I have bagels."

"Just coffee, but thanks."

His stomach couldn't handle anything in it right now. He'd lost what he'd thought he'd found in a blink of an eye, and he still couldn't believe Em had shut him out like that. She hadn't even tried to see it from his point of view.

When he went downstairs, his coffee was waiting. His mother was, too.

"What's going on Nick? Why aren't you at Em's?"

Adding creamer, he dropped into one of the kitchen chairs and stared into space. "She doesn't like my career choice."

"She doesn't like that you're a cop? She never had problems with that before."

"I'm going to be working for ICE for the next two weeks. See if I like it."

He heard the gasp and looked up. His mother's expression held surprise.

"You do know what the woman does for a living, don't you?"

"Even I'm not that obtuse."

"Do you know what this probably makes her feel?"

"She wouldn't be defending the type of people I'll be arresting. I don't see what the big deal is."

"The big deal is how Em sees this. I can't believe you're willing to put this ahead of your relationship with her. Did you bother talking to her about it or are you just charging in, like you always do?"

"What are you talking about?"

"You have an unhealthy habit of trying to save people. In fact, I think you go out of your way to find people who need fixing. What you end up doing is pushing them away."

"I'm not looking to fix anyone. I'm trying to prevent another plaza shooting."

"Immigrants are getting picked up just for living here. Can you honestly tell me you can detain someone like that?"

"If it means getting another Rojas off the street, yeah."

"How are you going to recognize the one out of millions who will turn bad?"

"I can't. That's why they all have to go."

"It sounds like you've become an avenger."

He bolted out of his seat, dumped the coffee in the sink, and was out the door before she could say anything else.

Why was revenge such a bad thing? He'd seen the carnage, had taken in the scene with a policeman's eye. White sheets littering the plaza, blood pooled like rain storm puddles. He was in the business of protecting people. Why wasn't Em seeing this for what it was? Why couldn't she see that there were some immigrants who were not welcome here?

He puzzled over this all the way to Alec's office.

Their meeting was short, the pleasantries taking up more time than the description of his assignment. Alec partnered him up with two of his officers, the insignia Boston ICE on the front of their shirts reminding him what he was doing. They sat strategizing and went out on the raids that were so controversial.

Over the course of the week, he was a witness to the detainment of a dozen illegals. Every one of them had committed crimes, from drug trafficking to spousal abuse and theft. He was feeling vindicated, positive that even Em would agree these men had to be deported. How could he convince her that he was doing a service to the country? He needed to do that somehow, but if she was unwilling to even talk to him…

Being without her was hell. He'd always missed her in the past, but now…knowing what they could have together made it even more painful. He knew what it felt like to wake up in her arms, what her lips tasted like, how he felt when he was buried deep inside of her. She had evoked feelings in him that he hadn't even known existed.

And in the blink of an eye, it was gone. Em, the joy, the easy companionship they'd always offered each other. A hole had appeared in his heart the moment she told him he had to move out, and it continued to grow wider each day they were apart. The nights had become too long without her, mornings arrived too early, the emptiness of the day ahead looming over him. He missed her with an obsession he didn't know how to break. He wanted to see her face, hear her voice, feel the love she so selflessly gave, but the day it happened…it had left him worse off than he'd been before.

He'd accompanied a couple of agents who were scheduled to testify at a hearing to the courthouse. She was sitting on a bench in the hallway and glanced up. Their eyes met and hung suspended for the briefest of moments before she turned her back on him. He hadn't missed the deep well of sadness in those beautiful hazel eyes. What hurt the most was that he'd put it there and it had cut like a knife, creating a scar he knew would never be healed.

By the end of the week, she was consuming his thoughts, and he wanted nothing more than to wrap himself around her and beg her to take him back. She'd win but…but nothing. This fight was being waged because of his own stubborn resolve. Maybe it was revenge, his need to get even with the man who had hurt her but if he was doing it to protect her, it was a mistake. She didn't want his protection. She had wanted his love.

She'd doubted him before…and he'd pretty much told her with his actions that she didn't matter, when she was his everything.

He made the decision to stay on for the next week because he'd made a commitment but then…he'd go back to the force, begin the life he wanted.

He needed her. It was that plain and that simple.

~·

Em spent the week in a fog. Wednesday the haze of seeing Nick at the courthouse cleared with Teddy's laughter and love. But there were also non-stop questions about why they couldn't live with her anymore. She had run out of reasons to give him. He missed her, the puppies, the house, his room. She was on the verge of tears all the way into her office on Thursday. The sadness was profound, and it was an uncomfortable fit. She didn't dwell on disappointment, she never got depressed, but Nick's betrayal to all she held dear had felled her. Even her walks across the plaza were easier. She didn't care enough to be afraid, her thoughts more on Nick than on the gunman. It was the only upside in the whole turn of events.

The families she was representing and the problems they faced should have made her feel better about her own. They were nothing in comparison. Hers weren't life-and-death, only soul chilling. She should have been able to put it in perspective, but she was having a hard time doing that.

Just this morning she'd gotten a call from a woman whose husband had gone outside to start his car at an inopportune time. Federal agents, seeing him, pulled into the drive-way and began to ask him questions. After Angelo provided his license and passport, the agents did a background check and found his old DUI and a sixteen-year-old deportation order. He was handcuffed and arrested on the spot. Deportation was imminent. The wife was a wreck, sobbing out, "He is my everything. My whole world is missing now."

Em had made some calls, tried to get bail, but it was denied.

Her mood had veered into dangerous territory.

With each call that came in now, she'd wonder if Nick was there for the arrest. If he'd been the one to put the cuffs on. If not today, then maybe tomorrow. He liked to think of himself as a knight in shining armor, but he'd turned into a rusty tin-man. He had a brain, but he'd lost his heart.

Unfortunately, she had, too.

~·

After walking into the break room, Cami and Jelani already there, Em was slow to smile.

"Still feeling punk, huh?"

Jelani was stirring her coffee, picking a piece of muffin out of the box that sat on the table.

Even perfect muffins had lost their appeal. They reminded her of Nick.

"I'll get over it. I always do."

"I knew Alec would be a problem. Didn't I tell all of you?"

"Alec didn't recruit him, Jelani. Nick decided this all by himself."

"But if Alec wasn't part of DHS, Nick might have thought about it longer. Having an in made it easy for him."

"I'm not sure. He mentioned it more than once after the rampage."

He'd talked about his conflicting emotions. The one he never mentioned was rejection, but she knew it had to be part of the mix, maybe at the top of the list.

Jelani took a sip of her coffee.

"Neither are getting an invite to your birthday party. Just sayin'."

She'd forgotten all about it. The party would be held at Jelani's just like every year. Nick had come to a couple of them, but it seemed those days were behind her. She was going to be another year older in just eight days. Her biological clock gave an incessant beep at the thought of it. Sure, more women were having children in their forties, but she didn't want to be one of them. That gave her a measly six more years to get to it. She could manage two in that amount of time, but she had to get moving. Next week would start the process and she was ready. Maybe it would stop the dam from bursting. The one that kept the churning waters of pain from flooding out. It looked like it was the only way she'd get what she wanted. A family of her own. It would include Teddy. She thought he might be excited with another little one around, and she'd never let a new baby interfere with her relationship with him.

~

Olivia came to dinner that night. She'd been checking in with her since Nick moved out, changing the bandages, helping her shower. Tonight, she came with news. Scott had proposed while they were at the beach and she was still thinking. She didn't tell her until they'd retreated to the family room after eating, sitting on opposite ends of the couch.

"That was days ago. How long are you going to keep him waiting?"

"At least I didn't say no outright."

"What are you afraid of?"

Em was shocked to see Olivia's eyes glistening.

"A lumber truck."

After scooting across the couch and hugging her, Em said, "You can't let that stop you from loving someone, Liv."

"You let it stop you from trusting anyone to be there for you. We both walked away with different scars. Mine are just as deep."

"I never knew."

Trying to laugh away the tears, Olivia said, "They shouldn't have been such good parents."

"You're right. If they'd been beasts, we could have weathered that storm with far less stress."

"I think I'm going to say yes. Am I crazy?"

"Crazy in love?"

"That, too."

"He's a good man, your Scott. I don't think you could do better."

"He's solid and he wants a family, Em. I wish—"

"Don't. I…I'm going to have one of them myself."

She reminded Olivia about the appointment at the clinic. Olivia thought it was still premature and did her best to talk her out of it. The main reason was Nick. When she explained that Nick had nothing to do with it, it sounded false to her own ears, but she'd come to accept that Nick was lost to her and she would never be involved with another man.

"I'm not spending my time like Jelani looking for a partner."

It was time-consuming and not worth the energy or disappointment. She'd been disappointed enough for a life-time.

CHAPTER THIRTY-TWO

Nick was assigned to a different team on the Monday of his second week, with Alec's cryptic message to watch his back. After only a couple of hours, he knew what Alec meant. The agents had an unhealthy attitude towards the immigrants and went by the book, the new book that had been written a few months ago. All black and white with no grey to soften the blows.

The first day, he'd stood by and watched a few detainees abused. Not only verbally, but the rough handling said something about the agents' mindset. The cops on the street who used to be his friends were steering clear, and all the community work he'd done as a patrolman had become wasted effort. The immigrants he'd come to know were avoiding him. He felt like a turncoat, for good reason.

The third day out, they got a call to arrest a man who was at home, sleeping. This was the call that put everything Em said into perspective. Miguel Ebenezer worked nights as a janitor and had only been home a short time when they knocked on his door, roused him from sleep. As they cuffed him with no explanation, his young son and daughter watched helplessly as he was led away. When his wife stepped forward to kiss him good-bye, the agents threatened to arrest her as well if she got any closer.

The little girl standing close by couldn't be older than Teddy. Big brown eyes produced tears as big as melons and she cried after her father. "Papi, come back, Papi." Looking up at her mother, fear glazing her eyes, she asked, "Will they take me, too?"

The mother hugged the child to her, kept her older son close, the devastation on her face mind-numbing.

Then she asked, her voice a low whisper, "Officer Nick, you are part of this now?"

He shrunk in size.

She knew who he was, had seen him at the convenience store, at the park playing ball with the kids in the neighborhood, or at the luncheonette. That was the way he wanted to serve the community, not ripping it to shreds. How could immigrants trust the law? They already lived in the shadows. Now they'd bury themselves deeper, refuse to testify in on-going trials, be unwilling to report theft, sexual abuse, and drug activity.

Em had told him all of this. He obviously hadn't been listening or he might have taken it more to heart.

He pulled at the arm of an agent.

"What are you doing? He's done nothing to warrant this."

"He's illegal, which means he's breaking the law. This is what we do, Nick. Get used to it."

"I thought we only went after criminals."

"I thought you understood. They are all criminals. They are here *illegally*."

He didn't know what he thought or understood any more. Ebenezer wasn't the type of man he'd deem a criminal. Was Hector Rojas? He'd been a factory worker. Had a home, a family. And they were taken away. If Teddy was taken from him, what would he do? Certainly not shoot up a plaza full of people, but he'd have other recourses, one of which was the court system. Which was where Em lived and breathed. She was their recourse. She was their avenger. He'd become the enemy.

Nick looked down at the little girl, the tears still falling down her cheeks. "Couldn't you have done this somewhere else?"

"No. This sends a message to anyone else out here who's undocumented. We're coming to get them."

Nick shook his head. He'd thought the same thing after the assault on the plaza and wondered where the momentary madness had come from and where all the good-will he'd felt toward the immigrants in the city had gone. Em might have been hurt physically, but he'd been impaired mentally. His brain cells had gotten clogged with propaganda, his own brand. He'd done this because of Em's wound, her fears, her pain. He was trying to fix her world, so she would be safe in it. He'd donned his armor and was on his charger, riding off into battle, but he was on the wrong side. He wasn't fighting for her, he was fighting against her.

As the two agents were walking Miguel to their car, jerking his arm as if he were offering resistance, Nick took note. He was going to report them to Alec and hope…

He glanced back at Muriel. There were tears in her eyes and she silently pleaded with him to do something. There was only one thing he could do that might help her. He needed to reach out, get her the representation she was going to need to face the coming fight. The call he made to Em went to voice mail.

Calling the firm, he asked for Attorney Spencer-Ronan and was put through without question.

When he heard her voice, he felt small inside.

"Em, they just picked up a man from his house. He left behind a wife and kids. You've got to help her."

The little girl was Teddy's age and Em had been right. He was as bad as Rojas if he was willing to do this.

The voice that spoke to him didn't belong to the Em he knew. It was civil and cold.

"I'll need her name and address."

"Muriel Ebenezer." He gave her the address and heard the click as she ended the call.

He stared at the cell in his hand, hearing past conversations he'd had with Em. How the kids of undocumented residents were under extreme levels of stress and that it affected their cognitive development. That even young children were aware that their parents could just vanish one day. How the new president had no clear factors in place for deportation, and without discretionary policies, everyone was at risk. She'd explained what kind of impact it was having on the communities. There was increased anxiety, less willingness to come forward to report a crime or seek justice. He'd believed her once and had tried to alleviate it by becoming a community advocate.

What the hell had he done?

How easy it had been to be seduced by the other side because of his fear for her safety. His need to serve was defective if he thought he could pick and choose whom to protect. It should include the most vulnerable. He preferred to be fighting on the same side as Em, standing united against the blatant targeting of those in jeopardy, working to create protections against the well-oiled deportation machine that had been put in high gear after the inauguration.

He pulled out his cell and called Juanita, asking if she could pick him up. Now that he'd straightened out his thoughts, he had to straighten out his life. He just hoped Em could forgive him.

⌒

Em scrubbed her face after she put down her phone.

Muriel Ebenezer was planning to hide. Burrowing deeper into the shadows. She refused to wait around to be detained. What that meant was Muriel could no longer go out, not to work, not for food, not to take her kids to school. She couldn't do anything for her if the woman wasn't willing to stick around to fight. With no avenue to pursue, her appointment at the clinic in an hour, she picked up her purse and let Heather know she'd be back before the end of business.

With a heavier heart than she'd started the day with, she arrived at the clinic, checking in with the receptionist before sitting down. There were other women here and she wondered if they had come to the same conclusion as she had. That a child would serve better than a husband. They looked professional, in suits and heels, texting, interfacing with the internet in some way. There was a woman sitting two seats over who was talking on the phone, joking about the sperm she was looking for.

"I want a donation from the jock bank, with a little intelligence thrown in."

Em stared at her for a moment, images of Nick filling her mind. He had more than a little intelligence. Or at least she'd thought h'de had, until this stupid idea he had of saving the world from the defenseless.

Filling out the forms, which were invasive, she paused to answer the questions as honestly as she could. The why behind her appointment the hardest to answer. Writing in, *to have a child* wouldn't be enough. The question spoke to her psychological profile, and maybe her lifestyle: a professional woman too busy to find love and marriage. The clients were called one by one as she continued to fill in the blanks. She glanced up in time to see the joker going in. What if they both picked the same donor? Would there be other children in the city who were related by DNA? Had she really thought this through?

"Ms. Spencer-Ronan."

Ready to run, she looked up to see a nurse standing in the open doorway.

Instead, she rose from her chair, handed the clip board over, and walked into the inner sanctum of the office, where the examination rooms were located. As she was led into one of them, the stainless-steel stirrups were the first thing that grabbed her attention.

Handing her a pee cup, the nurse said, "We'll need a urine sample. The bathroom is down the hall. When you're done, you can put it on the ledge by the door and someone will pick it up. Then you can undress and get into the johnny."

She did as instructed and then waited, her naked legs dangling off the edge of the table.

And waited.

It gave her long enough to rethink this decision. It was a cold and sterile way to produce an offspring. What she wanted was love. Nick's love. This was not going to get it for her.

She was so lost in her thoughts, she startled when the doctor came in.

"Ms. Spencer-Ronan, I'm Dr. Manning. It's nice to meet you."

She reached out to shake hands.

"Thank you, Doctor. It's nice to meet you, as well."

Dr. Manning stood, her hands tucked into the pockets of her white lab coat.

"From your paperwork, you came in to talk to us about artificial insemination, is that correct?"

"Yes."

"Well, you don't need it."

She stared at her, not understanding. Was there something on the questionnaire she filled out that had been deemed inappropriate?

"What do you mean?"

"You're already pregnant."

Her heart skipped a beat as the announcement found time to settle. She couldn't...

Non-plused, she choked out, "I'm what?"

"You obviously didn't know. You're in the early stages, and some women..."

"This can't be right. I'm still on the pill."

Or was. She was due to start a new cycle the day after the shooting. It had completely slipped her mind, until a few days later. Knowing she was considering getting pregnant, she'd dispensed with them but...the lapse couldn't have produced a pregnancy. Could it? They'd started using a condom several nights in. This couldn't be happening.

"I...was shot almost a month ago and I forgot—but I've been on them for years." She was having trouble breathing. "I was told I'd have to give myself three months off them before having the procedure to ensure the pregnancy took."

"That's usually the case. It seems not so in yours."

Her mind was whirling. This was what she wanted, wasn't it? Was why she was sitting in this office. She'd wanted a child of her own, yes. But now? With Nick? The complications were shooting like a boomerang in her head. And it always came back to she was having a baby and it was Nick's. What the fuck was she going to do now?

As if to herself, she muttered, "I knew I was late but...I thought it was due to the trauma."

"I'm assuming you want this baby."

She was distracted, nervous, agitated, until the doctor asked that question. She looked up, a wan smile on her face. The universe had played the ultimate joke on her.

"Yes. I just don't know what I'm going to do about the father."

"You know who it is."

"I do. I thought we were...had a future. I realized we didn't. That's why I kept this appointment. I know he'll want to participate, so the question is, do I tell him?"

"That will be up to you."

"Why don't you get dressed. You've already accomplished what you came here to do. I suggest you make an appointment with your OB-Gyn as soon as you can. Take care, Ms. Spencer-Ronan and good luck."

They shook hands, Em in shock.

She was still in shock when she got back to the office and went to Cami's door, which was open, indicating she was alone. After closing the door to give them privacy, she plopped down in one of the chairs, and she looked up.

Cami's eyes were intent on her.

"What happened?"

"I'm pregnant."

"Already? I thought..."

"I got pregnant a couple of weeks ago."

Cami leaned forward, a look of concern on her face.

"You're on the pill, aren't you?"

"I forgot to start the new cycle after the shooting. I didn't think to ask anyone to bring them to the hospital and then... What the hell am I going to do?"

"You've got to tell him."

"I fucking know that. Which is making me fucking crazy. I finally...finally...pushed him away and now this. What the hell?"

She could feel the tears fill her eyes, felt the moisture as they slid down her cheeks. Her misery was the quiet kind that pierced the soul.

Cami hesitated, as if she was unsure about what to say. She said it anyway.

"If I was my mother, which I'm not, but if I was, I'd say fate had a hand in this."

"I can't...do...this."

"Not alone. No. But you'll have all of us."

"I don't mean that. I mean I can't have a child with Nick."

There was a knock on the door and Liz peeked in through the window to let them know it was her.

Em brushed away the tears and nodded at her to come in.

Standing right behind her was Nick. When Liz realized she had a shadow, she turned and put her hand up to stop him from going any farther.

"Hey, you were supposed to wait out in the reception area."

He must have noticed Em's flushed face, the moisture gleaming on her cheeks. Rushing into the room, he asked, "Are you hurt? What's wrong?"

"Nothing. Everything. Just go away. Please."

He glanced up to see Cami examining him as if he had two heads. "Nick, you heard the woman. Now please leave my office."

"I have to talk to her."

"Not here, not now."

He was going to assert his obtuseness by ignoring their request.

He went to Em's chair, bent down on one knee and took her hand.

"Is it Muriel? Couldn't you help her?"

She snatched her hand out of his, the spark ready to ignite, something she neither needed or wanted.

"She's going underground. There's nothing I can do. Please, Nick. Just go away. I can't—"

"You were right. I've already talked to Alec, told him I have no intention of applying, and then I spoke to my supervisor. I've put in for a transfer, to the SWAT team. They have an opening and I'm set to start in a couple of weeks. I'll be working off my shifts with Juanita. Seems she's going to Narcotics. Said she couldn't work without me."

"Nick, I need some time. I can't..."

When he glanced up to see how Cami was taking the intrusion, she gave him the evil eye she was known for.

It didn't stop him.

"Em, please. I made a mistake. I've been miserable without you. Teddy's been miserable without you. I began to think this wasn't a good idea even before the Ebenezer fiasco, had already talked to Alec about the job. Told him...I thought I should work out the week. When I saw Muriel, and that little girl...I felt like scum. I betrayed them. I betrayed you."

Cami got up to leave, hesitating to make sure Em was all right with it. When she didn't object, Cami said, "I'll be in the break room."

"The why you had to do it is the crux of the problem, Nick. You still..."

After snagging her hand, he brought it up and kissed her palm.

"I don't. I thought I was going to protect people like you by getting people like them out."

He laughed sardonically. "People like *them*. Like Muriel and her daughter. Like Miguel."

"Like Hector Rojas."

"I can't look at him like that, Em. I'm sorry, but he almost took you away from me."

He let go of her hand, rubbed his forehead. "Shit. I'm the one who did that. Pushed you away, by trying to protect you from people like him. I know you think this has to do with... It doesn't. I love you, Em, more than I thought it was possible to love another person. I was afraid and angry. When I saw how terrified you were at the court house, I got all macho. Wanted to take out the bad guys who could make you feel like that. I didn't think about how it would affect me, us. Or the community. I want to be on the same side of things again."

"I knew I shouldn't have called you that day. That's one of the problems, Nick. You want me to ask for help, be less independent, but when I do, you go to extreme lengths to fix things. That's who you are. It's the one thing I can't live with. I'm an adult who can take care of myself. It doesn't mean I don't want to share my life with someone...but that someone will have to meet me on equal footing."

"I know that. Your independence is one of the things I love about you. I guess we both have to do some adjusting."

"Both?"

"Okay, I'm the one with the biggest problem. I love you so much I don't want anything to happen to you. I don't like seeing you hurt...or crying. Can you tell me what the tears were for?"

"Not yet. I need to think about some things. I've got to figure out what I want. It used to be you. Now, I'm not so sure."

It finally dawned on him just how much he'd hurt her with his obstinate behavior. He was willing to change for her, do anything he needed to win her love back.

He stood, looking down at her, his heart in his throat.

"You need time. I have that to give you. Take as much as you need. I'll be waiting."

He took her hand in his again and lifted her up. He pressed the lightest of kisses on her lips before wrapping his arms around her.

"This is where I want to live. I love you. Always have, always will."

After kissing her again, he let her go and walked away.

CHAPTER THIRTY-THREE

For two days Em struggled with what she was going to do. Not telling Nick about the baby would be unconscionable but...he'd want to rush to get married, take care of her, be her white knight. Damn it. She didn't need a white knight, didn't want one. She might come to depend on him and then what? That's what was so appealing about artificial insemination. She wouldn't have to count on anyone else. But that ship had sailed. And as she sat on the deck with the puppies chasing each other in her yard, she watched it disappear from view.

Calling for Lily and Ozzie, she rounded them up and crated them, needing to get ready for Teddy's visit. She'd agreed to keep him on Fridays so Nick could play hockey. It was at Teddy's request. He said he'd rather be with her than his grandmother and she'd acquiesced. Nick had texted, saying he'd drop him off, something she'd asked him not to do but maybe it was time to address the elephant that had shown up.

She hadn't seen or talked to him since the day before yesterday, when he made his grand gesture of resigning from ICE after the debacle with the Ebenezers'. She was glad he'd come to his senses. The respect she had for him had lost its shine and she'd been deeply disappointed. Not so much for his decision but the way he'd handled it with her. She insisted her voice be heard and he hadn't listened. He hadn't been noble, he'd been rash. And it had done some damage.

She didn't know how much yet, wouldn't until she measured his response to her news. She had to tell him, otherwise the weight of it would drag her down. She couldn't stop the laugh from bubbling out. She'd been eating non-stop since she found out and she didn't know if it was a reflex thing or if she really was hungry enough for two. It wouldn't only be the weight of the news dragging her down but her own voracious appetite.

The doorbell startled her. It got the puppies squealing, and they pawed at the crate, wanting out. Did they sense who was on the stoop? They loved it when Teddy was here. He played with them as only a child could. Full of energy and outright glee. Wiping her sweaty palms on her jeans, she walked slowly to the door and took a deep breath. When she opened it, Nick's back was turned but Teddy wrapped his arms around her legs in a familiar squeeze and ran into the family room to join his pack.

Her breath stuttered. Nick was a specimen. His broad back and tight ass a woman's dream. She swallowed past the lump in her throat.

"Do you want to come in?"

He shifted his footing, and then he was facing her, his expression causing her heart to stumble. It was visibly etched in pain.

"Am I welcome?"

She stepped back, giving him space to enter.

He was dressed in his tee and jeans, looking so good she had to fight off the urge to crawl into his skin. Why couldn't her love have disappeared with that ship? It would have made this thing so much easier.

He asked, with a voice raw and edgy, "How are you?"

"I'm...okay."

Teddy came running over. "Can I let them out?"

"Sure." She'd purchased a gate for in front of the stairs, so they couldn't get into too much trouble.

When she returned her gaze to Nick's face, she felt her heart beat pick up speed, as if cantering around a track. He stood there not saying a word, so she filled in the silence.

"How's the house going?"

Maks had told her that the whole hockey team was helping him get it updated so he could get it on the market. Cami had come over last night to hang out while Maks was over there. It'd felt like old times.

"Almost there. I've talked to a Realtor and I've signed the paperwork to get it listed. She said she doesn't think it will take long to sell. Now all I've got to do is find another place to live. I hate the thought of taking Teddy out of his school, but I may have no choice. It all depends on where I find something I can afford."

She wished she could offer to take Teddy, let him live with her, but she knew Nick wouldn't allow it. He loved his son and wouldn't be willing to let him live with anyone else. And asking to Nick to move in? It had its flaws. She'd been lonely without them. She'd thought the puppies would fill the empty space and they might have if she hadn't had Nick and Teddy here as well for so long. It seemed she needed all of them to complete the circle of family.

When he knew about the baby...

"Look, there's something I need to talk to you about. Something that's changed things for me. I'd prefer to do it without Teddy present, so I was hoping—"

"After he goes to bed? I could come back."

"I was thinking more about some other night... and don't you have hockey later?"

"I'll go late or skip it entirely."

Surprised he was willing to forego his night out with the guys and the game he loved so much, she wavered. She might as well get it over with. If she waited, she might lose her nerve and he had a right to know. "Do you want to stay for dinner? Driving back and forth makes no sense."

He blurted out, "I do," without missing a beat.

She studied him, his earnestness almost endearing. Backing away, she said, "Let me get it started. It shouldn't take long."

Their eyes kept a connection going as she continued to back up toward the kitchen.

"I'll be in with Teddy."

"I think the baseball game is on tonight. There's probably a pre-show on if you want to watch it."

"Sure. Thanks."

Her step faltered as she watched him head into the family room, his shoulders drooped as if he carried a heavy burden. This was going to be harder than she'd thought. He was acting differently. More civil than friendly. Was he willing to have this talk because he'd finally figured out he only wanted her as a friend? If they could go back to that...

Once in the kitchen, she put the water on to boil and got the jar of sauce out of the cabinet. She knew there were only so many things Teddy would eat, and spaghetti was one of them.

When they were finally seated around the meal, the only chatter taking place at the table was Teddy's, and when it was time, Teddy insisted she put him to bed. She left Nick to his game and the quiet.

⌒

The game was on, but Nick heard nothing but the blood pounding in his head. What did she want to talk to him about? Had she decided she couldn't cope with him and his fucking need to be needed? How could he prove to her that he was done with that? There was only one driving need right now and that was working his way back into her heart. He'd learned a valuable lesson this week. That there were more important things for him to worry about than the undocumented. Like his life, their life. He'd spent so many years settling, that it was more imperative than ever to grab happiness. He spelled it E-M, the word so intricately inscribed in his cells that he couldn't rip her out if he wanted to. The only person who needed fixing was himself. And he was on it.

If she'd just give him another chance to prove it, he'd show her. She'd always come first. He could give her that because she'd never use it against him. The distance she put between them had to do with her sense of right and wrong, not any kind of power play. She'd never once said *If you love e, you'd choose differently*. She'd never use his love as a bargaining chip. He knew that as well as his own name, but he'd demeaned her with his comment, disrespected her with his disregard for her feelings. If they were going to be a couple, it had to be a partnership. Wasn't that what he'd come to appreciate? They worked in tandem. They worked together. But he'd blown it by taking over, by forcing his point of view and relegating hers to the garbage heap.

She gave her life over to protecting the innocent and vulnerable. He knew how hard she fought, and what he'd told her with his actions was that it meant nothing.

He heard her footsteps fall softly on the stairs and he turned to see her looking at him. Was there fear in her eyes? As if what she had to tell him was something to be afraid of?

His stomach clenched as she made her way over to where he sat. Her fingers were grasped tightly together. And he braced for what he thought might be the end to any kind of relationship. He'd take scraps if that's all she had to give him, but he couldn't let her go.

After she took a seat in a chair opposite the couch, far enough away that he couldn't touch her, his heart began thudding in his chest.

She licked her lips, started to open her mouth, stopped, and started again.

"Over the weekend of Cami's wedding, I spent a lot of time trying to figure out what I could do to take my life back. I couldn't be at your beck and call anymore. It hurt too much."

Her fingers tightened, and he could see they were turning white.

"I made an appointment at a fertility clinic, thinking that if I had a child, I wouldn't have to settle for being backup to yours. Then…things happened that I didn't foresee."

He didn't think his heart could pound any harder, but he could feel it against his ribs, his pulse pounding in his head.

She'd decided to have a baby? Going through a clinic? Because she'd been his back-up?

The anguish built. If he'd gotten his head out of his ass, he would have been the one to provide her a child, a home, his heart. He had to convince her she'd always had his love. It was his own stupidity that had prevented them from finding what they had together, sooner.

Her fingers were trembling in her lap, her bottom lip trembling. For as much as he wanted to get up, go to her, hold her, he followed his own advice and kept silent. He was going to listen to what she had to say this time.

"After you told me about ICE, I knew you couldn't love me. Not like I needed to be loved. I went to the clinic on Wednesday, to ask questions, to see if it would work for me."

He wanted to yell that she was wrong, that she meant everything to him, that he did love her, so, so much, but he bit his tongue and let her finish, not knowing if his heart was going to survive.

"I'm pregnant, Nick."

He felt like a mule kicked him in the gut. The pain jelled into anger and he lashed out.

"Already? You didn't waste any time. It must have been the man you didn't want."

Her beautiful green eyes flashed a warning.

"You were the man I wanted, Nick. But…you loved—"

He jumped up, his hands going to his head, maybe to keep the top from exploding off. She still didn't know what she meant to him. He might have been prepared to listen, but this he had to address.

"You. I love you. I know it never seemed that way. I put so many things in front of you. I knew you'd always be there and I took advantage of that. You were the one I counted on, wanted to be with, entrusted Teddy to. I'm…sorry it took so long for me to see that…that… you are my heart."

He began to pace, all his self-made promises going up in the steam rising from his head. Okay, she was going to have a baby. It didn't have to mean the end of them.

He took her in. Her expression squeezed at his heart and the anger dissipated as pain came rushing back in.

"I can help you, Em. I promise I won't try to fix it, but I can help. I can raise it as my own, like you did Teddy. You've shown me how to do that…"

"Nick, I don't think you understand."

He stopped pacing, looked up to see what he didn't understand. His stomach had tightened in panic.

"I can't let you go, Em. You're too important to me. If you don't want me to help raise the child, then I'll be your friend. You can collapse with me after a night of colic, or I can help you get him or her back and forth to day care. I can—"

"Nick."

He went to bended knee, took her hand.

"You don't want me in your life at all. Is that it, Em?"

There was confusion in her expression, as if she wasn't following.

"Nick, the baby is yours."

His eyes sought hers out, and then he squeezed them shut.

Could this be happening? She was growing his child. It was nestled in her womb, and she was going to refuse him the gift of raising it. He already cherished it, another part of her he could… He couldn't take a breath, his lungs so constricted in pain.

"Where do I fit here, Em? Do I fit…"

She cupped his cheek. It created no shortage of sparks, but they had nowhere to go.

"I don't know. I thought you might want to…see if we can…come to…"

He opened his eyes, looked at her, wanting to read something different into what she was saying.

"Some kind of arrangement?"

There was a sheen in her eyes, something he so very rarely saw.

Her voice was small when she asked, "Have you changed your mind about us?"

Suddenly hope was staring him in the face, her beautiful eyes searching his.

"No. It's only gotten stronger. It…hasn't been good without you. It's never been good without you."

"You're not saying this so you can fix it, right? I don't need a fix. I need someone to share my life with. Someone who'll let me fall and help me up, someone who will listen, someone who I can count on to stand by my side, who won't push me into the background to protect me."

"I… I can do that."

She gave him a long, searching look, as if she wasn't sure she could believe him.

"I know you'll want and love this child. I need to know how you feel about me."

He tugged her up out of the chair and he caught her lips with his. "I love you. I never knew life, love could be this good."

He kissed her again, this time deeper. And then he ended it. "Can you forgive me? I lost it the day you called from the court-house. I hated seeing you so traumatized. I should never have rushed to judgment. I ended up being the villain in the story, not the hero."

"That's the thing, though, Nick. I don't need a hero. I'm not a princess and I don't need saving. If I'm stuck in a tower, I'll figure a way out. I wouldn't mind if you were at the bottom waiting for me. I might need a hug after all that work."

He brushed his fingers through her hair, his thumb caressed her cheek.

"It'll be hard for me not to try to protect you. I never want anything to hurt you."

"You're the only one who can do that, Nick."

He enfolded her in his arms, breathed in this woman who he could never live without.

Friend, lover, mother, wife…

"Will you marry me, Em? Or do you still need some time?"

"We should probably wait. It's so soon after…People might talk, Nick."

"It won't be the first time."

How many of their friends thought they were involved back in college? They'd already known what he'd yet to learn back then. They were good together.

"I guess it won't."

"So, before the baby comes?" He began mentally counting back. "When is it due?"

"I'm not sure. Maybe sometime in February. I've got to make an appointment with my doctor. But yes, before the baby comes."

He half growled, half laughed and pulled her closer, whispered in her ear, "Can I move back in? I don't want to spend another night without you."

He could feel the small nod against his chest and his heart exploded in happiness. There was one more thing that would make it more than perfect.

He held her by her shoulders and looked into her eyes.

"Will you adopt Teddy?"

Those pesky tears were back again, and he loved every one of them. They told him she loved him and was happy.

"Yes. I'd love him to be my son."

"He's always been yours, Em."

He told her about the day Teddy rubbed his heart and told him who was in it. "We can tell him tomorrow. He asked if you could be his mother right after… He wasn't real pleased I'd be the one to pick again. I can't think of anything that would make him happier."

"Are you ready for this, Nick? Two kids and two puppies are a lot to take on."

"I'm ready to take on the world with you. They're only the beginning."

EPILOGUE

"Happy Birthday, Em"

Nick snuggled her closer and she opened her eyes, still not believing that this was real. She turned on her side so she could face him, needing the visual. What she saw took her breath away. He was looking at her with such love and tenderness in his eyes she couldn't do anything but let go of all her reservations and inhibitions.

"Mhm, I can't think of a better way to start another year."

He kissed her eyes, her nose, his hands roaming her body, coming to rest on her stomach, still flat but filled with a gift that she could only marvel at.

"The puppies went out around two, but they probably need to go out again. You going to join me out there?"

She returned the kisses, butterfly kisses all over his face.

"Thank you. I never even woke up."

"I hope you don't mind that I let you sleep. You're going to have to guide me in this. I'm not sure what's right and what's wrong yet."

"I have to admit it helped when I didn't have to ask…for your help. This is going to take work on my part, too. I wouldn't have asked you to get up in the middle of the night, but I'm grateful that you did."

They both slid out of bed, pulled on their discarded clothes. He snagged her hand before opening the door, and they took a step out to the hall. Teddy came racing out to meet them, more than excited that Nick was back.

"Dad, what are you doing here? Didn't you play hockey last night?"

"No, pal. I skipped it. There was something more important to do."

She smiled a secret smile. He had been willing to miss hockey, which told her a lot.

"Wow. What was it?"

"We'll tell you later. For now, we have to get Lily and Ozzie out and then I'll make breakfast."

Teddy ran on ahead and was down the stairs, unlatching the crate and dancing with the puppies by the time she and Nick got there.

The three little ones barreled through the kitchen and to the back door and waited impatiently for Nick to open it and let them out. Before he slipped outside, Teddy asked, "Are you coming to the party with us?"

Nick cast her an arresting smile.

"I hope so."

"I consider your dad one of my presents."

She sat on his lap out on the deck, the sun already shining brightly, sharing its warmth. Resting her head on his shoulder, she said, "I don't think I've ever been this happy."

"That makes two of us."

There were three by the time breakfast was over.

~

Jelani was gracious when she answered the door to find Nick with them. Before the presents were opened, the cake sliced and eaten, the men went out back to kick around the soccer ball, giving her a chance to explain what had happened over the last couple of days.

"You're getting married, you're having a baby, and you're adopting Teddy. All of this a couple of weeks after you picked up two puppies. Nothing like cramming it all in before you turned thirty-four."

Jelani looked as if she was going to cry. Em felt bad but the feeling wouldn't hold. She was feeling too good about her life.

Nell offered, "I'm next up, so I better set a date. You're not beating me to the altar."

"I told Nick I think we should wait a few months. It might seem kind of quick for those who don't know us."

Arianna, who'd taken the day off the campaign trail to be here with them and who had the least amount of patience for men as a gender, said, "They'll just think Nick was another man who couldn't function without a woman."

"Been talking to Evan?"

"No, listening. The man has a Fruit Loop for a brain. He's spouting all this nonsense about tax reform, DACA, and health care."

"That's why you're the right choice for Massachusetts."

It had become her slogan, offered by Chloe and Keileh, who'd become her youngest volunteers. It was a play on Planned Parenthood and a woman's right to choose. A woman's right to govern.

And it had caught on.

"We're thinking September or October, which means your clock's ticking."

"In more ways than one."

Shaking her hair off of her face, deep in thought, Nell finally asked, "What's on everyone's calendar?"

Every one of them pulled out their phone and scrolled.

Mia was the one who asked, "What month are you looking for?"

"August. Mid. Anything going on?"

Arianna announced, "I'm away the first and last weeks, nothing in between except local stuff. I can re-arrange."

Mia said, "My kids will be at soccer camp the third week but it's Monday through Friday."

Cami laughed. "I need to get a life. I have nothing."

Jelani was the one who had a social life that most women dream of. "I will cancel anything for you, so pick your poison."

"Jack's on recess the whole month, so I don't have to check with him. How does August eighteenth sound for a wedding?"

They all said, "Perfect," in unison.

Em took in the group sitting at the table, all so different but intimately connected to each other. They were all in jeans, but even dressed down, Nell wore her intimidator shoes, four inches today of strappy sandal. Camille was elegant in her pink silk cami, looking fresh and feminine. Jelani, as always, went for the bold with a navy blue, three-quarter-sleeve shirt with colorful swirls of flowers in bloom. Her feet were bare, toenails splashed with bright hues. Arianna as the matriarch of the bunch, was coifed and dressed in more traditional attire, a blue and white-boat-neck-collared jersey and Mia who'd taken on the bulk of the work with her cohort on the road, had thrown on a white tee that said, NASTY WOMAN in gold. She had taken over the bad-guy role with Arianna off duty. It still amazed Em that she'd found these friends when she'd needed them and there was an effortless given-and-take between them.

Nate's voice came clear through to the kitchen from the back of the house.

"We're back. And ready to eat."

"Men," was all Mia could say.

The gab fest was over.

The buffet was spread out in the dining room, and as people mingled, Nick took her hand and led her to a quiet corner of the family room.

"I talked to Arianna, although I should have talked to you first. I didn't know if she'd be willing, and I didn't want to waste an argument unless I had to."

He kissed her, and she had a feeling it was to keep her quiet until he had presented his case.

"And?"

"I know we talked about waiting to get married, and we have to go through some paperwork, get blood-work, before we can make it legal but..."

She caught a gleam in his eye, the determined line of his jaw.

"But..."

"I thought, and if I'm overstepping my bounds here, let me know and we can do it another way..."

"Go on."

"Arianna is willing to officiate a ceremony today. It won't be legal. We'd have to repeat our vows later to get the state's blessing, but it will signify the commitment we've made to each other. Your friends are here and Teddy, Olivia, and Scott, and

I…" His thumb was tracing her cheekbones, and he leaned in for another kiss. She felt the shivers race through her body, still aching for what only he could give her.

"I want to be married to you, now, today. I want to be able to call you my wife. I want to get the paperwork started to make you Teddy's mother legally. I want our life to begin as soon as possible. How do you feel about that?"

There was such love in his eyes she was overcome with emotion. He was offering her what she'd wanted for so long.

"It might be the best present I've ever received."

"You're the gift, Em. I've been so blessed to have you in my life. To know you'll always be there…"

A warm glow filled her, and she gave herself over to his lips with a need she rarely let surface.

After the food was eaten, the presents opened, Arianna stood facing them, recited the words she'd often used as justice of the peace and proclaimed them husband and wife.

She looked down at the ring Nick had slipped on her finger at the appropriate time. It had been in a small box wrapped and waiting its turn to be opened and when she'd pried the velvet case apart, her eyes had filled with tears. It was a gold band with small diamonds encrusted along the edge.

"I wanted to be prepared in case you said yes."

"When did you buy it?"

"After I left your office the other day. I had to believe you'd forgive me, and I wanted nothing short of a lifetime."

"You didn't even know I'd agree."

"I hoped, and I went with that."

No one congratulated them more enthusiastically than Teddy.

"You picked good, Dad."

She watched as Nick put his hand on his chest and rubbed. "Know what this is, Teddy."

The four-year-old looked up and smiled.

"It's your heart."

"That's right. You and Em are in it."

When Nick glanced over, she gloried briefly in the shared moment before the festivities got fully underway.

Books by Faith O'Shea

Thrown for a Curve

The Scalera Family Series
Cold Sweat
Edge of Forever

Fire and Ice Series
Consumed by Fire
Skoli on Ice
Heart on Fire

HEART OF ICE

Jelani Ramirez had been looking for Mr. Right with fervor, the need to create a family the driving force. After losing her own to the immigration man, there was no way she'd let an ICE man take her heart.

Alec Cleland has just taken a job at the federal agency Jelani abhors, and he can tell from her insults she's not going to change her mind about who he is. It doesn't really matter. He doesn't want a family, or the white picket fence and he's heard through the grapevine that's what she's looking for.

When coincidence throws them together time and again, and Jelani begins to see beneath the surface to who he is, her principles are put to the test. Only when she uncovers some of Alec's secrets, does she realize it's not the job that's frozen his heart, but something he might never recover from. Even if she wanted to be the one to melt the ice, would he let her?

Excerpt of HEART OF ICE

Jelani Ramirez approached the federal court house in a tear, her three-inch heels making clicking noises on the concrete plaza. She glanced around, still feeling the aftershocks of the assault here just a couple of months ago. One of the partners at the law firm, Woodley and Fisher, had been shot during the rampage and they'd all been spooked by the event. They were more than grateful that Em had recuperated, in no small part, thanks to Nick's loving care.

The piercing sound of police sirens shot through her, putting her on red alert. There was a quickening of her heart rate as she raced toward the revolving doors.

Were they coming here? Was there another shooting? Inside this time?

None of the members of the law firm would ever feel safe here again, but they couldn't let that deter them. This is where they did their business and the fear skittling along her spine had to be ignored.

She could hear a cacophony of raised voices coming from the interior of the building, but there was no popping sound that would indicate that kind of trouble. Still, she hesitated before going in, took a deep breath, before pushing through the glass door and stepping into the lobby.

And stopped short.

The smell of fear almost gagged her, the acetic odor something she'd come to recognize. Chaos reigned, as a crowd jostled for position around a woman who they'd encased in their midst. Insults were being hurled, commands were being issued, and as she took in the scene, she knew why. The throng was trying to stop the Immigration and Customs Enforcement agents, the block letters ICE on their bullet-proof vests giving them away, from wading through the barrier that was three-men deep. It made her blood boil that these goons could trigger this kind of reaction and that they often seemed to embrace it. She paused, scrutinizing the agents and was struck by the way they were handling the detainment. It was as if they were wearing kid gloves. She'd been a witness to other arrests where the agents didn't care who they hurt if they were able to catch their prey. Was it the citizen protest that was having this effect? It did her heart good to see people standing up for each other.

As she scanned the area, her hackles went up when she saw another member of ICE directing the action. Why was he here?

Alec Cleland was a supervisor for the government agency and should have been managing things from his office, not doing a hands-on field run. By the look on his face, she could tell he didn't seem pleased with the way this was going.

Which meant she wasn't alone. It boggled her mind but didn't deter her from wading through

the melee. She tried to temper her anger but when she heard the shrew in her tone, even though her voice was a whisper, she knew she hadn't been successful.

"What the hell are you doing?"

She was standing toe-to-toe with the man who should be more friend than foe. He was making more of a stir in her life than she wanted, invading the inner circle, one wedding at a time. He was one of Nick's best friends, had been best man at Maks and Cami's wedding. The intensity of his expression had her take a step back. She had the guts to fight this kind of battle, but she wasn't a fool.

"We're detaining this woman for illegal residency."

His voice was cool and detached. She reproached him with a hostile glare.

"Here?"

He shrugged dismissively.

She wanted to claw his eyes out, or at least wipe the damn look of dispassion off his face. He didn't seem to care one whit that he was about to destroy someone's life. That it was happening in a court-house should have surprised her, but it didn't. In recent months, federal immigration agents had been hanging around court houses, hospitals, even seven-eleven stores, to get the jump on unauthorized residents. The head of Homeland Security had promised that ICE would be even more aggressive this year, and they'd already executed thousands of deportation orders. To be happening here, in this state, was egregious. Massachusetts was a stalwart of liberalism and refused to let the actions of the president dismantle what they'd worked hard to achieve: a safe place for immigrants to land.

"This is a federal court house, which demands a certain decorum. It is neither the time or the place for you to assail this woman of her civil rights."

"I'm sorry to disagree but federal law supersedes state law and we've been given the authority to arrest and remove any undocumented resident who ignores a detainment order."

His self-confident presence was pissing her off royally. He seemed so sure of himself and his place in the universe she wanted to throttle him. Instead, she did what she could to bide some time for herself and the woman in question.

"As her attorney, I'd like to see the order and I'd like to know where you're taking her."

He folded those thick, beefy arms across his chest, his expression one of skepticism.

"You're her attorney?"

The gulp was involuntary. And she couldn't stop the quiver than raced along her spine.

"I am."

Several men in blue had just come into the space, converging on the perimeter of the crowd. They were looking at each other, as if hesitant to make a move. They couldn't do anything to help the agents make an arrest. The Massachusetts Supreme Court had voted unanimously that law enforcement agencies had no legal standing to arrest or detain immigrants without a warrant. The judicial body felt any such actions would harm the officers and the communities they served. Alec knew this as well.

What the local police did have the jurisdiction to do, was break up the protest and it was probably why they'd been called in. If they did however, it would mean the immigrant would be left vulnerable, something the gathering crowd seemed disinclined to do. One of the cops was speaking into his radio, probably trying to get a higher-up's take on how to handle the problem. The current climate meant that every law professional stood on a fence, not knowing which way to fall.

Alec's eyes were hooded as he waited to see how this would play out. She couldn't tell by his expression what he was thinking, only that he was taking in the scene with a gravity she wouldn't have expected. He was throwing her off. It didn't help her balance when he glanced back at her. He searched her face as if trying to invade her mind. She shut him out as quickly as she could, demanding, "Can I see your orders?"

Without hesitation, Alec took it out of his inside pocket and handed it over. It looked legitimate which meant she'd have to back off. It wasn't something she did willingly.

"Where are you taking her?"

He hesitated. He didn't have to tell her anything. She might now be the attorney on record, but ICE had placed themselves above ethical principles.

The gruff voice almost startled her.

"Suffolk."

It was the holding facility located in Boston that housed the immigrants picked up for deportation. He had acquiesced to her demands, which surprised her. It allowed for a more amenable tone.

"Can I have a moment with my client, please."

His answer was a slight nod, before addressing his men, telling them to back off. They didn't seem pleased. He didn't seem to care. She reassessed him, before she weaved through the crowd to where her new client stood. The pale face and trembling limbs told her the woman was close to fainting. Jelani took her by the arm, before leading her to a quiet corner, away from the scrutiny.

"What's your name?"

"Carla Ngai."

"What are you doing here?"

"I came to speak to someone at the clinic about an appeal. My working visa expired. I need a new one."

"You're going to have to go with them, but I'll drop by the detention center this afternoon and make a request to see you. We can discuss the case then."

"I have no money, Miss..."

"Jelani Ramirez and that won't be a problem."

The relief on her face was evident.

"Thank you."

"Do you have a family? Is there anyone I can call for you?"

"I have a daughter. She is with my mother but..."

Carla bit her lip as if unsure she should go on. Jelani guessed why.

"Is she undocumented as well?"

Carla gave a slight nod.

"Did you put a contingency plan in place in case this happened?"

With the influx of raids and ICE activity, many of those at risk had put their lives in order, making sure their children would be taken care of. No one knew who would go and who would get to stay. It was like Russian roulette. The bullet hit at times, even though the odds were in your favor that the chamber would be empty.

Carla nodded again, her lips almost blue from fear.

Jelani pulled out her phone. "Can I have a number to call, tell your mother what happened?"

She added the number to her contacts and assured, "I'll speak to her as soon as I'm back at my office and I'll see you tomorrow at the latest."

Jelani placed her arm around Carla's shoulders and led her like a lamb to slaughter. She hated this, hated the people that made their living off the backs of the undocumented, hated the man standing there waiting for them, almost as much.

As the agents put the handcuffs on Carla, Jelani studied their movements, making sure she wouldn't need to file abuse charges. She glanced over to see Alec watching as well, his face etched in stone. What would he have done if she'd stepped in to stop the procedure? Cuff her, too? She'd done it before and had gone to jail for her efforts. It had been an impetuous decision. Standing on principle didn't help her client. And any look of satisfaction on Alec's face might goad her into committing an even more violent crime, resulting in a prison term...so she stood there as they led Carla out into the hot and humid day, feeling helpless and almost as vulnerable as she'd been years ago. Alec looked back, his expression not what she expected. There was no spark of triumph. Instead it held...remorse? How could that be? He applied for this job all on his own, knew what it entailed when he accepted the offer. Was he finally realizing what it meant?

After shaking the curiosity off, not giving a rat's ass what he was thinking, she collected herself and went off to find the client she'd come here to represent. This morning she was petitioning the court on behalf of Nadia Boza, a routine matter that she thought would get her in and out without incident. Wrong again. The law firm was taking on more clients with every trip to the federal building. The partners rarely got out of their pre-trial hearings without adding another file to their list of pending cases.

Jelani strode over to the bench where Nadia was sitting, just outside the court room where the petition would be heard. She was trembling and had curled herself in hoping to become invisible.

"I can't believe that just happened. How can they do this? I was so scared."

Jelani was, too, for all the DREAMERS who wanted citizenship and were being coerced out of the country they thought of as their own. The deadline for DACA applications was only months away and the immigrants who fit the guidelines were warned to prepare and arrange for their departure if they failed to apply in time. It was something that shouldn't be happening.

If the agents had started interviewing other people that were present at the courthouse this morning...Nadia could have easily been picked up even though she was gainfully employed, on staff in the emergency room at Children's Hospital. How could anyone think it imperative for the safety of the country to get the twenty-nine-year old nurse off the streets? Nadia had been living here since she was six, after her parents made the hellish journey into Texas, crossing remote and rugged terrain, led by a coyote, or human smuggler who charged exorbitant fees for his services. She'd told the gruesome story of what she witnessed along the way, skeletons lining the path, the intense heat and lack of water the right mix for death by dehydration. From there, the family had moved to Roxbury where her mother's sister lived. The stayed under the radar before the Boza's were arrested and detained, finally deported back to Mexico. Nadia was twenty when it happened, old enough to make the decision to stay, get her degree, hopeful there'd be a congressional resolution, so she could become a citizen. The DREAM Act was still languishing in Congress, had been for years and it didn't look like it would ever be passed. The majority saw it as a broad brush at amnesty and they weren't willing to vote for it, skeptics claimed that DACA denied jobs to thousands of Americans. It was bullshit and there was no evidence to support it. The last president had tried to circumnavigate the lack of progress of a congressional bill by signing an executive action called the Deferred Action for Childhood Arrivals as a shield to protect immigrants who came to the country as children from deportation. The current president was dismantling it. With DACA status getting fuzzy, her law firm was getting more and more frantic calls. Nadia's was the fifth one this week, the fear rising in the immigrant communities. Sanctuary no longer meant safe. She had a feeling it was only going to get worse and it was weighing all of them down in red tape and uncertainty.

Jelani felt a symbiosis with the young woman sitting beside her. She knew what it was like to have your family taken away and be left to your own devices. She was a natural born citizen, which had eased some of her worries, but she was still left to deal with the fallout. She'd promised to fight as hard as she could to get Nadia's legal status re-instated. But she'd warned her as well. Where the government was going with this was anyone's guess. The president was trying to force reform by ending these types of programs and Congress seemed willing to play games with those lives hanging in the balance. Nadia might find herself in the same predicament come fall and be living in limbo again.

As she sat there, watching the beehive of activity moving along the halls of justice, waiting with Nadia to be called in for the hearing, she was still feeling the repercussions from this morning's arrest. She could let her anger take over, but it was a useless commodity. Every immigration case she'd handled had been frustrating, and some were deeply worrisome. The government was taking an inhumane approach to the problem, and at times there was a fundamental disregard for due process. Why Congress couldn't get out of their own way to get a bill written and passed, constantly amazed her. There had to be an accounting, and every partner in the firm hoped it would come during the mid-term elections. If there was a majority where it counted, reform might be back on the front burner. It hadn't worked before, but in the last ten years immigrants were coming out and standing up in their own defense. The cogs of justice moved slowly but the marches and show of force was helping push them along.

There was another repercussion she was still dealing with, one she didn't want to analyze; her awareness of the man in charge and the delicious heat of attraction she felt for him. When his gaze had met hers, her pulse had flickered and leaped. It had been like that since the day she met him, but he was off the table. There was no way she'd be inviting an ICE man into her bed.

Relief flooded through her when they were finally called in to the courtroom. Her attention was back on her client, where it should be. She presented her case, provided Nadia's employment record and her references, one of which was a glowing description of her work ethic by her supervisor. She didn't need lady luck today, or a sympathetic judge. The facts dictated the outcome. The application was accepted, and Nadia's DACA status was in place. It would give her a couple of years before applying again. Hopefully by then…

She left the court house with another win under her belt, knowing there was another fight around the corner. One she might lose.

www.ingramcontent.com/pod-product-compliance
Lightning Source LLC
Chambersburg PA
CBHW060148180626
46813CB00007B/2679